ELENA RANSOM

AND THE UNEXPECTED
THE DISCLOSURE

by

J.S. WOOD

Illustrations by BRoseDesignz

Small Frye
Publishing

Atlanta, GA

ISBN: 978-0-9978908-2-2

Printed in the U.S.A.

To Amy and Darren

¤ Prologue ¤

"Joshua! Hurry now with the eggs," Abigail beckoned from the whitewashed, columned porch. "And bring Sassy when you come."

A cool breath of wind swept through the fields of tall amber grain, tossing it back and forth like waves in the sea, as Joshua's little legs ran across the yard. He pushed some black hair out of his eyes and pulled open a red barn door. A German pointer puppy charged through the entrance and tackled him to the ground, licking his face all over.

"Sassy! Sassy!" Joshua laughed. "Stop! Momma said to get the eggs quickly."

Joshua dislodged himself from the puppy and made his way through the barn. Several cows mooed. A few of the horses poked their heads through stall doors curiously. The cats purred from the rafters as he approached the far end of the barn where a row of nests lined the wall with a chicken perched atop each one.

Joshua eyed one of the chickens cautiously, and said, "Okay, Clucky, we're going to be nice this morning, right?"

His left hand slipped slowly into the chicken nest. He retrieved an egg with his two-year-old fingers and placed it carefully into a small wicker basket.

"You're lucky you don't have to do this, Sassy," he said to the puppy that was now pulling at the cuff of his pants with her paws and teeth.

Joshua placed six more eggs carefully into the basket and turned from the chickens. Being very careful not to spill, he stepped through the barn door and called over his shoulder, "Come on, Sassy!"

The puppy came barreling out of the barn and clipped one of Joshua's legs. The boy tumbled to the ground, dropping the basket as he went. In a panic he looked, expecting to see broken yokes, but the eggs were still whole. Joshua heaved a sigh of relief, thankful that he didn't have to brave the chickens again. He picked up the woven container and walked back to the sprawling plantation house that was set against an orange, yellow sunrise.

Sassy was waiting for him on the porch, wagging her tail and looking mischievous. Joshua climbed the steps carefully balancing his load, and the door to the kitchen slid open automatically.

"Joshua, I thought I asked you to be quick about bringing the eggs," said Abigail as she wiped her hands on her apron and took the basket from her son.

"Momma," said Joshua in an adult-like manner. "Clucky nearly pecked my finger off last time I took eggs from her nest, so I would appreciate a little more patience."

Abigail smiled, and said, "Yes, of course." She turned toward Joshua's oldest sister and said, "Ruth, dear, bring the blueberry muffins to the table and grab the milk from the fridge."

Ruth obeyed as Joshua turned toward the living room. His younger sister, Rebekah, was painting on canvas and his older brother, David, was wrestling on the floor with his dog, Bugle. Sassy bounded into the room with her caramel ears flapping and pounced on David and Bugle. Joshua couldn't resist a wrestling match. He darted across the room and jumped into the middle of the flailing mess of arms and legs and dog hair.

Moments later, the booming voice of Joshua's dad filled the house.

"Is everyone ready to eat?"

Joshua took off running, back toward the kitchen and watched his dad heave a dead turkey onto the counter. Then, he pulled off his hunting gloves and overcoat.

"Jonathan," Abigail said to her husband, "please wash your hands *first thing* this time."

Jonathan leaned over the sink, and Joshua watched him wash quickly. Then, he slipped an arm around Abigail's waist and tucked his fingers through the gold chain that hung around her neck. He tugged her toward him and pecked her on the lips.

"Daddy, how was it?" Joshua asked, hugging his dad around the knees in an attempt to interrupt his parents.

Jonathan released his wife and tossed Joshua onto his shoulders. "All the traps were full. The animals are very plentiful this year. We have much to be grateful for."

Ruth reached up to tickle Joshua under an arm. "I guess that means we'll have the best Thanksgiving Day yet."

Joshua laughed and wriggled as Jonathan ran him around the kitchen with Ruth chasing behind them.

Abigail giggled. "Alright, you hoodlums, time to eat breakfast."

As the family gathered around the table for a farm house style meal, Abigail said to Jonathan, "After school, I was thinking that the girls and I could harvest the garden. So, would you please take the boys out to the orchard? We'll need apples for the pies and pears for the dressing tomorrow."

"Of course," Jonathan said as David let out a low moan. "What's the matter, David? I thought pie was your favorite part of our feast. We can't make it unless we get the apples."

"Yes, sir," David replied respectfully. "I'm just glad tomorrow is a holiday."

"Why is that?" Abigail asked.

"Because we don't have school or chores, and we can fish all afternoon if we want," said David.

"I wish it was warm enough to swim," Joshua said longingly as he watched Sassy lick the sides of Jonathan's boots by the back door.

"Before fishing," Jonathan said to David, "you and Joshua are coming out with me to learn snares. Then, we'll pick berries for pies."

"So, we do have chores," David grumbled with a disappointed look.

"Learning snares and picking berries is hardly a chore," Jonathan said with a smile. "But you could do your regular chores instead of snares if you'd like."

"No, no," David said abruptly. "Snares and berry picking is fine."

Joshua noticed his parents share a knowing look and a smile. He smiled, too, and stuffed his mouth with a muffin.

After breakfast was eaten and the dishes were cleaned, Joshua gathered in the book room with Abigail and his siblings. Joshua sat at his desk, and Ruth helped him identify sight words and mathematical equations while Rebekah helped David with a scientific experiment. Then, David moved to another table to assemble a complex patterned mosaic as Abigail taught Ruth and Rebekah from a book of history.

Joshua sat with David, but instead of watching the puzzle, he watched his mom very carefully. She spoke slow and steady, inflecting her voice when she was making a point. And, the entire time she taught, she fiddled with the chain around her neck.

The end of the chain carried an oddly shaped looking instrument that was threaded with strumming strings and was carved with strange symbols that he didn't understand. But, Joshua knew his dad had given it to her on their tenth wedding anniversary to remind her of how their love filled his life with music.

"Joshua." Abigail called, forcing him from his thoughts. "You'll want to get started building that model if you want your lunch."

The next morning after breakfast, David and Joshua pulled on their hunting boots and stood at the back door waiting for their dad.

"Bring our boys back in once piece," Abigail told Jonathan, and he smiled at her in a mischievous way before pecking her on the cheek.

Jonathan led David and Joshua out the kitchen door, through the pastures and fields, and to the wooded area at the farthest section of their property.

"Okay, boys," Jonathan said, pointing to an area of soft ground between the trees. "Here is a fine trail for hunting rabbit."

Joshua saw a little funnel of sticks, rocks, and small trees on the ground. He noticed animal prints in the soft earth.

"What you want to do is tie the wire just so," Jonathan said, as he pulled a sturdy wire from his pocket and looped it through his fingers. "Then, we're going to tie the snare across the path where the rabbit runs."

He began to tie the wire to a durable but small tree trunk.

"We're going to leave this snare about four inches above the ground. The next time the rabbit runs through here he'll get all caught up in it."

"Dad, why do the animals run into the snares?" Joshua asked. "Are they dimwitted?"

"No, son. Animals have very good instincts," Jonathan replied. "But they can't smell or see a wire and have no understanding of what it represents."

Joshua followed Jonathan and David around as they set twelve more snares, and then they tromped back through the woods, filling a woven basket with multi-colored berries along the way.

"Dad, why does the sun go to bed so early in the winter but stay up late in the spring?" Joshua asked as they walked.

"The position of the sun on the earth has to do with the tilt of the earth's axis. In the winter, the earth is tilted away from the sun so it gets dark earlier."

"What's an axis?"

"Imagine one of your momma's sewing needles," Jonathan said patiently. "And then imagine a ball stuck to one end. The ball can tilt back and forth on the needle. I'll have momma show you when we get home."

Joshua followed his dad and brother through the tree line to the sprawling lake not far from the house. Today, the water was a deep blue, and there was not a single ripple on the surface.

"Come on, now," Jonathan said. "Let's get fishin' so we can turn David's frown upside-down."

"I'm not frowning," David said defensively. "I'm just ready to fish."

"Dad, why do fish smell so stinky?" Joshua asked as Jonathan pulled three fishing poles and colored lures from the storehouse near the lake.

"Fish are actually odorless." Jonathan handed a fishing pole to David. "They only smell when they've been out of the water too long."

David rolled his eyes. "Dad, may I fish over there?"

"Yes, son," Jonathan replied. "Here's a tackle box for you."

Joshua watched his brother walk quite a ways from them and sit with his back up against a tree.

"Dad, why does David fish over there?"

Jonathan looked toward David and said, "David likes it quiet, like your momma. He's not as talkative as we are. He likes to keep his thoughts to himself."

"That's weird," Joshua said thoughtfully. "Dad, why do fish bleed when you cut them open?"

Jonathan smiled kindly and went on to answer every single question Joshua asked him over the next hour until, finally, the fishing basket was full. David and Joshua helped their dad put away all the gear before heading back to the house.

The warm kitchen was thick with the smell of fat dripping from the turkey. Joshua set a basket of berries on the counter. Then, he watched Ruth and Rebekah roll dough and fit it into round tin pans.

Joshua stuffed berries into his mouth. Then, he walked into the sitting room where his dad and David had already set up their favorite board game. Joshua liked to watch them play.

Hours later, the entire family gathered around the dining room table wearing their best clothes and clasped hands for a prayer. After Jonathan had given thanks for the food, platters of cranberry-pear stuffing, pole beans, smashed potatoes, baked corn pudding, and turkey with gravy were passed around the table.

"In keeping with tradition," Jonathan said, "we'll go around the table one at a time and say what we're thankful for. And this year, we'll go youngest to oldest, which means that Joshua can go first."

"And you go last, daddy?" Joshua questioned.

"Oh, no..." Jonathan smiled. He winked at Abigail. "I married an older woman."

"Easy on using the word 'older' when referring to me," Abigail replied with a twinkle in her eye.

Joshua thought for a moment and then said, "I'm thankful for Sassy and for blueberry pie."

"Joshua!" said Ruth, half laughing. "You're supposed to say something like 'I'm thankful for my family.'"

"Joshua, it's very fine to be thankful for your dog and pie," Jonathan interjected. "I'm also thankful for pie."

"Your turn, David," Abigail said in a direct way.

"I'm thankful for the lake and for fishing," David said. "Today I caught a spotted bass, and it's going to taste so good when momma fries it up."

"Sounds like you're more thankful for momma's cooking the fish than the actual catching the fish," Jonathan said. "Rebekah, what are you thankful for?"

"I'm thankful for my art pencils and brushes," Rebekah answered quietly.

Ruth straightened up in her chair and said, "I'm thankful for this family and for our friends."

"Oh, I thought you were going to say that you were thankful for Michael Swanson," Rebekah said. "I saw him watchin' at you at church last Sunday."

Ruth blushed as Abigail said, "That's enough. We won't be teasing each other about boys."

"I'm thankful for peace," said Jonathan. "It brings me great joy that we can live here without interference."

"What's *interference*?" Joshua asked.

"It's a big word that we can discuss at another time," Abigail said, thumbing her necklace through her fingers. "I'm thankful for all my kids...and their many questions."

The rest of dinner was filled with laughter as they told stories about past Thanksgiving Day celebrations and made plans to go cut down their holiday tree. Joshua spent a fair amount of time telling anyone who would listen about the list of toys he wanted for Christmas. Then, he crawled into his warm bed and fell asleep to the sound of his momma's voice.

The next afternoon, the sun burned brightly making for an unusually warm fall day. Joshua ran up and down the ramps on the play structure that Jonathan had built on the opposite side of their house. Sassy raced around him, nipping at his heels until finally he stopped and looked over at his mom. Abigail hung wet clothes along a line of string in the yard with a grin on her face.

"Momma," Joshua called from the playground. "Why do you hang the clothes outside to dry?"

"Because I like the smell of sunshine in our clean clothes," Abigail replied.

"I didn't know you could *smell* sunshine," Joshua said in an amazed tone.

Joshua's sisters just laughed, but he didn't bother to ask why because he noticed that Sassy was crouched low, glowering at something not too far away. Joshua followed her line of sight to a white rabbit just on the edge of the grain field.

A second later, Sassy sprang from the playground and dashed off after the rabbit through the fields. Joshua couldn't help but run after his puppy.

"Joshua, you be back here by suppertime!" Abigail hollered after him. "You hear?"

But Joshua was running too hard to hear her. Sassy sprang through the rows of grain, but the rabbit darted in and around so quickly that the puppy could never catch it.

Finally, Joshua jumped through the field on the far side of the lake. He couldn't see where Sassy or the rabbit had gone, so he picked along one of the streams that flowed into the lake, throwing stones and sticks and taking sips from the water.

In the thicket upstream, he noticed a deer with her new fawn. He began to think about all the things he'd need to ask his dad when he got back home, like why did deer scare so easy, why did fawns have freckles on their hinds, and why did animal noses always look so wet.

A long time passed before Joshua realized that it was beginning to get dark. He thought about how his momma would scold him for being gone so long. He started back toward the house, making up excuses in his head.

When he finally got back to the edge of the grain field he noticed a strange hovercraft parked in front of his house. Joshua had only ever seen his dad's hovercraft and the supply hovercrafts that were driven by traders selling products in town, but this vehicle was very different; it looked heavy with armor and stood taller than Joshua's house. But the most peculiar part was the presence of a dozen robotic soldiers that were standing along the front of the house with positioned weapons.

Joshua slinked along through the grain field to the backside of his house and ran as fast as he could to the porch. He crawled along the decking to one of the back windows and peeked through it into the kitchen. His eyes widened as he saw that the members of his family were tied to chairs around their kitchen table.

An imposing figure stood before them, shrouded in a black cloak and wearing a silver-studded mask. Joshua could hear a deep, menacing voice as the masked figure talked to his dad. He noticed that Ruth and Rebekah were crying and that David wore a frightened look on his face.

As Joshua's eyes landed on his mom, he realized that she'd already been looking at him.

"Momma!" he mouthed at her through the window glass.

Her eyes seemed relieved to see him as a single tear escaped, running quickly down her cheek.

Joshua fixed his eyes on his dad, who was watching the stranger closely. However, as soon as the man in the mask turned away, Jonathan's eyes found Joshua's face. Jonathan calmly tilted his head ever so slightly, and Joshua knew from his dad's eyes that he was supposed to leave.

Joshua ran as quickly as his stout legs would carry him back into the grain fields and found a spot to hide. He sat for a long time, scarcely daring to breath. He wondered about the robot soldiers. He wondered about the cloaked figure that was talking to his dad. He wondered why his family had been tied down. But most importantly, he wondered how long he should wait in his hiding spot because he was getting hungry.

A short while later, a dark cloud appeared in the twilight. Then, a strange smell filled the air, reminding Joshua of the fires that Jonathan had taught David and him to build from dried wood. He hurried back toward the house but fell to his knees at the edge of the field. His house was engulfed in flames!

As fire seared the sides of the house, Joshua could hear Ruth calling out for him. He could hear the screams of pain searing the night. He saw the masked man and the soldiers standing just outside the house for a long while, watching it burn, yet none of them moved. Joshua wondered why no one was trying to help, but he stayed very still and quiet, not wanting to be seen.

Finally, when no more voices came from the house, Joshua watched the man in the mask climb into the hovercraft. The robotic soldiers followed him, and a moment later, the hovercraft disappeared into the setting sun.

Joshua ran to the barn, weeping and feeling terrified. He threw open the barn door but fell over as Sassy bounded on him. He pushed the puppy away roughly and crawled into the nearest haystack. Sassy cuddled in beside him as he sobbed. Joshua cried until the questions he had about what was happening ceased into stillness.

Darkness had fallen over the entire farm when Joshua heard the sound of a hovercraft pull into his yard. He tiptoed to the edge of the barn and peeked through the door. He saw a man with a pencil-thin black beard and a long waistcoat step from the vehicle. The hololights from the man's hovercraft shone brightly on the ruins of Joshua's house, but the boy couldn't bear to look at it.

"Jonathan!" the man yelled loudly, as he frantically ran around. "Abigail!"

Joshua watched the man walk into the remains of the house, continuing to call for his family. He even heard his own name being called, but Joshua was too afraid to come out of hiding.

Then, Joshua noticed the man turn toward the barn and stare. The stranger started across the lawn in his direction. Feeling panicked, Joshua climbed a ladder to the loft and wedged himself between the low hanging rafters.

The man in the waistcoat entered the barn, and Joshua watched him pull back the cuff of his sleeve to reveal a round object attached to his wrist. A tiny object the size of a drop of water flew from the device, and an Optivision screen appeared holographically in midair.

Joshua watched the water droplet fly around the barn with small beams of light surveying all the stalls until it finally came to rest on him. The stranger walked slowly to the ladder and looked straight up into Joshua's eyes.

He smiled kindly and said, "Hi, I'm Truman."

The man with the pencil thin beard held out his hand, but Joshua buried his head in his hands shyly.

"Come on, kid. I won't hurt you," Truman pleaded.

Joshua looked into the man's gentle eyes and tears burst from his own. "My parents...my family is gone."

Truman looked back through the barn doors toward the house.

"Yes. I sure am sorry about that, but we've got to get you to a safe place. So, come along. Let's get you out of there."

Joshua climbed out from his hiding place and watched in amazement as Truman began to open the stall doors and let all the animals out of the barn.

"What are you doing?" Joshua shouted angrily.

"If we leave your animals in the barn they will die. But, if we set them free they'll be able to make a new life for themselves."

With a little sadness, Joshua watched as all the chickens scattered away. Then, he pulled his puppy into his lap.

"But what about my Sassy?"

"Sorry, kid, but the dog can't come where we're going," Truman said.

Joshua tried hard not to cry as he followed Truman over to his hovercraft, leaving Sassy alone by the barn.

"Get on in and strap yourself down," Truman instructed, and Joshua obeyed.

Truman navigated the hovercraft toward the lake. Joshua was curious and terrified as they drove into the water and disappeared under the waves. The boy had never considered how deep or wide the lake was, but it seemed as vast as an ocean, and it was filled with fish and reefs and long reeds of green.

Just as Joshua was beginning to feel weary from the length of the trip, bright lights suddenly popped up along the deep. He saw the outline of a structure. Then, a building appeared under the lights.

"What's that place?" Joshua asked.

"This is called Smuggler Station," Truman replied.

Joshua watched in awe as the hovercraft dipped below the building and surfaced into a pool surrounded by a cement wharf. He gawked disbelievingly at a dock, which was lined with a dozen steel plated doors.

"What are we doing here?" Joshua whispered.

"We're here to get something that belonged to your dad," Truman replied. "Just wait here, kid. I'll be right back."

Truman stepped from the hovercraft, and Joshua watched him walk along the length of the dock and disappear behind an ironclad door. Joshua's imagination began to race, wondering what the man would bring back.

Moments later, the man who called himself Truman returned to the hovercraft and handed Joshua a round, silver object with an odd symbol carved in the center.

"This is a neurolizor," Truman explained. "It belonged to your dad. Will you keep it safe for me?"

Joshua took the disc into his hands; it was the only thing he had left of his family. He felt suddenly overwhelmed and began to cry again.

"Don't worry, everything is going to be alright now," Truman said in a reassuring tone, and he patted the boy's forearm gently. "Come on, let's get you to safety."

"Where are we going?" Joshua asked between gulps of air.

"First, we have a mission in New York City," Truman said. "And then I'll take you to your new home, where you'll become invisible so no one can hurt you again, kid."

"Why do you keep calling me 'kid'?" Joshua asked. "I have a name."

"Actually, I'm calling you by your *new* name," Truman replied. "Kidd Wheeler."

Thirteen Years Later

Unexpected Mission

Elena Ransom shivered between the folds of a fleece blanket as she stared out the front window of the Independence command bridge. Mount Ararat stood, still looking cold with its icy peaks at the summit. Feeling slightly afraid, she fiddled with the necklace that her dad had given her on her thirteenth birthday.

She looked at the multidimensional star, with its angles and crevices and smiled as she remembered the look on his face when he gave it to her. A lump began to rise in her throat, so she dropped the necklace quickly and tucked some of her red curls behind her ears. Then, she searched her left hand for a good fingernail and began to chew.

"We can't risk going to Istanbul!" Kidd Wheeler yelled at Austin Haddock for the third time in the last twelve minutes of their argument. "We only have two functioning engines. If we make a detour to Istanbul we might not be able to get back home."

Days ago, Elena and her friends left Grimsby School of the Republic and illegally crossed the ocean to search for an artifact that they'd learned about after stealing information from their classmate, Melly Linus.

The Tablets of Destiny was only one of the artifacts that Elena and her friends needed to locate. The Ransom Dossier and the Catalan Atlas confirmed that the Tablets were hiding on Mount Ararat in the country of Turkey.

Only twelve hours had passed since they'd found half of a giant Ark, the same boat that they'd learned about in Advanced Historical Analysis class, hiding in a crevice of the mountain.

As they were on board the ship, Declan Bowen had been injured. Then, they were forced to make a quick evacuation without finding the Tablets because the centuries old boat broke apart, causing an avalanche that damaged their hovercraft.

"What happened to the third engine?" asked Abria Bowen as she walked through the door onto the command bridge.

"Didn't you see?" Elena asked incredulously. "The landslide clipped the bottom of the Independence."

"Oh, I totally had my eyes, like, closed for the duration of the avalanche scene," said Abria, combing her long, blonde hair through her fingers.

Even with the minor cuts that she'd received as they attempted to escape the avalanche, Abria still had one of the most beautiful faces that Elena had ever seen.

Elena couldn't blame Abria for keeping her eyes shut. It had been beyond terrifying as the ancient boat began to sway and make spine-chilling groans as it crumbled from the mountain. Closing your eyes and pretending to be someplace else would have been preferable to accepting that your life was about to be crushed by an Ark. But Elena had not shut it out. And, unfortunately, she relived the nightmare again and again.

"Well, the third engine was, *like, totally crushed*," Kidd told Abria in a mocking tone. "And I just don't know if I can get it all the way back home. I haven't even had enough time to assess the entire ship. The Independence could be damaged in other places. We won't know until I can get outside to check her out. Doing anything else right now is reckless."

"But Istanbul was the largest manufacturer of hovercrafts in the entire world fifteen years ago," said Austin practically.

"How could you possibly know that?" Kidd asked in disbelief.

"Fergie and Pigg accessed the information on the global server before we left school," Austin said. "I asked them to research everything about Turkey before we came here so we'd be prepared."

"That is accurate," said Fergie Foreman, who was sitting in a captain's chair with dozens of Optivision screens open and ready for commands. Her short raven black hair was twisted in a fancy braid because Abria had said that she needed to do something to help take her mind off the fact that they'd almost died.

"Istanbul isn't far. If we get there we can see if there's any material that can help us repair the Independence," Austin said calmly as Pigg handed him a steaming mug.

In the hours after the crash, Pigg had started cooking in the galley and hadn't come out. But now he was passing out rations of hot chocolate. Elena accepted the beverage gratefully. She wrapped her hands tightly around the mug and felt warmth spread through her fingers.

"You just want to go there because we decoded that thing in the Ransom Dossier about the possibility of an artifact being in Istanbul," said Pigg flippantly as he handed a cup to Abria.

"What?" Kidd blurted in disbelief.

This was news to Elena, too. She noticed that Pigg's brown eyes filled with regret, like he'd just told a secret that Austin didn't want shared.

Kidd ran his fingers through his spiky, black hair in a frustrated sort of way.

"This is about those artifacts? I can't believe you want to risk our lives over those dimwit diaries AGAIN! I already told you that the Tablets weren't on the ship. And I thought I made it clear that I'm not going to help you look for any more artifacts."

"Is anyone else tired of, like, traveling?" Abria asked, turning the mug in her hands and avoiding eye contact with everyone. "I mean, honestly, after the huge wooden ice boat almost killed us you'd think we'd deserve a break."

"We can't take a break," Austin said. "We've got to get the ship fixed so we can get back to school before someone notices."

"I thought that was the point of having Decoys," said Abria, referring to the exact replica body doubles that Fergie's parents had created to take their places while they were searching for artifacts outside the protection of the domed cities where they'd grown up. "Kenneth and Anne Foreman built those Humanoids to look like us so that no one would notice that we're gone."

"We've still got to get back to school at some point," said Austin. "We can't live out here forever."

Elena was suddenly weary from all the talking and arguing.

"Stop! Stop talking." She sighed deeply and set her mug down so she could press her palms against her eyes. "Wheeler, how likely is it for us to go the seven hours back home?"

Kidd looked at several of the open Optivisions. He touched them so that red lines of warning appeared, indicating the areas of the hovercraft that had been damaged. He considered the images closely.

"There's maybe a fifty percent chance."

"How likely is it that we can make it to Istanbul?" Elena pressed him.

"We could definitely get there using just the hover systems instead of using the aeronautic capabilities," Kidd said. "However, have you noticed that every time we go anywhere together we're almost killed? When is it going to be enough? Does someone have to actually die?"

"Look, we can't get home, but we can get to Istanbul," Austin said. "We need parts. It's as simple as that. Please help us. We won't mention the artifacts again."

Kidd scowled but said, "I'll ready the Independence for departure." Then, he stomped out of the command bridge.

"I'm so sorry for telling him about the artifact," Pigg groaned. "It just kinda slipped out when I wasn't thinking."

"That's alright," Austin said, as Elena asked, "Yeah, what's all this about another artifact?"

"I was planning to tell you about it later," Austin said. "And by later I mean not in front of Wheeler..."

"Again, so sorry," Pigg squeaked.

"Pigg was tinkering with the Ransom Dossier while I was wo
Declan's ribs, and he found something. I'm going to the research
now, and you're all welcome to join me."

"I'm just going to check on Declan again, actually," Abria said. "He said to
bring him news as soon as possible. I think he feels left out because he has to be
in bed. Maybe we should start having meetings in his room?"

"I'm going to make another snack," Pigg said, completely ignoring Abria's
suggestion before he hurried out of the room.

As they left the command bridge, Elena followed Austin down the hall with
Fergie by her side. To Elena, the Independence had always felt like a moving
city with its dozens of cabins, galley, command bridge, research lab, and cargo
bay. In addition, the hovercraft was also beginning to feel like home to her.
They'd spent so much time traveling, and now, when they were most desperate,
it was a safe place to rest while the wintry air crept around the mountain
outside.

As soon as they reached the research lab, Fergie got to work accessing
several Optivisions that hovered in midair above the pupil station: one with a
map of where they were, one with a map of where they needed to go, and
another of the safest route to get there.

"Guess what the city of Istanbul was once named?" Austin said to Elena.

Elena looked at the second map that Fergie had opened and recognized it
immediately.

"Constantinople! We just studied the Byzantine Empire at school."

Austin nodded. "And look at this," he continued as Fergie accessed yet
another screen.

The image of a massive building with a rotund roof appeared. Smaller
buildings, barren trees, and four towers that stood like points on a compass
flanked the larger building, which looked like it had been constructed of red
sand.

"Hagia Sofia?" Elena said quizzically. "We just studied that, too. It was the
cathedral constructed during the reign of Justinian the Great."

"That's right," Austin confirmed. "In the earlier part of this century, the
building was converted into a manufacturing plant."

"What does that have to do with the artifacts?" Elena asked.

"When we came back from the Ark empty handed, I asked Pigg to read through the dossiers to see if he could find anything we missed."

As he was speaking, Fergie pulled the Broadcaster from her wrist and set it on the pupil station. Then, a tiny Touchdot flew from the device, and an Optivision screen appeared holographically in midair. This new screen displayed scans from the ceiling in Truman Ransom's office.

"As Pigg was looking through all this, he was able to decode part of the ceiling in your dad's office." Austin rubbed a finger over the scar on his chin, which Elena understood as a sign of concentration mixed with uneasiness.

"Please observe," Fergie said as she pulled the Ransom Dossier toward her.

She flipped the diary open to a specific page and accessed an Optivision from the center of the page.

"I didn't know the diary had Optivision capability!" Elena said, leaning closer.

"Pigg found that, too," said Austin.

Fergie layered the Optivision screens from the Catalan Atlas and the Ransom Dossier with the ceiling scans from her dad's office. A dot appeared in Istanbul, which Austin pointed to.

"Because of this spot, our theory is that one of the artifacts is hidden in Istanbul," Austin said. "We think that a Station was built underneath Hagia Sofia."

"Do we have any way of knowing which Renegade put an artifact there?" Elena asked.

"No, not yet," said Austin. "But, if we can find an artifact in Istanbul, that would give us three artifacts. And with that number collected, I'm hoping that Wheeler will take what we're doing more seriously. Then, maybe we could convince him to help us get the Tablets of Destiny from Tavington's farm," Austin said optimistically. "And then we'd only need eight more!"

"You say 'only eight more' like it's going to be easy to get those artifacts," Elena scoffed. "May I remind you that we've had one disaster after another since Hopper told us that Imperator enslaved the entire human race inside the domed cities?"

This one conversation with their Resident Advisor, Hopper, had unraveled too much truth for Elena. The truth about a secret organization called the Renegades that her parents were involved with to help fight against the ruthless dictator, Imperator. The truth about her parents' unexpected murder. And the truth that unless Imperator was removed from power none of humanity would live in freedom.

"We almost drowned in quicksand when the Independence was swallowed in New York City, we were attacked by Humanoids outside the White House in Washington D.C., and now we've almost been crushed to death by an avalanche."

"You sound like you're panicking a little bit," Austin pointed out.

"Yes, and won't you join me?" Elena replied.

"As you know, my parents insist that we need all the artifact codes assembled in order to defeat Imperator," Fergie reminded her in a tone of formality. "We already know that the Renegades hid the artifacts around the world. At some point, it will be essential that we recover all of them."

Elena bit her bottom lip to keep words from exploding from her mouth. In the beginning, she wanted to know about the secret artifacts because she wanted revenge for her parents' murder. But now, Elena felt the whole journey was getting out of control.

Plus, given that there were some truly fatal consequences to pursuing this quest, Elena suspected that Kidd would never help them get all the artifacts they needed, no matter how much Austin wanted to believe it.

"Hey, Brainiack." Kidd's voice echoed unexpectedly over the ship's communication system. "Could you get up here so we can get moving?"

Elena rolled her eyes at the nickname he'd used, but Fergie jumped up immediately and left the room.

"I wouldn't get your hopes up about Wheeler ever helping us," Elena told Austin.

Austin shrugged, and pulled the Alpha Manuscript toward him from across the table. He stared longingly at it.

"I find my father's writing so fascinating. I just wish that we could unlock some of its secrets like we've been able to for the Ransom Dossier."

Elena could tell by Austin's face that he was more excited than ever about following up with the work their parents had been doing with the Renegades. But she was beginning to feel pressed in on all sides. She wished she could be strong like him, but all the days of traveling, not sleeping well, the confusion she'd felt when they didn't find the Tablets of Destiny, and the almost dying left her feeling weary.

Elena rubbed her eyes tiredly and said, "I can't look at this stuff anymore. I'm going to check on Bowen, okay?"

"Sure," Austin said. "I'll be over in a little while to give him another check up."

As Elena walked into the corridor she felt the Independence begin to move. Knowing that they were on their way to Istanbul filled her insides with unfamiliar tension. Random thoughts began to race through her mind: What if they couldn't find the materials they needed to fix the Independence? What if they could never get back to school or home to Atlanson? And even if they made it home, how were they ever supposed to return to their normal lives?

"Hey there, Sunshine," Declan Bowen said weakly as Elena entered his room. "I've been waiting for you to show up and give me some news."

Elena was always amazed at how much Abria and Declan looked alike in the face, though his piercing blue eyes had a distinct look of playfulness that was uniquely his own.

"How are you feeling?" Elena asked, eager for an excuse to talk about something else.

"Fine, fine. Austin said that I just need bed rest for these dimwit broken ribs, but no permanent damage. I don't even get a cool scar to go with my injury."

Elena tried with great difficulty to smile at his lightheartedness. "Where's Abria?"

"She said something about needing to do her hair or nails or something."

"Yeah," Elena said dolefully as she sat on the edge of his bed.

Technically, she should still be angry at Declan. He'd helped Austin tie her up and leave her behind so they could search the Ark alone.

But soon after, she'd been scared to find him pale and helpless, lying on a heap of broken wood after he'd fallen through the ship. Then, they'd almost died during the avalanche. So, keeping a list of people to be mad at seemed like too much work for her today.

"You're very cheery today." Declan forced a smile.

"Austin wants to go to Istanbul to get parts for the Independence so we can fix the engine. Apparently, there was a hovercraft manufacturing plant there. But he also thinks he found another artifact because Pigg found a new module in my dad's dossier.

"But we're not supposed to tell Wheeler that we're searching for an artifact because he gets ridiculously angry every time we bring it up. You should have seen his face when Pigg let it slip why we're really going to Istanbul. I'm pretty sure that he wishes he'd never met any of us.

"And then Pigg, I mean, the boy is cooking everything on the ship. I'm kinda afraid that we'll run out of food, and he'll start cooking our mattresses or something to make soup." Elena stopped talking after she noticed the expression on Declan's face. "Sorry. I'm rambling."

"Yes, you are," Declan confirmed. "What's going on with you? It's not like you to be fearful."

Fearful. Fearful? Was that the strange feeling she had in the pit of her stomach? But what was she afraid of? Maybe it was the thought of losing everyone like she'd already lost her parents.

"Don't worry so much, Ransom," Declan said, breaking her thoughts. "We'll figure it all out in the right time."

"When did you become so optimistic?" Elena said sarcastically, because Declan was the most easygoing, optimistic person she knew besides Abria.

"I don't know," Declan said mockingly. "Maybe it's because I almost died yesterday."

Elena wanted to smile, but she couldn't.

"When I was growing up all I wanted was to get outside the domes and see the world. But now, I would trade every dream to be able to snuggle up on the couch with my parents and tell them about my boring life." She sighed. "You know, as Austin and Fergie were going over all the diaries and scans and everything I was just thinking that I wanted to know what it all meant so we could be done. It's frustrating to not know all the answers."

"You don't have to do this, you know?" Declan said.

"Do what?" Elena asked, feeling confused.

"Look for clues and artifacts, search for answers to crazy questions, try to be the superhuman that saves the world. You could choose to just be a normal, sassy, sarcastic girl."

Elena rolled her eyes at him.

"I guess I could try to be *normal,* but I was so looking forward to having superhuman powers."

As Declan began to laugh, Elena felt an abrupt vibration beneath her feet and struggled to maintain her balance as the Independence pitched sharply to the side. Elena exchanged a wide-eyed look with Declan and then, instinctively, grabbed the straps from the sides of his bed.

"What are you doing?" Declan said as the hovercraft pitched again.

"Strapping you down so you don't fall out of bed," explained Elena. "I've got to go see what's happening."

Declan grabbed her forearm tightly. "Don't leave me!" He pleaded as she clipped the straps to his chest.

"I'm sorry," Elena said sincerely, yanking her arm from his grip. "I'll be right back."

Elena crashed into the wall on her way out of Declan's cabin. She stumbled down the hall toward the bridge as the Independence swayed back and forth violently.

"What's going on?" Elena hollered as she stepped through the door to the command bridge.

"The Independence is going down," Kidd said. "The ship must have more damage than I thought."

Elena looked nervously at Austin and then to Fergie, who confirmed with a nod of her head that the ship was going to crash.

"How far are we from Istanbul now?" Austin shouted above the noise of the failing ship.

"Seven miles. But I've lost almost complete control!" Kidd took a moment to look back at Austin. "I don't know if I can get us all the way there."

Austin looked at Elena and the others. "Better get belted."

"But what about Declan?" Abria said frantically.

"He's okay," Elena replied. "I strapped him down."

Elena ran to the nearest captain's chair and jammed the seat belt on. She watched Kidd's fingers move quickly over the dozens of Optivisions that were hovering above the control panel. Fergie was on her feet beside him doing her own work, but all the screens were lit up red, and different alarms were sounding in all directions around the command bridge.

"I could try to switch on the two working engines to see if that will stabilize the ship," Kidd told Austin.

"Try it!" Austin ordered.

As Kidd started to open several new screens, Elena saw a vast, dense cityscape come into view through the front window. Tall buildings were stacked closely together, only wide enough to allow foot traffic. Elena felt a vibration when the engines turned on, but then the Independence began to rotate wildly.

"I don't see any place to land!" Kidd shouted. "It's only buildings down there. I'm going to switch to full manual operation to see if I can regain control."

Elena watched him grab the control yoke and could tell that Kidd was straining, but his strength wasn't enough to maintain control. The Independence careened wildly. Elena felt a lot of pressure in her chest and was dizzy from all the spinning.

"Brainiack, elevator trim and wing flaps!" Kidd yelled at Fergie, who began to do something on one of the screens without hesitation. But whatever she did, it clearly wasn't enough because Kidd hollered, "We're going to crash! Prepare for impact!"

▢ 2 ▢

Boots on the Ground

Elena thought it was dimwitted for Kidd to tell them to *prepare* for impact. How could she ever be *prepared* to crash? But the Independence was out of control, and there was nothing to be done about it. Kidd tried his best to swerve through the city, but Elena could still feel the hovercraft scraping against the sides of the buildings.

All at once, a body of water appeared out the front window.

"There's a bridge!" Kidd sounded almost relieved. "I'm going to put us down right there."

Elena saw the bridge getting ever closer. The scene suddenly felt like it was happening in slow motion. She could see that Kidd was yelling something. He and Fergie were trying to maintain control of the ship, but there was a sharp ringing in Elena's ears that negated all other noise.

Elena looked at Austin. He was trying to say something, but she couldn't hear him. She held her breath and released her grip on the chair rests so she could hold the Kairos around her neck. Any moment now she would meet her parents in the world where only spirits live.

Then, her head slammed back into her seat and forward to her chest as the Independence made impact. She felt the ship tremble as it skidded for a long stretch, vibrating dangerously. The ship plowed through the dozens of hovercrafts that had been abandoned on the bridge, yet they were still sliding.

And then, just as it seemed that they would smash through the guardrail and plummet into the waters below, the Independence stopped abruptly, coming to rest. Elena felt a momentary appreciation for Kidd's flying and, more importantly, landing ability.

"Everyone alright?" Austin called.

"Worst landing, like, EVER!" Abria managed to choke out. Her face was stained with sweat and tears.

"I think my heart stopped," Elena replied as she unclipped her belt.

She slid unceremoniously out of her chair and landed in a heap on the floor. Feeling surprised and confused, she looked around. The entire ship was tilted to one side, and anything that hadn't been bolted down had created a field of debris throughout the entire room. Plus, several of the wall panels had popped free, exposing wires and control boards.

"Why are we, like, crooked?" Abria asked.

"We must have hit a couple of those abandoned hovercrafts on the bridge," Kidd said. "But we won't know for sure until we get outside."

"I've got to go, like, check on Declan," Abria said.

"I'll come with you," Elena said. "I need to find Pigg."

But, getting down the now crooked hallway was a real challenge. Chairs from the galley, random articles of clothing, combat boots, and mattresses from some of the cabins were scattered about.

"My lipstick!" Abria said, picking a round cylinder up off the floor.

Elena paused by the galley for a moment. Pigg didn't answer when she called out for him, so she and Abria moved on down the hall toward Declan's room.

"I can't believe you left me!" Declan blurted as Elena walked through his door.

Everything in his room looked surprisingly normal except that all the drawers along the wall were open, and clothes were laying in a haphazard mess all over the floor. And there was Pigg, sitting against one of the walls with his hand clutched over his heart.

"I wish I hadn't left," Elena said honestly. "After the crash on Ararat, I probably shouldn't have watched us go down again. I guess it's more bad dreams for me."

"What happened?" Declan said.

"Wheeler figures the Independence has more damage than he thought, so we've crashed on a bridge. But at least we're in Istanbul. Yay..." Elena said dryly.

"Can you take me back to the command bridge with you?" Declan asked.

"I don't see how we could get you there," Elena said. "The hallway is blocked with junk. But I'll go find out what Austin wants to do and be right back."

"I'll just wait here," said Abria.

"Come on, Pigg," Elena said, hoisting him up by the arm. "We've gotta get you up and moving around."

Elena helped Pigg pick his way back down the hall to the command bridge where she announced, "Bowen's fine."

"Oh, that's just fantastic," Kidd said shortly. He was flipping through several of the Optivisions that were open on the control panel. "So can we focus on something that's actually important? I've got to check out the whole ship now, okay? I need to make an assessment of all the parts we need from the manufacturing plant, and now that we've crashed again, I'm thinking it's going to be extensive."

"Do you need any help?" Austin asked.

"No," Kidd said curtly as he held up his Broadcaster and activated the Touchdot. "But it would make it easier for me to check the ship if everyone could pick up the stuff that got thrown around during the crash."

Then, without another word, Kidd took his Touchdot and left the room.

"Pigg," Austin said, but Pigg's eyes were a little glazed over. "Pigg?" He snapped his fingers in Pigg's face. "Are you okay?"

"I'm just a teeny bit traumatized actually," Pigg replied weakly.

"Well, I need you to get it together, okay? I need you to check over the ship to make sure that all the programs are running correctly and that none of the control systems are damaged? Just don't get into Wheeler's way. Can you do that?"

Pigg's eyes slowly slid into focus. "Can I get something to snack on first? Because I always work better when I'm not hungry. And if you want me to stay out of Wheeler's way, I think I'll start on the side of the ship with the galley anyway because chances are that he'll be in the cargo bay first so that he can get outside to look at the exterior. And then, I think that maybe I should…"

Austin put a hand on Pigg's shoulder in a kind way to interrupt him. "Go in whatever order you need to, just make sure that the systems will operate so we can fly out of here once Wheeler fixes the engines, okay? Take as much time as you need."

Pigg gave Austin a salute and left the bridge.

"Perhaps I shall accompany Pigg," Fergie suggested. "He seems to be experiencing a small degree of shock."

Austin nodded and then looked at Elena as Fergie left the room. "Are you alright?"

"I'm a bit traumatized," Elena said honestly. "But I've learned that being your friend comes with special perks like that." Austin smiled admiringly, but Elena kept on. "So, how did we get stuck with janitorial duty?"

"Maybe because we're the least qualified on the ship to actually do anything useful in a situation where our primary mode of transportation has crashed?" Austin said playfully.

"Hey, I can be useful at fixing the ship," Elena said as she and Austin moved down the hall, picking up articles of clothing and mattresses along the way. "I would just need some training on basic concepts and I think I could…" But Austin was shaking his head in a disbelieving way. "Okay, fine! I'm a complete dimwit. Is that what you wanted to hear?"

"You're not a dimwit. And I actually need your help with something that is," Austin lowered his voice to a whisper, "equally as important as fixing the Independence."

"Oh? Are we going to lie and tell Pigg that we ate all of his favorite snacks? Because that would be so fun." Elena was excited about the possibility of doing something normal like teasing Pigg. "Remember that time in Sector Seven when he'd hid all those snacks from his mom, and we said we ate all of them?" She smiled at the thought. "He had that panic attack, which included copious amounts of shaking, if I remember correctly."

"No," Austin replied, shaking his head disapprovingly but also smiling just the same. "I wanted to talk to you about how we go about looking for the next artifact without letting Wheeler know that's what we're actually doing."

Elena's face fell. She thought about how Declan had mentioned the word *fearful* to her. Now that she'd had a little time to think on it, she realized why she wasn't excited to talk about more artifacts with Austin.

"What's the matter?" Austin asked.

"Huh? What do you mean?"

"You're frowning, which isn't entirely in itself a weird thing because you frown a lot, but this kind of frown means you're thinkin' on something," Austin said. "So, what's going on?"

Elena shrugged. "It's just, earlier today Bowen said that I was acting fearful. And since we've crashed again, I've realized that he's right."

"What are you afraid of?"

"I don't exactly know how to say it," Elena admitted. "But growing up in Atlanson made me feel like I was mostly in control of my life. I mean, I had parents to respect, but we basically went where we wanted, when we wanted to, right?"

Austin nodded.

"But ever since dad and mom died, and we found out that Imperator keeps us under constant surveillance, and we started looking for these artifacts, I've just felt like I've had less control over everything."

"Less control means more fear," Austin said in an understanding sort of way.

"Exactly!" Elena said. "And now that we've almost died twice in the last couple days, I'm starting to realize that the more I try to hang on to control, the less I actually have. I can't even control my stupid dreams, which have been downright terrifying, by the way."

Austin set the mattress he was holding up against the wall and grabbed Elena's hand.

"Look, if it's too much, I'll go alone to find the next artifact. You can stay here and look after Bowen. Or you can come with us and help the others find machine parts. Then, we'll get back to school and slow down on all this artifact stuff."

"Yeah, that's *if* we ever get home. It's looking doubtful at this point," Elena said. "I mean, we're standing in a hallway that is tilted. Things aren't looking great for us right now."

"I'm sure that Wheeler will be able to fix the ship," Austin said. "We made the right decision coming here."

"How do you know?"

"I just know it," Austin said, but Elena looked away moodily. "Do you trust me?"

"Of course I trust you," Elena said without delay. She looked into his face. "I can't let you go looking for an artifact alone. If I lose you then I'd be alone with everyone else. And I have no confidence that Wheeler and I could get along well enough to get us all back home alive."

"You don't give yourself enough credit," Austin said. "I'm sure if you tried just a little bit you could get along with Wheeler."

But, hours later, Kidd finally returned to the command bridge with a sweaty brow, torn clothes, black smudges on his face, and a temper that could rival Marshall on a bad day. Elena felt certain that she'd never be able to deal with Kidd in a courteous way.

"It's pretty bad," Kidd said gruffly. He went over to the control panel and pulled up several Optivisions, accessing different areas of the ship's operating systems. "So, we know that one of the engines was already crushed. And I'm going to need a new turbine and carburetor to fix that. But with the last crash we're going to need new aircraft cables, tri-fold rivets, fuel lines, fuse panels, a new aileron, a compressor for engine 2, and a horizontal stabilizer. Plus, it wouldn't hurt to have a twist grip throttle kit with friction lock."

Elena stared at Kidd with her mouth hanging open. "How are any of us supposed to know what you said?"

Kidd rolled his eyes. "I don't expect any of you to know what I said, which is why you'll each have these *pretty little pictures* on your Touchdots of the parts we need." He indicated the screen from his own Touchdot that displayed images of the parts.

While Kidd wasn't looking, Austin turned to Pigg and raised his eyebrows in a way that Elena knew meant he wanted confirmation that everything Kidd said was all that they needed.

After Pigg nodded his head ever so slightly Austin said, "Listen, it's getting dark. Let's rest now and leave out of here at first light. We'll hike to the city, get everything we need, and be back as soon as possible so that we can get started fixing the Independence."

There was a murmur of general consent, and then the room cleared quickly, leaving Elena and Austin alone.

"Okay, so give me this brilliant plan for how we're going to find the next artifact," Elena said to him.

Before the sun was up the next day, Elena crawled out of bed slowly. She pulled on her infantry training uniform and combat boots. Yawning, she walked down the hall toward the galley and pulled her curls into a knot on her head.

"You look awful," Pigg said as she entered the kitchen.

"Thanks for the info."

"I just meant that you look like you didn't sleep well," Pigg said, looking embarrassed.

"Did you sleep?" Austin asked, standing from his place at the table to pull out a chair for her.

"I think I did sleep a little bit, somewhere between the dream about crashing the hovercraft I was flying into the side of a mountain and the dream where I caused an avalanche that then covered me over so I drowned in the snow." Elena yawned again and stretched her arms above her head.

"There you are," Abria said, coming into the kitchen and looking at Elena. She looked rested and was glowing with a fresh application of makeup and lip shimmer. "I came by your room to get you. I'm surprised to see you awake so early."

"Who says I'm awake?" Elena grumbled into her cereal bowl. "I wonder how cold it is outside. I almost froze to death on Ararat."

"The thermal scans on the control panel indicate that it is approximately 50 degrees Fahrenheit." Fergie had entered the room, but Elena didn't even look up. "We are approximately eight kilometers to our target, so I am confident that light clothing would be appropriate for hiking. We should include a rain poncho in our tactical pack and a light lunch."

"Thanks, Fergie," said Austin.

"Personally, I don't worry about the weather," Pigg said after taking a rather large bite of dry cereal. "I worry about us starving to death. We're running low on food."

"How is that possible?" Elena said. "I thought you stocked the galley for a month of traveling. We've only been gone four...five days at most."

"Oh, well..." Pigg looked guilty. "After the whole thing on Ararat I had a snack fest to calm my nerves. It got a little out of hand. But I knew that we were in trouble when I realized I was eating a box of uncooked noodles. On a side note that's actually completely food related, I'm a little nervous about the hike to Hagia Sofia. I just get so hungry, and when Fergie said we'd need to pack a *light* lunch I have to be honest, I got a little sweaty."

Austin shook his head and smiled. "Pigg, will you stay here and look after Bowen?"

"Really? Oh, thank you, Austin," Pigg said gratefully. "I was hoping I'd get to stay behind. I'm really not up for any more adventures."

"I'll just take Declan some food before we leave," Abria said. "I'll tell him that you'll be staying here, Pigg, in case he gets lonely."

"I'll come, too," Elena said.

Moments later, Elena stepped into Declan's stateroom and said, "We only have dry cereal and powdered milk this morning, but maybe we can scrounge around town for food when we go out."

Declan was propped up on some pillows. He was looking better than the day before.

"How are you feeling?" Abria asked him in a singsong voice.

"Fine, fine." Declan eyed Elena for a long moment while Abria set his breakfast tray down. "What's wrong with you?"

"Oh, are you curious about my gaunt look and the dark circles under my eyes? Bad dreams kept me awake," Elena explained.

"So, what's the story?" Declan asked her.

"Well, we're leaving now to go see if we can find the next artifact," Elena folded her arms over her chest. "Though we're not supposed to tell Wheeler that because he'd go crazy. He's going to give us a list of all the machine parts we need, so Fergie and Abria will look for parts while Austin and I search for the artifact. And Pigg will stay here with you."

"I wish I could go," Declan said moodily.

"I know," Elena said, but then added with a smile, "Don't worry, we'll get into plenty more trouble before we're done finding artifacts."

"I don't want to get in trouble," Declan said. "I just want to be with yo...y'all...all of you. You know. E-ver-y-one."

"Okay, that was weird," Abria said, smiling brightly. "Get some rest, Declan. We'll be back soon."

Elena gave him a fleeting smile. She followed Abria out the door and down the hallway into the cargo bay. Several tactical packs were lined along the floor, and Kidd was tossing a canteen into each one.

"Oh good, you're here," Pigg said brightly to Elena and Abria. "Okay everyone, gather 'round and I'll show you the improvements I've made to the packs."

Pigg picked up one of the tactical packs for display.

"The packs are still fitted with a high glide compressed air tactical parachute and an emergency floatation device, which I won't demonstrate again because of that time you had to cut if off me so I wouldn't suffocate. But hopefully you won't encounter a scary situation that involves any kind of drowning. There's also a snack compartment and a canteen pocket."

He then turned the pack around to show them a little zipper on the side.

"But, I've added this little compartment here for a reflector blanket. After the disaster on Ararat I didn't want anyone to freeze to death if we got stuck outside."

"That's really brilliant, Pigg!" Austin praised.

"When did you do all this?" Elena said, clapping him on the back in approval.

Pigg put his eyes on the floor in an uncomfortable way and looked for a moment like he didn't want to say, but making up lies was not one of his qualities.

"After I finished my evaluation of the Independence's condition I had some extra time on my hands and since we're running low on food. Which is totally my fault" — he added quickly after receiving a look from Elena — "I decided it would be best to tinker down here."

"You *evaluated* the ship?" Kidd growled at Pigg. "Who asked you to do that, huh?"

Pigg looked away, but Austin said, "I asked him to inspect the ship while you were doing yours. He didn't get in your way, so what does it matter?"

Kidd gave Austin a look of disgust, but he didn't reply, except to say, "Stand back, away from the main floor."

As Elena moved to one side of the room, Kidd reached out for a small lever on the wall panel. Then, a section of the floor the size of a two-person stretcher rose up in the air leaving an indentation like a missing piece of a puzzle.

"These are called hover-transporters. You control them with your Broadcaster. The whole floor of the cargo bay is lined with them so we'll have plenty to use if we need to take out more."

"This is amazing!" said Austin, beaming at Kidd with appreciation. "How did you find these?"

"I found it when I was making *my evaluation* of the ship," Kidd replied nastily.

"Are we going to do this all day?" Austin asked directly. "I was kinda hoping that we could get along for the amount of time it takes to find the parts at the manufacturing plant. Can we leave the attitude here?"

Elena had never heard Austin speak so directly to anyone about their behavior before, besides her. She was curious to see how Kidd would take it and, in truth, she'd already gathered her fist into a ball in case he decided to hit Austin. But, Kidd simply surveyed Austin for a quiet moment and then nodded his head.

"Just scan the side of the hover-transporter here," Kidd continued, and Elena shook her head, silently wondering if she'd ever understand boys, "and it will assign to your Broadcaster so that you can operate it. We'll walk these out to the manufacturing plant and load the machine parts on top of them."

Then, Kidd and Austin began to pack the hover-transporter with grappling hooks, climbing rope, tactical knives, and other supplies.

"They don't look it, but each of these transporters can carry a ton of material. We'll be able to pile all the parts we need," Kidd said.

"How do you know that these can hold so much weight?" Austin questioned.

"We use these at the racetrack in Harleston Village," Kidd replied. "The transporters hover up and down the grease line bringing spare parts and recycling old parts. One time, after I'd won my twelfth race, the transporter carried all the parts I'd won to..."

He'd been smiling as he recalled the memory, but suddenly Kidd made a face like he'd shared too much personal information. He frowned, and said grumpily, "Can we just go?"

"Allow me to place my Touchdot to scan so that we may record images of the city," Fergie said as Kidd opened the exit to the cargo bay, and a surge of frigid air pushed into the ship.

Elena gave an involuntary shudder. "I'm gonna just grab an extra jacket."

Kidd led the way down the loading plank with his hover-transporter floating beside him. When Elena finally stepped foot on the bridge she noticed that the Independence had indeed crashed on top of several abandoned hovercrafts. She couldn't help but wonder how they'd ever be able to move their hovercraft off the bridge.

She set off behind Austin and Fergie who were following Kidd, with Abria bringing up the rear. The forsaken belongings that had been left to decay in the sun made it difficult to forge a path, but Kidd never hesitated as he brushed things aside or navigated his hover-transporter around vehicles.

Toward the city, Elena could see where the seawater had receded from the coastline. She remembered Fallon telling her once, while they were at the Statue of Liberty in New York, that the sun was eroding the supply of water on the earth.

"This place is totally creepier than, like, New York," Abria said as if she could hear Elena's thoughts.

Abria had made an excellent observation. The city did remind Elena of New York with its discarded belongings, broken shop windows, and weeds growing rampant. But, they'd experienced most of New York in the comfort and safety provided by the Independence.

Walking along the vacant city of Istanbul with only the thud of their footsteps echoing off the brick streets was a little unnerving. Not even the sun-bleached banners that hung from the street lamps provided any sound.

As Elena turned around to ask Abria if she thought Fallon would jump out from behind one of the buildings, she noticed that her friend was sitting on top of her hover-transporter. Elena stopped dead in her tracks; the scene reminded her of a book she'd once read about a magical flying carpet.

"What are you doing?" she asked, rolling her eyes.

"Oh, just riding on the hover-transporter," Abria said. "Remember when you made those, like, sleds during our third quarter exam last year so we didn't havta, like, walk? Well, this is my version of a sled. But, ya know, totally better because we don't havta push it." She giggled and tossed her hair. "I just thought I'd save my energy for lifting heavy objects."

Elena looked at Austin, who shrugged and then jumped onto his own hover-transporter. A couple seconds later, they were all flying through the city atop their individual magic carpets toward the huge, towering cathedral complex that lay before them.

Elena felt minuscule as they made their way through courtyards of naked trees and overgrown sidewalks toward the rotund buildings and towers that formed the Hagia Sofia compound. The façade of the main structure was faded yet still portrayed its own rustic beauty.

"This is the manufacturing plant?" Kidd said skeptically. "It looks like a cathedral."

"It was a cathedral," Elena replied. "The emperor Justinian the First brought in material from all over the Byzantine Empire for the construction, and over ten thousand people were employed to build it. He had large stones from quarries in Egypt..."

"I didn't ask for a history lesson, Freckles!" Kidd rudely interrupted. "Let's just find a way to get inside."

Elena rolled her eyes and walked on with the others in silence. All the outer doors and windows were firmly boarded up from the inside. However, after a long walk around the building, Kidd finally found an upper window that had already been broken out.

He pointed one of the grappling hooks above his head and shot it through the opening. Moments later, Elena followed him up the rope toward the top of the building.

Elena's mouth fell open as she climbed through the window and straight into the main gallery. The dozens of windows all around the room gave light to towering marble columns, glittering mosaics, and richly painted domed ceilings. As she began to slide down the rope, she noticed long rows of dust-covered hovercrafts; it looked almost like a showroom.

"This is totally, like, amazing!" Abria said, her voice echoing all around as they rappelled into the room below. "I can't believe they turned *this place* into a, like, manufacturing plant."

As her feet touched the floor, she said, "So, this room is filled with hovercrafts. Can't we just use one of these to, like, get home?"

"None of these hovercrafts possess aeronautic technology," Fergie said knowingly. "However, and more importantly, the Independence is linked to a private Orbitor so that no one may ascertain our position."

"Oh, right...Orbitor," Abria said, rolling her eyes like it had never occurred to her to remember a piece of information that she found useless. "Totally forgot."

"Does everyone know what we're looking for?" Kidd asked impatiently, and they all murmured in agreement. "Good. Let's stop the chit chat and get going."

Kidd moved off in one direction with a look on his face like he'd already spotted something they needed.

Abria looked at Fergie helplessly and said, "I know we have pictures, but you know I still need help because all of it looks the same to me."

"Lena, follow me," Austin whispered as Fergie led Abria away from them.

Elena watched the Touchdot fly from Austin's Broadcaster, and a scanning screen opened. They set off together down one gallery with the laser scanner in front of them. Then, they descended a flight of stairs and hurried through a maze of machine parts that were drowning in dust.

"Fergie, we found a room full of machine parts on the south side of the building. Just follow the stairs down one flight," Austin said into his Broadcaster, but he and Elena didn't wait for her reply. They kept on, pursuing hall after hall of the abandoned building.

"It really, really smells terrible," Elena said, covering her nose with the sleeve of her jacket.

"I haven't seen anything yet, have you?"

"Besides these long, ridiculously boring hallways, no."

"Has your Kairos moved at all?"

"Nope," Elena said, sounding bored. "It's been just as still as everything else down here. Are you sure there's an artifact here?"

"Of course I'm not sure," Austin said. "I can't be sure of anything since the failure on Ararat. But, I am hopeful."

Elena wished that she felt hopeful. But since the directions up to this point had been more like guesswork it was hard for her to be optimistic about something she didn't understand.

At long last, Elena and Austin came to a small, insignificant room that was aligned with cubicles and office furniture.

"Oh, fantastic! A dead end," Elena said, feeling frustration creep over her. "We must be miles below the city, and now we'll have to turn around and go back."

"No! This is it!" said Austin suddenly. "I see it there!"

He pointed at something Elena couldn't see.

"The light from the Touchdot is shining just right. I can see weakness in the wall of the simulation."

Austin appeared to be reading from the Touchdot and then moved his fingers in a non-distinct way along the vacant space directly in front of him. A moment later, Elena watched as the wall of the simulation began to break down, melting away to reveal a darkness that was so absolute it seemed to spill out toward her feet.

"I still wish I could understand how you can see these things," Elena said, feeling awe-inspired.

"Me, too," Austin admitted as he activated his Touchdot. "Fergie and Pigg were able to improve the cryptology programming so that it will record straight to the Independence. We have really smart friends."

Elena removed the hololight from her tactical vest and held it high above her head. Her mouth fell open. They'd stepped inside a grandiose tunneling system that was supported by hundreds of marbled columns; some of the columns were round and plain, but others were richly ornamented with carvings of leaves.

"This is called Basilica Cistern," Austin read from his Touchdot.

"Oh, yesssss," she said thoughtfully. "It was constructed in the sixth century during the reign of Justinian to bring drinking water to Constantinople from Thrace."

"The technology is impressive."

"And also a little overwhelming," Elena said. "How are we supposed to find an artifact down here in the dark?"

"We'll just follow the Touchdot," Austin said. "It will go in front to scan the room, and we'll see if we can find anything."

However, trying to keep track of where the Touchdot was scanning was harder than it sounded. The little device shot off in one direction, but it also raced around the columns quickly, never pausing for more than a moment. The sound of their footsteps echoing off the stone floors and walls was beginning to confuse Elena. She lost all sense of direction.

"This is less like following and more like chasing," Elena said as she ran, winding through the columns with her hololight aloft.

CHAPTER 2

At long last, Elena noticed a face appear in the distance. She almost dropped her hololight out of fear, but then quickly realized that the façade wasn't moving. She stepped slowly toward what was actually a statue. Holding up one of the columns was an upside down head of a woman with sightless eyes. Instead of hair, the statue had snakes carved on its stone head.

"Check her out!" Elena called to Austin. "She's totally creepy."

"You sounded like Abria when you said that."

Elena shoved Austin hard in the arm, and he gave her a sideways smile. But then he gasped, and she knew why without even asking because she'd felt the movement from her necklace.

She pulled off the Kairos just as the sharp angles of the star necklace were automatically unfolding. Finally, a clock-like surface with multi-tiered faces appeared. The globe-tipped hand and the sun-shaped hand began to spin wildly while the various symbols lit up at different intervals.

After a moment, Austin cried out, "That's it! The artifact is somewhere inside that column."

He reached forward slowly as though touching it might inflict pain, but there was no need to do anything. The sightless eyes on the statue were already beginning to open. Then, the rest of the face slid around, shifting like pieces on a puzzle. Before Elena could blink, a purely white statue of an angel with a horn to its lips appeared.

As Austin reached forward to take the angel, Elena felt the ground quake, sending a violent vibration up her spine. She watched in awe as a column on the far side of the row crumbled from the top to the ground, pulling part of the ceiling with it.

"I guess by now we should have been prepared for the surprise ambush portion of collecting artifacts," Elena said dolefully as she grabbed the Kairos, and strung it back around her neck.

Austin crammed the statue into his rucksack.

"And we're running!" he urged, grabbing her hand as several other columns crashed to the ground.

❑ 3 ❑

Cave-In

Elena and Austin raced between the columns, which fell unceremoniously, trying to get back to the place where they'd entered. But the ground shook as the ceiling crumbled, and there was no clear path that Elena could see. The everlasting darkness of the underground began to fill with swirling dust. Soon, it was clear that their movements were hopeless.

"The way is blocked!" Elena hollered.

"Come on," Austin said, turning around. "We'll go back this way."

Elena tried to follow Austin, but the falling columns thundered in her ears. Her hololight was no match for the marble powder that was now crushing her lungs.

"Running is useless!" Elena coughed into the collar of her shirt. "I can barely see. And we don't know where we are."

Austin held his hololight high up in the air.

"Trauma Module!" he yelled as if he'd just remembered something important. "Fergie showed me how to use the Trauma Module on the Touchdot last week."

The Touchdot flew out from his Broadcaster, and he accessed an Optivision screen. Elena was relieved to see the light from the screen spread out in all directions. Austin selected a program, and it started working immediately.

"It will lead us to the best way out," Austin said.

Elena didn't even think to question it. She took off after Austin who was chasing after the quick moving Optivision that was attached to the Touchdot. Running still felt pointless because of the ever-increasing cloud of debris. Plus, she kept tripping over falling columns. She'd already skinned both her knees and was certain that there was skin missing from her left arm.

But then Austin suddenly shouted, "Look! A stairwell."

Elena and Austin bumped into one another as they clamored up the stone steps. Then, she heard an overwhelming thunder behind them. She couldn't turned and immediately wished she hadn't. A slow motion wave of terror tingled through Elena's body as the entire cistern ceiling began to collapse. She knew instantly that it was too late to escape. She fell to her knees against the wall of the stairwell, shut her eyes tightly, and covered her head with her hands.

Moments later, Elena felt the support against the stairwell begin to collapse. She felt like she was falling and rolling at the same time. When she finally landed, a sharp pain shot through both her legs. She couldn't help but cough as dust swirled into her nose and down her throat. The sound of crushing rock pressed out any other sounds.

"Austin!" she cried out, but she could barely hear herself call his name.

She felt sick at the thought that she hadn't grabbed his hand. The sounds of roaring and collapsing continued on for a long while, but the noise still couldn't block out the images of Austin's crushed body that flashed through Elena's imagination. Complete darkness consumed everything around her. She lost all concept of time and space.

But then, after a long while, Elena finally heard Austin's voice. "Lena! Where are you?" He sounded far away.

"I'm over here!" she shouted as loud as she could, but her voice sounded mute and strange.

"I can hear you," Austin called out. "Keep talking. Try to move toward my voice."

Elena tried to move, but she could barely lift herself onto her elbows. "I can't move. I can't see a thing. I have no idea where I am or how you're going to find me."

"Just keep talking so I can follow the sound of your voice."

"Keep talking!" Elena said as loud as she could. "Do you want me to tell you about my recent vacation in Istanbul? Because it was a smash!"

A second later, she began to see a light coming from between some cracks in the rock.

"I can see your hololight right now," called Elena.

"Are you alright?" Austin asked, though she still couldn't see him.

"I don't know. I can't find my hololight. I must have dropped it."

"I'm going to send my hololight through a hole," Austin said. "Let me know if you get it."

Elena heard a tapping as, she assumed, the hololight was falling down the rock toward her. Then, quite suddenly, the hololight bounced off her head.

"Ouch! Seriously?" she grumbled.

The brightness from the hololight lit up the entire area. She could see rock all around, and where her legs had been pinned just above her knees.

"Yep, my legs are definitely stuck," Elena called to Austin.

"Can you feel them or move them?"

Elena thought about wiggling her toes. She waited earnestly for the sensation, but it never came. "No!"

"Okay, well don't panic," said Austin.

"Yeah right, because I'm so good at not panicking in stressful situations," Elena said derisively.

"I can't get to you. The columns and ceiling have fallen all around you," Austin said. "I'll have to go back for help. Hopefully, Wheeler, Abria, and Fergie are still gathering parts inside Hagia Sofia."

"I'll just wait here," Elena said dolefully, and she could almost see Austin smile at her sarcasm.

"I'll leave my vest out here so I can find you again," said Austin. "Be back as soon as I can."

Elena tried to shift her body this way and that, but it was no use. She reached into the side pocket of her tactical vest, and retrieved a canteen of water. She rinsed her mouth. She washed her sweaty face, and then took a large gulp, which dropped like a stone into her stomach. Hours had passed since breakfast, and she couldn't reach the snack in her pack. She made a mental note to talk to Pigg about adding a snack pocket to the vest just below the chin.

She laid her head against the wall behind her and sighed. What if she'd never be able to use her legs again? She'd be sent home from school, but to do what? Live with Grandpa and Grandma Haddock for the rest of her life?

Then, it occurred to her that she'd never actually seen a crippled person in Atlanson. Since her mom's hospital was at the forefront of medical advances, maybe that meant that she wouldn't lose the use of her legs.

Over time, Elena was less concerned about walking and more concerned about the fact that she was finding it harder and harder to breath. She had the terrible thought that she could asphyxiate on the dust before anyone could even get back to her location. She knew that it would take Austin at least twelve minutes to walk back to Hagia Sofia, and then it would take another twenty to get back to the Independence. And who knew how long it would take to gather the supplies they would need to dig her out of the rubble.

Elena looked at her nails, but the thick layer of dirt made them unappealing. She pulled the Kairos from around her neck.

"I wonder what Dad would say if he knew where I was," Elena said slowly as she imagined herself curled up in his arms reading one of their favorite stories with her mom cuddled beside them.

But then, Elena began to question if there were books in the spirit world. And that made her think about the feelings she'd had just before the Independence crashed on the bridge.

At that moment, Elena felt sure she was going to die and be reunited with her parents. However, she'd never actually considered what happened when a person died. Her parents had never discussed such topics with her, and she'd never thought to ask. Fear and desperation consumed her.

She'd just about passed out from exhaustion when she heard Austin's voice suddenly through the wall of rock.

"Lena! I'm back. Lena! Can you hear me? Are you okay?"

"I'm still here waiting to be rescued," Elena managed to choke out, but she didn't even bother to open her weary eyes.

"Are you hurt bad?" Elena heard Declan's voice shout from the other side of the rock.

Elena's eyes flew open. "What are you doing out of bed, Bowen?"

"We tried to stop him, but he insisted," Abria called out.

"But it's good that he came because I think we'll need everyone to shift the rock to get you out," Austin said.

"Actually, this is a simple matter of Physics," Elena heard Pigg say. "If we apply the right amount of pressure to the correct rock then the others should fall correctly, and Elena will be free."

"That is an accurate assessment," Fergie said. "However, we would need to be precise in our calculation because an incorrect movement of the rock could be catastrophic. My Touchdot can scan the fallen debris and will inform us as to where we need to apply the pressure."

"We don't need a geological study," Kidd said gruffly. "We just need to start moving the rock."

"Look at those blocks," Austin said assertively. "They must weigh a ton. There's no way we can move them. Unless you have some super human strength that we don't know about. Plus, we risk hurting Elena more. We'll take the time to study where she is and what to do before we try to move anything."

Elena thought she heard Kidd say something nasty, but then Austin called, "Lena, we're going to scan the area now. It will be a few minutes."

She heard a lot of mumbling and talk of equations and estimations. The intelligence of the verbiage being thrown around would have made Instructor Copernicus proud.

At long last, Austin said, "Lena, can you cover your face? Maybe with your vest?"

Elena unzipped her tactical vest, but it wouldn't move up or down her body. "No! I can't move enough to get it off."

"Okay, can you pull your shirt up to cover your nose, at least?"

"Yes, okay."

"Here we go," Austin said. "Just be as still as possible."

Elena heard some strange sounds, similar to what the boys sounded like when they were lifting too heavy a weight during Basic Training class. She realized that she was holding her breath in anticipation of the entire ceiling of rock to come crashing down on her head. But then, quite magically, the stones fell away.

Elena saw daylight and Austin's face blur into her line of sight. Then, she felt the weight on her thighs being removed.

"Don't move yet!" Austin ordered.

Before she knew what was happening, Austin reached over and clasped a stiff cone around Elena's neck.

"What's this?" Elena asked warily.

"I found it in the cargo bay. This rigid collar will support your neck for now. When we get you out I have another brace that will stabilize your spine until we can get you back to the ship and I can see how much damage there is."

Elena couldn't have guessed how they managed it, but one of the hover-transporters came so close to her that Declan, Austin, Kidd, and Abria merely had to slide her on top of it. Austin encased Elena's body in some kind of plastic framework that made her feel like a mummy in one of the tombs in Egypt.

"So," Kidd said loudly. "If you're done getting into trouble now, I'll go back to get the rest of the parts we need to fix the Independence. That is *why* we came here in the first place, right?"

He gave Austin a pointed look but, when Austin didn't reply, Kidd walked away in a huff.

"Let's get you someplace safe," Austin said, placing a hand on Elena's forehead.

The journey back to the Independence was long and slow. Austin was being very careful not to bump Elena's hover-transporter. Plus, she could tell that Declan was in pain as he stepped over the debris that littered the streets. By the time they got to the bridge, Abria and Fergie were half carrying him.

The moment Elena's hover-transporter passed through the door to the Independence's cargo bay, Austin said, "Bowen, you need to get back in bed right now."

"I'll go as long as someone comes to give me an update on Ransom as soon as possible," Declan said.

"I'll give you the update myself," Elena replied. "As soon as Austin fixes me."

Declan flashed a toothy grin at her stubbornness and hobbled down the hall holding tightly to his sides.

Elena's stretcher hovered easily down the hall with Austin by her side directing it. They entered a sizeable room that she'd never used before.

"I was hoping I'd never have to use the Medical Bay," Elena grumbled.

"I'm sure we'll all use it at some point," Austin said. "But it's only temporary. Later, we'll move you into the captain's quarters with Declan."

Austin, Abria, and Fergie slid Elena's rigid body onto a flat table.

"I'm just gonna take off your boots and socks," Abria said. "Let me know if it, like, hurts and I'll stop."

Elena shut her eyes tightly expecting to feel excruciating pain, but she didn't feel anything.

"Before we start," Austin said, interrupting her fears about being paralyzed. "I'm going to prick you with my Suturand, starting with your toes and moving up your legs to your belly. Just let me know when you feel something."

Every second or so, Austin asked if she felt it when he pricked her, but she couldn't feel a thing. She was too afraid to ask how far he'd gone up her leg when suddenly she felt a zap just below her bellybutton.

"I felt that!"

"Very good," Austin said. "Okay, I'm gonna get started now. Be as still as possible."

Tears leaked from her eyes and slid down the sides of her face. Crying was completely pointless because it wouldn't change anything, but she couldn't help it. Abria grabbed one of her hands and Fergie the other. She felt more and more helpless as the minutes ticked by slowly. Waiting to hear if she would ever be able to walk again was excruciating. Again, her thoughts drifted to the possibility for the Healing Surgeons in Atlanson to figure out a way to help her walk.

Finally, Austin looked Elena straight in the eye and said, "Your tailbone is badly bruised. But, miraculously, your legs weren't crushed. You'll make a full recovery."

Elena let out her breath as if she'd been holding it for a long while. "If I'm not paralyzed, why can't I feel anything?"

"Because of the bruise," Austin said. "It will heal, but I'm not sure how long it will take for you to regain the sensation in your legs and feet. I'm going to give you a pain blocker so that you won't feel too much as your body begins to recover. But, I promise that you will get better."

Elena couldn't contain the smile that spread across her entire face.

Austin smiled too, but then he said in an authoritative voice, "You need to start physical therapy right away. And you'll need to stay off your feet for the rest of the trip to keep the swelling down in your legs and back."

"Sure, whatever you want!" Elena said, feeling euphoric.

"I'm serious!" Austin said, giving her a face like he didn't believe that she'd take it easy. "I have to do spinal traction to pull your bones back into their proper place. Then, you'll need a cooling bath to help the swelling go down. And you'll need to do lumbar stabilization exercises so that your back muscles are exercised to teach your spine how to stay in the proper position. It's not going to be easy work, and you're going to need to do everything I ask of you. It will be painful."

"Austin, I'm just so thankful that I'm not paralyzed. I promise I'll do anything you ask of me."

"Even stay in bed?"

"Yes, even stay in bed."

Austin nodded his head. "Okay, then. Pigg will bring some dinner in here. After that we'll move you to the captain's quarters where you need to go right to sleep and rest your back."

"Whatever you say," Elena said as she rubbed her face with the palms of her hands and screamed with relief.

"This is the happiest I've seen you in days," Declan said as Elena was later directed into the captain's quarters. "Austin said we're going to be roomies."

Elena smiled genuinely, but sarcastically said, "I couldn't think of a more annoying person to have to recover with."

"I've known you for two years now so I think it's safe to finally ask you this very important question." Declan eased into a chair. "What's your favorite food?"

She stayed up way too late talking with Declan so that when her eyelids finally closed it barely seemed a minute before Abria's tinkling voice filled her ears.

"Time to get up!"

Elena opened one eye slowly. Her vision was blurry from sleep, but she could tell that Declan was already wide awake, looking at her.

"You were snoring a bit," he said.

"Don't tell her that," Abria rebuked him. "Girls don't want to hear stuff like that about their sleeping habits."

"It was cute-ish," Declan said with a playful smile, but Elena was too groggy to even scowl at him.

"Abria, what are you doing?" Elena asked impatiently as her friend began to pull back the blankets and sheets that were covering her body.

"Today you start physical therapy," Abria said, her words laced with cheer. "And since Austin is going to be away part of the day working with Wheeler on the hovercraft, I'm going to help you start your exercises."

"How do you know what you're doing?" Elena asked suspiciously.

It was one thing to have Austin help her through physical therapy because he understood the human body better than most adults, but to allow Abria to coach her through it when Abria spent most of her free time grooming herself seemed absurd.

"Don't worry, don't worry, Austin set it up for me. Last night, Austin had Pigg access everything about spinal injuries on the global server, and the two of us worked together on what you would need to do. He showed me each step and I saved all the directions on my Touchdot. So, we'll just follow right along with the routine that he planned out and we should get along just fine." Abria accessed an Optivision screen from her Touchdot and reviewed the notes. Then, she read, "So, we're going to start with a, like, lumbar stabilization exercise."

"Can't I eat breakfast first?" Elena asked.

"Pigg is making it now and will bring it in soon, but Austin wants you to start the day by getting your muscles warmed up so it's easier to move," Abria said. "So, we need to find the position that allows you to feel most comfortable, and then we'll exercise your back muscle so your spine will learn how to stay in the neutral position."

"I'm going to need help sitting up and moving around," Elena said.

Declan moved toward her at once.

Abria looked closely at the notes on the Optivision screen, and read, "*We need to keep Elena from getting atrophy*. What on earth does that, like, mean? Oh, here it is...*which means that her muscles would gradually decline because of not being used enough while she's in recovery*. Well, that doesn't sound good, does it?"

Abria brushed some hair out of her eyes and continued reading Austin's notes. "*We need to exercise the muscles that support the spine, including the back and gluteal muscles, the abdominal and iliopsoas muscles, and the obliques*. Okay, he put a lot of words in here that I don't even, like, understand."

Elena couldn't help but smile at her effort.

"I can't believe you got her to smile! It's not even 0700 hours yet," Declan said in a disbelieving tone.

"I got her to smile by being brainless," Abria said flippantly. "That's not really anything to be proud of."

"You're not brainless," said Elena. "I wouldn't know it either except my mom was a Healing Surgeon and Austin is a child prodigy. Most of our conversations growing up were about medical things."

"I wish your mom were here," Abria said, looking over the screen with a look of hopelessness. "She'd be much better at this."

"You'll be fine," Elena said kindly. "Now, come on. Let's work up an appetite."

They started slow, but it was still exhausting work. The physical therapy routine was long and detailed, putting strain on Elena's body, even though she was flat on her back for most of it and couldn't really feel her legs. Declan helped as much as he could, but they had to stop often so that Elena could interpret the medical verbiage for Abria.

After an hour, Elena felt frustrated that she still couldn't feel anything. Fortunately, Pigg soon arrived with a breakfast tray.

"Where did you get all that amazing food?" Elena exclaimed after she noticed the flapjacks with blueberry compote, egg scramble with mushrooms, and mixed berry salad.

"Oh, I commandeered it from a few different stores in town," Pigg said proudly. "When everyone came back here yesterday I took one of those hover-transporters and went into the city determined to find food. Plenty of stuff was expired, but then I found a whole storeroom full of canned supplies and, surprise! I was able to put together a breakfast fit for a king. Well, maybe not a king but good enough for a raggle taggle group of gypsies like us."

Abria laughed loudly.

"What a funny little, like, saying."

Pigg blushed. "It's what Elena's mom used to call us."

Elena smiled sadly at the memory.

"Thanks so much, Pigg. I'm starving."

Elena also ate her lunch and dinner that day sitting up in bed. Declan and Abria kept her spirits up with funny stories and silly jokes. But, in the back of her mind, she was starting to have a nagging question.

"So, the ship is still tilted to one side," Elena said to Abria as her blonde friend helped her get ready for bed. "Any word from Wheeler as to how he can get the Independence upright?"

"He said something about using the engines to propel the ship into an upright position," said Abria. "But he also said he might want to land it on top of some of the other vehicles on the bridge so that he could look at the hull or something like that. I don't know. When the boys start talking about machine parts and fixing the ship, that's when I start thinking about new ways to wear my hair."

Abria pulled Elena's blanket up to her chin. "Don't worry your pretty, little red curls about it. I'm sure that Wheeler and Austin will work it all out."

The next morning, Abria came again to wake Elena early.

"Argh! My back is so stiff," Elena said, as she pushed up on her elbows.

"That's why we're going to start with stretching exercises today," Abria said. "We'll try to see how much flexibility we can get in your muscles, ligaments, and tendons. We also need to, like, activate and strengthen muscles not directly involved with the injured area.

"For example, hamstring tightness limits motion in the pelvis and can place it in a position that increases stress across the low back, so hamstring stretching is an important part of alleviating lower back pain."

Elena and Declan stared at Abria with their mouths open.

"Don't look so, like, shocked," Abria said. "I was tired of being the dumbest person in the room so I stayed up late to study all this stuff."

They started right away with Elena flat on her back in bed, and Abria pushing on her legs. And then Abria moved quickly into low-impact aerobic exercises, all done with Elena in a seated position. They worked hard until Pigg brought them breakfast and then got right back to it until lunchtime when Austin arrived, looking tired.

"Hey stranger," Elena said. "You look awful."

"Sorry I didn't really come see you yesterday. Wheeler and I have been working non-stop on the ship," Austin said. He yawned loudly. "How are you feeling today?"

"I still can't really feel much of anything," Elena said honestly. "And I'm super tired."

"Alright, let me check your spine to see how the physical therapy is working."

Abria and Declan helped Austin flip Elena onto her stomach. She waited patiently while he took Suturand scans.

Finally he said, "Very good progress. I'm going to give you another pain blocker just in case."

Elena felt the pressure of his hand into the small of her back, though she really couldn't feel the needle.

"So, how's it going with fixing the ship? Abria doesn't say much about it because she's so worried about her hair."

"Hey, Austin," said Abria. "Can you give her a pain blocker in her mouth to stop mean things from coming out of it?"

"Ha...ha..." Elena said drearily, but Declan laughed out loud and nodded. "Everyone is so funny today."

Austin smiled softly. "The repairs are slow and frustrating. At least, Wheeler seems frustrated, so I'm taking that as a bad sign."

"He's always in a bad mood." Elena shrugged. "I would worry if he was any different."

"Okay, boys." Abria clapped her hands together loudly. "You've got to leave the room now."

"What?" Declan said. "I thought we were doing all this therapy stuff together."

"Yes, we are. Except the next part of Elena's therapy will include skin, bladder, and, like, bowel training," said Abria. "No one wants you here for that."

Declan made a funny face like he'd smelled something pungent and said, "Okay, I get it."

"Come on, Bowen," Austin said. "You can't do anything strenuous, but maybe Wheeler has something you can do from a seated position."

As the boys left the room, Elena asked, "Abria, why are you doing all this for me?"

"Because you're my friend." Abria smiled. "And you'd be a totally miserable human being if you weren't able to use your legs for the rest of your life. So, I guess when you really think about it, helping you get better is totally selfish on my part."

Elena smiled genuinely. "Thanks for all your help, Abria, no matter what the reason."

However, after the third day of exercising, Elena was beginning to feel nothing but annoyance at her friend. She tried her best to remain calm in front of Abria, but as soon as she left the room for lunch Elena turned toward Declan in frustration.

"If Abria asks me to do one more low-impact aerobic exercise with her happy, little face I'm going to choke her."

But, then she caught the look on Declan's face and said, "Sorry. I wouldn't actually choke her, but she's just so ridiculously happy all the time. It's getting on my nerves."

Declan smiled sympathetically and said, "She's just trying to help so you aren't paralysed."

"Well, when you say it that way I feel like a bully," said Elena. "But I just don't think I can do this a day longer. I feel a dull pain all the time now. And I'm frustrated with how slow my recovery is."

"Slow? Slow! It's only been about four days since you were injured."

"I know, but they have been very, very LONG DAYS," Elena said.

"Time for a walk!" Abria said, bouncing in the room. "And I have a surprise for you."

"If you say that we're going to paint our nails or braid our hair I might find a window to jump through," Elena said dryly.

"No, come on, silly girl," Abria said. "Wheeler built something for you."

"Huh?" Elena and Declan said together.

"Just come on," Abria said as she and Declan helped Elena onto the hover-transporter.

Moments later they entered the cargo bay where, in the far corner of the room, one of the hover-transporters had been removed from the floor. A wall of steel had been welded around the space in the floor, and the space inside had been filled with water.

"It's for water therapy," Abria said happily. "Apparently, this kind of therapy is really good for spinal injuries. Wheeler even built a motor that will simulate movement in the water to help with resistance. Isn't it amazing?"

Elena nodded, feeling perplexed by the gift. In fact, she was so confused that she couldn't sleep later that evening as she lay in bed in the captain's quarters on the Independence. She looked over at Declan who was asleep on his camp bed. He was snoring slightly. She smiled. But her thoughts were consumed with Kidd.

Elena decided that she wouldn't be able to relax unless she spoke to him. Therefore, after a lot of false starts, she got herself to the hover-transporter. Then, she navigated it out of the room and down the hall to see if she could find the boy who built the pool.

⌑ 4 ⌑

Physical Therapy

Elena had never considered how still the Independence could be at night, but as her hover-transporter moved down the deserted halls, she felt that it was eerily silent.

She wasn't sure if Kidd had ever chosen a cabin as his own, so she had no idea where he slept. But, she knew that he did stay up late and liked to eat alone, so she looked in the galley first. When she didn't find him there she went back to the command bridge. After that she tried the research lab, even though she didn't think he'd stepped a foot inside the room before. And finally, she went out to the cargo bay, where she found Kidd asleep on one of the Speedsters.

Her presence must have startled him because he jumped awake. Kidd looked around for a moment like he didn't know where he was.

"Sorry to wake you," Elena said, and she meant it.

"Oh, it's you," Kidd said groggily. "What are you doing?"

"I was looking for you, actually," replied Elena. "But we can talk tomorrow."

Kidd stretched and yawned loudly. "No, it's fine. What do you want?"

Elena felt unsure whether or not she really wanted to talk to him now that she'd woken him up, but he was staring at her with anticipation so she asked, "When did you have time to build me a pool?"

He considered her in silence for a moment.

"I don't really sleep much at night, and I can't really go banging around the ship while everyone else is sleeping, so I just stayed in here for a couple nights putting it together."

Kidd's answer didn't really satisfy what was actually bothering Elena. "But, *why* did you spend the time to put it together in the first place?"

"I read that water counteracts gravity, which makes stretching movements easier. So, you know, your recovery wouldn't be so painful." Kidd's attitude seemed to be of genuine concern, which bewildered Elena even more.

They essentially couldn't stand one another. So, why did he care about her recovery? Why was he helping her?

As her brow narrowed in confusion, Kidd's face clouded over with irritation, and he said, "I was getting tired of all the complaining and moaning coming from your room when Abria's in there helping you exercise. At least this way you'll be far away from where I'm working."

And there he was, the boy that she knew and expected.

"Well, thanks for the pool," she said shortly, and then she directed the hover-transporter back out of the room.

Kidd had gone to the trouble of building her a device that would help her get well. Yet, he still acted as though she was an annoyance to him. She shook her head sadly. In that moment, Elena decided that she wanted to try and be nicer to Kidd, no matter what he acted like to her. She felt she owed him that, at least, for the gesture with the pool.

"We have to try and walk today," Abria said the following morning after she and Declan had helped Elena finish the standard stretching routine on her back.

"But, I can't feel my legs," Elena remarked.

"I know, but Austin said we're supposed to walk you for twenty to thirty minutes as part of your aerobic conditioning. But let's just see how long it takes before you get tired."

The three of them started down the hallway slowly, but after only a few minutes, Elena was starting to feel an extreme amount of pressure in her lower back.

"I can't do it," Elena said through gritted teeth. "Everything feels wobbly."

"Can you try to walk back to the room?" Abria asked.

As they turned to go back down the hall, a piercing throb of pain shot up Elena's back to her neck. Her knees buckled, and Abria almost dropped her. Declan immediately grabbed Elena and shouldered her under his arm.

"Let's not overdo it," he said, as he winced slightly.

"You shouldn't be lifting my side," Elena scolded him. "You're still healing from your own injuries."

"I'm fine," Declan said, though Elena felt like he was limping slightly. "Abria and I can support you down the hall. Let's get you into the pool to see if that helps any."

So, they went to the pool. Elena practiced kicking her legs slowly back and forth, then side to side. Then, she got out and stretched more. And she attempted to walk again before it was time for lunch. But still she couldn't go far, and Declan ended up half carrying her back to bed.

Soon enough, Pigg arrived with a tray of food. Fergie came with him so that they could have a leisurely lunch together. However, even with the extra company, Elena was beginning to feel trapped in the bedroom. A sense of uselessness kept creeping up on her whenever there was silence lasting longer than seven seconds.

"I've been in this room forever," Elena told Declan late that afternoon. "I hate being in bed while everyone else is working."

"Now you know how I feel," Declan said, folding his hands behind his head and grinning like a cat.

"Really? You're going to try and make me feel bad about going to Hagia Sofia without you again?" Elena said, sounding frustrated. But Declan only continued to smile. "Well, I'm not staying in here all day again."

She pushed up on her elbows, swung her legs over the side of the bed, and said, "There must be something I can do from a seated position."

"Easy, easy," Declan said, standing to support her.

"If you can get me something to lean on I can walk myself," Elena said, the edges of her words assertive and bold.

"Don't be a dimwit, you can't walk," Declan replied. "But I'll let you lean on the hovertransporter, and you can walk until you're tired. Then, you can ride the rest of the way."

Elena eagerly accepted his offer and set off down the hall with Declan on one side and the hovertransporter on the other.

"What are you two doing out of bed?" Austin asked minutes later as Declan and Elena arrived on the command bridge. He looked exceptionally tired, and even though he smiled, his eyes were consumed with anxiety.

"We want to help do something, anything," Elena said, almost begging. "We're so bored."

"Actually, I'm not bored because Ransom's feisty, quick wit is wildly entertaining. I mean, you should hear some of the things that come out of that mouth when Abria helps her do that stabilization exercise," said Declan as Elena shot him a dirty look. "But she was determined to get out of the room, and if I stayed in there alone I really would be bored. So here I am. Put me to work too."

"Fine," Austin said smiling. "Bowen, you can go help Pigg do some welding in the cargo bay." Then he dropped his voice to a whisper. "But make sure to remind him to wear the safety goggles and protective gloves. And don't stand too close to him while he's working. Oh, and there are three fire extinguishers around the table where he's working."

Declan laughed. Then, he meandered out of the room holding his side.

"Elena, you can help Fergie in here," Austin said, leading her hover-transporter to one side of the command bridge. "She's working on the wiring and making sure that all the command programs are operating correctly."

"Are you sleeping?" Elena asked him suddenly.

"What?"

"You look really tired," Elena said. "Are you getting enough sleep?"

"No, he is not logging appropriate amounts of rapid eye movement sleep," Fergie said formally. "He and Wheeler have been working virtually non-stop for days."

Elena looked at Austin's face and considered him silently for a moment. "I know you're too busy to help take care of me, but the least you could do is take care of yourself."

"I'm alright, really," Austin replied. "I can sleep when we get back. Or at least when we get away from here. I just can't relax here. There's too much to do." He looked at her with shame etched on his face. "I'm sorry that I haven't been around to help with your recovery."

"Don't feel bad," Elena said soothingly. "Abria has actually been really awesome."

Austin squeezed Elena's shoulder tightly. "I figured she would be. So, I have to go again."

She clicked her tongue loudly, disappointed that he was leaving.

"I know, I know," Austin replied. "But I promise we'll have dinner tonight, okay?" And with that he left Elena alone with Fergie on the command bridge.

"So, how much longer do you think it will take to fix the Independence?" asked Elena.

"The estimated time of completion has not been discussed with me," Fergie replied. "Wheeler seems to want to work on the hovercraft alone, but Austin and Pigg are constantly trying to help. Their involvement generally leads to an argument of some variety."

"Wheeler is just so...complicated."

"I suppose we each have an obstacle to overcome in the realm of our disposition," said Fergie. "Except perhaps for me."

"What? Your parents didn't *write* you a personality? I beg to differ," Elena replied. "Austin's probably the only person I know who doesn't have one major defect."

Fergie shook her head. "Perhaps you are correct, unless you count *selflessness*."

As Elena began to laugh, she heard an echoing of several pairs of heavy-booted footsteps disturbing the hallway outside.

"The indicator is indicating some indication problems," Kidd said distractedly as he walked suddenly onto the command bridge. He was looking at a program on his Touchdot but walked determinedly to the control panel.

"Those are comforting words," Elena said sarcastically before she could stop herself. She really did want to try and be nicer to Kidd, but sometimes it was still hard to not have an attitude around him.

Kidd turned pink around the ears. He looked up as if he realized that what he'd said hadn't made any kind of sense. "What I mean is that I still don't understand everything that's broken."

"I told you that you should let Pigg have a look," Austin said as he entered the room with Pigg and Declan following closely behind him.

"I already had a look," Kidd said rudely.

"But, if you'd let me try…" Pigg started, but Kidd interrupted him.

"Do you think you're smarter than me, Big Ears?"

"I know I'm smarter than you," Pigg said rather boldly at first, but then he cowered away as Kidd gave him a nasty look.

"Maybe in a world of PocketUnits, microchips, and programming simulations you might be smarter than me, but in the world of fixing hovercrafts, I'm the one who knows what to do."

"You do realize that this hovercraft is made of microchips and can be operated by a PocketUnit, right?" Austin said to Kidd. "So, let Pigg have a try."

Kidd threw his hands up in frustration and stomped out of the room.

"What was that all about?" Elena asked.

"We got into an argument in the cargo bay about the correct procedure for reloading some of the programs that were damaged," Pigg said. "So, I said that we needed to power everything down and then power up with a new program I wrote to help redirect energy based on the parts of the Independence that were damaged beyond the point of repair. But he said that he didn't need my dimwit program and that since the ship belongs to him that we're going to fix it correctly. And that he'll go back to the manufacturing plant as many times as he needs to until he gets all the parts he needs." He paused for a moment to take a breath. "He was really mean about it."

"Wheeler wants to do everything his way, so let him," Austin said. "But Pigg, there might come a time when we have to use your plan. So, we need to make sure that the program is working perfectly."

"I'll check it again, but I know that if we use it we could have the ship ready to go as early as tomorrow."

Austin looked at Elena. "I guess that means we need to get you walking again, Lena."

After that, Elena spent all her time either stretching with Abria, exercising in the pool, or trying to walk down the hallway.

By the end of the third day of nothing but exercise, she could almost walk the entire hall without having to hold a hand. Declan managed to find her a sturdy walking cane from one of the abandoned homes in the city, so she practiced walking the ship with the support of the cane from morning until night on the fourth day.

"We're going home!" Abria said gleefully as she bounced into Elena's room.

She and Declan were almost finished with a game of Stratego on Pigg's PocketUnit, but Elena looked up at Abria suddenly. They'd been grounded for at least seven days, so Elena was surprised to hear that the Independence was ready to launch.

"What happened?"

"Well, Austin finally told Wheeler that we couldn't wait any longer for him to keep getting supplies from the city and that, like, Pigg already knew how to fix the ship and that Wheeler was, like, completely out of time now and that we were just going to, like, fix the ship Pigg's way."

Elena's mouth fell open.

"I mean, Austin said it all, like, nice and stuff, but Wheeler still got mad and said it couldn't be done. Then, Austin was like, 'What's the harm in trying it Pigg's way?' and Wheeler was like, 'Maybe nothing, but what if he ruins my ship?' and Austin was like, 'Then I'll buy you a new one.' And that's when I started giggling so hard that Austin asked me to leave the room. But anyways, so Austin and Pigg are working on doing the whole power-down thing so that they can, like, upload Pigg's program. But they say we'll be ready to fly in about fifteen."

Elena couldn't believe her ears. "I'm relieved to be going home."

"So, Austin doesn't want you to, like, come to the command bridge, but he does want you to get belted in. And he says that he'll come see you once we're in the air."

Elena rolled her eyes at Declan. He helped her get into bed, and then clipped on the makeshift belts that he'd attached to the sides of the bed.

"You know, I think that Wheeler's attitude has shown drastic improvement over the past few days," Declan said dryly as he strapped one belt over Elena's legs.

She clipped the other belt across her chest. "I couldn't agree more. Maybe when we get back we can all go shopping together and get dinner at my favorite restaurant."

Declan laughed and pulled a jump seat down from one of the walls. He clipped his belt on just as Elena felt the Independence begin to vibrate with energy. A moment later, she could feel movement. She closed her eyes tightly, hoping that they wouldn't plummet to the ground. But in next to no time, Austin had arrived at her cabin door.

"We're up and staying up!"

She hadn't seen Austin so happy in days.

"Pigg and I will be in the engine room for a while to monitor things, but Wheeler and Fergie are flying, and Abria said she'd try to make dinner."

Somehow the idea of Abria cooking seemed ridiculous to Elena. So, she asked Declan to walk with her to the galley. When they arrived, she was relieved to see that Abria was simply opening prepackaged cans of food and heating the contents up on the warmer.

Elena sat at the table with Declan while Abria chattered about school and Frankie Smiley's dimples. Finally, Fergie, Austin, and Pigg arrived. Over bowls of beef stew, they talked and laughed and swapped stories until Elena yawned loudly.

"Oh, we should get some sleep if we can," Austin said. "We've still got a few hours left in flight. And Lena, you should really rest before we have to be back at school in a couple days."

Elena couldn't disagree. Leaning on her cane, she hobbled back to her room where she fell into a deep and peaceful sleep.

■ ■ ■

"We're home, like, safely!"

Elena opened her eyes to slits, feeling groggy.

"What's going on?"

"We're home, silly. Oh, I'm glad you two were able to sleep," Abria said.

Elena looked over and noticed that Declan was just beginning to open his eyes as well.

"Do you want to come to the command bridge with me?" Abria asked. "Austin's going to tell us what we should do next."

Elena felt slightly stronger just knowing that they were home safely. As her feet touched the floor, Declan brought her a cane to lean on.

Declan and Abria walked on either side of Elena as they came down the hall toward the command bridge. But soon, she could hear Kidd's loud voice echoing off the walls. He sounded really angry.

"We're all going to die one day," Austin was saying calmly to Kidd as Elena entered the room. "What matters is how we choose to live. Hundreds of thousands of people are enslaved by Imperator, including all of us. Don't you want to help save everyone? Don't you want to be free?"

"No!" Kidd said forcefully. "What I want is to forget that I know you. Now that we're back, we're going separate ways. I don't want the Independence anymore. I'm ending our agreement. And, I know we're in the same Unit, but feel free not to speak with me during school unless you have to."

"But won't you even consider helping us with Taving…" Austin started, but Kidd held his hand up.

"I don't know how to make this any more clear to you," he said angrily. "You keep asking and I keep saying 'no.' My answer will never change."

Elena watched Kidd pick up his already packed rucksack and storm out of the command bridge.

"What was that all about?" Elena asked.

"Oh, hey," Austin said as if he just noticed they were standing there. "I was just trying to talk to Wheeler again about Tavington's farm." He lifted his shoulders slowly looking thoroughly defeated. "Bowen, how are your ribs feeling?"

"Still a little sore, but better."

"And Lena, how are your legs?"

"Stiff and sore," Elena said, but she had no interest in discussing her health. "So, what do we do now, Austin?"

"Everyone is scheduled to be back at school tomorrow," Austin said. "Our Decoys will return to school with everyone else."

Elena imagined Grandpa and Grandma Haddock walking her and Austin's decoy Humanoids through the station to the Grimsby Channel.

"Fergie has already sent them instructions to come to the Firebird Station when they get off the train. So, we'll just wait here, and then trade places with them."

The Firebird Station was just as comfortable as they'd left it a few weeks ago. Pigg got to work right away in the stainless steel kitchenette as Elena and the rest of her friends dropped into a cluster of cushiony chairs that surrounded an Optivision pupil station in the main living area.

Austin pulled the purely white statue of an angel that he and Elena had found in the cistern under Istanbul out of his tactical pack and set it on the table. The sight of it made Elena's back tingle with pain.

"So, with everything that's happened we haven't exactly had a chance to talk about the artifact we recovered," Austin said to the others. Then, he looked at Fergie. "Do you want to take a guess as to what this is?"

Fergie reached for the statue. She held it for quite a while before she said, "I am not sure what this object is. However, I have only this minute realized a more significant hindrance than not retrieving the Tablets of Destiny."

"Oh, please don't say that," Pigg groaned from the kitchen.

"My parents said they created the codes to be engraved on the artifacts and that those codes could not be recreated. But they did not specify how we are to read the codes after we have retrieved all the artifacts."

"So, you're saying we have no way of processing the codes and therefore won't be able to use the artifacts the way they were designed?" Austin asked.

Fergie nodded. "That is precisely correct. I will contact my parents directly and ask them if they have a program to read the code. If they do not possess one already, I will ask that they help us develop one."

After everything that had already happened, Elena wasn't expecting the disappointment that they technically weren't any closer to knowing how to defeat Imperator.

She closed her eyes in frustration and blurted, "Okay, well I'm going to go exercise now. There's no sense in me being a cripple my first day back at school."

▭ 5 ▭

Back to Reality

In the first month, on the first day, Elena waited anxiously at the Firebird Station kitchen table with her friends until she finally heard the front door squeak open. Austin's identical twin Humanoid walked inside the room, followed closely by the other Decoys. The robots were smiling and talking and acting so human-like that Elena felt an odd sensation creep up the back of her neck. It was the first time she'd ever considered the possibility that a robot could replace her in real life. For the rest of her life. And no one would notice.

"Hey, Brainiack!" Kidd called to Fergie. He appeared from the back hallway, and Elena suddenly wondered where he'd been all night. "How do I shut my Decoy off so I can get outta here?"

"Don't you want to watch the playback?" Austin asked. "How else will you know what your Decoy did on fourth quarter break?"

Kidd didn't even bother looking at Austin. He just stared at Fergie until she said, "You will need to scan your Trademark against the Decoy's Trademark and give it a command. In this case, you could tell it to return to the closet and power down."

Kidd wasted no time. He marched right up to his Decoy and told it, "Go back to your closet now and shut down. Got it?"

Kidd's Decoy made a face of pure loathing at him, a face that Elena had seen many times on the human Kidd's face. Then, it turned and walked down the hallway where, Elena assumed, it climbed into the closet to shut itself away.

Elena turned to say something nasty to Kidd about his attitude, but the door to the Firebird Station was already closing. She shook her head disapprovingly, and then noticed that her own Humanoid mimicked her in exactly the same way.

Austin approached his Humanoid steadily and asked, "So, how did it go?"

"It was fantastic!" Decoy Austin exclaimed. "Atlanson was awesome. And your grandparents were really nice. Grandma Haddock makes the most delicious food. She made some kind of strawberry, infusion cake for Elena's birthday that melted in my mouth."

In all the busy preparation for their fourth quarter exams, and the chaos on the trip across the ocean, Elena had forgotten about her birthday. She'd turned fifteen nearly two weeks ago and hadn't even noticed."

"Did everyone treat you *normally?*" Austin inquired. "I mean, as if you were really us?"

"Everyone seemed fine," said Decoy Elena.

Austin looked expectantly at Fergie's Decoy for confirmation that everything had gone well in the Galilee Province.

"We did not detect any usual feelings toward our presence," the Decoy Fergie replied formally. "Though, in fairness, the Foremans created us so the other Humanoids knew to expect robots."

"At least we know they, like, work," Abria said appreciatively as she smiled at her Decoy.

"We should not waste time," Fergie said. "We need to examine the Decoy's memory drive so that we can make our way to registration."

Fergie led Elena and the others back to the Research & Development room where she and her Decoy stood at one of the pupil stations.

"Observe the following procedure, and then repeat with your own Decoy," said Fergie as she accessed an Optivision screen.

She and her Decoy each scanned their Trademarks against the screen. Then, a laser scanner engulfed the Decoy's head. Elena saw images begin to fill up the screen that was hovering in midair.

Elena repeated the directions with her own robot. Through the Decoy's eyes, she watched the familiar train ride back to Atlanson. She noticed that the conversation between Austin and Pigg was fairly normal; the robots spoke with ease and laughed together.

She experienced the greeting from Grandma and Grandpa Haddock; her birthday party; going with Austin to different Simulabs on Meeting Street; riding the elevator up and down their resident tower; and meeting with school friends in the square to eat and shop. The tone and voice inflection when her robot spoke to other people was a perfect match to her own.

And though the Decoy Austin didn't have a scar on the under part of its chin, Elena noticed that it often thumbed that area in exactly the same way that Austin did when he was feeling contemplative. However, when the two robots were ever alone they sat in silence, never engaging with one another.

"That was, like, too weird," said Abria, bringing Elena back to the reality of where they were. "My Decoy went to parts of the city that I've never even seen before. It was like watching a traveler do all kinds of fun stuff that I never even do when I'm at home."

Decoy Elena turned toward her and pulled off the coat it was wearing. Elena recognized it immediately because the piece had come from her own closet back in Atlanson.

"Here, you'll need this," said the robot. "It's really cold outside."

"Thanks." Elena looked at her Decoy uneasily. "Erm…you can go back to the closet now and power down with the others. Thanks for all your help."

As Elena watched her Decoy walk off, Austin said, "We'll exit the forest at different locations and at different times just like we normally do so that no one notices us returning to school. Hopefully, they haven't changed any of the surveillance around on us."

Moments later, Elena pulled on her coat and stepped out of the Firebird Station door into the Grimsby forest with Austin. She grabbed his arm suddenly for balance.

"You doing okay?"

"Yeah, I'm just a little stiff," she replied. "This is the first time I'm gonna actually hike since getting hurt. I think my body is already rebelling against the activity."

"You'll be fine," Austin said reassuringly as they started into the crisp, cool woods. "The last scans I took of your spine showed vast improvements. By the time we start Basic you'll be even better. We won't have Gauntlets for a while, so you'll have plenty of time to make a full recovery."

"You know, those Decoys didn't go to Sector 7 once," Elena said, changing the subject so they wouldn't have to talk about Marshall.

"Yeah, they acted more normal than we do." Austin laughed.

"I can't believe I missed my birthday," Elena said. "What a weird thing to forget. And why didn't you remember it?"

"I always remember your birthday," Austin said. "But with everything going on it felt weird to have a celebration. I'm really sorry. From now on we'll always celebrate, no matter what else is happening."

From the tree line, Elena noticed the four Grimsby resident towers looming on the horizon. Each building was distinctly postmodern with a triangular but also rounded façade outlining the different floors. Elena knew that the glass Grimvators hurrying up and down on the outside of the building were delivering students to the recreation lounge, pools, resident floors, Simulabs, Telepost Office, Media Room, Uniform Lockers, and Mess Hall. Elena remembered feeling awe-inspired the first time she saw the campus, but now she frowned.

"This place is beginning to feel more like a prison everyday," Elena grumbled.

"Remember, how we talked about how we need to pretend that everything is normal," Austin said.

"Yeah, but what do you think will happen if anyone finds out that we left school again?"

"No one's gonna find out," Austin said. "Unless Pigg says something."

"Why isn't it hard for you to come back to this life after we go outside the domes?" Elena asked. "I like the feeling of freedom when we're away. Coming back here when I know we could easily go live in New York City with Fallon seems counterproductive."

"I like feeling free," said Austin. "But everyone else has a right to have freedom, too. Not just us. Plus, we need the school's technology for research."

"Hey, Ransom!"

Elena and Austin turned together to see that Frankie Smiley was coming across the lawn toward them.

"Oh, hey Smiley," Elena replied.

"What happened to you?" he asked, looking curious about the way her arm was draped through Austin's elbow.

"Oh, I tripped over my own two feet when I was stepping off the train," Elena said, and then she forced a fake laugh. "I'm getting as bad as Pigg."

"Hey!" Pigg arrived at Elena's side. "I resemble that remark."

"That's why I said it," Elena said, punching him lightly in the gut.

"Well, have you seen Abria yet?" Frankie asked.

"Not yet," Austin said. "But she, Bowen, and Fergie usually meet us in the quad."

"That was a pretty good lie, especially for you," Elena whispered to Austin after Frankie had waved and walked away from them.

"I've been practicing." He smiled and winked. "I'm trying to be as good as you."

"Oh, you'll never be that good," Elena said slyly.

"Oh look!" said Pigg excitedly causing Elena to jump. "They have the little refreshment carts out again this year. I want to get a couple of those little quiche thingies because I'm starving."

"Of course you are...we've just finished breakfast," Elena said.

"Oh, please, please stop for a bit!" Pigg said. "Just look at all that butter and cinnamon pouring out of that baked apple? Delish!"

Elena rolled her eyes as he continued.

"I miss proper food. Not that I'm a bad cook, but we had such meager ingredients on the trip. I could really go for the confit salmon rillettes with horseradish cream on grilled sourdough that Blakely makes in the kitchen."

"You know the name of someone that works in the kitchen?" Elena said, feeling amazed.

"Obviously, it's an entire staff of Humanoids, but the culinary brilliance comes from the main robot that's called Blakely," Pigg said. Then, he lowered his voice to a whisper and leaned toward her, saying, "Sometimes, the Humanoids let me come in after classes and they teach me how to make my favorite dishes."

A smile appeared on Elena's face. "Why are you whispering?"

"Oh, because technically students are restricted from certain parts of the resident towers, like the staff areas, kitchens, maintenance tunnels, and all, but I think they really like me in the kitchens."

"Hey, guys!" Declan said, coming up suddenly with Abria and Fergie behind him. "It's great to see you. It's been *so* long."

Elena wanted to smile at his joke, but her back was starting to scream at her for a break.

"I don't want to eat. I'm just gonna get my uniform."

"Oh-wah," Pigg whined. "Isn't anyone else hungry?"

"I'll wait with you, Pigg," said Austin.

"Me, too!" Declan said. "I saw some kind of apple cider latte over there with my name on it" But then he looked at Elena abruptly, "Unless you need some help walking to your room, Ransom."

"She'll be fine with us," Abria told him as she looped one of her arms around Elena's elbow.

As they began to walk, Elena noticed groups of new Level 1 students walking up and down the breezeway. She had a twinge of nostalgia as she remembered her first day at Grimsby.

"Those unfortunate students have no idea how hard their first week of school's gonna be," Elena said. "Or how awful Marshall is!"

"Those poor ones look lost," Abria said, pointing at a group of girls. She moved in their direction, saying, "Hey, there! Your resident tower is over that way."

"Why did we have to be friends with the friendliest person at school?" Elena asked Fergie impatiently.

"I detect some underlying ailment as the cause of your impatience," Fergie said smartly. "Care to discuss it?"

"My back is hurting," Elena said quietly. "I just want to get to our room."

Minutes later, Elena convinced Abria to leave the younger students alone so that they could get going. They stepped inside the foyer of their resident tower. The shining floors reflected the dome ceiling far above. Hundreds of windows looked out and down upon the dozens of leisure seating areas. The hallways on either side of the foyer were filled with students loitering.

The three friends stepped onto the nearest Grimvator and immediately selected the Uniform Locker option from the Optivision screen.

"It's so nice to be back. I can't wait to see Frankie Smiley," Abria said to Elena and Fergie. "Those dimples of his get me every time. And I totally need to work on my nails tonight. They're, like, nasty looking." She scrutinized her hand carefully.

Elena looked at her own nails. She'd chewed them all raw when she was lying in bed waiting for her back to heal.

Soon, Elena and her friends arrived at the Uniform Locker floor, which had a long corridor lined with doors. She hobbled to the nearest available stall and scanned her Trademark. After the stall door opened she entered a small room with a mirror and dozens of thin panels instead of walls. Once the door locked behind her, Elena's face appeared holographically on an Optivision screen in midair. Then, laser lights scanned her entire body.

After this was complete, a drawer popped open from the wall. Elena removed an armor wear combat shirt, an aviator suit, bomber jacket, and jump boots.

Last year, they'd given her a wet suit uniform, and all year Marshall put the Firebirds through swim training.

The year before that they were given buckle breeches and combat boots, and they spent a lot of time on the ground with their faces in the mud.

Elena didn't even want to try and guess what Marshall was planning to do to them as she held the aviator suit in front of her.

Carefully, Elena bent down to pull off her shoes. But the hike through the woods and campus had pushed her back past some kind of limit because her body was rejecting every movement.

Pulling her shirt and trousers off was near excruciating, and it was even harder to get into the one-piece aviator suit.

Eventually, Elena was able to place all the pieces of her new uniform onto her body correctly. Then, the laser lights came on again and scanned her body once more.

A Telecaster appeared holographically. "Elena Ransom, please remove the uniform and place it neatly inside the drawer. You may get dressed in your regular clothing. Your wardrobe will arrive in your room shortly."

Several long minutes later, Elena exited the stall and found that Abria and Fergie were already waiting for her.

"I almost knocked the door down to come get you because you were taking so long. Are you, like, okay?" Abria asked.

"Yeah, it's just the first time I've had to undress myself in a few days. I need to lie down soon. I feel awful."

"We will go back to the room now and rest," Fergie said. "We can update our Smartslates later."

"I just love our new uniforms," Abria gushed, grabbing one of Elena's arms gently, but so that Elena could put part of her weight on her friend. "Don't you just love them?"

"You say that every time we get a new uniform," Elena said.

"I guess it's because I just look good in everything," Abria said with a tinkling laugh and a flip of her hair.

"Did you notice we got jump boots?" Elena said. "I feel so bad for Pigg. He's already afraid of heights. I bet Marshall will have us swinging by vines like monkeys."

The three friends got onto another Grimvator and moved slantways until it arrived at a circular vestibule. Red, orange, and yellow patterned cozy couches were placed around the room and a row of charcoal colored writing tables sat in front of a picture window that looked out over the lake.

The Firebird, a bright orange bird of prey, was etched into every nook and cranny of the space. The logo was even carved into the bedroom door where Elena scanned her Trademark. The door slid open silently. She hobbled through the comfortably furnished room and eased carefully onto her bed.

Meanwhile, Abria scanned her Trademark to open one of the doors to her wardrobe.

"Hello, closet," she said as the doors folded open. "Oh, hello clothes."

She rubbed her fingers through the hanging material and then caught her face in the mirror.

"Eek! Have I looked like this all day?"

Abria's frivolous enjoyment over her clothes actually made Elena feel a little better. She smiled slightly as Abria smoothed her fingers through her hair and then rubbed some gloss on her lips.

Then, Elena watched her blonde friend grab one of the poly bags from her bed and tear it open, removing the armor wear shirt that was packaged inside.

Elena was just beginning to smile as her gaze fell on Melly Linus's bed, which was still untouched. She wondered what their first encounter would be like because the last words they'd exchanged seemed to indicate that Melly wanted to destroy her. She could hear Melly's words in her head:

"I lifted your fingerprints from the photograph. The one inside my wardrobe. You drugged me and then used my Trademark to gain access. Is this ringing any bells?"

"Has anyone seen Melly yet?" Elena asked Abria and Fergie tentatively.

"I have not," Fergie said. She was also depositing uniforms in her wardrobe.

"Me neither...thank goodness," Abria said. "Remember how scary she looked the last time we, like, saw her? I know she was smiling and all, but she also looked like she could have peeled our skin off with her eyeballs." She shivered. "Elena, what's wrong? You're grimacing."

Elena tore her eyes away from Melly's bed and replied, "Huh? Oh...my back hurts a bit."

Abria dropped her things instantly. "Okay, time for some stretching."

Elena spent the next twenty minutes on her back as Abria pulled and stretched her leg, arm, and back muscles. At first, it was shear torture, but gradually Elena began to literally feel her strained tendons loosen and relax. She was just starting to feel a little better when the bedroom door slid open.

Vivienne Castellow and Olivia Nelson walked in, practically looking like twins.

"Oh, you got matching haircuts!" Abria squealed, as she abandoned Elena and skipped over to their roommates.

"Do you like it?" asked Vivienne, combing her fingers through her now very short blonde hair.

"Love it!" Abria gushed.

Olivia's blue eyes sparkled as she said, "Yeah, over break we decided that it was time for a new look. We even got our nails and toes done the same, see." She held out her fingers, and Abria grabbed her hand.

"Stunning. I'm totally, like, jealous!"

Elena was just about to roll her eyes when Fergie said, "Our orientation with Hopper starts in twelve minutes, forty-seven seconds. Perhaps we should start down to the Firebird common room now."

Elena felt nauseous on the Grimvator ride to see Hopper. Vivienne and Olivia chatted with Abria about everything they'd done over fourth quarter break. Abria asked tons of questions and giggled freely at all their stories. Elena stood by the door feeling miserable as she watched the different floors pass, each filled with students laughing, talking, and having a good time.

In minutes, the doors slid open to the courtyard that was designated for the Firebird Unit common area. A loud wave of yelling hit Elena in the face. The boys were having some kind of wrestling match in the middle of the floor, right between the modern furniture, pupil stations, and lounging chairs.

"What are you boys, like, doing?" Abria asked, giggling so hard that she could barely speak.

"Just causing a little ruckus," Declan hollered just before Frankie Smiley head rushed him in the gut. "Ahhh!" He groped his ribs.

Apparently, Pigg had attempted to wrestle, but he was presently sprawled out flat on his back taking deep gasps of air. Austin had Crosby Gamble in a headlock until Frankie launched into them and knocked them to the floor. That's when Elena noticed Kidd sitting far across the room completely engrossed with his Smartslate.

Ignoring him, Elena fought the urge to join in the wrestling, and it was a good thing because a second later a mess of rainbow colored hair rushed through the courtyard and collided with the Firebird boys. With their Resident Advisor joining the fight, Declan stepped away holding tight to his sides.

Hopper's wildly curly hair swung around. Instead of his usual baggy style clothing he was wearing an Instructor uniform. She'd never seen him wear one. And though a uniform made most people look smart, his was wrinkled and untucked.

"Jump in, Bowen," Hopper called to Declan, who Elena noticed was now standing away from the wrestling on the other side of the common area.

Declan just laughed and waved his hand, holding tightly to his sides.

"Okay! Okay!" Hopper finally yelled after he tossed Austin, Frankie, and Crosby half way across the room. "That's enough."

Elena felt suddenly nervous as Hopper stood to address them. She knew that if the Decoys hadn't convinced Hopper that he would have told Hannibal that she and her friends were outside the domes again. She also knew that Hopper would have noticed the Independence was gone from the Firebird Station if he'd been down there during break.

Last year, after they'd been caught coming back from New York City, General Hannibal had defended the Firebirds at a tribunal. But Elena wasn't confident that Hannibal would try to protect them again. She also wasn't sure that he'd keep their trip secret from Headmaster Worthen Bentley, which meant it was possible that they'd be sent to prison for illegal activity. But, Elena was determined not to give them away, so she put on a friendly smile as he caught her eye.

"Hey, rugrats, everyone come around here and get close," Hopper said loudly as he held his arms out and waved them around until everyone was gathered. "So, I have some sad news to start us off. Pamela Linus will not be returning to Grimsby this year. Her parents have decided it would be best to continue with schooling at home."

Elena felt her face grow red. She averted her eyes from Hopper to the rich red and warm golden banner that was stretched across the wall, which bore the Firebird logo. What did it really mean that Melly wasn't back at school? Elena cut her eyes at Austin. He looked just as concerned as she felt.

"This leaves our Unit one member short. However, we can't replace Melly at this point because it's too late in your studies. So, we'll have to be a Unit of eleven instead of twelve. But I'm confident that you'll be able to rise to the challenge.

"This is your last year of Basic Training. After this year, you'll move to your new resident tower, and I will no longer be your Resident Advisor. But don't start crying about that, yet, you rugrats. We still have this last year together.

"At the end of this year, Headmaster Bentley and Hannibal will assess your entire performance and grades over these first three years of core studies. From that assessment they'll decide if you'll stay in your Units during Level Four studies or if you are able to advance to Special Ops training. Only six of you in the Firebird Unit will advance. So, keep your grades up, and perform well during Basic Training."

"What is Special Ops?" Pigg squeaked.

"It's an elite class of the best students. But, we won't spend time talking about what all that means right now. This year, the Aves Company will take every single class with your two sister companies, Animalia and Maritime. In addition, your exams in Basic will put you against your sister companies.

"During part of our lessons together, we will watch playbacks of the last two years of the Animalia and Maritime Basic Training classes so we can learn their strengths and weaknesses. But, we don't need to cover all this now. You know where I live, so come see me if you need anything. Have a good dinner, and I'll see you in class soon."

After Hopper's speech all the other students walked toward the door where they'd go to dinner, but she marched straight up to Hopper.

"What's all this nonsense about Melly not coming back to school?" Elena questioned in a whisper.

"It's just like I said, her parents wanted to homeschool her."

"But why? Doesn't that seem a little odd to you after she spent a full year here? Did they give any reason why they didn't want her to come back?"

"They worked it out with Headmaster Bentley, and he informed me last week. I don't know anymore than that," said Hopper. Then eyed her suspiciously and asked, "Why? What did you do to her?"

"Why do you assume that I did something to her?" Elena said, trying to sound innocent.

"I don't know…maybe because you're always punching people and causing a scene. Come to think of it, Melly did end up in the infirmary a few weeks ago due to some questionable circumstances. You wouldn't happen to know anything about that, would you?

"No!" Elena said unconvincingly. She blushed, knowing full well that she and her friends had drugged Melly so that they could look through her closet.

"Uh huh…" Hopper smiled at her in a quirky way. "Try to keep your nose out of trouble this year, Ransom. Now, I've got to head off and make myself presentable to the Level One rugrats. And, I got to get my motorbike so I can scare the stuffing out of them." He barked a laugh. "See you around. And stay outta trouble."

Dinner was a fabulous affair. The students were served air-dried meats with fancy cheeses, luscious fruit, and diced tomato that was mixed with fresh mozzarella and olive oil on pagnotta bread. For the main course, roasted goosnargh duck was served with garlic mash and tender stem broccoli, but Elena's mind was consumed with thoughts of Melly.

Part way through dinner, Austin leaned toward Elena and whispered, "Are you alright?"

"Sure. Why?"

"You've barely touched your dinner."

Elena looked down at her plate. She hadn't noticed that she'd been absentmindedly pushing food around as her friends made guesses about what their first few days of classes would be like.

"I didn't realize this was going to be our last year in Basic," Elena told him. "I mean, I guess I'd heard about it, but I never really thought about what we'd do in Level Four. We have to move to a new resident tower and room with new people. Plus, what if I'm not good enough for Special Ops? There have been a lot of times that I didn't give full attention to my homework or an exam. I didn't realize every single class was all counting toward such an important placement in the program."

"I guess we should have talked through the finer points of the Grimsby Initiation memorandum," Austin remarked.

"And what's all this that Hopper said about Melly not coming back?" Elena continued. "Is it weird, in the earth shattering kind of way, to you? Because it is to me."

Austin nodded. "I know."

"Oh, how I've missed this," Pigg said loudly, interrupting all the conversation at the table. He stuffed a large bite of the layered, rich chocolate torte into his mouth, closed his eyes, and moaned. "I wonder if Blakely would teach me how to make this."

Elena looked worriedly from Pigg to Austin and whispered, "What if we don't all make it to Special Ops together?"

"We'll all make it," Austin replied, using a tone of reassurance that he used often to calm her. "We'll do our best, and we'll make it together."

6

Level 3

"After wrestlemania last night, Austin had to give me a pain blocker, Ransom," Declan said the next morning as Elena and her friends walked to their first class after breakfast. "I slept like a teen on third quarter break."

"I wonder what class is going to be like today," Pigg said nervously. "Hopper said that we'd have lessons with the entire Aves Company. I wish we didn't have to. Hunter just can't seem to leave me alone when we're in class together. And he always makes mean comments when I walk by him in the hall."

"I can't wait for Special Ops," Declan said. "This is our third year doing the same schedule so I'm sorta bored with the routine."

"That's funny, I was just thinking that I finally feel like I know what's going on, and I don't want anything to change," Elena grumbled.

"Oh, come on," said Declan. "We get to move to a new resident tower, no more writing with pointers on Smartslates, no more group work during class, and no more Marshall."

Elena did like the sound of not seeing Marshall on a weekly basis.

"But aren't the academics, like, way harder?" Abria asked.

"In point of fact, once we finish our Level 3 studies we should have enough basic academics and should therefore experience a marginal levity in the intensity of the class work," Fergie said.

As they rounded the corner, Elena noticed a group of students from the Aves Company crowded around the entrance to the classroom. Then, she saw Oscar Hunter standing almost in the center of the assembly.

"We're in accelerated training now," Oscar was saying. He had a slightly intense look on his face. "We're in direct competition with Animalia and Maritime this year. Our scores matter more now than they ever did...each and every one. I, for one, want a top spot in Special Ops. I know that we're always going to have certain setbacks as a Company because of dimwits like Pigg, but that just means the rest of us need to work harder. I don't want to be held back by any of you."

Elena noticed Pigg's face turn a violent shade of red. She thought seriously about diving through the crowd to punch Oscar in the nose, but Fergie actually stepped up to him boldly.

"Logically speaking, each Company will have an equal ratio of students with similar attributes and skill level. At this point, the determining factors for selection into Special Ops will be based on the quality of our leadership. Thus far, Hunter, your competence in this area has been severely lacking."

Oscar looked for a moment like he'd taken a bite of something bitter. Elena took a step toward her friend in case he decided to throw a punch. But, instead of even replying, Oscar turned and walked into the classroom followed closely by all the members of the Raptor Unit.

"What's up with him?" Elena asked Austin. "I mean, he was never exactly nice, but that was just cruel."

"Some people lead by show of force," said Austin, lifting his shoulders to a shrug. "He may think that people will be drawn to the perception of his power and influence over others. Don't be surprised if he's mean to you from now on. He knows you're a leader so that makes you his competition."

"I'm not a leader!" Elena said incredulously. "You are."

Austin laughed loudly and wrapped an arm around her neck.

"Oh, Lena…maybe one day you'll see yourself for who you are instead of how you think you should be."

Elena and Austin entered an enormous, white-walled room that seemed to have no beginning and no end. The floor was inlaid with red molds in the shape of feet, eight rows down and six rows across.

"Aves Company!" Instructor Booker's voice carried through the entire room, though Elena couldn't see where it was coming from. "Take a pair of footprints anywhere in the room that you'd like."

As Elena took a spot between Austin and Pigg she noticed that Kidd was standing about as far away from the Firebird Unit as he could get.

As soon as her feet were positioned securely in the floor molds a pupil station appeared, and Optivisions came alive all around her. Then, Instructor Booker's façade, complete with crew-cut black hair and bushy black eyebrows, appeared holographically across one of her screens.

"Welcome to your Level 3 studies," said Booker's hologram. "This will be your classroom every first, third, and fifth day of the week from now until the end of term. All of your classes will be conducted in here until lunch each day, and then you will go out to the hydroponic farm for your afternoon lesson with Instructor Emerald."

This change in their school schedule seemed odd to Elena, but Instructor Booker didn't allow any time to ask questions.

"Now that we've moved to Level 3 studies your work load will increase. However, the length of historical time we study will only be in increments of one to two hundred years instead of the five hundred years. Can anyone tell me why this is?"

Fergie's face popped up first on yet another screen at Elena's pupil station.

"Because written records increased after 1000 AD and even more after the invention of moveable type printing in 1456 AD," Fergie's hologram answered.

"That is correct," said Booker. "Today we will begin a journey through 1000 AD and will finish through 1200 AD by the end of the first quarter."

And with that simple direction, Instructor Booker launched into his lesson. He'd never exactly taken it easy on the class, but Elena noticed right away that his expectations of their retention and comprehension of the lecture were more than they had been in her previous two years.

Within the first seven minutes of class, Booker lectured on the three principal trade routes that were used to bring merchandise from the Orient to the Mediterranean between 1000–1200 AD.

Elena's pupil station was alive with maps, trade route lines, and a detailed list of the manufactured goods that were bartered. He went on to tell them about the primary centers of trade on the local level in Europe and the large-scale international trade that was popular.

Booker also addressed the money practices of the Medieval Church and the contributing factors to the growth of towns in Medieval Europe.

Before Elena felt that she'd had time to properly understand all he'd said, his hologram disappeared and a list of questions materialized on one of her screens. She was given instructions to either speak her answers aloud or use her pointer to answer the questions on the screen. Suddenly, the drone of dozens of students talking began to echo around the room in such a loud manner that it was hard for Elena to concentrate.

She had to rewatch part of his lecture so she could even answer the questions about the four basic freedoms that were shared by townspeople, and also so she could list the three classes of members in the crafts guilds for trade fairs.

Then, before Elena could even finish answering all the review questions, her screen went blank and Instructor Niva's hologram arrived in a whirlwind of energy.

"Welcome back students!" Niva said in Russian dialect. She pushed a plait of black hair off her shoulder and said, "We already studied the beginning of Russian history, which began with the Eastern Slavs and the Finno-Ugric people. Now, we'll begin to see what influence the Byzantine Empire had on the culture and development of language."

Elena's screen filled with Niva's lecture notes. Then, the Instructor went on to teach the entire lesson in one of the first forms of the Russian dialect that was very hard for Elena to interpret. In fact, she only caught one out of every three words. And since she'd been standing the entire time since Booker's class had started, the heaviness in her legs and the odd twinge of pain in her back were making it nearly impossible for her to focus.

In the end, Instructor Niva set a homework essay about the two greatest writers of the late Medieval period, which had to be written in the original Slavic language. Elena was expecting to now be excused to go to lunch. Instead, Instructor Copernicus' hologram appeared, her short, spiky hair looking whiter instead of its usual blonde.

"Good morning, students," said Copernicus in her normal, peppy voice. "As you know we are all about studying the Middle Ages this quarter. Unfortunately, scientific knowledge was lacking in the 11th century in Europe. Medieval science was clouded by magic and superstition. But the during the 12th and 13th centuries, Greek and Muslim works began to circulate in Europe making way for new and exciting discoveries for arithmetic, astrology, and physics."

Copernicus went on to lecture for the next hour, barely pausing to take a breath. And Elena could do nothing but stand and stare at her ever-changing Optivision screens, feeling hopeless and exhausted.

At lunch, Elena slumped down at the table, staring at a plate of something the kitchen had called farmhouse terrine with piccalilli, which sounded fancy but to her it looked like a loaf of multicolored meat and vegetables.

"That was brutal!" she complained to Austin after he dropped in the seat beside her. "I wasn't expecting to have to stand for the entire three hours of class. You'd've thought they could've given us some warning before they changed the entire way we have class."

"They did tell us, in the Grimsby Initiation memorandum on our Smartslates," Austin said. He looked just as tired as Elena felt. "Though nothing could have really prepared you for that even if you had watched it."

"I'm so hungry!" Pigg exclaimed, stuffing the last bite of his cheddar and rye bread in his mouth as he sat down. "We stood for three hours. THREE hours!"

"I know. They crammed all the subjects together. How are we supposed to spend three hours with Emerald?" Elena asked gloomily.

"Emerald's class is only one hour," Fergie said as she joined them. "We will be off for the rest of the afternoon to begin our homework."

"We weren't really given any homework," Elena said.

"You really need to start reading the syllabus before the new school year starts," Austin said patiently. "The Instructors won't technically tell us if we have homework or not. We have to go to the Media Lab after classes to see if anything has been assigned."

"This day just gets better and better," Elena grumbled.

"Is it just me or does this bacon wrapped meatloaf look amazing?" Declan asked as he also sat down.

"So, three hours of, like, standing in the same spot is a lot harder than it sounds," Abria said as she joined them. "My back actually hurts. How's your back, Elena?"

"Fine," she mumbled, but truthfully, it was throbbing.

In fact, pulling on her aviator jacket after lunch and walking across the simulated snowy grounds to the geodesic glass dome for Instructor Emerald's class was almost too much for Elena to take.

After she entered the greenhouse, she walked along the hallway with the entire Aves Company and into an endless room of clear tubing that was secured to the ceiling. Plants sprouted from every tube, and it smelled like cucumber salad in the springtime. Pathways paved in brick wound through the building with small streams of trickling water and dozens of pupil stations.

When Elena reached the end of the brick walkway, they found Instructor Emerald, as usual, standing atop a bucket wearing his pristinely white lab coat.

Emerald smoothed his fingers through his greasy black hair and said, "Welcome to your Level 3 studies. Now that we're well versed in farming and agriculture, we'll take a journey across land and sea to study the trade routes that merchants used to transport goods."

As Emerald led the class through the building, he added, "We'll also learn to manufacture some of the collateral they used for trading."

Then, Elena and the other trainees entered a room that was lined with docks, ships, crates of goods, stocks of animals, and artisan welding tools. To one side of the room there was a caravan of camels and to another a series of maps hovering in midair. The room was alive with people speaking in different languages as they bartered away their trinkets.

Emerald climbed atop one of the ship planks, and suddenly all of the simulated activity ceased to complete silence.

"Now, as the 11th century progressed, agricultural surplus stimulated the foundation and growth of towns in Europe. Once a week, traders met along highways, in church courtyards, or in village squares to trade in silks, pottery, crops, and other goods.

"Feel free to move around the room, learn from the traders and the artisans, and be sure to make plenty of notes because we'll start our hands on lesson next class."

Elena didn't feel free to move anywhere because her back was in such pain. Even the following morning she lay in bed struggling to feel conscious after the Telecaster hologram woke them at 0600 hours. Her entire body felt stiff and achy, so Abria helped her stretch before breakfast.

After a filling meal of baked eggs with wild mushroom gravy, Elena followed a procession of students back to the classroom they'd been in the day before. She expected Hopper's hologram to begin the class, but instead she was happy to see that he was there in physical form.

"Come in, dudes," Hopper said excitedly to everyone. "Welcome to Tactical Analysis. So, we're basically finished now with all our survival training and will only have one refresher course at the end of this year to prepare you for Level 4 studies. In this class, we'll strictly be studying military tactics to help you prepare for Special Ops."

Hopper clapped his hands together loudly.

"So, dudes, the motif for your Level 3 studies is war, war, war! We have five hundred years of war to cover this year to prepare you for the Age of Exploration in your Level 4 studies."

Elena's pupil station screens crowded with dozens of maps and men dressed in a variety of different uniforms.

"So, the Crusades were a series of wars concerned with the recovery and defense of lands that had been lost to Muslim invaders. The Crusades were important because it weakened the feudal system in Europe, it expanded commercial activities primarily through trade with the Orient, it strengthened the leadership of the papacy, and the contact with the East helped introduce new ideas and civilizations.

"Today, we'll discuss the First Crusade and how the crusaders altered the political balance in the Eastern Mediterranean for many centuries."

As always, Hopper taught his class in a way that was very easy for Elena to understand. And after the rigmarole that she'd experienced during class the day before, she was happy to study troop movements, the weapons that each army used during battles, and how the Crusades were beginning to shape a new culture.

However, after the second hour of standing, Elena began to feel a tingle up her spine. Being on her feet put a tremendous amount of strain on her body, and she began to feel anxious about what might happen during Basic Training to make her back worse.

"This year is your final year of Basic Training!" Marshall barked in greeting after roll call later that afternoon. Years of disappointment were creased on his face and evident in the furrow between his black eyebrows. "You completed infantry training during Level 1 Basic. In Level 2, you completed maritime training. This year, our focus will be on aeronautic training from which we get your Company name, Aves. You will train as a Company on every single Gauntlet this year. A Lieutenant will be chosen at random at each class so we can continue to build a leadership profile on each of you."

When Marshall said the word "Gauntlet" a quiver of energy shot up and down Elena's body. She remembered the first time she'd seen the practice field during their Level 1 studies, a challenging obstacle course that was equipped with everything needed to strike fear in the hearts of children. Then, during their Level 2 studies, the Gauntlet had morphed into a course that was soaking in pools of water.

But, they'd never started their first Basic Training class at the Gauntlet. So, she wondered desperately what the new course would look like and what they'd be expected to achieve on their first day. Her back ached just thinking about it.

"During some of the classes you will work together as a Company to accomplish a task, and sometimes you'll be required to compete against each other in your individual Units, as you've done in the past," Marshall continued. "However, no matter what the classes are like, you will all be in direct competition with your sister Companies as they will be given the exact same exams and class work.

"At the end of the year, Hannibal and I will assess your performance over these three years of Basic. If you have scored well, you will advance to Special Ops training for Levels 4, 5, and 6. If your scores are average you will remain with your current Company and be combined with the rest of the trainees in Levels 4, 5, and 6. Your academic scores will play a part as well as our assessment of your leadership skills. Work hard! And train even harder! Because only six members out of each Unit will be given the opportunity to advance to Special Ops. You'd better make this year count!"

Elena could feel her insides squirm.

"Our day will begin with routine stretches. Then, a Lieutenant will be chosen, and it's right on to the Gauntlet."

Elena cut her eyes at Oscar, who was already looking at her with his face set in a grimace. She thought it would be a disaster if he was chosen to be the Lieutenant, but she pushed her feelings aside because she knew that if she didn't focus all her energy on stretching there was no way she'd be able to get through the Gauntlet.

"The stretching feels good on my back and legs," Elena whispered to Abria. "But I'm not sure about going on the Gauntlet yet."

"I'm sure everything will be fine," Abria said, her words laced with positivity.

"I'm really grateful for your help and patience during all the physical therapy," Elena replied. "I couldn't have made it this far without you."

"Well, not to brag or anything, but I did tell Austin that I think I'd make a pretty good nurse," she said with a wink.

Before long, Marshall stood in front of an Optivision. Elena watched it flicker with the faces of the different students in the Aves Company. Finally, the images stopped rotating and a girl's face appeared holographically in midair on the screen.

"Abria Bowen!" Marshall barked. "It looks like you're our first Lieutenant of the year."

Abria called the entire Aves Company into formation right away, and they began the mile long hike out to the obstacle course. In next to no time, Elena saw several strange pilings rising in the air in the direction of their hike.

When she finally reached the crest of the hill overlooking the obstacle course, she saw that the Gauntlet had been transformed into a forest of climbing towers and platforms that rose twenty, thirty, and over forty feet in the sky.

Each climbing tower was layered seven high with landing platforms. Then, each of the dozen towers were connected by ropes, nets, zip lines, swinging rings, balance beams, wooden slats, rope bridges, and floating discs.

Marshall's face appeared holographically at the entrance to the course.

"Your objective is to get up the towers and cross through the obstacle course without anyone falling. If you fall, you will be disqualified. So, everyone grab your harness gear and get suited up."

As the students began to move toward the equipment, Elena gripped Austin's arm tightly.

"How am I going to survive this."

□ 7 □

The Gauntlet

"At least there isn't a puddle of, like, mud to slosh through," said Abria as her gaze traveled up the massively high towers.

"And I don't see any crazy, small tunnels or pools of water, so I think we're going to be okay," Declan said hopefully.

"Speak for yourself," Pigg whined. "You'd think by now that I would have stopped having a fear of heights, but it's actually getting worse. Do they really want us to go up there with no training?" He pointed a shaky finger at the obstacle course.

"Nah, Big Ears," Kidd said scathingly. "We're just supposed to look at it."

Elena opened her mouth to say something nasty to Kidd, but Oscar Hunter arrived with the rest of the Raptors and said loudly, "I can't believe a Firebird got chosen to lead first. What a joke!"

"Bowen, what are our orders?" Austin said loudly as he cut his eyes at Oscar.

Abria stepped forward and with an edge of superiority said, "It's always worked well for us to pair people that are afraid of heights with a person who isn't. So, pair up in your Units."

Elena groaned under her breath. Abria's instructions meant that she would be headed up the Gauntlet with Pigg above or below her. Her back and legs gave a shudder just thinking about it. Her physical therapy had gone really well, but this was the first time she'd be doing such a strenuous activity since she'd bruised her spine.

As Elena reached for the rack of harnesses, Declan grabbed her by the elbow and whispered, "I'll come with you up the tower. Castellow said that her climbing is much better now."

"Thanks, Bowen," said Elena. "I wasn't sure how I was gonna get me and Pigg through today."

"What do we do after we're paired off?" Elena heard Oscar holler at Abria.

"Oh, it's taking all my strength not to punch Hunter," Elena whispered to Declan.

"You'll have to get in line behind me," Declan said. "If he's awful when we're up there I'll push him off. Just focus on getting up to the first platform alive, okay?"

Elena smiled, thinking of Oscar falling from the tower, and nodded.

"Just give me a minute to look over the map, Hunter," Abria told Oscar shortly.

Abria was standing in front of an Optivision that Elena had never seen at a Gauntlet before. The screen displayed a map of an extensive course, far beyond what Elena could see with her eyes.

"So, there are basically four different options for advancement. Each of the four towers has four base posts. Each post has hand grips for climbing. Harriers, I want you to go up the North side, Falcons to the South, Raptors to the East, and Firebirds to the West. We'll see you at the top of the first twenty-foot platform and go from there."

Declan helped Elena shimmy into her harness. Then, he attached her screwgate locking carabiner to a long, buddy-system of climbing cables.

"Okay, Ransom, up you go," Declan said, helping her up onto the first climbing rung. "Just don't look down."

Elena used her legs to push her body up the tower, but almost immediately her legs began to tremble, and her back began to ache. A steady sweat broke out on her forehead and under her arms. Pigg was just above her, grunting and struggling with every single step. She looked up, hoping silently that he wouldn't fall because there was no way she'd be able to help him.

Periodically, Declan called out from below her, "You're doing fine, Ransom," or "You're almost there, Ransom."

However, by the time she'd climbed to the first landing platform, she was positively exhausted, in severe pain, and in imminent threat of losing her lunch all over her boots. She leaned up against the nearest pole to catch her breath.

"Ransom! Are you okay?" Declan asked urgently, coming straight to her as he cleared the top of the platform.

"Fine," Elena managed to say between heaving gasps of air. "Why?"

"You're as white as a sheet," Declan said. "Plus, my sides are killing me so I can't even imagine how you must feel. Do you need to rest?"

Elena felt awful, and even though Declan was standing in front of her, he seemed fuzzy and far away. She tried to smile, but she could tell that Declan wasn't convinced.

"Haddock!" Declan called just as he'd reached the top of the landing platform. Then, before Elena could stop him, Declan whispered, "Ransom isn't doing so well."

Austin made his way to Elena without delay. "What's the matter?"

"It's my back," Elena whispered. "I'm in so much pain. And my legs are shaking so bad that I don't think I can go on."

Austin reached into his shirt and, Elena assumed, into his body bubble because he withdrew a familiar looking needle. He pressed his hand into the small of her back. Similar to what she'd experienced before, there was a pinch of pain and then instant relief.

"Better?" Austin asked.

"So much better. Thanks," she replied.

"How are we supposed to, like, get up there?" Elena heard Abria say in a slightly panicked voice. "There aren't any more climbing holds."

Elena noticed that Abria was pointing above her head to the next tower platform that was six feet above them. Above that were a series of towers with platforms every six feet but no ladder.

"Why are we waiting here?" Oscar called loudly from the Eastern tower.

Elena noticed that all forty-seven of the Aves Company were now standing on the individual platforms awaiting Abria's next instructions.

"In case you didn't notice, there aren't any hand grips to get up to the next platform, Hunter," Abria said aggressively.

"Well, figure it out," Oscar bit back.

Austin looked at Abria steadily. "Think about it, Bowen. Think about what we'd need in order to get up to the next tower without hand grips."

"I don't know," Abria said slowly. "It would take some kind of problem solving skills that I absolutely don't have."

Austin simply watched her, as if he were waiting for her to come to the answer herself. But Elena thought they'd have a better chance of actually finishing the task if Austin just told her what to do because waiting for Abria to arrive at it seemed like it might take forever.

"The Harriers! They're the best with Physics," Abria said. "Maybe they can tell us how...think up some kind of plan..."

Abria moved toward the Harriers at the North tower and began yelling orders at them. Elena slid to the ground, glad for a moment to rest and stretch her muscles. She could hear the students muttering about getting up the tower, but Elena was too tired to listen carefully.

At long last, Stacia Bassi from Harrier said, "So, basically we've come up with a similar concept to the human ladder. We'll lift each student in an upside-down and backward motion. I'll go first to demonstrate."

Elena watched Stacia stand at the edge of the platform with a boy on either side of her. The boys grabbed her back and waist and hoisted her into the air. Then, they flipped her up. At the same time, she pulled her legs back toward the platform above, and finally, she slid backwards onto it on her belly.

"Ugh..." Elena groaned.

"Oh, come on," Declan said, putting his arms around Elena to help her up. "You've done much harder things than this before."

"I really don't think that's true," Elena muttered.

"Great work!" Austin called to the Harriers as the Aves Company began to take turns lifting each other up to the next platform.

Finally, it was Elena's turn. She felt Austin's and Declan's hands press firmly on her back.

"Easy does it," Austin said as Elena was lifted into the air.

She pulled her feet up, over her head. She did a backwards, upside down flip up to the wooden platform above her. Elena felt her knees and belly scrape as she slid against it. She did a push up/stand up and waited for the rest of the Firebirds. Then, they moved up to the next platform using the same technique until they all finally reached the seventh platform.

Elena looked down over the side of the tower, feeling nauseous.

"You're doing a great job leading us," Elena told Abria. "But could we try to hurry this along? I feel awful."

"I know, I know," Abria said sympathetically. Then, she turned toward everyone else and shouted, "Okay, everyone, good work. It looks like we need to attach our clips to the pulley system."

Elena looked up to see a rope strung across the course with a slender, one-foot wide beam at their feet.

"We'll move across these beams to the next platform. Let's go slow, okay? Marshall said we'd be disqualified if we fall," Abria warned.

Abria clipped her hook to the rope above her head and eased out onto the beam, using her arms to help balance her. More students followed after her, but when it was Elena's turn she noticed at once that walking on the tiny beam was awkward to navigate with the harnesses. Plus, trying to keep steady with everyone else crossing the beam at the same time was extremely difficult.

"This is bumpy," whined Pigg from behind her. "The bar is shaking. How can Marshall expect us to walk?"

Elena tried to concentrate on Declan's boots in front of her, but even looking down a little made her dizzy. She grabbed hold of her harness hoping it would steady her and tried with all of the strength left in her body, but she couldn't hold on any longer.

The rope slipped through her fingers, and she fell from the beam. The harness caught her sharply. Back pain. Shoulder pain. Neck pain. Elena could feel every throbbing ache as she was lowered down to the ground with Pigg right beside her.

"Ransom and Pigg, strip off your gear and get back into formation!" Marshall barked at her when she landed.

Feeling defeated, Elena slowly peeled off her gear. But then she noticed that most of the Aves Company was already standing at attention, gazing up at the towers.

Austin, Declan, Kidd, Oscar Hunter, and a few of the other boys from Falcon and Harrier were still moving steadily over rope nets, across zip lines, and floating discs. But, when they finally reached the swinging rings, it was too much. In turn, they each fell and were lowered to the ground as the others had been.

"That was a disaster!" Marshall screamed. "Not one of you managed to cross the beams. What am I training you for if you can't do the simplest thing?"

Elena rolled her eyes because it hadn't been simple at all.

"The Aves Company is going to have to do better than that if any of you expect to make it to Special Ops."

Even with Abria helping Elena do physical therapy every morning and night, the next few classes with Marshall weren't any easier on Elena's body. Pigg had eventually resorted to crawling on his hand and knees during a few of the challenges on beams. Oscar Hunter was becoming increasingly hostile toward everyone. He yelled every chance he got and pressed the Aves Company with angry words and belittling remarks.

Meanwhile, the class work was harder than both Level 1 and 2 studies combined, which was startling since they'd only just began their studies and they hadn't made it through 100 years of history yet.

Instructor Booker tossed around words like bishop and clergy, saint and pope, knighthood and nobles. Niva was now teaching every single class in a different language, and it was always a surprise when they arrived for the lesson as to which vernacular she was going to use.

Instructor Copernicus began to teach about the two styles of learning that were popular during the Middle Ages. The Quadrivium view included a formal education in the understanding of music; therefore, she spent a fair amount of her lectures teaching them the plainsong liturgical music of the Roman Catholic Church, and they studied the physics of sound and music theory.

Instructor Emerald forced the Aves Company into group work using one student from each Unit to make up a group of four. During the next several weeks of his classes, Elena experienced a wide variety of personalities and work habits. But easily the worst group was when she shared the four person pupil station with Stacia Bassi from Harrier, Garrett Vaughn from Falcon, and Ernest Darnell from Raptor. Every time she got stuck with them it took her a while to work up the courage to join them.

On one such day, Elena walked to the pupil station cautiously but discovered that the others hadn't waited for her to begin their work.

"I've already decided who's working on what," said Ernest Darnell shortly.

"How can you just let him assign us all the tasks?" Elena said to Stacia and Garrett.

"He was very clever," Stacia said, her brown eyes glittering in the lights from the Optivision. "He exploited our complete lack of interest in choosing the assignments for ourselves."

"And since you took so long to get over here," said Garrett from Falcon. "No doubt because you were goofing off with Austin or whatever, you can't really complain."

Elena didn't feel like arguing, so while Stacia mapped out a trade route from Byzantine and Muslim merchants in the Mediterranean, Garrett added the Italian merchants with their flag fleets and detailed how they became the middlemen in trade between Europe and the Orient. Ernest showed how the Silk Road connected Constantinople with Beijing, China, and Elena completed the list of all the markets and fairs that were available.

When class was finally over, Elena was ecstatic to get away from the students in her group. She was just beginning to leave the hydroponic farm when she saw Oscar pursue Pigg at the door.

"Pigg, I wanted to talk to you about Marshall's class tomorrow," Elena heard him say in a rude tone. "I've noticed that you haven't gotten any better at the towers even though we've practiced dozens of times. In fact, the last few classes I saw you crawling around on your hands and knees." Oscar crossed his arms over his chest. "You need to try harder! Practice more. I don't want to be held back by you."

"What do you expect, Hunter?" Kidd said nastily as he passed them. "Pigg crawls around like a baby because he's afraid of heights. You can't do anything about that dysfunction."

Elena's face flushed with anger. It was bad enough that Oscar gave Pigg a hard time, but he didn't need a member of his own Unit to pick on him, too. Irrational rage began to boil in Elena's insides, and she knew exactly who to take it out on. Leaving Pigg with Oscar and all her friends behind, Elena pursued Kidd across campus and back toward the resident towers.

"Hey, Wheeler!" Elena shouted when she felt she was in earshot. "You don't have to be so awful to Pigg!"

Kidd spun around, looking surly.

Elena approached him and lowered her voice to a whisper. "He helped you fix the Independence and took all your attitude problems without saying anything in return. He should get a medal for keeping his temp..."

Kidd held up an index finger in Elena's face before she could even finish speaking.

"First, he wouldn't have needed to help fix the ship if we hadn't been on one of your dimwit adventures to begin with. And second, and most importantly, our deal is off. So, I refuse to listen to you tell me how I'm to treat anyone."

"That reminds me," Elena said, folding her arms over her chest. "Now that the Independence is back to its rightful owners, you should go get the junk you left on board." She scowled at him for effect. "Unless you'd like me to toss it for you."

Kidd's eyebrows creased together in a frown. "You're a selfish brat, you know?"

Elena couldn't even respond. She simply stood, gaping as he walked away. For some unexplainable reason, she actually felt shame. Was she really selfish? And a brat?

"Wheeler is the selfish brat." Elena tried to tell herself. "I'm just reacting to him."

Yet, she began to wonder if what he said was really true. She also began to feel confused about why Kidd's words bothered her so much. Elena stalked off toward the nearest Grimvator, and it moved slantways. Then, she entered the Media Lab in a bustle of energy and found Austin sitting at one of the pupil stations.

"Do you think I'm selfish?" Elena demanded before even sitting at the table.

"Yes," Austin said without hesitation and without bothering to look up.

"What?" Elena said indignantly, stamping her foot like a child.

Austin moved his gaze from his Smartslate and caught the look on Elena's face.

"Oh, um...when you said *selfish* I...I thought you were being rhetorical," Austin stuttered.

"Then, why did you answer?" Elena said, plopping down in the chair across from him.

Austin smiled sheepishly. "Why the awkward questions?"

"Wheeler told me I was a selfish brat because I told him to get his stuff outta the hovercraft."

"Why do you care what he says about you?"

"I don't care," Elena said, looking down at her fingernails. "I just don't understand why he has to be so mean."

"You don't think it was mean of you to tell him to move his stuff?"

"No, the Independence is ours now," Elena said defensively. "The quicker he gets his stuff out, the less I have to see him. He was so awful to Pigg today. And that was *after* Hunter had already said a bunch of mean stuff about Pigg right to his face."

When Austin didn't reply, she watched him work for a few minutes in silence. Then, she dropped her chin in her hand.

"What are you working on?"

"Phonology for Niva," Austin said. "You should get started on it, too."

"I'm too grumpy to work on that now," she replied. "Besides..."

But before she could say another word, she heard Pigg's voice carry across the room. "Elena! Austin! I'm so glad I found you."

He hurried over toward their pupil station but tripped over his own feet and fell head long into the table. The resulting sound indicated that Pigg had hit his forehead quite hard.

"Are you alright?" Austin asked, standing to help him up.

"Yes, yes. I'm fine." Pigg rubbed his forehead with his palm. "I need you, though, and this is very urgent. I heard a rumor that they put an aeronautic simulation in the Simulab because we're supposed to learn how to fly an aerocraft sometime this year!" He looked a little green in the face.

"I heard that, too," said Austin, turning back to his work. "Apparently, besides the standard Simulabs, new simulations have been added that offer a wide range of games and exercises that are done high in the air to prepare for aeronautics. It's really not any different than the previous years. Remember how they had all the hand-to-hand combat Simulabs the first year? Then, last year they had water simulations?"

"But this is different," said Pigg. "I'm terrified of heights. I don't see how I'll ever learn to fly. I've watched Wheeler operate the Independence. It seems really hard. Too many steps to remember."

"Well, I was thinking I'd ask Wheeler if he'd tutor me in operating so I'd have a head start," said Austin. "Want to come with me?"

Pigg shook his head furiously, so Austin looked at Elena expectantly.

"Seriously? After what he just said to me!" Elena said incredulously. "I refuse to take any kind of lessons from Wheeler."

"But if he gives us lessons it may help improve our scores later on," said Austin.

"There's no way I'm asking for his help," Elena said stubbornly. "I'll just practice on the Simulabs like everyone else."

"Oh, can I come with you?" Pigg asked.

"Right now?"

"Please, Elena!" begged Pigg. "I'd feel so much better if I could get some practice in early so I don't look like a dimwit later."

Elena looked at Austin, but he only shrugged. "I'd love to, Pigg, but I really need to start on my homework. Booker gave us a million sections to read about self-contained farming communities that were worked by peasants, and I still haven't even started on the origins of the Arabic language for Niva."

Pigg fell to his knees at her feet. "Please, Elena, please help me!"

"You don't have to do this right now because of what Hunter said," Elena told him. "I know he hurt your feelings, but he's just mean to everyone so you're gonna havta get over it."

"No, it's not that," said Pigg until Elena made a face of disbelief. "Okay, it could be partly that. But I need to practice this so that everyone doesn't make fun of me later. You know how clumsy I am. *Please* HELP ME!"

"Fine! Get up!" Elena said impatiently. She gave his shoulder a shove. "But you'll have to help me with my homework later . . . and I don't want to hear any complaining no matter how long it takes."

"Thank you. Thank you," Pigg said breathlessly.

They took a Grimvator sideways and down to the Simulab. The room was massively deep, with ceilings so high Elena couldn't see the parameters of the room. Dozens of simulated activities were spread out along the walls and down the center, making up rows and aisles of familiar games like kickboxing and Stratego, but there were also several new aeronautic simulations and problem-solving Simulabs that dealt with heights.

Pigg led Elena to a cube shaped Simulab that was fitted with two captain's chairs and a large operating screen.

"Could you go first? You know, just so I can see what it's like," Pigg asked.

"Sure," Elena said as she slid into the pilot's seat.

The central screen came alive. Elena opened several Optivisions from the control panel and accessed the operating manual so she could read up on the steering directions, many of which displayed hand/eye coordination details.

After she was familiar with how the aerocraft operated, Elena selected a practice module at the beginners level. The central screen showed a view of the main road while another screen showed the controls and direction. There was also a screen with a small map of the course, and yet another that had a side view of what the aerocraft looked like as it was in motion.

Elena felt the aerocraft hum with energy as it galvanized. She grabbed the control yoke eased onto a straight stretch of roadway. She swerved around cones, made right and left turns on curved streets, and drove through darkened tunnels. The simulation was so straightforward that she was able to finish it rather quickly.

"That was pretty easy," Elena said after about three minutes of flying. "Do you mind if I try something more challenging before you start?"

"Sure," said Pigg. "Take as long as you need. I'm going to study your every move."

Elena selected a course with a curved road and narrow bridges, but it seemed far too effortless for her to try again. She decided on one where different obstacles flew in front of the aerocraft so that she had to swerve often to avoid a crash. Finally, she chose a cityscape with rows of tall buildings and narrow streets with tight corners, which reminded her a little too much of New York City.

"That was really great!" said Elena after she'd finished the fourth simulation. "I like driving a lot. Okay, your turn."

Pigg plopped down in the pilot's seat, and Elena slid into the passenger's seat. He opened an Optivision screen from the control panel just as Elena had, but instead of going for the easy course, he chose the one with the narrow bridge. He was sweaty and twitchy, tapping his fingers against the control yoke nervously.

"Maybe you should start with an easy simulation," Elena suggested. "You seem really nervous."

"Nah, I liked the scenery in this one," Pigg said. "Besides, if I don't challenge myself I might panic later, and then I'll never hear the end of it from Wheel...I mean the other students."

"Okay, well just relax," said Elena, eyeing his compulsive finger-drumming with a little apprehension. "It's just a simulation."

"So, I know the general mechanics of how this operates," Pigg said weakly. "And we're starting on one of the beginner courses, so everything should be fine...or close to fine. I mean, you just completed it, so how bad could it really be, right?" Pigg looked at Elena expectantly.

"You're *asking me?*" Elena said. "How should *I* know? But your little pep talk to yourself isn't inspiring confidence." She clipped her belt on tightly. "It says the total simulation should take three minutes when driven correctly. So, just get started slow, okay?"

Pigg nodded and swallowed hard.

"Sure. Slow. It's going to be fine."

The simulation began with a screenshot of a classic city street with a boat harbor to one side and residential buildings on the other. As Pigg put the vehicle into drive, it lurched forward, and Elena's head slammed back into the headrest. He cut the steering column hard to the right, and it crashed into the side of a building. The entire vehicle shook.

"I wasn't expecting the crash to feel so real," Elena groaned, rubbing the back of her neck. "That was worse than landing in Istanbul." She sighed, trying to remain patient. "Okay, let's try again, but this time when you put the hovercraft into motion, try not to jerk the control yoke so hard. The thing flies straight with barely any pressure."

Pigg started again. This time he was able to ease out onto the road, but soon the course curved in between the building, and he lost complete control.

First, he smashed into the building on the left. Then, he overcorrected and hit the building on the right. Somehow, he managed to hop the curb and fly the aerocraft through a shop, running down the shopkeeper.

The screen kept lighting up with different suggestions for a change of direction or a red warning sign, but nothing helped Pigg. Every single time he hit something, the entire vehicle shook and made noises like it was going to fall completely apart.

At long last, they reached a tunnel. Elena held tightly to the sides of her seat as he entered a dark passageway, especially as other aerocrafts with hololights began to speed by them.

"Being in the dark is really scary," said Pigg.

"Just in case you were wondering, being in the dark is not the scariest thing in this tunnel. Turn your lights on," Elena tried to coach him.

But when he tried to access the lights from the Optivision screen, he lost complete control of the aerocraft again, and he crashed into several of the vehicles that were passing through the tunnel.

At long last, Elena saw light coming from the other end of the tunnel.

"Oh, there it is!" Pigg said excitedly. He was so excited, in fact, that he accelerated the aerocraft so they could get out quickly.

They flew through the mouth of the tunnel, spun out of control, and crashed into the side of the bridge. For a moment, the aerocraft hung as if suspended by a string, but then it tipped over the edge. Elena felt the sensation of falling a long way. The aerocraft hit the water below with such force that she knocked her head into the dashboard. They were both sprayed with a copious amount of water.

With stinging eyes, Elena watched a side profile view of their vehicle from one of the Optivision screens. The entire vehicle slowly submerged.

"I guess I failed the simulation," Pigg said slowly.

A red screen appeared with a message that read, "Pilot and passenger fatality."

"I'd say you impressively failed it," Elena groaned.

"Do you want to go again?" Pigg asked feebly.

"*Again?* Again! How could I possibly ride with you again? I'd get brain damage."

"Please come with me, please!" Pigg begged. "That was just my first try. I know I'll get better."

Elena sighed. She had a terrible headache but agreed to go again. In fact, she went three more times with him and, if it was possible, he got worse.

"I just don't understand how you did your simulation so perfectly the first time," Pigg said as they were walking from the Simulab an hour after they'd started.

"It was really hard. My brain had to tell my hands when to turn," Elena said sarcastically as she rubbed the back of her neck with the tips of her fingers.

"Don't be so arrogant, Elena," said Pigg. "It's really hard."

"I'm not being *arrogant*, Pigg," Elena replied moodily. "I'm just feeling a little unstable from the concussion that I have right now."

"I said 'sorry' a go-zillion times," said Pigg, and then he heaved a great sigh. "I know I'm always a disappointment."

"Hey! You're not always a disappointment," Elena said, trying to encourage him, though her head was pounding. "I'm just grumpy today."

Pigg shrugged. "Come on, I'll help you start on our homework."

❑ 8 ❑

Meeting with Truman Ransom

The weeks pressed on at a hurried pace. Elena's brain was a haze of dates and facts. Details about merchants, bankers, craftsmen, and skilled laborers were competing in her mind with timelines of how the Byzantine and Arab civilizations exposed Europe to new ideas and functions of government.

In between classes, Elena's hours were spent on writing lengthy essays to summarize her interpretation of medieval literature. Fergie tutored Elena in Phonology and in the fundamental forms of musical composition because, even after a lot of practice, she just couldn't understand how to read the curvy notes on the page.

A few times, Austin attempted to have a conversation with Elena and the others about the Tablets of Destiny, but as Fergie rightly pointed out, there was no reason to discuss it without Kidd's help. And, since they didn't have any new leads on possible artifacts, they didn't visit the Firebird Station during their first few weeks back at school.

As always, Instructor Emerald kept the group work in his class in constant rotation. Elena was forced to work with Oscar Hunter a few times and had to endure more of Stacia Bassi. It didn't seem to matter who she was in a group with, whether they were minting coins or firing pottery, she just couldn't get along with any of them. And, she wasn't the only one having trouble with the group work.

"I've missed doing group work with only Firebirds," Declan said to Elena, Austin, and the others one afternoon while they were on their way back to the resident towers after Emerald's latest class. "The girls in my group today were annoyingly flirtatious."

Elena grabbed one of his cheeks and pinched it. "Oh, poor little Bowen. Too popular and handsome for his own good."

"I'm trying to be serious," Declan said, shoving her hand away. "I have a real, actual problem. There's this one Falcon girl that I think is *following* me. It seems like everywhere I go she's there. She has an odd smell...some kinda perfume I guess. Ugh! I don't know what she's thinking, but I hope she doesn't have any ideas about asking me to go to Harleston Village or something."

Elena laughed out loud.

"Frankie Smiley got wood glue in my hair during apprenticeship skills lab today for Emerald and he didn't even say sorry," Abria said. "He just laughed."

"That dimwit," Elena said dryly.

"Oh, he's not a dimwit," Abria said earnestly. "I just wish there'd been time for him to help me clean it, like, out."

"Anybody want to Simulab with me? Hint, hint...Elena," Pigg interrupted.

"Pigg, we've done that aeronautic Simulab almost every day and we still haven't had any classes on aeronautics. There hasn't even been an announcement that we're even going to have lessons on aerocraft operation this quarter," said Elena. And then, after remembering their last class in Basic, added, "If you're going to Simulab you should really do the ones that deals with heights to help your acrophobia."

Pigg did agree to practice in the Simulab. However, nothing he did seemed to help conquer his fear of heights. In fact, he almost seemed to get worse as the classes with Marshall intensified.

In keeping with the theme of their team building exercises done on tall towers, the eleven Firebirds were hooked together side-by-side on a forty-foot high platform during their next Basic Training class. A massive wooden log was suspended above their heads on a track. As a Unit, they were tasked to push the log down the track while also stepping in sync on wooden beams that were spaced three feet apart.

During another training class, ten of the students were blindfolded while Frankie Smiley had to talk them through an obstacle course of rope ladders and bungee cord mazes. And in yet another Basic, the Firebird Unit had to get all the members across a bridge comprised of dangling ropes and wires.

By the end of the first week of the second month, Elena slid under her bed covers feeling overwhelmed and exhausted. Abria was perched on the edge of Fergie's bed gossiping about Stacia Bassi and Garrett Vaughn, but all Elena could think about before her eyes closed was how ready she was for a couple days off school and that she'd be at the Firebird Station the following day with her friends.

"Time to wake up, Sunshine."

Elena rubbed her face in her pillow and smiled. She hadn't heard her dad's voice in a long time. Bleary eyed, she looked up into his handsome face, which seemed to be glowing.

"Good morning, Daddy."

"Come now, we have a lot of work to do."

Elena felt curious about what he could mean by "work" as she crawled out of bed to follow him. She crossed the marbled halls and followed him into his office. Truman walked around to the other side of his desk toward an elaborate bookcase that stretched the entire wall. The shelves were oaken and embroidered with rounded emblems.

He pushed open the third emblem from the left and inserted his finger into a hole. A moment later, a portion of the bookcase swung away from the wall, revealing a secret room.

As Elena stepped toward his secret library, she caught her reflection in the gleam of his desk and felt instantly confused. In her mind, she felt fifteen-years-old, but the little reflection looking back at her was only five.

"Elena, come on in," her dad called.

Elena walked through the entrance and into a room that was filled from floor to ceiling with books placed on shelves, stacked in piles on the floor, and lying lazily over cushioned chairs. The book bindings were so familiar that her concern about her age quickly faded away.

"Now, what do you suppose this is?" Elena's dad asked. He held his hand open.

When she saw that he was holding a star necklace with sharp angles, Elena exclaimed, "The Kairos!"

"Yes, that's right," said Truman Ransom. "Now, watch very carefully as I turn to page forty-seven in my dossier."

As he opened his diary, the sharp angles of the necklace began to slide automatically. Eventually, it unfolded to reveal a multi-tiered clock-like face with a dozen hands. Everything on the clock began to spin wildly.

Page forty-seven of the Ransom Dossier had strange letters and symbols that were scrawled along the binding, corners, and edges of the page. But the most bizarre component of their encounter was that the ceiling in Truman's office also began to light up in certain places.

Then, in midair, a twisted structure appeared holographically; two strands of colored pearls were woven together in a complex pattern, and those strands were connected by dozens of other beaded lines.

"Lena, this structure is called a double helix," said Truman. "The helix is the key to locating information about the Firebird Disc. When the disc and all the codes from the other artifacts are joined together, we will know how to defeat Imperator forever."

This information made Elena feel impatient. "I already know that, Daddy. How do I find the Firebird Disc?"

"That I cannot tell you," he replied patiently. "Your knowledge of that will come in *time*."

Elena jolted straight up in bed inside the Firebird girls' dormitory.

Typically, her dreams slipped away the moment she opened her eyes. But this had been something entirely different. The images from her dad's office were at the forefront of her thoughts, which were perfectly clear, almost like she was experiencing a *memory*. She wasn't sure how to feel, but she was certain that she needed to go look at the Ransom Dossier right away.

Elena noticed that Abria was still sleeping soundly, which meant it was still very early. She scanned her Trademark into her wardrobe, and a little light blinked awake. She dressed in silence and pulled on her aviator boots.

Elena headed down the hall to the balcony off the washroom. She swung her leg over the side of the porch railing, ignoring the dull pain in her back, and began to climb down the side of the building as she'd done many times before.

Minutes later, she skirted along the edge of the building where she knew the surveillance wouldn't catch her and made her way out into the woods.

At length, she stopped in front of a myriad of trees that were covered with creeping plants. She pulled on a handful of foliage to reveal the steel plated door to the Firebird Station.

Once inside the Research & Development room, Elena set her Kairos on the table. She opened the Ransom Dossier to page forty-seven. Then, she pulled up an Optivision screen and accessed the scans of the ceiling in her dad's library. She was expecting everything to light up and start working just as it had in her dream, but after a few moments she decided that something must be wrong. Everything remained still.

Elena turned each page of the diary slowly, hoping that the Kairos would transform as it had in her dream. However, after several long minutes that turned into an hour, the dossier and Kairos on the table were still motionless.

Feeling impatient and hungry, Elena carried the open dossier with her to the kitchen and set it with the Kairos on the counter. She poured a bowl of dry cereal. As she crunched on breakfast, she flipped through the diary pages, again hoping for some kind of miraculous transformation.

As she sat, she began to wonder why Austin and her friends hadn't come down to the Station yet. Shouldn't someone have noticed that she was missing, and then guessed where she was?

She felt urgency pressing on her. She needed to talk to Austin. She was tempted to get his Humanoid out of the cabinet, but she knew she couldn't turn it on without the real Austin's Trademark. Suddenly, she realized that the next best thing to Austin was herself.

Elena hurried back to the cabinet in the Research & Development room. She scanned her Trademark into the arm of her Decoy. The robot immediately awoke. It gazed at her with a look of irritation.

"Sorry to wake you," Elena said honestly. "But, I need you to be the best version of me for a few minutes. Could you do that?"

The robot nodded slowly.

"Kenneth and Anne Foreman created you to be just like me, right?"

"Yes."

"To think like me? Reason like me?" Elena said. "But you don't have my memories, do you? Because the Foremans wouldn't have been able to access them. You'd only be able to create new memories or, I guess, data."

"Yes."

In shorthand, Elena explained everything to her Humanoid about the dream and her dad's office. She showed her robot the research that she and her friends had collected.

"So, I'm thinking that my dad gave me these memories, or whatever they are, so that I could find the Firebird Disc. Maybe it's my family artifact. What do you think?"

"I don't know," Decoy Elena said. "We need Austin and maybe even Fergie's help."

"I guess I was wrong about needing help from you," Elena said grumpily. "You're so much like me that I can't problem solve with you." The Decoy looked offended, but she ignored its indignant expression. "I wish we could wake their Decoys. Though, when I didn't show up for breakfast, Austin should have come looking for me. Especially after, I'm sure, Abria told him that I wasn't in bed when she woke up. I wonder what's keeping all of them."

But at that moment, Elena heard the door to the Station open. She hoped that Austin had finally come to find her, but Abria appeared from the hall, her face stark white.

"Elena. Come quick!" She was slightly out of breath. "Fergie's parents have died in an explosion."

▭ 9 ▭

Death of D.E.S.

Elena ran along the gleaming Grimsby hallway behind Abria. Tightness was building steadily in her chest. Abria had just said that Fergie's parents were dead, and if that was true, Elena knew exactly where Abria was leading her.

Abria's pace slowed to a walk at the end of the hallway, and Elena watched the door to Headmaster Worthen Bentley's office slide open silently. She drew a deep breath.

The last time she'd been there, the Headmaster told her that her own parents had been killed in an accident. She didn't want to go inside. But, Fergie was her friend and her parents were dead. Even though it was painful, Elena stepped over the threshold. Instantly, her brow furrowed in confusion.

She was surprised to see that the room was filled with adults she didn't recognize. Some were grouped around the Headmaster, talking in low voices, while others snacked from a table of refreshments. When her parents had been murdered, only Hannibal, Hopper, and Austin had been in the room.

Before Elena had a chance to fully contemplate the meaning of all the men and women talking to Headmaster Bentley, her eyes fell on Fergie. Declan's arm was around her shoulders, and though she wasn't crying, her face was drawn into a deep frown. She watched Abria join Declan and Fergie's embrace.

To one side of the room, Austin was talking quietly with Hannibal and Hopper. Pigg was off in another corner eating from a modest buffet of bite-sized sandwiches and cubed fruit. No one noticed Elena enter the room, and she was grateful. She slinked over to join Pigg.

"Oh, Elena," Pigg said, stuffing his mouth with a cube of white cheese. "This is just awful. We missed lunch to come here, but all they're serving is tea-time crackers, fruit cocktail, and these little finger sandwiches. I've tried all the ones on that platter, but don't have the one with the darker crust because it tastes like sauerkraut." He gave an involuntary shudder.

Elena sighed and shook her head.

"Sorry," Pigg whispered. "I know it's not right to talk about food at a time like this, but I get so hungry when I'm upset and then I say the wrong things when I'm nervous, you know?"

Elena did know. At her parents funeral, Pigg had eaten an entire table of food all by himself. Then, he went on to tell anyone that would listen that Elena had gotten into so much trouble in just their first few weeks of Level One that Marshall had her running laps after every class for the whole first quarter of school.

"Have you heard anything about what specifically happened to Fergie's parents?" Elena asked him.

Pigg shook his head. "Just that a hovercraft accidentally flew into the D.E.S. building and the whole thing blew up and burned to the ground with her parents, all the Humanoids, and all their work inside. They say that the building literally collapsed into dust."

Elena covered her hand over her mouth so that no one would hear the loud gasp that came from it. Her mind went into overdrive. She'd never heard of anything so ludicrous. How was it possible that a hovercraft could crash into a building the size of the D.E.S. lab and that it would burn to the ground? The structure had been massive, a colossal engineering masterpiece with its forest green rotund roof and marbled hallways.

"Hey," Austin said, putting an arm around Elena's shoulder. "You doing okay?"

"Why are all these people here?" Elena asked.

"Apparently, they have a vested interested in the D.E.S. lab. The Headmaster is on the Board of Directors. I guess they want to know what's going to happen to their investments."

"Have you heard anything more about what happened?" Elena said.

"More than the building burning to the ground with Fergie's parents and all their work? No."

"How likely is it that the entire building would burn up into ashes from one hovercraft flying into it?" Elena asked very quietly.

"Well, that's the thing with *accidents*...they can seem unlikely," Austin whispered back.

"Technically, it does deny the laws of physics for a building of that magnitude to burn to the ground," Pigg mumbled, his mouth filled with green grapes. "Especially since it was built with the most advanced technology available and able to withstand fire, water, and pulverizing weaponry. Kenneth talked me through everything when we were there last."

"That's what I'm saying. So, what do we think *really* happened?" Elena said.

"I have a few theories," Austin admitted. "But we can't talk about it here."

"Hey," Declan appeared suddenly at Austin's shoulder. "We're going home in the morning for the memorial service. The Headmaster gave permission for you three to come with us, if you want to. I know it would mean a lot to Fergie."

"Where will you stay now that your home is gone?" Austin asked.

"There's an innkeeper in town that was friends with our families. She'll let us stay there now and anytime we come home."

"We'd be glad to come with you," Austin said.

Declan looked at Elena. She gave him a half-hearted smile and a nod. He grabbed her hand and squeezed it as if to say he was grateful. Then, he walked back to Abria and Fergie with a somber expression.

"I want to go to the D.E.S. lab when we first get to the Galilee Province so I can look through the debris," Austin whispered to Elena.

"Why bother with that?" Pigg asked.

"To see if there are any clues as to why the building fell."

"But, how can we tell the others we want to do that?" Elena asked. "It might be too hard for them to even see the site, much less dig through the remains."

"We won't tell them," Austin said. "We'll go to the inn, drop off our things, and then make an excuse about giving them space or whatever. I just have to see what's left of that building."

That night, Elena watched Abria brush Fergie's hair as she sat on the edge of her bed. They hadn't gone down to dinner; Hopper just sent sandwiches to the room. Vivienne and Olivia hadn't even come back yet. Elena assumed it was because they wanted to be respectful and give Fergie some space.

Normally, it would have been torture for Elena to watch Abria doing hair, nails, and makeup, but she didn't have the heart to leave her friends. In fact, she even agreed to let Abria do her hair when she was finished with Fergie's nails.

They'd been mostly silent all afternoon, leaving Elena alone to think of her parent's death and how much it had changed her. Much in the same way she had, Abria had to wipe tears from her eyes every other minute. Plus, she was constantly blowing her nose, which caused Elena's heart to ache with pity.

Conversely, Fergie didn't seem any different. She was steady, quiet, and indulgent when Abria talked to her. Fergie didn't really seem upset, more like she was concerned that a transaction had gone through incorrectly. Elena wondered if Humanoids felt pain the same way humans did.

Finally, Elena realized that she hadn't actually spoken to Fergie since she found out her parents had died. She felt like she should offer some kind of condolence, but she didn't know what to say except, "I'm sorry about your dad and mom."

"Yes, it is unfortunate," Fergie replied. "I was relying on them to contribute to our efforts until the end of our *operation*."

Elena felt perplexed by her response. "But aren't you sad at all?"

"Elena!" Abria said in a shocked tone.

Fergie looked at them both seriously and said, "I am disappointed that they were not able to write a program for reading the codes on the artifacts before they passed on."

"They didn't *pass on*," Elena said steadily. "They were murdered!"

"You can't say that for sure, Elena," Abria said harshly. "A hovercraft flew into the building and caused an explosion that collapsed the building. That can happen."

"Oh, puh-lease!" Elena said. "You can't tell me you actually believe that story."

"Well, I guess we'll find out more tomorrow when we get there," Abria said, wiping a tear from her cheek. "But I don't feel like discussing it any more right now."

"Abria," Fergie said kindly. "What did my mom always say about life and death?"

Abria hung her head. "We are all given a purpose. We're given a supreme moment in this life to die once our purpose is complete."

"That is accurate," Fergie said. "My parents would not wish for you to weep for their death, but rejoice that they have moved on to the next phase of their journey."

"I'm just going to miss them," Abria said.

Fergie put her arms around Abria's shoulders awkwardly, almost as if she were trying to hug her.

Elena turned her back on her friends and put her head on her pillow. If *destiny* and *supreme purpose* meant that the people you loved died horrible deaths long before it was their time, then destiny sounded like a cruel idea.

The next morning, Abria was more subdued than normal. She didn't really speak to anyone as they rode the train to the Galilee Province. Declan also didn't seem himself. He even snapped at Pigg when he accidently spilled juice on the breakfast table, which was an almost daily occurrence that Declan usually laughed off. However, Fergie seemed completely normal. She carried on with regular conversation as if they were going for a shopping trip in Harleston Village.

At long last, the Grimsby Channel rose out of the ground above an extravagantly lush and vibrant city. The train continued along a rail line that was built on the outskirts of the town. Tree-topped mountains encircled the tall city buildings that were adorned with multi-colored rotund roofs.

Soon, Elena and Austin were winding through the emerald and vibrant floral streets behind Abria. Declan and Fergie walked slowly, arm in arm, while Pigg lagged behind them, picking up snacks from vending carts along the streets. They walked through a vast stone courtyard with rows of quaint shops with apartment homes above.

At length, Abria pushed open the door of Number 129 Cherry Hill Avenue, and Elena heard a little bell ding.

"Ah! Ciao. Entra, miei piccoli tesori." A very beautiful woman with long, sleek black hair and a light, flowing dressed appeared. She swept across the room as if she'd floated there on a cloud and enclosed Fergie, Abria, and Declan in a generous hug. "You bring the sunshine with you!"

Declan managed to peel himself away from the woman and said, "Elena, Austin, and Pigg, we'd like you to meet Contessa. She's our oldest family friend."

"Dio mio!" Contessa blurted, looking at Elena intently. "Is that your real hair?" Elena couldn't help but blush. "Just look how gorgeous you are. Oh! And all these freckles. Do you know I always secretly wanted freckles? For several months when I was fifteen I painted them on my face. But it was just so much work I had to stop eventually." Contessa the innkeeper wiggled her finger at Elena and said, "Spin! Spin!"

Elena was forced to turn in a circle several times as Contessa made noises of extreme admiration.

"Help me," Elena mouthed to Austin as Contessa grabbed her hand and began to pull her around.

"Mind if I join in?" Declan asked, as he grabbed one of Elena's hands and somehow managed to squeeze his body in between them so he could dance with them both at the same time.

"My personal space has been violated and there's nothing I can do," Elena called to Austin.

Then, she caught the somber looks on Abria and Fergie's faces. They'd come to the Galilee Province for a funeral, but being in Contessa's presence had made her forget that they were grieving. Declan must have caught his sister's face, too, because he suddenly stopped spinning.

Contessa looked around at their faces. "Come, my little tesori! Let's not mourn the dead today. We'll have plenty of time to grieve tomorrow. You should go and rest. Tonight I will cook a feast and we'll light candles for the lost. Then, tomorrow we will say good-bye."

"Elena, Pigg, and I will go walk for a bit," Austin said. "Let you have some time to talk about the arrangements for tomorrow. What time would you like us back for supper, Contessa?"

"When the sun goes down, tesoro," the innkeeper said in a breezy voice. "And we will dine in the garden tonight."

"Tell me again why we have to do this today?" Elena asked Austin as they stepped onto the street. "I'm so tired. I didn't sleep well last night and tomorrow is going to be emotionally exhausting." She thought back to her feelings during her parent's funeral. "I wouldn't mind just going to sit someplace quiet for now."

"Me, too," Pigg agreed.

"I have to see the site before they clear everything away," Austin said, sounding urgent.

"Austin, the D.E.S. lab was a huge building. It will take weeks or months to clear it all way."

But Austin clearly didn't want to hear any protesting from Elena because he quickened his pace. She thought, for a moment, how peculiar they must look to everyone else who was casually strolling along the marbled Galilee walkways.

The boulevards of olive trees, manicured hedges, fields of honeysuckle, and vines of hanging yellow flowers passed by in a blur as Elena tried to keep up with Austin. Pigg even tripped a few times, but Austin never even looked behind him.

"Austin, slow down," Elena finally called. "You're walking too fast. Pigg and I can barely keep up."

"Sorry, I'm just distracted. We're almost there." Austin slowed his pace a bit.

"I get that you're all crazy about getting to the building, but if we could just wait until tomorrow after..." But Elena stopped short, her stride ending in a stumble.

They'd just arrived at the crossroads where the *Destro Electron System* facility had once stood as an imposing structure with a forest green rotund roof. Now, there was nothing. Not one thing. The building was completely gone, along with any traces that it had ever existed to begin with.

"H...how is this p...possible?" Elena stuttered. "There's nothing h...here. How could they have cleaned it up so quickly?"

"They couldn't have. Or they *wouldn't have* needed to unless they were trying to hide something," Austin said. He looked deep in thought for a moment as he thumbed his chin. Then, he said, "Pigg, when we get back to the Firebird Station I'm going to need you to hack into the global server to see if you can access any surveillance footage of the D.E.S. building before it crumbled to the ground."

"Why do you want to see that?" Pigg asked.

"Because it may give us answers to what actually happened."

"Okay, but what should we do now?" Pigg asked.

Austin looked at Elena sorrowfully. "Nothing. We can't do a thing right now, except go to the funeral tomorrow."

A couple days later, Elena sat on the Grimsby Channel with her friends on their way back to school. Her thoughts were consumed with Kenneth and Anne Foreman's memorial service, which had been completely unlike her parent's funeral in every way.

First, it was held outside near the water. Friends of the family took turns sharing memories about Fergie's parents at random. Doves were released, symbolizing something that Elena didn't understand. Then, Fergie scattered her parent's ashes into the water.

"You okay?" Declan asked Elena as she stared out the train window in silence. "You have a weird look on your face."

"This is how I look, okay?" Elena said, trying to be funny. "I'm hoping I'll grow out of it one day."

A faint smile appeared on his face. "Me, too."

"How are you doing?" she asked.

"I've basically lost another set of parents," Declan said seriously. "I'm not really sure how to feel."

"As Austin says, there can be no consolation in this life for the loss of a parent," Elena replied in a kind way. "For myself, I'm starting to learn that I grieve so much because I loved so much. All the love that I want to give my parents in kisses and hugs and time can't go anywhere now, so it comes out in tears and anger and frustration."

Declan grabbed Elena's hand tightly, but he didn't say anything and he wouldn't look at her. And that's when she realized, even Declan knew that sometimes the grief of life had to be experienced in silence.

When they got back to school, Elena and Austin wasted no time. They headed straight for the Firebird Station with Pigg to hack the global server.

Within minutes of their arrival, Pigg had already located the file they needed. He pulled the surveillance footage up on the main Optivision screen so that they could get a larger than life view. Then, as if it were happening right in the room with them, Elena watched a hovercraft fly into the D.E.S. building. She watched a ball of fire erupt from the windows after the initial explosion and pieces of the structure fall to the ground below.

"Would you play the impact scene again, but slow it down to .05 frames per second?" Austin requested.

Pigg did as he was asked. Elena watched it for a second time. And then a third. She could tell that Austin was waiting to see something specific, but what it was exactly he didn't say.

"Thanks for that," Austin said. "Now, fast play that footage until right before the building collapses."

The playback raced forward at a sickening speed and finally stopped, recounting a tragic scene of the building collapsing, as if it'd been built out of crackers.

"Play back to right before the building falls and enhance the footage of the windows. Then, slow it down to .05 frames per second," Austin ordered.

Pigg did as he was told. His fingers moved the vantage point closer to the building windows. When he started the footage again, Elena distinctly saw tiny puffs of smoke burst on each floor as the building collapsed on itself floor by floor.

"What are all of those little puffs?" she asked.

"A series of explosions."

The sound of Fergie's voice made Elena jump and turn. She saw Fergie standing in the door frame with Declan and Abria behind her.

"Explosions? But what does that, like, mean?" Abria asked.

"It means that this entire event wasn't an accident!" Austin said in astonishment. "From the hovercraft hitting the building to it collapsing, to the fact that it'd all been cleared away only hours after it'd happened. None of it was an accident. It was a controlled demolition."

"I can't believe what my eyes are, like, seeing," Abria said as she watched the footage play another loop.

The third time around there was no mistaking it; the floors were being blown up one by one until the entire building turned into ash.

"There are witnesses on the ground," Pigg said, pointing to some people standing near the building. "How could they get an entire city to believe that it was an accident if there were people standing there to hear the explosion?"

Austin shook his head and looked at Fergie. "Why would Imperator want your parents dead? And why would he ruin the entire stock of Humanoids in the process?"

"The real question is: why did he want it to look like an accident?" Declan said.

"I know why," Elena said aggressively. "To keep people under control. Think about it. Imperator can't make murder look like anything except an accident or else people would be outraged."

"But why do this now?" Austin said. "Why was he after Fergie's parents after all this time of them working for him?"

"It is probable that Imperator found out that my parents were aiding us," Fergie said. "Or he could have discovered that my parents were including a fail safe module in each of the Humanoids that, when used by the correct program, would turn them all into warriors for the Renegade cause."

Elena shared a look of astonishment with Austin.

"Why didn't you tell us that before?" Austin said.

"For one simple reason, I did not know before the information before my parents' death," Fergie said plainly. "Apparently, their death activated a fail safe in my own mainframe. I have been acquiring new data in the days since their death. In essence, I am only now just learning the true nature of my being. Yet, I still do not have access to all the information."

"Do you know anything now about the Tablets of Destiny?" Elena asked.

"I confess I do not," Fergie said. "But that does not mean that I will not, at some point, gain access to it."

Austin paced up and down the room.

"Your parents' death has created somewhat of a delay in answering some of the questions I have about the artifacts." He told Fergie. "The greatest of which is knowing how all the codes on the artifacts fit together."

"I will attempt to finish the program on my own..."

"No, no, that's not what I meant," Austin said gently. "And I'm not trying to sound callous about their death. It's just that, for the first time, I've realized that we're all, essentially, orphans now. There aren't any adults with intimate knowledge of the Renegades' actions that can help us, unless we go to Pigg's parents, which he says is out of the question."

As Elena began to absorb the fact that they were now going to have to pursue all the artifacts without any type of help or guidance, Austin said, "I think we should go visit Melly in Crowfield Plantation. We need to ask her about the photograph from her closet and see if she knows anything about the Renegades or the Tablets of Destiny."

Abria dropped her head in her hands. "Why would you think that Melly would even, like, talk to us about that photo?"

"If she won't, then we need to see if her parents will talk to us."

"Melly was awful. Her parents must be at least as bad as her . . ." Elena started to say, but Austin was already interrupting.

"We need to know if they were Renegades. If they were, we'll tell them that we know that the Tablets of Destiny are at Tavington's farm. And we'll ask if they can help us with anything else."

"They could be really terrible people, Austin," Elena said. "How can we know if we can trust them with what we're doing?"

"So, we'll make up a version of the truth to protect ourselves," Austin said. He looked at Elena. "You're the best at making up stories. So, make one up. But we've got to try something, right?"

Elena looked around at the unconvinced faces of her friends. She felt grieved for Fergie, who'd just experienced the worst tragedy; for Declan and Abria having to put on a brave face even though their parents were wasting away in a hospital; for Pigg, as scared and timid as he was, having parents that didn't care enough to get involved with his life.

They'd all lost or, in Pigg's case, didn't have important people in their life. They only had each other now.

"I'll go with you, Austin," Elena said. "Of course I'll go with you. But you're right, we're gonna need a really good story."

▭ 10 ▭

Cognicross

"Today, there are no harnesses! There are no nets!" Marshall barked as a greeting in Basic Training. "You will be up on the towers for class. Your only objective is to get to the end of the Gauntlet. If you fall from the tower," Marshall smacked his hands together in a way that made half the Aves Company jump, "SPLAT! So, Pigg, don't embarrass the rest of us by falling."

Elena rolled her eyes. Then, she looked over at Pigg to give him a smile of encouragement, but his eyes were trained on the ground and he was trembling slightly.

Marshall stood in front of an Optivision screen that was filled with the faces of every single student in each Company. Elena watched it flicker with the faces of the different students in the Aves Company. Eventually, her image was joined by Garrett Vaughn and Adrien Segars from Raptor, Stacia Bassi and Herbie Clucas from Harrier, Ernest Darnell and Moriah Kirkley from Falcon, and Pigg.

"You will notice team groupings on the screen," Marshall said roughly. "When you are in the Gauntlet, these people will be your support system to stay together. Dismissed!"

Elena looked at the students on her team as they came together in a group. They all had black hair and brown eyes and had varying looks of disappointment or fear etched on their faces.

"Everyone should know each other by now," Garrett said instantly. "It's clear we're not excited about the group exercise, but let's try to make the best of it."

"That was a really inspiring pep talk," Elena said shortly.

"Vaughn's just trying to be honest so we're all clear where we stand," Adrien said defensively.

"It's always clear where the Raptors stand," Stacia Bassi said gruffly.

Elena hadn't paid much attention to many of the students in the other Units, but she decided that she liked Stacia Bassi from Harrier.

"Let's not start fighting," Ernest Darnell said. "It sounds like this Gauntlet is going to be challenging enough. Kirkley and I want to be supportive, but there's no denying that we each have an agenda, and that's to make the best possible scores."

"Yeah, so let's just get on with it," said Herbie from Harrier.

They all turned to start walking the mile trek to the Gauntlet, but Pigg grabbed Elena's arm and held her back.

"I don't trust them," he said earnestly.

"Of course you don't trust them, we barely know them." She tried to give Pigg another encouraging smile, but he still looked terrified. "Don't let Marshall get to you. And don't worry about those other dimwits. We'll take care of each other, right?"

"Like we always do," Pigg said, looking a little more confident.

"Yes, like we always do."

Elena swung an arm around Pigg's shoulders, and they headed off after the others toward the Gauntlet. Before long, they'd arrived at the edge of the grassy knoll, and Elena stared up at the tall towers with handgrip challenges. Her back gave an involuntary shudder.

"Are you ready?" Garrett called to her and Pigg.

"Sure," Elena said more confidentially than she felt.

Elena and Pigg walked together toward the first insufferably tall tower. She let Pigg climb first behind Moriah Kirkley. As Elena used her legs to push her weight up the tower, she felt thankful that her climbing had gotten better since their first Basic Training lesson. Recently, she and Pigg had spent a lot of time in climbing Simulabs so she could increase her stamina and Pigg could conquer his fears.

Still, when Elena finally reached the first landing, she fell to her knees feeling foolish for being in such poor shape.

"What's that noise?" Herbie blurted suddenly.

At first, Elena didn't hear anything. But then, a current of air swept through the tower, blowing her red curls wildly around her face. She stood cautiously, and that's when she realized that a wind simulation had begun.

The crushing sound of the blustery weather was so enormous that her head physically hurt. Elena's palms slid up to cover her ears. Afraid that the wind would knock her off the platform, she sank back down to the ground.

She noticed that Garrett was calling to the rest of them, but the gusts were so loud she couldn't hear him. Finally, he made a hand motion that indicated he was moving on, so Elena helped Pigg to his feet. Using him for support, Elena half directed him after Garrett across a bridge that was suspended by some type of cabling.

The airstream was so violent that the entire bridge shook and swayed. Elena was beginning to feel sick and dizzy. And because she was now clinging to the sides of the bridge so she wouldn't be blown away, her eardrums felt like they might explode.

Miraculously, the mouth of a cave appeared at the end of the bridge. She watched Garrett, Stacia, and the others hurry into the cavern. She tripped in after them, clutching to the rock walls for support. Fortunately, the cave provided complete protection from the wind, but her ears were still throbbing.

"What do we do now?" Moriah Kirkley asked.

"It's obvious, isn't it?" Garrett said impatiently. "We're going through the cave."

Garrett didn't even pause for everyone else to recover. Soon, he was out of sight. Elena clicked her tongue impatiently.

"He's a really bad leader," Pigg whispered. "So, how do you feel? Because my whole face is chapped and I feel like my ears are going to explode."

"Me, too," Elena said. "Come on, though." She eased away from the wall and linked her left arm through Pigg's right. "We should get going before Garrett finishes the Gauntlet without us."

Arm in arm, Elena and Pigg began to take short, steady strides through the cave. It was cold and damp, but at least it wasn't windy. Far too soon, Elena began to feel a twinge of pain in her lower back. The stress of climbing coupled with being unsteadied by the wind had clearly caused some kind of stress.

Garrett and Adrien from Raptor were already so far ahead that Elena couldn't see them. But the Harrier and Falcon students were pacing steadily. She felt that as long as she and Pigg could keep up with them, they'd get through the Gauntlet in a satisfactory amount of time for Marshall.

The cave was becoming steadily darker, and Elena began to wish that they'd been allowed to pack a hololight with their tactical vest before the course began. She started to bump into Pigg, or trip over rocks that were pushing up from the ground, or scrape her shoulder against the walls of the cave. Then, unexpectedly, she noticed a small light dancing around the wall as Moriah Kirkley and Herbie Clucas walked ahead.

"Look at this!" Elena said excitedly even though her head pounded, making her dizzy. She hurried over to the strange light and opened an Optivision that was rather small.

"Whoa!" Herbie said. "How did you know there was an Optivision screen there?"

"I didn't," Elena said. "I just saw the light as you passed by it."

She looked over the screen and noticed instantly that it featured a map of the entire Gauntlet course.

As she followed the map with her eyes, she vaguely realized that Moriah was calling down the tunnel to Garrett and Adrien to come back and join them. The Gauntlet, it turned out, was a complex maze of paths, challenges, and traps.

"Too bad I can't read a map to save my life," said Stacia.

"There are seven different routes to choose from," Elena told the others. "They each have a different challenge. Apparently, the wind is the first challenge. As we keep moving, there will be more."

"That one," Pigg said pointing at a path on the map before Elena had a chance to really inspect any of the choices fully. "That's the easiest one. Let's go that way."

Elena continued to examine their choices in silence. Pigg's suggestion was the easiest, but it was also the longest. If she had to guess, she would have said it might take them three times as long to take the route he wanted to go. The most direct route was steep with a variety of climbing and balancing exercises.

"We can't go that way" Garrett had returned to their group and was looking over the map with a confused expression. "It's too long. We'd never finish."

"Let's go this way," Elena suggested, pointing to shortest course on the map, even though she knew it would be harder for Pigg.

"Are you joking?" Pigg said. "I'll never make it that way! Do you see how hard it is? I was barely able to get up here."

"It's the best way," Moriah said aggressively.

"Come on," Elena pleaded with Pigg as Garrett and Moriah already started back through the cave toward the rest of the course. "Vaughn's right about your way being too long. I'll get you through it. I promise."

In truth, Elena wasn't sure if she was strong enough to get them both through it, but she wanted to get off the course as soon as possible.

"We don't have parachutes or harnesses," Pigg argued. "You heard what Marshall said...SPLAT!"

"You won't fall," Elena said, feeling desperately impatient as Adrien, Stacia, Herbie, and Ernest Darnell also began to clear out. "No one has fallen in weeks. You'll be fine."

Pigg finally agreed, but just barely. By the time Elena and Pigg reached the mouth of the tunnel, she could see that the others had started out into another maze of balancing platforms that were high off the ground. As it turned out, everyone had thought wrong about the wind simulation ending. In fact, it seemed to have gotten worse.

"Elena! Look at all those teeny tiny, skinny little balance beams. We have to walk across *those*? I can't do it," Pigg hollered over the rushing wind. "I want to go back to the cave."

"Pigg, we have to go this way," Elena said, feeling exasperated and exhausted. "We can't go back. That would just take too long now."

At the snap of a finger, the wind simulation suddenly stopped. Elena and Pigg were suspended in silence.

"That was too weird."

Then, slowly a wave of fog gathered beneath them. Before long, it was impossible to see anything in front or behind them, much less the ground below.

"Okay, feet steady on the beam, Pigg," Elena said. "Let's get going."

"This seems really dangerous," Pigg whined. "I mean, what are the chances that I'll make it through without falling?"

"I'm right here with you," Elena said in a reassuring tone. "The wind has stopped. I know we can't see anything, but at least we won't be blown off the beam to our death."

She pushed Pigg a little in the back to start him down the beam, but he immediately lost his balance. Elena reached forward to try and steady him, but he fell forward, causing the beam to sway dangerously. Then, he slipped off the side, hugging the beam desperately with both his arms.

"I'm gonna die!" Pigg screamed so loudly that Elena was sure everyone on the course could hear him.

"Everything's going to be okay," Elena said uncomfortably. She dropped to her stomach and slid down the beam toward him. "Stay focused, Pigg! I'm going to grab your arms and get you."

Elena tried her best to lift him, but she didn't have enough leverage on the slender beam to pull him up to her. And, since he was dangling his full weight, Pigg was unable to help with the rescue mission.

"I'm gonna die! I'm gonna die!" Pigg screamed out again.

"You're not gonna die!" Elena shouted at him.

A thick sweat broke out under her arms and across her forehead. She knew she couldn't lift him, but she wasn't about to let him go. So, she did the only thing she was able, she held him as tightly as she could.

"Could you try to crawl up my arms?" Elena asked.

Pigg made one attempt to grab her arm, but once his weight shifted they both hollered a loud cry: her because he'd about ripped her arm out and him out of fear. A slow minute eked by. Pigg still clutched the beam as well as he could while she continued to support his weight with her own arms.

As she was just starting to curse the other members of their team for leaving them, Elena saw a strange movement in the clouds. Austin suddenly appeared. She felt a surge of hope that gave her strength enough to hold Pigg a little tighter.

"You know," Austin started as he eased out onto the beam. "This is not really the point of the exercise."

"How did you find us?"

"I could hear Pigg screaming from all the way across the course. I got here as soon as I could. Where's the rest of your team?"

"They left us!" Elena managed to shout with a resentful edge in her tone.

Elena watched Austin lower his body down on the beam. He grabbed Pigg under his arms. Just as Elena and Austin began to pull up their friend, she felt her body slip awkwardly off the beam. She let go of her grip on Pigg so she wouldn't fall, but then something unbelievable occurred. Both Austin and Pigg fell from the bar and were swallowed whole by the fog below.

Elena blinked. She clung to the bar and pulled herself into a sitting position. She gazed into the fog, trying to make sense of what had just happened. One moment her friends had been there, the next they were gone. Elena tried to imagine how high she must be now. She guessed at least one hundred and twenty feet in the air. No one could survive that fall. No one. Then, she had the thought that maybe they simply fell to a lower beam.

"Austin! Pigg!"

When there was no reply, Elena began to panic. She didn't know exactly how long she screamed their names, but eventually she heard movement to her left. Kidd suddenly emerged from the fog on a beam adjacent to her.

"What happened?" he called.

"They fell!" Elena screamed, feeling out of her mind. "Austin and Pigg fell!"

After she said the words out loud, she realized for the first time that they really must be dead. Tears began to stream down her face, and moans of grief filled the Gauntlet.

"Freckles, get up!" Kidd ordered. "We've got to finish."

"Maybe I could climb down after them," Elena sobbed, completely ignoring him. "Or I could use the rope ladders to swing my way down."

"No!" Kidd said. "We've got to go on! We'll find Marshall and see what's going on."

"Marshall." Elena clawed her face with her stubbed fingernails. "Marshall! Why didn't Marshall give us harnesses? How could he be so careless? Especially with Pigg?"

"Freckles, look at me," Kidd said, but Elena refused to look anywhere but where her friends had fallen. "Stand up! I'll walk on my beam and you can walk on yours and we'll get outta here together."

"They're dead!" Elena cried. "And it's all my fault!" She buried her face on the beam and sobbed.

A moment later there was a sharp vibration on Elena's beam. She looked up and was startled to see that Kidd had joined her.

"What the..." Elena started.

"I jumped over here."

Elena looked at the beam from where he'd come from, and it was at least six feet away.

"Are you crazy! You could have been killed coming from there."

"I'm not leaving here without you, Freckles," Kidd said, pulling her to her feet.

Elena barely registered the fact that she was hurrying through the Gauntlet with Kidd directing her. Somehow he was able to get her across the maze of obstacles. She didn't even know how long they'd been going, but eventually they reached the final part of the task.

Kidd convinced her to belay down the wall at the end of the track in order to exit the course. When she reached the ground, Declan, Abria and Fergie were waiting for her, but Elena wanted to see only one person.

"Marshall!" Elena yelled, starting down the field after she noticed him standing with a group of students, including Fergie and Abria. "How could you do that?" she screamed in his face. "How could you let us up there without safety harnesses or nets."

"Excuse me?" Marshall said indignantly.

"I know that you know they fell!" Elena screeched. "Where are Austin and Pigg? Are they hurt?"

"They fell from one hundred and ten feet in the air," Marshall replied. "You do the math."

"*Are they hurt?*" Elena was shaking all over in anger and grief.

"Are you finding it hard to accept that you made a bad decision for your teammate? And that he fell to his death because of you?"

At the word "death," Elena took a faltered step away from Marshall.

"You were selfish and stubborn. You made an immature decision when you knew Pigg's limitations. It was your fault he fell."

Elena's face burned, and her insides seared. "I suppose you think Austin's fall was my fault, too!"

"No, Haddock made his own immaturely, selfish decision to try and save Pigg from falling."

Elena lunged at Marshall, but Declan caught her around the waist and held her back. So, instead she screamed, "Don't you dare talk about Austin!"

"Accept responsibility for your mistake, Ransom!" Marshall roared. "And move past it."

"No!" Elena said firmly. She stopped struggling against Declan and took a calm step toward Marshall. "It was *your* fault. We didn't have harnesses or nets. You should have made sure we were safe."

"Lena!"

Elena turned sharply at the sound of Austin's voice. She saw Austin and Pigg striding out of the fog. They were unhurt, without a bruise or scratch.

She blinked, not fully comprehending what was happening until Marshall said, "Ransom, haven't you learned by now that this program is designed to challenge the boundaries of your identity? I hope that next time you'll make a less self-centered decision. You might just save a life."

Elena turned from Marshall and ran to Austin. She wrapped her arms firmly aground his neck.

"I thought you were dead!"

"Nah, I'm immortal," Austin said with a laugh.

Elena released him. "I can't believe Marshall would allow me to think you died."

"The program is designed to disorient your thinking," Fergie said formally. "We must constantly be aware of the fact that they will deceive our minds."

Elena turned toward Pigg and said, "I'm glad you're okay. I'm sorry. I'm so sorry. It was my fault that you fell. I knew you couldn't do it, and I pushed you anyway. We should have taken the longer way even though everyone else..."

"Elena, it's fine." Pigg interrupted her. "We all make mistakes. Life's too short to hold grudges. But, right now, I'm so hungry. When can we eat?"

That night, Elena stood atop a grand hill. The gusts of wind caused her body to tremble with fear. Pigg stood on her left. Declan, Abria, Fergie, and Kidd stood behind her, but their faces were fuzzy and distorted. A little higher on the hill in front of them stood Austin with his face brighter than the sun. He was speaking, but she couldn't hear a word.

Elena's ears and body ached all over. Then, the earth gave a shudder that caused her teeth to chatter. She wanted to fall to her knees and cry out, but the ground began to open up and she watched helplessly as Austin vanished through the earth.

Frantically, she raced to the spot where he fell. Austin was lying in a hole on his back, looking up at her with a grieved expression. Before Elena could even think of what to do, a clump of earth fell on Austin's stomach. She looked around wildly as more earth fell on him. Her friends each carried a shovel and were filling dirt upon Austin's body.

"He's still alive!" She wanted to say, but when she opened her mouth no words came out. As her friends continued to layer on the dirt, she said, "Don't do that! Help me get Austin out!" But again, she couldn't even hear herself speaking.

She looked at Austin, hoping he would tell her what to do, but he said, "Help them, Lena. Help them cover me."

Without understanding, a shovel appeared in her hand. She raised it to the earth and dumped gravel on her friend until the hole with Austin's body was completely covered over.

Elena startled awake, feeling sweaty and anxious about the dream. She tried to tell herself that it hadn't been real. But something about it reminded her of the dream that she'd had about her dad before Fergie's parents died. Again, the dream had felt like a *memory*.

She lay in bed for the rest of the morning, feeling sick to her stomach and too afraid to go back to sleep. At breakfast, she pushed her food around and dodged questions about her sullen attitude. That day, her classes felt like a complete blur as she tried to sort out her feelings about the dream. Why had the dream felt like it had already happened? Why did it feel like a memory she was reliving?

"What's the matter?" Austin finally asked her as they walked alone out to the hydroponics farm for class with Emerald.

"Nothing," Elena mumbled.

"Come on," Austin urged. "You're not still upset about me and Pigg falling yesterday, are you?"

"Sort of, but not entirely," Elena admitted. Then, she told him about the haunting dream. However, she was underwhelmed with his reaction.

"It was just a dream," he said dismissively. "You were just upset because you thought Pigg and I died yesterday. Your brain manufactured a scenario of trauma."

"No, it was more than that," said Elena moodily.

"What do you mean?"

"I can't talk about it here," Elena said, eyeing the other students walking to class.

"Let's go to the Station before dinner," Austin suggested. "Then, you can tell me all about it."

Elena agreed.

Instructor Emerald's class was a haze of information, and soon enough she and Austin were sitting alone at the Firebird Station.

"So, I had this dream a few weeks ago about my dad," Elena began. "We were in my house. He took me to his library to show me something in his diary. When I woke up, it felt like the whole thing had been a memory. So, I came down here to see if what he'd showed me in the dream was real."

"Why didn't you tell me that before?"

"Because that was the day we found out Fergie's parents were killed," Elena said sadly.

"Have you had any other dreams like this before?"

"Just one last year when we were out in the wilderness. I dreamed that I was at the ocean with my parents. I was swimming and saw a huge building under the water. Then, an octopus swam up and grabbed me. When I woke, Wheeler was trying to wake me up."

"And, that dream felt like a memory?"

"Well, I didn't realize it at the time because I was so distracted by the fact that Wheeler was there and I hate him," Elena confessed. "But looking back on it now, it definitely wasn't a normal dream."

Austin sat in silence for a moment looking deep in though. "The only thing I can think to do is scan your head with my Suturand to see if there's anything unusual."

"I'll try anything at this point," Elena said.

She laid her head back in the chair as Austin got into position. He moved the Suturand to her head. Out of the corner of her eye, Elena saw an Optivision screen appear. For several breathless moments, she thought about nothing but her head exploding.

"Extraordinary!" Austin breathed.

"What? Is my brain superhuman, or something?" Elena laughed nervously.

Austin smiled slightly. "Not superhuman. Remember when we went to see Declan and Abria's parents at the hospital?"

"Of course I remember. I'll never forget how angry Abria was after she found out that the Foremans knew that her parents were intentionally being kept there. It was almost...unnerving. And then she and Bowen learned they're twins. I mean, talk about keeping secrets and..."

"Remember how I said that the machines their parents are attached to are keeping them in a state of neural interactive simulation?"

Elena nodded.

"They're locked in their minds," Austin said. "You have a similar situation going on in your brain, except instead of a machine simulating an environment, you have a device that triggers these *dreams* for you."

Elena felt more confused than ever.

"Most likely the device is programmed with stories that were created specifically for you to know. The program that controls Declan and Abria's parents is called *Cognicross* because it combines a cross between human cognition and a simulation. Maybe you have a hybrid of it in your head."

Elena felt her face grown uncomfortably warm.

"Remember how Fergie mentioned that the fail safe in her mainframe activated after her parents' death? So, maybe this is your failsafe," Austin suggested.

"Take it out! Right now!" Elena ordered.

"I can't take it out!" Austin said incredulously. "I'm not a brain surgeon. I would kill you in an instant."

"But who would..." Elena's voice failed her.

There was only one person she knew that could have put such a device in her brain or, at the very least, had a brain surgeon implant it for her.

"Why would my mom put a Cognicross in my head?" she asked slowly.

Austin didn't speak at first, and Elena could tell that he was trying to understand it himself.

"Maybe your parents wanted you to know something about the Ransom Dossier or the Renegades or whatever it is that they were doing. Maybe they figured the only way to keep the information safe was to put it where no one else would think to look for it."

"But, then why did my dad write me that letter in his diary telling me to put the dossier away and never speak of it to anyone?"

Austin shrugged, looking grim.

"And why would they write a program of you being buried alive? It's hard to believe that anyone would do something so cruel. And even harder to believe that my parents would agree to have that scenario put in my head."

Austin put an arm around her shoulder.

"It's still possible that your dream last night was simply a dream. Just because there's a device in your head doesn't mean it's working *all* the time. How about you start keeping a journal of your dreams?" he suggested. "You can make a record so you don't have to worry about them any more. Then, you'd also have the details all in one place in case something starts making sense."

Elena nodded. "That sounds like a good idea."

An internal battle was beginning to rage inside Elena. She was confident that her parents had created the device specifically for her mind, which meant that all the programs on it were a warning or a clue or a piece of information that they wanted her to have.

If she didn't have any control over when she got the information, how would she be able to tell the difference between her actual thoughts and what she was programmed to see? On the flip side, if she were only dreaming about her worst fears, would she be able to figure out a way to control those thoughts as well.

◫ 11 ◫

Crowfield Plantation

On the sixth day of the third week of the third month, Elena, Austin, and their friends gathered on the Grimsby Channel to take the hour-long journey to Crowfield Plantation.

The day before, the Aves Company finished the weeklong first quarter exam process. The hours upon hours of standing at her pupil station to answer questions that covered dozens of societies, languages, and religious practices from two hundred years of history had made Elena feel anxious and exhausted.

And now, as the train sped along, she felt a whole new type of panic building in her chest. She didn't want to see Melly or meet her parents, but she couldn't deny that it was probably the only way they'd learn what they needed to know about the Tablets of Destiny.

"Would you just look at the state of my nails?" Abria said. "They got all chipped when we were doing that last Gauntlet. Ugh! What I wouldn't give for a manicure. They actually have some great health resorts in Crowfield Plantation. Maybe we can find some time so I can get my nails done?"

"Sure, Abria," Austin said indulgently. "We'll make time after we see Melly."

"I'm thinking about getting my hair cut, too." Abria pulled a large chunk of hair through her fingers and looked at it cross-eyed. "What do you guys think?"

"I never think about your hair," said Elena glumly, staring out the window at the simulated range of fields and wishing she could sit somewhere else.

"I do," Pigg said absentmindedly while playing his PocketUnit. But then he blushed and looked up, seeming to realize what he'd said out loud. And, for some crazy reason, he kept talking. "It smells nice. And it bounces when you walk."

Abria's smile stretched across her entire face. "I'm glad that one of my friends can appreciate the effort I take in making sure that I always look presentable."

Before long, the view out the window changed from rows of cotton fields to dozens of houses with whitewashed columns that reminded Elena a lot of Washington D.C. However, instead of overgrown weeds, the city was in bloom with purple and fuchsia colored flowers.

"Ew...the air is sticky," Elena complained as they stepped from the train onto an open-air platform that was lined with rocking chairs.

"Yep, it always feels like the inside of Emerald's hydroponic farm," said Abria. "At least, it did every time we visited in the past."

Elena felt the humidity increase as she followed Abria and Declan through cobblestone streets that were lined with three story dwellings. The salt in the air settled onto her face and skin. The city was alive with insect noises but also with pedestrians strolling casually, giving Elena shifty glances that made her feel very out of place.

On Market Street, Elena saw women weaving baskets of straw and saw dough being fried in iron skillets. Non-intrusive sales people staffed tables of boiled peanuts, shepherd's purse, jams and marmalades, and spices. Baskets of pink lady apples, collard greens, bamboo shoots, rutabagas, okra, and jars of antifungal remedies lined the boulevard.

As they continued, they passed large oak trees with hanging moss, posh homes with people rocking on covered porches, a fountain shaped as an overgrown pineapple, and a harbor with seven-man porch swings.

"At least we know why Melly is so weird," Elena said. "I'm getting the strangest looks from people. And that guy back there told his companion that he didn't know the devil was female."

"Melly wasn't *that* bad," Abria said kindly, completely ignoring Elena's comment about someone thinking she was the devil.

"Are we talking about the same person?" Elena said. "Melly...the girl who tricked Pigg into thinking that she liked him, spread rumors about me crying about my dead parents, and then there was that really awesome time when she lied to Instructor Booker about Fergie and I not letting her help with the class group work."

"Well, of course when you say it that way it sounds bad." Abria lifted her shoulders into a shrug.

At the first window dimensional they could find, Austin scanned his Trademark and spoke the Linus family name into the clear glass. However, instead of Melly's face appearing alongside her parents, a red screen appeared with the message: Information Not Found.

After that, the friends agreed to split up and each take a different store to ask the shopkeepers if they knew how to find the Linus family. Elena put on her best smile at the first three shops she entered, but no matter how kindly she asked for the address or contact information for Melly, everyone seemed closed off and snobbish. At the last store she came to, Elena was finished being respectful.

"Hey," Elena said shortly to the man behind the counter. "I'm looking for someone and no one can give me answers, not even the window dimensional. It's like this whole town is prehistoric." She rolled her eyes for good measure. "Is there anyone in this place that can answer my questions with intelligence?"

The man smoothed his blonde hair back on his head, and said, "If you need to find someone, just go on over to the capitol building, and give them the name. They know where everyone is."

Elena hurried to gather all her friends together from the surrounding stores. Soon they arrived at the capitol, yet another white columned building that reminded Elena of the White House in Washington D.C.

Elena and Austin walked shoulder to shoulder up a steep flight of stone stairs. He walked resolutely through the front doors and straight to the first reception desk in the lobby.

A very pretty young woman with blonde hair and blue eyes said, "Good morning, what may I do for you?"

"Hey there," Austin said, leaning up against the desk in a casual way. "We were wondering if you could help us find a friend?"

"Of course, Sir," the woman replied.

"We were looking for our friend from Grimsby, Pamela Linus. Her parents work here in a local government office."

A look of confusion appeared on her sweet face. "I must apologize, but I do not recognize that name." She pulled up an Optivision screen and searched the mainframe. Then she said, "I do not have a record of anyone named Linus ever working in the local government or even living in the city limits. Are you sure you have the correct city, Sugar?"

Austin slapped his palm to his forehead. "You know what? I think Melly told us that she lives in the Galilee Province. Sorry to have wasted your time."

"Not a problem, Sugar. Have a nice day."

Elena exited the capitol building with her friends feeling thoroughly confused.

"What was that all about?" she asked Austin.

"Either the Linus's do live here and they don't want anyone to know where they live," Austin said. "Or they don't, which begs the question, *where do they live?*"

"Or they do not even exist," Fergie said in a tone of practicality.

"Either way, we shouldn't attract any more attention," said Austin.

"So, what do we do now?" Declan asked.

"I'm starving," Pigg whined. "Can we puh-lease stop to eat somewhere?"

"Oh, I know the perfect place," Abria said, her voice tinkling like crystal. "It's just over here on the harbor. The entire restaurant is actually *under* the water, isn't that amazing?"

Without waiting for a reply, Abria added, "Uncle Charles...I mean...my dad's favorite breakfast was cheese grits with poached eggs. For lunch, always the shrimp po'boy with bean-jicama salad. And for dinner, low country shrimp boil with the most amazing spicy sausage and cob corn, plus hush puppies, fried green tomatoes, carrots in a syrup bath, and for dessert, peach cobbler. He wasn't a big man, but he ate like a horse."

Elena was completely confused by the sudden change in topic. One second they were talking about the fact that Melly didn't seem to exist in Crowfield Plantation, and now they were discussing lunch options. She was too dumbfounded to even speak, so she followed along behind her friends feeling sulky and despondent.

"I sense that you are feeling apprehensive," Fergie said in Elena's ear as they pursued Abria through the city. "I am available if you need to talk."

"It's just," Elena said in a low voice. "Pigg and Abria don't seem to care about the fact that we couldn't find Melly. Isn't it weird?"

"Absolutely. Her absence here means that we were lied to, either about where she lives or about her true purpose for being at Grimsby."

Elena hadn't even considered that. She'd been so focused on the fact that Melly wasn't where she said she'd be that she completely missed the simple reality that Melly being at school could have been an anomaly. Pamela Linus had only arrived after Kate Bagley (and her family) were murdered.

"I understand your reaction to the news," Fergie continued, breaking Elena's thoughts. "But if you believe that Pigg and Abria should share your feelings, then your expectations are tragically misguided."

Elena decided not to bite her tongue as they walked out on a long wooden pier where fishermen cleaned fish of all shapes and colors.

"Can we please stop for a second to talk about what's really important here?" Elena said impatiently as her friends turned to face her. "We came here to find Melly, which we haven't managed to do."

She sighed deeply, feeling despair creep up on her.

"My parents are gone. Austin's parents are gone. Fergie's parents are gone. We can't find Melly or her parents. We can't talk to Bowen and Abria's parents.

Wheeler won't work with us. And Pigg...well, his parents just won't or maybe shouldn't be involved. Everything feels like it's falling apart."

"Maybe we could mention this to Hopper?" Declan suggested. "See if he knows where Melly went."

"That's not a bad idea, as long as we keep it vague," Austin said. "Our second quarter starts in a few days. Maybe a couple of us can ask him after a class when he's distracted."

"Good idea," Declan said. "Though Ransom probably shouldn't be one to talk to Hopper. She's not great at being vague."

Elena only rolled her eyes as a response.

■ ■ ■

Second quarter classes began on the first day of the first week of the fourth month. The Instructors launched into their lessons with a high level of enthusiasm, but Elena was still feeling rather curious about the mystery surrounding the Linus family. She could barely stand to wait to ask Hopper after their class with him the following day, but they'd agreed that it would be best to approach him in a casual way.

So, Elena sat through Booker's lecture about Marco Polo's journeys with the Mongols during the Golden Age of China with a fake smile on her face; she barely listened to Instructor Niva explain the importance of John Wycliffe and the first English translation of the Hebrew Bible; she had a hard time staying focused as Copernicus took the class through the ancient kingdoms in Africa and their contributions to mathematics and science; and she was so distracted during Instructor Emerald's explanation of agriculture during the Ming Dynasty in China that she was forced to replant her entire tea plantation simulation after class ended.

The following morning, Elena stood at her pupil station. She was having a hard time focusing while Hopper lectured about the Hundred Years War between England and France. The Optivision screens that encased her were alive with troop movements and fields of battle, but she could only think about what Hopper might say when they mentioned the fact that Pamela Linus didn't actually exist.

At long last, Hopper's class ended. As all the Aves Company began to file out of the room, Elena followed closely behind Austin as they approached their resident advisor.

"Great lesson, Hopper!"

"Thanks, Dude." Hopper smiled.

"Um...I wanted to ask you something," said Austin.

"I hope it's not about your exam grade because I'm not really supposed to tell you," he said with a wink.

"No, it's not about that," Austin said. "I went to go see Melly in Crowfield Plantation over first quarter break."

"Oh? I didn't know you were close. How is she?"

"She wasn't there," Austin said.

"That's a shame, I guess," Hopper said absentmindedly as he began to get distracted with closing out different Optivision screens. "Did you at least shake hands with her parents?"

"They don't exist. Any of them," said Elena.

"Huh?"

"I tried to look them up, but no one in town had ever heard of them," Austin said. "There actually wasn't a record of anyone by the name of Linus having ever lived in the city," said Austin. "What do you think that means?"

Hopper scratched the scraggly hair on his chin thoughtfully and said, "It means the Headmaster falsified her transcript and arranged for her to be here and leave secretly."

Elena hadn't even had time to fully absorb what Hopper said before Austin asked, "Do you think it has something to do with the Renegades?"

"It must, but I don't know how," Hopper whispered. "Look, I don't know what you two are up to, but you should stop. Everyone has secrets. And you can bet that if the Headmaster wants to keep Melly Linus a secret, then he's going to. It won't do you any good to go poking your nose around in things like this."

"You're probably right," Austin said indifferently, though Elena noticed Hopper give him a shifty grin.

After lunch, Elena and the entire Aves Company entered a white-walled classroom that she knew would eventually transform into a Grimsby field training course after Marshall was finished assigning them their tasks.

"Today is a relay race, of sorts, where you will be in direct competition with the other Units," barked Marshall after calling the Aves Company to attention. "You will be assigned to one of four towers: North, South, East, or West."

An Optivision screen appeared with a map of the entire course that they were required to finish.

"At the start, the first person in the relay will move along the balance beam and collect a flag for your Unit from the first tower platform.

"Then, the lead person will move along to the next platform to free the next person from your Unit. If they don't release in time, you will suffer a three-minute penalty. You will move along through the course together collecting members of your Unit and one flag for each member. Firebirds, you will have twelve flags to recover even though you have a team of eleven, so you'll have to work extra hard!

"The support object that will be used is a jouster." Marshall held up a four-foot long staff with a cylinder pad at each end and said, "You can use the jouster for balance or to knock an opponent off the tower. If you fall from the beams, you will be transported to a holding cell where you will remain until a member of your Unit releases you.

"The objective of today's lesson is to get every member from your Unit to the Red Keep."

An image of a tower in the middle of the course appeared on the screen.

"The team that unites the twelve flags in the Keep first wins. Now, essentially, there are no rules to this game, which means that your flags can be stolen from the Keep. My only advice is to hide your flag from the other Units so they're not taken. You have three minutes to choose your positions before the session begins."

The Firebird Unit was moved off to one side. Declan, who'd been chosen as Lieutenant, assigned each student to an area of the course at the start. Elena was given the first position at the North Tower. She walked to a hologram on the floor that was marked with her destination. Soon, the lights faded to black. When they turned back on, her insides squirmed.

The room had been transformed into a forest of towers, with the tallest ones over one hundred feet high. Elena was standing atop one tower with Oscar Hunter on a platform to her left. Stacia Bassi from Harrier and Ernest Darnell from Falcon stood on the two platforms to her right. The four of their beams branched out and converged into a single, larger platform where Elena could just see the Firebird orange red flag dangling from a dais.

An Optivision appeared out of thin air with instructions:

Pick up the jouster.
Wait until the horn sounds to move into the course.

Elena found a jouster attached to one of the posts. She balanced it in her hands, learning it's weight, and then she threw a couple practice swings. The Optivision screen counted down from ten. After a horn blasted, Elena progressed forward down the beam, using the jouster for balance. She moved swiftly, crossing her feet one over the other in a steady, consistent motion. From the corner of her eye, she could see Oscar Hunter advancing down his beam so she sped along and reached the platform first.

As Elena reached up to scan her Trademark into the niche to release the Firebird flag from the podium, she felt a sharp blow to her side. She stumbled toward the edge of the platform and nearly fell off, but she recovered her balance. She whirled around and noticed that Oscar was stuffing the Raptor flag down the front of his shirt.

"Got to move faster than that if you're going to beat me, Ransom!" Oscar sneered at her.

Heat rose to Elena's face. As Oscar turned to run down the next beam, Elena swung her jouster around her head and knocked him in the side. He lost his balance completely and fell off the side of the tower.

"Was that fast enough for you, Hunter?" Elena hollered after him.

Then, she turned to see that Stacia and Ernest were getting closer to the platform. She hurried to release her flag, but then had a thought. She scanned her Trademark into the Falcon niche and, to her surprise, she was able to grab their flag. She grabbed the Harrier flag as well, and then pitched them both over the edge of the platform.

Elena looked toward the next podium where Abria stood, very far away. She rushed across a lane of floating discs to free her friend.

"What are you, like, doing?" Abria asked before Elena had even landed. "Why did you knock Hunter off? And why did you take the other Unit flags?"

"Marshall said that there weren't any rules. If they don't have a flag to collect, they won't be able to win this challenge," Elena replied.

"That was totally, like, brutal," Abria said. "Are you supposed to do that?"

"Who cares?" Elena said impatiently. "Come on, let's go."

Elena moved toward a series of rope nets similar to what they'd trained during their Level 2 studies with Abria following closely behind her.

"But, where did Hunter go?" asked Abria.

"I'm assuming he got transferred to the holding cell just like Marshall said he would," Elena said. "Hunter won't be able to get out of there until someone from his Unit frees him, which might be a while because I'm planning to knock all the other students off their pods, too."

Elena saw the next tower in front of them where several students were waiting, including Frankie Smiley and Adrien Segars. She was sure that Adrien hadn't seen her knock Oscar off the first platform, so she had a good chance of catching Adrien from Raptor off guard.

As Elena neared the platform, she swung her jouster around hard and knocked Adrien in the legs. An ear splitting scream of fear as she fell from the platform soon replaced her cry of pain.

Out of the corner of her eye, Elena saw the blunt part of a jouster coming for her head. She ducked out of the way and rolled across the platform. She turned just in time to see Abria bump Moriah Kirkley from Falcon and Herbie Clucas from Harrier off the platform. Elena reached over, grabbed all the other Unit flags, and pitched them over the side.

"Okay, now that that's done, would you mind telling me what you two are doing?" Frankie asked. "Why did you knock everyone off the platform? And why did you throw all those flags over the side?"

"We're winning this challenge," Elena said aggressively. "No one else will be able to beat us if all their flags are gone."

"You need to calm down," Frankie said in a steady tone.

"This *is* me being calm," Elena almost shouted. "Come on!"

Without even waiting to see if Frankie collected his flag, Elena hurried through the next set of balancing obstacles. Then, she crossed a staircase of logs that each rotated freely on a lateral axis. After that, she came to a series of platforms that were tilted at a forty-five degree angle above nothing but sky.

"I guess if we fall from here we're going to the holding cell," Elena said to Abria and Frankie. "So, just try to be careful."

In a few seconds they'd jumped across the platforms successfully. But now, they reached a landing dais that divided into a dozen different directions.

"Where do we go, like, now?"

"I don't know," Elena replied. "How about we head for the Keep to see if anyone else has made it?"

Climbing up to the Red Keep was easily the hardest part of the simulation because the stairs were steep, narrow, and in constant motion. When Elena finally managed to catapult her body up the last few steps, she landed with a thud on the floor.

"Lena!" Austin said, pulling her to her feet.

"Abria and Smiley are behind me," Elena said, after taking a loud breath as if she'd just run a marathon.

"We'll help them," said Austin, and that's when she noticed that Declan and Fergie were also there.

"What's going on down there?" Austin asked after Abria and Frankie had been pulled safely into the Keep. "It seems like complete mayhem."

"Ransom has been stealing the other Unit flags and pitching them over the side," Frankie said as he joined them. "Not to mention the fact that we've been knocking everyone off the platforms to send them to the holding cell."

Everyone looked at Elena in stunned silence.

"What?" Elena said, shrugging her shoulders. "Marshall said there weren't any rules."

Declan's face spilt into a wide grin. He held up a hand and said, "Up top on that one."

Elena smacked his outstretched palm with her own and looked at Austin. "What's the deal with the holding cell?"

Austin shook his head. "We haven't tried to go there yet. Look, the holding cell is there." He pointed off the edge of the Keep wall where Elena could look down onto the maze below. "And over there, Nelson and Wheeler were making their way across the swinging rings to the base of the Keep."

"So, Gamble, Castellow, and Pigg are in the cell," Elena said. "I think most of us should stay here, but if a couple of us go, we could each take a different route to the holding area and free our friends. I'll go."

"I'll come with you," Austin said. "But let's split the flags between us so one person isn't carrying them all."

"And I'll go, too," Declan offered as Elena began to distribute the flags she'd collected to the Firebirds.

Elena, Austin, and Declan left Abria, Frankie, and Fergie and climbed down from the Keep and back out onto the main maze structure.

"I'll go this way," Austin said, pointing to the path on the left. "And Lena, try to stay outta trouble."

Elena winked at him mischievously. Then, she took off running through the next set of obstacles. After crossing a series of spinning cones, she jumped and grabbed onto a vertical wall that was spinning around a central vertical axis. She held tight until she reached the platform on the other side.

Elena continued at a steady pace until just as she was coming through a maze of electrified cords, she heard a low rumbling sound like it was coming from the mouth of an enraged animal.

"RANSOM!"

Elena spun around wildly. Oscar Hunter advancing on her from one of the beams to her right. She took off quickly, but not in the direction she needed to go. She was simply trying lose herself in the maze.

Eventually, she realized that if she continued going she'd end up back where she started. So, she climbed up on the railing and jumped feet first down to the next tower over. Then, she shimmed down a flagstaff onto yet another beam and began to advance back into the maze.

The path to the holding cell was extremely complicated to navigate. In fact, it took her walking back and forth at one section of the course about seven times before she realized that there was a hidden Optivision screen that she needed to access. The screen displayed a brain teaser program that had to be solved before a secret door opened. Then, yet another riddle had to be answered, and one more after that.

Elena finally arrived at the door to the cell feeling tired and frustrated.

"Elena!" Pigg yelled through the gaps in the bars when he saw her. "So glad to see you. The door is encrypted from the outside, so we can't break out on our own. Gamble, Castellow, and I each gave it an unsuccessful try."

Pigg relayed the encryption to Elena through the bars. Within moments the door melted away, and she was reunited with her Unit.

"Okay, this way to the Keep," said Elena to the others.

The Firebird captives followed Elena through the maze until, at long last, they arrived back in the Red Keep. To her extreme relief, all the others in her Unit were already there.

Each of them united their flags on the dais and scanned their Trademarks. Then, the simulation morphed. Elena found herself standing in the white-walled classroom. Declan immediately let out a yelp of joy. But, just as Elena began to celebrate, she heard her name called out yet again.

General Hannibal was standing in the doorway in his pristine military uniform. His salt and pepper hair and strongly pronounced chin were the same as ever, but his normally kindhearted eyes seemed distant.

"Elena Ransom, please come with me."

Hannibal said nothing as they took the Grimvator to his office. She wanted to ask him what they were doing, but he looked so serious that she was afraid to speak. She followed him into his immaculate office.

"Please, sit down," Hannibal instructed her.

"If you wanted to congratulate the Firebirds on our win, you could have just said something down there," Elena began, rather boldly, as she sat in the chair across from his desk.

"You took flags from the opposing teams so they were unable to complete the class work today," said Hannibal.

"Yeah..." Elena replied slowly. "Well, Marshall said there weren't any rules."

"But there is common decency," Hannibal said steadily. When Elena didn't reply, he continued, "You hit Hunter in the back."

"He hit me first!" Elena said defensively. "And then later he looked like he wanted to kill me on the course. Did you happen to see that?"

Hannibal didn't reply. He simply gazed at her with disapproving eyes.

"So, what? Are we disqualified or something?" Elena said. "Did we fail? You know, we were the only Unit to get all of our flags to the Red Keep."

"Ransom, this year is not about one Unit," Hannibal said. "I am trying to prepare you to work together as a Company."

"Then, why did you put us against each other?" Elena asked. "Why did you tell us that we were in competition to see which Unit would win? And why would Marshall say that there weren't rules?"

"To observe your behavior. To critique your competency. To judge your character when there were no rules applied."

Elena looked down at her nails, suddenly feeling slightly ashamed. The entire exercise had been a test to see how well she could lead, direct, follow, and compete with integrity. If she had to guess, she'd say she impressively failed.

Hannibal stood from his desk and summoned her with his index finger to stand. He walked toward the wall of window glass in his office. She peered through the window, which morphed into a myriad of Optivisions, each one displaying a different student from the maze.

Without speaking, Hannibal enlarged her portion of the training. Then, he enlarged Austin's recording. She could tell right away that she'd been reckless, impatient, impulsive, and dismissive. But Austin had been steady, confident, and encouraging to those students with obvious weaknesses.

"If you're trying to get me to be more like Austin, you're wasting your time," Elena said dolefully, turning away from the screen. "I can never be like Austin. I don't have the temperament for being kind to everyone."

Hannibal smiled sadly and said, "I didn't show you Austin's playback because I expect you to be like him. I wanted you to see how a true leader uses the talents they've been given to help the others on the team rise and use their own unique gifts. Do you know what I see when I look at these two performances?"

Elena shrugged and looked at him.

"I see two very competent, exceptional minds for tactical advancement," Hannibal said. "But I also see a boy who encourages the entire Unit to use their individual skills to accomplish the same goal, and I see a girl who is only out for what she can do, what she can prove, and what she's trying to achieve."

Hannibal paused, and Elena sensed that he was trying to choose his next words carefully.

"You can never be like Haddock because you're different people. But, you can learn from his example. Next time you go out there, take a moment to think about how best you can serve the Aves Company with *your* unique skills. Then, take an extra moment to think about how you can encourage the others to use their skills. If you learn to do that well, Special Ops will gain another qualified leader."

After Elena left Hannibal, she was determined to be more in control of her attitude during their next training simulation, but the following four classes with Marshall kept the Aves Company busy with jump training.

During their first lesson, Marshall gave each student a tactical vest with a pressurized parachute in the back, similar to the ones that Elena and her friends used to parachute out of the Bowen's apartment building in New York City.

For hours, the Aves Company stood in long lines on an elevated platform just ten feet in the air as Marshall taught them balance, jumping from a fixed position, and landing with both feet firmly on the ground while bending their knees.

Throughout these lessons, Elena noticed a definite shift in the attitudes of many of the students from the other Units. She had never been popular by any means, at least not compared with Austin, Declan, or Abria, which meant that she went largely unnoticed by her classmates during the schooldays. But now, she distinctly heard her name being grumbled sometimes when she walked by students chattering as they waited for jump training.

"I know that everyone is being mean to me because of what I did during that last training exercise," Elena told Pigg as they climbed into yet another flight simulation. He'd been making her come with him to do as many aeronautic Simulabs as she could tolerate. "I just don't know how to make it better."

"Now that Marshall has us in jump training, do ya think that he'll teach us how to operate an aerocraft now?" Pigg asked.

"I don't know, and I don't care," Elena said as she put her feet up on the dashboard. "But would you please watch where you're going? We're about to drive off the bridge again."

By the third week of the sixth month, Marshall still hadn't mentioned aeronautic training. Instead, he had the Aves Company jumping from two hundred feet above the ground in aerocrafts that were flying around and around in a continuous circle above the school.

When it was Elena's turn, she stood in the doorway of the craft and looked down. The ground looked very far away. She had a fleeting thought of smacking into it at full force. Then, as she jumped, the wind caught her breath. She experienced a comfortable sensation of floating until the opening shock of the parachute deploying.

Just before Elena touched the ground she braced her entire body. Then, her feet made contact, and her knees bent together perfectly.

"Oh, that's what it's supposed to feel like when you land, like, correctly," said Abria as she stopped beside Elena. "Much better than the first time I parachuted."

Elena smiled as she remembered the first time they'd parachuted. Kidd had pulled her out the resident tower window when they were in New York City trying to escape being captured by Fallon's men.

Now, she watched Kidd land on the ground easily beside Declan, and her smile faded. After all they'd been through, Kidd Wheeler still wouldn't talk to them.

Elena and Abria had just gotten back into line to wait for their next turn to jump when she saw a strange movement in the crowd. Oscar Hunter appeared, and making sure to catch Elena's eye, he kicked Pigg full on in the back. Pigg didn't even have time to brace his fall. His face went straight into the dirt.

"Payback for stealing our flags, Ransom," Oscar said maliciously.

Elena's temper rose in an instant. She leapt toward Oscar and wrapped her arms around his throat. She felt hands close on her shoulders in that same moment. Then, she was thrown to the side by one of the Raptor boys.

Elena noticed a flash of blonde hair just before Declan put his fist into the boy's face. Abria pulled Elena to her feet. Then, they both jumped Oscar together. Even with her friend's help, Elena felt a blow to her face and back that caused white spots to pop in her vision.

Suddenly, a commanding voice ordered, "Aves Company! Stand at attention!"

Elena was sure that Marshall had found them. She turned slowly, expecting to be punished for fighting. Instead, her mouth fell open in surprise. Austin was standing on the dais where Marshall usually made the announcements. He was looking down on them with disappointment on his face.

"Aves Company! Stand before me at attention!" Austin ordered again because everyone was still watching him with mouths hanging open.

However, on this second command everyone formed rows, many of them wiping blood from their noses and mouths and holding together torn uniforms. Elena realized one of her jump boots was missing as she limped to her own spot. Finally, the Firebirds were in formation with the Raptors, Harriers, and Falcons flanked around them. They were a pitiful group of tattered children.

"Perhaps Marshall didn't make this clear, so I'll remind you now," Austin said in a steady voice. "Not all of us will move to Special Ops, which means that we all have to work hard on our individual scores *and* our Company performance. If we don't stop fighting, they may just decide that Aves is too immature for Special Ops." He looked pointedly at Oscar. "Hunter, do you want to be in Special Ops?"

"Yes," Oscar grumbled.

Then, Austin looked at Elena. The anger was gone from his eyes. He looked at her with nothing but compassion, which actually made her feel worse somehow.

"Ransom, do you want to be in Special Ops?"

Elena licked her fat, bloody lip. She wasn't sure she wanted to be in Special Ops, but looking at Austin standing there she was sure he'd get selected. She knew she wanted to be with him wherever that was.

"Of course."

"Alright then," Austin said. "Let's pull ourselves together and make this a winning Company."

Elena climbed into bed that night feeling thoroughly exhausted after the fight. Her eyes closed in sleep almost immediately, but then it seemed only moments later that she heard a strange rumble and felt a vibrating sensation on her bed.

"Abria!" Elena said sharply, not bothering to open her eyes. "Whatever you're doing STOP IT or I'm going to pummel you!"

But the noise and the shaking continued. Elena sat up quickly, planning to hit Abria. But, instead, she smashed her head into something hard.

▭ 12 ▭

The Islands

Elena massaged her forehead angrily. She opened her eyes wide. Then, she shut them again tightly and rubbed her lids furiously with her palms.

"This is just a dream," she said aloud. "Wake up, wake up!"

Elena opened her eyes once more, but she was still in the same place. She was strapped to a chair, sitting beside Stacia Bassi from Harrier. Across the aisle from her sat Garrett Vaughn from Falcon and Ernest Darnell from Raptor. They all appeared to be sleeping. Elena looked around. She was sitting inside some kind of aerocraft.

She'd hit her head on the pilot's chair in front of her. And, now she noticed that there was also a co-pilot's chair, control panel, and a control yoke at the front of the craft. She could see nothing but dense white through the small window on the right side of Stacia.

"Fantastic, I'm on some kind of aerocraft with no idea how I got here or what I need to do," Elena said bitterly.

Then, as if the aerocraft heard her, an Optivision screen appeared out of thin air. Slowly, words began to fill the screen, but they weren't just any words, they were instructions:

> Take whatever supplies you can carry.
> Jump from the plane.
> Parachute to one of the islands.

"Take whatever supplies?" Elena said slowly.

She unclipped her harness and turned to see an entire cargo bay that was filled with crates, tactical vests, canteens, and other survival supplies.

Elena read the Optivision screen again. She peered out the window. All of the sudden, the stark whiteness that had been obstructing her view melted away, turning into blue sky.

She reached over and shook Stacia's shoulder.

"Hey! Wake up."

As Stacia began to show signs of rousing, Elena reached across the aisle toward the boys. "Hey! Vaughn. Darnell. Wake up."

Soon, the others were awake and asking the same questions that Elena had.

"Where are we?" Stacia said.

"Not sure," said Elena. "But I'm going to venture a guess and say that this is our second quarter exam."

"What does *parachute to one of the islands* mean?" Garrett asked after looking at the directions on the Optivision.

"I'm not sure," Elena said, climbing back to the cargo bay. Then, she noticed a door with a scanner niche.

Holding her breath, she scanned her Trademark. The door slid open silently. A gust of wind engulfed the entire craft, sending Elena's fiery curls flying in a hundred directions. She grabbed hold of a grip mount and leaned through the door as far as she felt was safe.

Below her, beside her, all around her were a dozen islands floating in blue sky. In front of her and behind her, eleven other aerocrafts similar to the one she was on were also flying. They all seemed to be following one another, around and around in a circle. She scanned her Trademark again, and the door slid shut.

"Whoa!" Ernest breathed. "So, we have to jump to one of the islands?"

"Apparently," Elena said through gritted teeth.

Feeling angry, she started through the cargo bay, tossing things around unceremoniously. She found a sleeping bag, several filled canteens, a medical kit, and four tactical vests.

"What are you doing?" Ernest asked impatiently.

"I'm checking the supplies," Elena said. "The directions say we have to jump with what we can carry."

Elena opened one of the crates and saw that it was filled with food. She opened another crate and fingered through a pile of knives, machetes, and firestarters.

"We need everything on this aerocraft. Except there's no way to jump with it all."

Elena moved back through the aerocraft toward the pilot's chair. She watched the other aerocrafts that were circling the islands. Fear rose up inside her like a monster. Here she was again, with no control over her circumstances. Elena was constantly at the mercy of other people making decisions for her.

But slowly, an idea began to creep through her mind. She'd practiced dozens of the flight simulations with Pigg. Could this aerocraft be any different from those simulations? She couldn't be sure, but she knew she didn't want to waste any more time thinking about it.

"We're going to fly this aerocraft to one of those islands below," she said triumphantly.

"Excuse me?" Garrett said sharply. "We're doing what?"

"Actually, we won't be flying anything. I'll be flying this to one of the islands for us," replied Elena.

"We can't do that," Stacia said nervously.

"Yes, I think I might be able to," Elena said. "In fact, I think it's even what they might want us to do."

"How do you figure that?" Ernest asked.

"Didn't you notice that half the Simulabs are programmed to teach us flight simulations?" Elena said as she jumped into the pilot's chair and strapped herself in.

"I think we can all agree that you're not the best person to make decisions for all of us," Garrett said forcefully.

"Yes, you are slightly impulsive and irrational at times," Ernest said.

"And you've been known to endanger the lives of the people in your own Unit," Stacia added.

"Thank you all for being so blatantly honest about my character flaws in this highly stressful situation," said Elena as she accessed all the Optivisions that she needed to control the vessel. "But we don't have time to discuss this now. I've got to figure out how to get this aerocraft out of whatever procession pattern it's locked into."

"The reason we are here is to learn how to perform to the school's standards. Why would we ever need to do anything differently from the directions they have provided?" Garrett questioned.

"Aren't you ever *just done* with doing everything the way they tell you to do it?" Elena asked, her voice thick with frustration. "You're worse than cyborgs. But I really don't care. Just do whatever you want. I'm flying this thing outta here."

Elena's hair suddenly bounced around her face again. She turned to see that Garrett had opened the cargo door. The wind rushed through Elena's ears, but she still heard Stacia say clearly, "We're going to jump."

Before Elena could blink, the others had thrown on parachute packs and jumped without so much as a canteen of water. She leapt up from her seat and hurried over to the open door. As she watched the tops of their canopies, she noticed that they were headed toward an island that was covered with jagged rock. She closed the door and shook her head.

"Robots."

After Elena was strapped back into the pilot's chair, she heaved a deep breath. Without worrying too much about the consequences, yanked the control yoke.

The aerocraft soared easily out of its rotation. However, she realized quickly that it had very little manual control. The vessel took a sharp nosedive that caused her stomach to plummet.

After a few minutes of maneuvering, she was finally able to steady the aerocraft, and just in time because one of the floating islands was looking ever closer. Before she even knew what was happening, Elena saw a solid sheet of ice and decided in an instant that it was the only place she could land. She tried to brace herself for the impact of hitting the ground, but it was no use.

As the aerocraft touched down, she slammed her face into the control panel. The vessel stopped so suddenly that she felt completely disoriented. A stab of pain shot up her legs and back. Then, Elena could feel something warm and sticky seeping down her face.

Declan appeared suddenly at the side window of the aerocraft and startled Elena out of her boots.

"Geez!" Elena yelled, slapping her hand over her heart. "You scared me!"

"I saw you crash. Are you alright?" Declan called through the window.

"Oh yeah, I'm perfect!" Elena said sarcastically. "I crashed...hit my head. I feel awesome."

"You're bleeding!" Declan looked concerned.

Elena's fingers moved instantly to the warm sensation she felt on her face. When she pulled her hand away, she could see that it was covered in blood. She felt a little dizzy at the sight.

"Just wait a sec. I'll get you out of there," said Declan.

Elena watched Declan move away from the window. She looked around for something to sop up her face, but all the supplies were in the cargo bay. She unbuckled her belt and used the seat to help steady her as she slowly began to stand.

A moment later, Declan arrived back at the window. "The door is jammed."

"How am I going to get out of here?" Elena called.

"Think I could break the passenger's side window?" Declan suggested.

"No, break one of the back windows. There's only cargo back there."

From a secured position at the front of the vessel, Elena watched glass shatter all over the cargo bay. Slowly, she walked along to the back of the aerocraft using the seats for support. She pushed a couple aviator jackets through the broken window and the medical kit. Then, Declan grabbed her around the arms and helped her climb through the space. Her boots touched down into a drift of deep snow.

"I can't believe we're in the snow again," Elena grumbled. "You'd think they'd be a little more creative in the simulations."

"Hold still," Declan said impatiently. "You're still bleeding."

When Declan touched her face, she winced in pain. He opened the medical kit quickly and pulled out some gauze and sanitation wipes.

"How bad is it?" Elena asked after a few seconds.

"It's not too bad," Declan said. "But I wish Austin was here to fix you up. That Suturand could zap this cut in a second. As it is, you're going to have to wear a bandage until the bleeding stops and then we'll just have to see. Come on, sit down. It'll be easier for me to put the bandage on."

Elena pressed her back up against the aerocraft. She slid to the ground.

"So, we're stuck inside another marvelous simulation without any directions for how to get back to school," Declan said as he wiped her face. "I'm super excited, aren't you?"

"I told you they were feeding us better," Elena grumbled.

Declan smiled wildly. "Yeah, yeah…you're really brilliant about following clues. It was smart of you to take the whole aerocraft. I was a dimwit and followed the directions. We only got out with a parachute each and a few supplies that would only last a day or so."

"We?" Elena looked around and saw Herbie Clucas from Harrier, Moriah Kirkley from Falcon, and Adrien Segars from Raptor standing at the far side of Elena's aerocraft.

"Well, they're all friendly and helpful," Elena said sarcastically.

"I think they're scared of you." Declan smiled again. "So, I think you're the only one who took the whole craft."

"Why do you say that?"

"I watched almost everyone else jump. Not all the islands have snow or even look like landforms. When you're feeling better, I'll show you."

"I'm fine," Elena said, using the side of the aerocraft to help her stand. "Show me what we're up against."

Declan pushed through the snow, leading Elena up the side of a steep hill. The air was glacial. Snow blew around them thick and heavy. Within minutes, Elena was frozen to her core. She also felt a strange sensation in her feet, like they were remembering the frost nip she'd had the year before.

Eventually, they came to the side of a cliff that fell decidedly into nothing but more deep blue sky. Elena took a deep breath as she counted eleven other islands floating in the sky. She noticed one island with trees that looked like they belonged in a jungle and another with a flat desert. There was a mountain spewing with lava on yet another island and one with forests of crowded trees.

"So, what do you think we're supposed to do now?" Elena asked.

"I don't know. Find everyone?"

"Find *everyone*? That would take forever!" Elena said angrily. "We don't even know how to get off this island. And I don't even see land anywhere, do you?"

"Duh!" said Declan, giving her a toothy grin. "There are at least eleven islands out there."

"Ha...ha..." Elena said derisively. "I meant *below* the islands, you know, on the actual ground."

Declan looked down, and Elena watched his eyes scour below them.

"Nothing. There's nothing." They were quiet for a few moments and then he added, "We need to find Austin. He'll know what to do."

"Now you're talking sense," Elena said. "So, how are we going to get over to the other islands?"

"Let's check the aerocraft to see if we can fly the thing off this rock," Declan suggested.

"Good idea," Elena said, pulling the hood of her aviator jacket tight around her ears. "Besides that, we've just got to get off this island before we freeze to death. Which island do we start with?"

"Pick one, my lady," Declan said, gesturing toward the other islands.

"I don't want to go to the desert. That one," she pointed, "looks like a forest. That other one looks like a jungle. Jungle or forest? Which do you think would be easier to land on?"

"If we can find a beach off the jungle, we could put the aerocraft down fairly easy."

"A beach!" Elena said incredulously. "It's a *floating* island."

Declan smiled at her in a boyish way. "You have something better to do? Look, I saw a few people land there so, we may as well fly around and give it a look."

"Okay, but how are we going to convince the others to go?"

"I'll just tell them they're coming with us," Declan said simply.

Elena couldn't help but roll her eyes at his confidence. However, as soon as they returned to the crash site, Declan had put on his most winsome grin.

"So, everyone," Declan clapped a hand firmly on Herbie Clucas's shoulder. "We've decided to fly the aerocraft to that island there."

"Huh?" said Moriah.

"Fly what?" Herbie said at the same time.

"We're going to fly off this island to the one that looks like a jungle so we can look for everyone else that parachuted down," said Declan as he flashed his dimples at Moriah, who blushed and looked away quickly.

"I don't know if we should leave yet," Adrien said, though her teeth were chattering. "We haven't been given any directions. Plus, what if there are others that landed on *this* island? We shouldn't leave them."

"No one else landed here," Declan said. "Believe me, I watched everyone touch down. Well, that is, I watched everyone I could see. But some of those islands are blocked from our view."

"I'm still not sure we should..." Adrien started, but Declan moved toward her and threw an arm casually around her shoulder.

"Come on, Segars," he said smoothly. "You don't want to stay here in the cold, do you?"

She shook her head. "I guess I'd rather try a different island."

"Yeah, I think we could go." Herbie nodded, and then climbed through the shattered out window.

The other girls shrugged at one another, and then climbed in after him. Elena's mouth fell open. "How did you do that?"

"I was *nice* to them," Declan said. "Something you clearly need to work on."

"What do you mean?"

"Oh, come on," Declan said impatiently. "I saw all the other students come out of your aerocraft before you flew it out of rotation. What did you do? Push them out?"

"No!" Elena said defensively. "They had a melt down when I said I was flying the aerocraft. Some *blah, blah* excuses about following the directions we were given."

"Dimwits!" said Declan. "Woulda saved all of us trouble."

"Let's get outta here." Elena's teeth chattered uncontrollably. "Would you mind flying though? My head..."

"Are you feeling dizzy?" Declan reached forward to touch her cheek, but Elena pulled away abruptly.

"I'm fine," she said shortly. "I just don't feel like landing again."

"You'll let me know if you get dizzy though, right?"

Elena nodded curtly. Then, she crawled back inside the aerocraft. She and Declan worked to cover the missing window with some of the sleeping bags. Then, Declan cranked the engine and activated the Optivision screens as Elena belted herself into the co-pilot's chair.

"I hope you know what you're doing," said Herbie from behind them.

"Don't worry," Declan said. "After I noticed that Elena and Pigg were logging dozens of hours in the flight simulation I started doing some myself. I may not be able to fly as well as Ransom, but I can certainly land better than her."

Elena punched him in the arm as the aerocraft rose out of the snow and zoomed away from the icy island. They flew steadily through the blue sky, toward the tree-topped jungle. She was impressed by Declan's knowledge of the control panel, so she sat in silence and peered eagerly out the window. Then, suddenly she saw a long streak of golden ground below them.

"Oh, look," Declan said mischievously. "There's a beach. Imagine that, a beach on an island with a jungle."

"Alright, alright!" Elena conceded. "You were right and it was a good idea to check."

"Hang on." Declan closed his eyes as if he were savoring a delicious meal. "I just need to save what you said in my memory..."

"Open your eyes, dimwit!" Elena laughed. "You're going to crash us."

Declan's roaring laughter filled the hovercraft, and Elena couldn't help but laugh herself as the aerocraft dropped from the sky toward the sand. Moments later, Declan had touched them down rather gently on a long stretch of sand.

Herbie Clucas yanked on the cargo bay door, which opened at once.

"It must have been jammed from the snow," he said. "Glad it's working now, though."

Elena stepped onto the sand. In less than a minute, beads of sweat formed on her brow. She pulled off her bomber jacket and tossed it aside.

"Ugh...it's miserable out here," said Declan wiping his own forehead on Elena's shoulder sleeve.

"Who did you say landed here?" Elena asked, trying to shield her face from the blinding sun.

"I couldn't really tell," Declan said. "But maybe three or four landed somewhere."

"Should we look for them?" Moriah asked.

"We shouldn't go tromping through the jungle right now," Elena said, pulling her sweaty head of hair into a bun. "It looks like it could get dark soon. We should make a camp and eat something."

She looked toward the waves that were rolling in on the shoreline. Beyond that, blue sky continued until the next island began.

"It's so strange to see water and a beach in the sky," said Adrien. "Do you think we'd fall off the edge of the island if we go in it?"

"There's only one way to find out," Declan said.

Declan took off running for the water. He jumped in before Elena could even holler at him to stop.

Elena looked at Herbie and the other two girls. Then, they ran for the water as well. Declan still hadn't surfaced by the time they arrived.

Elena was suddenly worried that he had fallen straight through the island. Then, she wondered if that meant they'd failed the exam. She slowly walked ankle deep into the water.

"What are you doing?" Adrien asked. "He hasn't even come back up yet. What if you fall through?"

Ignoring her question, Elena leaned down toward the water in the place she thought he'd jumped in. Without warning, Declan's head popped up. A fountain of water spewed from his mouth straight into her face.

"Gross!" Elena shouted, wiping with her sleeve.

"Come on, Ransom! Get in!" Declan beckoned.

Elena smiled. It had been so long since she'd done anything truly fun. And the water was such a pretty color blue that she felt she could get lost in it forever and feel completely happy.

Before she could stop herself, Elena bent down and splashed a hand-full of water in his face. Declan beckoned the others to join them, but Herbie, Moriah, and Adrien simply shook their heads and moved back toward the aerocraft. Elena didn't care.

She and Declan splashed one another for a long time. Then, they swam in the deep blue. They climbed the trees along the shoreline and built a little castle out of the warm sand. When they were hungry, they ate bananas from a nearby tree and learned to open coconuts.

At long last, Elena and Declan made their way back over to the others, who'd set up a small camp around the door of the aerocraft.

"We're going to sleep here tonight," Herbie informed them. "Inside the aerocraft."

"That's going to be miserably hot. Let's go camp over there under that hanging tree so we get a bit of a breeze," said Declan quickly.

"With our backs to the jungle?" Elena questioned. "I don't think so. Anything could be in there. Besides, we should stay together."

"But what if the tide comes in or a sea monster comes out of there?" Declan said playfully. "Come on, you don't want to sleep in that hot tin can, do you?"

"I know what you're trying to do," Elena said. She'd just watched Declan manipulate the others into getting off the island of snow.

"Is it working?" Declan sounded eager to know.

"Well, I definitely don't want to sleep with those dimwits," said Elena. Herbie looked offended but didn't reply. "Let me just get some stuff outta the cargo bay so I can feel like we have some kind of campsite."

"Good job being nice," Declan whispered sarcastically as they entered the cargo bay together.

"What?" Elena slid a tactical knife into the pocket on the side of her aviator boot.

Declan grabbed a tactical pack and began to fill it with prepackaged meals, water, and medical supplies. "You called them dimwits to their faces."

"I don't know why Clucas looked surprised," Elena said honestly. "I can't be the first person to ever call him that."

Declan laughed jovially as they walked over to the hanging tree and tossed the supplies into the sand.

"You really need to learn to say things politely."

"Yeah, I know, I know," Elena said hopelessly. "Austin's been telling me that for years. It's just hard for me to make friends easily."

"We're friends."

"Yeah, and look how long that took," Elena said. "Actually, I probably never woulda been friends with Abria, but she was so insistent."

Declan tossed a pouch of trail mix at Elena's face, but she caught it before it hit her.

"This food makes me actually miss Pigg," Declan said absentmindedly.

Elena smirked. She couldn't understand it, but at the mention of Pigg's name, she suddenly missed home. She imagined her mom working at the hospital and saw her dad working in his office.

She swallowed the lump in her throat. "Can I ask you about your parents?"

Declan's smile faded. "Sure. Anything."

"How old were you when they went to the hospital?"

"Abria and I had just turned three. Fergie's parents were great, though. They took us in right away and really helped us through the grieving process."

"Was it hard for you when Fergie's parents died?"

"Yeah. I know you didn't really get to spend time with Kenneth, but he was a good dad. Not as good as mine, but better than most."

"My dad was really great, too," Elena said. "And my mom. I actually think Austin might miss her a little more than I do because he could always talk with her about the hospital and medicine."

The sun was setting now over the water, casting orange and yellow hues in the sky. But Elena's thoughts carried her far away to another lifetime.

"Whoa! You...your..." Declan pointed at Elena's head as he stuttered.

"What? Are you going to tease me about my hair? I know it's frizzy, but it's so humid here."

"No!" Declan screamed. "The tree is attacking us!"

Elena had been so distracted by their conversation that she didn't even noticed vines from the hanging tree had encircled them completely. One of the vines reached out quickly and attached to Elena's ankle with the speed of a venomous snake.

▱ 13 ▱

Saving Kidd Wheeler

The creeping vine grabbed Declan's tactical knife and absorbed it into the jungle before he had a chance to react. Then, the wild plant continued to wrap itself around Declan and Elena's legs, arms, and bellies.

"Help!" Declan called out in the direction of the aerocraft. "Clucas! Help!"

Elena quickly pulled a tactical knife from her boot. She cut the vine off at the base of her left foot and then started on her right arm.

"That was a nifty little trick!" Declan said lightheartedly, just as Herbie, Moriah, and Adrien came running for them.

"Don't get sassy with me!" Elena hollered. "We're in this mess because you *had* to sleep under the tree."

"What should we do?" Herbie asked, looking at the ever-expanding vines with horror on his face.

"Run back and get the other tactical knives and machetes from the supplies," Declan ordered.

Herbie took off in an instant. Elena reached toward Declan to start cutting him free, but by the time she'd released one of his legs, more vines were crawling on them.

"Ahhh..." Moriah screamed out as the vine grabbed hold of her ankle and yanked her to the ground.

Adrien screamed and took off running back toward the aerocraft.

"She's a brave girl," Elena said bitterly as she struggled against her bonds.

Suddenly, a hololight appeared at the edge of the jungle. Then, Fergie jumped rigidly through the foliage, brandishing a machete.

Elena's mouth fell open in surprise.

Without a word, Fergie began to hack at the plant. Herbie also appeared holding several knives and two machetes. He handed out the weapons, and together they all cut the vines away. The work was long and tiresome, but finally Elena, Declan, and Moriah were able to get free enough to run. Elena hurried back to the aerocraft with the others, gasping for breath and feeling tired.

"How did you acquire the aerocraft?" Fergie questioned. She was not out of breath, but did appear anxious.

"Ransom flew it out of the rotation and landed it on that island over there," Declan said, pointing back toward the snowy island.

"A very brilliant, strategic move," Fergie said, though she still seemed distracted by something. "I am grateful to find you. I have been searching for this beach for several hours. I watched you land. I made my way here directly."

"What's wrong?" Elena said. "You seem tense."

"I had to abandon Wheeler," Fergie said. "His parachute caught in a tree. I was unsuccessful in my attempts to free him."

Elena sighed heavily.

"What's the point of all this?" Herbie said grumpily.

"The point is the same as last year," Fergie said wisely. "To see if our teamwork and innovation can get us out of the simulation,"

"That's funny, I didn't look at the frozen wilderness that positively," Moriah said. "Cause it really felt like they were just trying to kill us."

"That doesn't really matter now," said Declan. "We've gotta get Wheeler out of a tree. Fergie can take me."

"Certainly," Fergie replied, as Elena reached for a tactical pack.

"What are you doing?" Declan asked.

"I'm getting ready to go with you," Elena said plainly. "You saw what that plant just did to us. And who knows what else is inside the magic jungle. Face it, the more people that go with you, the better."

"Maybe someone else could go with us instead," Declan said, looking expectantly at Herbie.

"I think I should stay here with Segars," Herbie replied. "She got spooked by the vines. She's hiding in the aerocraft right now. I don't think it would be good if we all leave her here."

"I'll stay with her, too," Moriah offered.

"Fine." Declan didn't look irritated, but Elena felt frustrated by the lack of help the others offered. "Ransom and Foreman, let's get as much as we can carry from the cargo bay so we can be on our way."

Minutes later, Elena followed Fergie and Declan into the jungle with a tactical pack secured comfortably on her back. She was armed with a hololight in one hand and a machete in the other, but since Fergie was already using her machete to cut them a path, Elena's weapon was ready for protection against anything that might come at them in the jungle.

"How long did it take to hike here?" Declan asked Fergie.

"Three hours, twelve minutes, and twenty-seven seconds," Fergie said. "However, I was attempting to follow your Trademarks using my limited tracking abilities. The jungle is dense with creeping plants and crawling vines. Therefore, it took me a while to navigate. I am certain that I can get us back through the foliage without it taking that long."

"Oh, you have your Touchdot?" Elena said excitedly.

"No," Fergie replied. "I was using my internal mainframe."

"Where's Austin?"

"He is a long way from here," Fergie said. "And Pigg is even farther."

"Ugh! Why can't we ever find Austin first?" Elena said grumpily. "You know, last year we did water training, but they dropped us in a frozen wilderness. This year we have aero training and they drop us on an island. It seems so chaotic. I wish they'd make up their minds about what they want to teach us."

"If you feel disoriented, then that is how Grimsby wants you to feel," Fergie said. "But make no mistake, the exams are methodically planned. All of the training we have received in every single class since the moment we arrived here has been designed for optimum retention and long-term physical endurance."

"Well, the whole thing seems completely random to me," Elena complained. "And I thought we'd have a little more time in class to prepare for a simulation like this. Last year, Marshall didn't torture us this way until the third quarter."

"Ransom, maybe you could conserve some of your energy by not complaining," Declan joked.

"Fine. But I'm only saying what I know everyone else is thinking."

The three friends were silent for a long time. Elena's head was beginning to viciously pound, but she didn't dare tell the others. Also, she was starting to feel a painful tingle at the site of her previously bruised tailbone, and she began to worry if she was pushing her body too hard. She kept wishing that Austin were there so that he could tell her what they should do or at least help fix up her head so it wouldn't hurt so badly.

"Can we stop for a bit to rest?" Elena said after a couple hours of silence. "I need some water."

"If you could wait, Wheeler is just up here between the trees," said Fergie. "Perhaps another ten minutes."

Elena mumbled a "yes" as they continued on until the dense jungle opened into a small field of bamboo shoots. Fergie stopped along the edge of the clearing where she looked up into one of the taller palm trees. Elena could see a parachute canopy tangled up in all the branches. And there, hanging like a trapped animal, was Kidd.

"Are you hurt?" Declan called up to Kidd.

"No," Kidd replied. "Just extremely thirsty."

Elena stepped toward the tree and said, "I'll climb up and cut him down."

"Are you sure you should?" Declan said, grabbing her forearm. "You already hit your head. And we walked hours to get here. Maybe you should rest."

"Who else is going to climb up there? Fergie said she couldn't get him down, and you're not as agile as me," Elena said practically. "I'll just head up this adjacent tree and reach over to cut him free."

"Okay, but don't carry anything with you," Declan said, taking Elena's pack. He handed her a machete, which she slung across her back. "Wheeler can have water when he gets down. And call out if you're feeling dizzy, and I'll try my best to climb up after you."

Elena nodded and began her ascent. She was barely seven feet up in the tree when she knew it was a mistake to volunteer. Her head began to spin, and her eyes became fuzzy. Her arms and legs were strong, but trying to maneuver between the vines and the rough sleek tree trunk was complicated. After long, hard work, she finally was in a position where she could reach Kidd.

"You should have picked a taller tree to get stuck in," Elena said sarcastically as she pulled the machete from over her shoulder. "I would have appreciated a little more of a workout today."

"You could certainly use more of a workout, Freckles," Kidd said scathingly.

"Look, I already regret that I have to come get you, but you helped me out with that pool when I was injured so how about we call it even."

Kidd didn't even have a chance to nod before Elena cut his parachute lines abruptly. He let out a yelp and skidded down a fair portion of the palm trunk before he was able to catch himself from falling all the way to the ground. He looked up at Elena with malice in his eyes.

"Oops! The machete got away from me," she called down to him.

Once everyone was safely on the ground, Declan said, "Should we start back for the beach?"

"Oh, can we just stay here for a few hours rest?" Elena almost begged. "I'm exhausted. And I doubt any of those other dimwits would be able to fly the aerocraft, so we're not in danger of them leaving us here."

"Elena has sound advice," Fergie said. "We should rest and make our return journey at first light."

"Where exactly are we supposed to sleep out here?" Kidd grumbled.

Elena sat right down on the ground and pushed her back up against a tree.

"You're not afraid of a little dirt, are you Wheeler?" Elena crooned in a mocking tone. She put her hands behind her head in a relaxed sort of way and added, "Besides, it's warm here. It's not like we'll freeze to death. I don't even think we'll need to light a fire."

Declan smirked at Kidd, and then he sat down beside Elena.

"Would you give us a detailed account of the events that transpired that led you to land on this island?" Fergie asked Elena and Declan as she sat stiffly on the ground as well.

Elena noticed a look of reluctance on Kidd's face as he also sat beside them. Then, she and Declan took turns explaining about how they'd flown the aerocraft from the frozen island and crashlanded.

"Well, that sounds like a real interesting adventure," Kidd said dryly when they'd finished. "Too bad the vines didn't eat you."

"Too bad we were here to cut you out of that tree," Elena bit back. "I'm sure it would have been fun getting down all by yourself. Except, had you been able to do that, you could have certainly managed it before we hiked *all the way* out here to get you."

"So, Ransom," Declan interrupted. "It's late, and we are tired from hiking all day. What do you say if we just..."

"Stop talking now," Elena inserted. "Yeah, let's do that."

She rolled away from all of them feeling tired, slightly frightened, and still extremely bitter that they hadn't found Austin first.

The next morning, Elena and the others arrived back at the beach and were surprised to see that Vivienne Castellow and Frankie Smiley had joined Herbie, Moriah, and Adrien at the aerocraft.

"Hey!" Declan said genuinely, shaking Frankie's hand and clapping him on the back. "Glad you could join us."

"Me, too," Frankie said. "I think we must have landed about as far from this beach as possible. But we were up high on that hill and saw your aerocraft land."

"Please tell us you have some kind of plan," said Vivienne as she looked directly at Elena.

"Me? Have a plan?" Elena said curiously.

"Yeah, Clucas said you were the only one to fly the aerocraft," Frankie said. "That makes you the smartest one of the group."

Elena noticed that a few of the others smirked unkindly at his comment.

"Yeah, so you have a plan for how we're going to get outta here, right?" Vivienne asked.

"Not exactly. We've talked," Elena indicated Declan and Fergie with her finger, "about how it's possible that all the Aves Company has to be together for the simulation to end. If that's true, then we need to get to the next island to see if we can find anyone else."

"And hopefully we won't have to go to all the islands," Declan added.

"Think that aerocraft will fly with all of us in it?" Frankie asked.

Elena looked around at their party. The aerocraft had seats for six, but now they were a group of nine.

"I don't know," Elena said. She looked at Kidd. "What do you think?"

Kidd frowned at her and said, "I think we'll be lucky to get to the nearest island." He pointed past the shoreline toward the only three islands that they could see from their position. "That one with the forest of trees. We'll have to clear most everything out of the cargo bay and, even still, the aerocraft might not support our weight."

"Well, we've got to try," urged Declan.

"Agreed," Elena said. "So, how about we pull everything out. Then each person can pick what they need, and we'll leave the rest on the beach."

After everyone else agreed, the work began. Some of the crates inside the cargo bag were extremely heavy, so they had to be partly emptied before they could even be moved. Some of the more important equipment included climbing gear, jet propelled wings, and zip line tackle. All the tactical vests were equipped with a high glide compressed air parachute, but they were able to fill the vests with food, water, and medical supplies as well.

After everything was out of the aerocraft, each of the students chose a tactical vest with mediocre supplies.

"I'll fly," Kidd volunteered.

"And I will navigate," Fergie added in a way that made Elena remember their recent trip from Istanbul.

"The rest of us will sit in the cargo bay so that the girls can have the seats with belts," Declan said.

"Thanks for volunteering us," Herbie said bitterly to Declan as they all moved into their positions on the aerocraft.

Elena eased into a seat beside Adrien as Moriah and Vivienne buckled her restraints.

"Okay, here we go, Brainiack," Kidd said as Elena heard the engine crank.

The aerocraft rose at a steady pace. Then, they eased forward off the edge of the island toward the forest of thick trees out the window.

But suddenly, the aerocraft plummeted into a sharp nosedive. Shrill screaming filled Elena's ears as Kidd pulled the control yoke to keep the craft steady. She couldn't even close her eyes.

Before she understood exactly what was happening, Kidd said, "We're *under* the island."

Pieces of rocks and trees jutted out to the point that it looked like they were flying through an upside-down mountain. And suddenly, the mouth of a cave appeared, and Elena knew there was nothing they could do. She heard a piercing sound erupt from her own mouth, and it burned her throat as the aerocraft crashed through the mouth of the cave. The vessel slid out of control until it finally caught on a tangle of tree roots, stopping abruptly.

"Everyone okay?" Elena called out, turning quickly to look at the guys in the cargo bay.

A general murmur of wellbeing echoed around the vessel. Declan was first to the door, but he couldn't push it open. Herbie, Kidd, and Frankie moved to help him, but it was no use.

"Are we trapped?" Adrien asked in a slightly panicked voice.

"No, we're not trapped," Kidd said impatiently. He walked back to the cockpit and a second later was able to pop out the windshield using only a machete blade and leverage.

"That was impressive," Declan told him admiringly.

"Yeah, whatever!" Kidd replied as he leaped through the now open windshield.

Elena rolled her eyes at Declan, who smiled in a boyish way. "At least there's a way out."

Elena climbed through the window after Declan, and together they combed the small space in the cave around the aerocraft. Rocks and hanging tree roots filled almost every inch. The crashed vessel blocked the way they'd entered, but after a little searching, they noticed a side chamber that seemed to lead away from where they were.

"Oh, terrific! We've landed in the center of a floating island. How are we ever going to get outta here?" Herbie asked.

Elena couldn't have explained the calm she felt, except that so much had already gone wrong it almost seemed impossible that it could get any worse.

"I think we should load up with as much as we can carry and start walking," she suggested. "We'll follow the cave along and see where it leads. I'm sure we'll figure something out, but we can't stay here."

"Ransom is right," said Declan. "We've got to go on as far as we can. We'll head into the tunnel with all our hololights on."

He climbed back into the aerocraft and, a moment later, supplies started flying through the missing windshield at their feet. Elena quickly grabbed and tactical vest and strapped it on.

"Take it easy, Bowen," Kidd barked. "You just tossed a machete at us."

Elena picked the blade up and waved it around lightheartedly. "What's the matter, Wheeler? You afraid you might get a little hurt?"

Kidd made a face at her but said nothing else.

Elena turned toward a grouping of tree roots. She firmly grasped the handle of the machete with both hands and took a giant swing. The roots cut easily away from the mouth of the cave.

"I believe you are the definition of my hero," Fergie told Elena in a dry, formal tone.

"Feel free to keep telling me that all along the way," Elena winked at her. "It will keep my confidence up as I receive dirty looks from Wheeler."

"Okay, everyone ready?" Declan jumped out of the aerocraft with another machete in his hand and a tactical pack secured on his shoulders.

"I am," Elena said as she took another chop at the vines.

Elena and Declan began to cut open a path through the narrow cave using their machetes against the tree roots. At first the roots were easy to cut, but soon they grew thick and stubborn across the opening so it took a lot of effort to cut them. Often, Elena and Declan had to take a break and let Kidd, Frankie, or Herbie use the machetes.

In addition to this, the cave began to grow extremely cold. Even though Elena was sweating under her bomber jacket, she could see every breath that heaved through her mouth.

The hours stretched on slowly, but since they didn't know how far they had to go, or even where they had to go, Elena kept on without talking or complaining. The tunnel was very cramped, and she was beginning to fear that they'd never get out of the tiny space. Plus, the increasingly frigid temperature reminded her too much of their Level 2 exam in the wilderness, which made her feet tingle uncomfortably; whether from the memory of almost having frostbite or because she was actually getting it again, she didn't know.

After a long time, Adrien Segars finally said, "We've been walking forever! Can we stop for a break?"

"Wait!" Kidd called from the front of their procession. He'd been cutting tree roots for over thirty minutes, but wouldn't pass the machete to anyone else because he said he was bored just walking. "Look at this!"

Elena followed along the narrow path behind Fergie until, quite suddenly, it opened into a circular area with dozens of hanging roots. Elena and the others spread out around the cave with their hololights aloft.

"I don't see an exit," Elena called out.

"None over here," Herbie replied from one side of the room.

"Not here either," Moriah said from another side.

They all came together in the center of the cave and, without a word, collapsed to the floor. Canteens of water were sipped and snacks were taken out of packs. They were silent for a long time. And in the silence, Elena's brain was working overtime.

The exam was a test of willpower and intelligence. She was certain that Marshall would never put them in a situation that they couldn't get out of, but then perhaps he didn't factor in the possibility that they would have crashed an aerocraft *under* an island.

"But, there was that one test I did under the water," Elena said out loud.

"Huh? What did you say?" Declan asked.

"Remember, I told you that Austin and I were stuck under some kind of sheet of ice," Elena said excitedly. "And the only way out was…"

"Up!" Declan finished her sentence.

Elena was on her feet in an instant. She used her hololight the best she could, holding it high above her head.

"I see it!" Declan pointed. "Just there! The hanging roots continue up instead of growing straight out from the wall."

"You think we have to *climb* out of here?" Herbie asked, looking at Elena.

"It's the only thing that makes sense," Elena said. "We're stuck down here. The only way we'd ever be able to find everyone else is if we climb back up to the surface." She looked around at the group. "So, who's the best climber?"

"Kirkley and I are," Herbie said confidently.

"Then, you should go first," Declan said. "And the rest of us will partner up based on our skills."

In the end, Moriah and Herbie started up the tree roots first with the tactical climbing gear to help make their ascent a little easier. Adrien and Kidd followed them, grasping onto the rope that Moriah and Herbie had secured on their way up. Then, Frankie and Vivienne paired up to go next with Fergie and Elena behind them. Declan climbed last.

If Elena thought the tunnel had been narrow, the climb through the tree roots was even worse. Often she felt her face scratched or her feet slip. And, instead of it being terribly cold, it was now miserably hot. Brow sweat dripped into Elena's eyes as she tried to manage holding her hololight plus the roots and the climbing rope. And worse than that, tree bark and falling debris showered down from the climbers above her.

"Tree roots have to be the worst climbing material in the history of time," Elena grumbled to Fergie as the group finally reached a place of solid footing where they could take out canteens for a quick break.

"Remember when I said we should make my resident tower in New York our summer home?" Declan said reminiscently. "I take it back. This would be much nicer."

Elena couldn't even smile.

As they continued upward, Elena's limbs began to shake and a headache formed at the base of her skull. But, just as she was getting so depressed that she actually considered climbing all the way back down to see if she could fly the damaged aerocraft out of the cave, she heard a trickling of voices from above her.

"Blue sky!" Frankie yelled. "Clucas said he sees blue sky."

"What's that he's saying?" Declan asked from below Elena.

"He says Clucas can see blue sky," Elena said, feeling relief wash over her.

"Pity," Declan said dryly. "I was just beginning to enjoy it down here."

▭ 14 ▭

Into the Earth

In next to no time, Elena was blinking and squinting in the blazing sunlight. Fergie grabbed one of her arms and helped Elena climb the last foot out of the whole. She was standing at the base of a mammoth tree that was a tangle of massive roots. From the shade of the tree, Elena could see that they'd arrived on a long flat plain of grassland with a forest on one side.

Herbie, Moriah, and the others had already collapsed inbetween the tree roots and were searching for snacks and water in their packs. Elena grabbed Declan's arm to help him out of the tunnel.

"Wow, it's nice here. Have we died or something?" Declan teased.

Elena smiled a little. "We could only be so lucky at this point." She crumpled to the ground, taking large gulps of water from her canteen.

She'd just finished stuffing her mouth with her third snack bar when Herbie said, "What's that sound?"

Elena heard a low rumble. Then, the ground began to tremble. She leapt up, but felt completely off balance.

"Earthquake!" yelled Declan with panic in his voice.

"Seriously?" Elena hollered, stamping her foot on the ground. "This has been one hugely awful disaster after another. Can't we get a little break?"

"Don't stop to complain!" Kidd yelled at her. "Just run!"

Elena had no idea which way to go, but the ground was dangerously unstable. The other students had run off in different directions, but Declan and Fergie stood beside her. She could see nothing but flat prairie land and a cluster of trees to the far side of the island. There was literally nothing to protect them.

"What do we do?" Declan shouted over the rising sound of the earth falling apart.

"We have no clear choices for safety given the terrain," Fergie said.

"Except one that we don't want to admit," Elena hollered. "We've got to climb back down into the tunnel."

"Of course!" Declan slapped his palm to his forehead. "Too bad the others..."

But a blood-curdling scream stopped Declan from finishing his thought. Elena saw the ground split apart in the exact spot where Frankie Smiley and Adrien Segars were running. Try as they might, they couldn't outrun it. They disappeared from sight as the earth swallowed them.

"Hurry!" Declan said, pushing Elena and Fergie down the mouth of the hole under the tree.

Elena clutched the tree roots until her knuckles turned white. She barely dared to breath as she waited to see if the earthquake would push them further down the hole. Dirt crumbled all around her. Then, a minute later, everything was suddenly quiet.

Elena, Fergie, and Declan emerged slowly from the hole and made their way over to the area where Adrien and Frankie had fallen. Without thinking about her own safety, Elena danced along the edge of the newly formed cavern. Her eyes searched the black hole, but she couldn't see them.

"Segars! Smiley! Where are you?" Elena called as she fell to her knees.

"We're here!" Adrien yelled back. "We're stuck!"

"She means, there's nothing for us to climb on so we can get out," Frankie added.

"Bowen, do we have any rope left?" Elena asked.

"No, we left it tangled up in the vines on that last island," Declan replied.

Elena looked around, feeling truly helpless.

"Look!" Declan shouted and pointed, startling Elena out of her boots.

The students that had run away during the earthquake were striding back toward them, followed by Olivia Mickel, Crosby Gamble, and a group of other Aves students.

"Declan!" Abria hollered, her voice carrying across the prairie.

Abria jumped into Declan's arms and said, "I'm so glad you're safe! How have you been?"

"We're okay, but Segars and Smiley are stuck down this cavern," Elena pointed. "Do you have any rope?"

"No, most of our supplies got lost in the last earthquake," Abria said. "An earthquake occurs every few minutes here, but they come so randomly we never know when or where it's going to happen."

"And there's no food or water on the island, at least not that we've found," Crosby added.

"We don't have much food or water left either," Declan said.

"Well, at least we know that we'll dehydrate, like, together," Abria said with a smile.

"Has anyone seen Pigg?" asked Elena while the others shook their heads. "I'm worried about him. I'm sort of imagining him tangled up in a tree, swinging from his parachute straps like Wheeler."

She pulled off her tactical vest and dropped it on the ground as Kidd made a face at her.

"That sounds like a fun story," Abria said leadingly.

So, Fergie explained how she and Kidd had landed on the jungle island and how he'd gotten his parachute stuck in a tree.

"And this one here," Declan said, nudging Elena lightly in the shoulder, "Flew the aerocraft to the island instead of jumping."

"Of course she did," Abria said.

"So, all the Firebirds are together now, except Pigg and Austin," Herbie said. "And we're still missing two from Harrier, three from Falcon, and Hunter."

"What are we going to do now?" Moriah asked. "Especially about Smiley and Segars down that hole?"

"I don't know," Elena said. "Without rope, I don't see how we can get them out."

"It's been one thing after another without any kind of real break," Vivienne grumbled. "It's like Marshall's really trying to kill us this time."

"Yeah, even with our rations we've basically been out of food and water for a day now," Abria said.

Elena sat in a heap. Her head dropped onto her tactical pack like it was a pillow. "I just need to sleep for a bit before we have to worry about finding water. Is that okay?"

"Me, too," Abria agreed as she also sat. "At least a twenty-minute nap would be great."

Elena was about to say that a two-hour nap would be better when she felt a rumble vibrate her eardrum. She sat up quickly as the earth began to tremble. Mighty rocks began to spring up from the ground like jagged spears.

"What do we do?" Declan hollered at Elena. "Should we try to run?"

Elena was up and felt ready to run, but the ground shook so violently that it was difficult for her to remain steady.

"We can't go anywhere!" Kidd called.

Elena's eyes locked with his. But before she could respond, Abria called, "Hey! Um...something is like..."

Elena looked over and noticed a strange look on Abria's face. She looked down at her feet. Before Elena could blink, the ground opened up and swallowed Abria whole.

"Abria!" Declan hollered as he tried to run toward the place where she fell, but the ground trembled with such force that they could barely stay on their feet.

In horror, Elena also watched Stacia, Kidd, and Crosby slip through the terrain, followed by a couple other students.

Minutes of uncontrollable shaking continued until finally the earth finished with a low grumble. Elena stood slowly while taking inventory of all they'd lost.

"All the tactical vests are gone!" Vivienne said hysterically.

"And most of our team," Elena added as shear desperation began to drown her insides.

Then, she noticed that Declan was crouched on the ground beside a deep cavern.

"Is Abria okay?" Elena shouted.

"No!" she heard Abria call from a place she could not see. "It's really dirty and gross down here!"

"What are we going to do now?" Declan asked.

"I don't know," Elena grumbled.

Then, she remembered that there was someone that could tell them what might happen next.

"Clucas! What happened last year when the Harriers couldn't finish the exam?"

Herbie looked at her with confusion on his face. "I'm not really sure. The simulation just kinda melted away. We *appeared* suddenly in one of the classrooms."

Elena felt discouraged by this news. If they couldn't figure a way out of this not only would they fail the exam, but she'd also suffer the embarrassment of not being allowed to finish.

"We should make a list of the fallen," Fergie said, breaking into her thoughts. "And then we should talk with the others about our options."

However, even after talking through many possible scenarios, no one from the Aves Company had come up with a single idea that could work. Elena curled her knees to her chest feeling tired and moody.

"We've been here almost a day with no water," Elena said. "It's over. We're going to fail."

"Well, we haven't failed yet because we're still here," Declan encouraged. "That means there must be something we can do to get out of this."

Elena closed her eyes, ready to admit defeat. "It would take a miracle."

Then, as if the rocks could hear her, a rumbling noise filled her ears. She thought it must be another earthquake until she noticed that the ground wasn't moving. Her eyes flew open and she was up on her feet. She recognized the noise.

"Help!" she screamed into the sky while waving her arms frantically. "Help! We're here! We're here!"

Then, an aerocraft appeared out of the blue and flew around the island. In the next moment, Declan and Fergie were on their feet also waving and screaming. Elena began to climb the nearest rock formation, hoping to get high enough to see if there was any kind of straight, flat place for the aerocraft to land. But before she could even finish climbing, the vehicle came down like a drop of rain on the earth, silently and with very little effort.

Elena's jaw dropped. Pigg was sitting in the pilot's seat waving excitedly at her.

¤ 15 ¤

The Savior

"Pigg!" Elena exclaimed when the door to the aerocraft opened and he stumbled out. "You're here!"

"Just barely," Pigg said. "Where's Austin? I need to show him this cut I have on my arm."

"No one has seen him," Elena said breathlessly. She was still in shock from seeing Pigg there with an aerocraft. "Do you have any rope in your supplies?"

"Yes, we have tons." Oscar Hunter's rough voice came from behind Pigg.

Elena watched him shove Pigg slightly out of the way. Then, Oscar stepped out and took a survey of the surroundings.

"Vaughn! Get over here," he hollered as he walked down a pile of gray boulder.

Garrett walked in Oscar's direction at once. Elena didn't even have time to feel angry as all the Raptors headed off in one direction as a group.

She hurried up to the aerocraft and threw an arm around Pigg's neck. "I was worried about you."

"I was worried about me, too," Pigg admitted as the other missing students of the Aves Company began to file out of the aerocraft.

Elena hurried into the cargo bay and began to frantically search through the supplies as Pigg dug into his pocket and pulled out a snack bar. She began to toss rope and climbing equipment out of the cargo bay door toward Declan and Fergie.

"Would you start to pull the others out of the cavern?" Elena asked them.

Without delay, her friends did as she instructed. After a tremendous amount of work, all the students that had been swallowed during the earthquake were pulled to safety.

Then, the Falcons moved off in one direction together and Harriers in another. The Firebirds all circled around Pigg begging him to tell them how it was that he came to fly the aerocraft.

"I was forced to make a terrible choice," said Pigg in earnest. "Jumping or attempting to fly it. I chose the thing that frightened me the least."

"Pigg, I'm impressed," said Declan. "Ransom was the only other person that thought to take the aerocraft."

"I think the word you're searching for is *shocked*," Kidd said rudely. Even though he'd just been rescued from one of the caverns he was still standing outside of their circle like he didn't want to be involved.

"At least he *flew* the aerocraft," said Elena sassily to Kidd. "Shouldn't that have been your first thought?"

"Pigg has done better than the rest of us and that warrants praise," Fergie said in an attempt to crush the ensuing argument.

"I'm glad to be back as a proper team." Pigg slid to the ground as if he were exhausted. Then, he tore the packaging off another snack bar and filled his cheeks. "Takes the pressure off having to make decisions."

"You had to *make decisions*?" Elena said incredulously.

Pigg nodded, looking nauseous at the memory.

"How did you convince the others to fly the aerocraft with you?" Abria asked as she sat beside him.

"All I said was I didn't want to starve to death and I didn't think I could carry enough of everything," said Pigg. "Then, I explained that I'd been taking

Simulab lessons with you, Elena, and they all seemed to feel a little more confident about my plan after that. Still, it wasn't an easy landing. Plus, I think Hunter might have wanted to choke me after the first night when I snuck into the food rations and ate all the trail mix."

Elena burst into giggles at the thought, and Abria and the other girls joined in for good measure.

"So, which island did you land on?" Declan asked.

"The one with lava," Pigg said. "It was absolutely terrifying. The first night we didn't really know that the mountain was going to spew lava and we were sort of sitting in the wrong place, so we had to climb back into the aerocraft and I attempted to fly it away from the lava, which sort of worked, except that there were too many of us and the aerocraft was overloaded with stuff in the cargo bay, so we came down like a rock on the island that was basically a desert wasteland with poisonous creatures. But the ship wasn't too badly damaged so we flew it outta there and have been searching for the rest of you ever since."

"So, how do we get off this island?" Frankie asked, looking at Elena.

"Yeah, how do we end the simulation, Ransom?" Vivienne asked.

"How should I know?" Elena said. "Why are you asking me?"

"Because without Haddock here you're sorta the leader," said Vivienne.

Elena blushed slightly and said, "At this point I think that ideas from everyone are absolutely necessary."

"May I suggest that we locate the nearest coastline?" Fergie said in a formal tone. "If we follow along the edge of this island at least we will be in sight of the other islands. We are still searching for Haddock."

"It's a better idea than staying around here to wait for the next earthquake," Elena said as her eyes scanned the thick forest on one side of the island. "Any thoughts on which direction to go first."

Declan shrugged. "I guess it doesn't matter."

"I would suggest we choose the easiest route," Fergie said.

"How are we going to convince the others to come?" Abria asked as she eyed the other Units.

"Well, Hunter will fight us no matter what we say," Declan said. "But we don't have to convince them. We just need to tell them what we're doing. If they want to come, they'll come."

"You've completely lost your mind!" was the first sentence out of Oscar Hunter's mouth when Elena relayed their idea to the entire Aves Company.

"We can't go walking around. What if we have another earthquake and lose everyone in a cavern?" said Ernest Darnell.

"We have to take some kind of risk. We can't stay on this island forever," said Elena.

"Plus, we need to locate a water source," Declan added.

"Not to mention the fact that we have no way to get to any of the other islands now," said Abria. "We need to find out where we are and where we need to be."

"We have all the supplies we need in the aerocraft!" Oscar said forcefully. "We should stay here and wait for more directions. I'm not going to allow you to lead the Raptors on a pointless quest through dangerous terrain."

"Listen Hunter!" said a voice, and Elena was surprised to see that Herbie from Harrier had stood up in the center of the group. "All the Harriers have acknowledged that Ransom's leadership tactics have gotten us this far. She showed bravery and sound judgment during this entire...whatever this is. Therefore, the Harriers have agreed to follow the Firebirds into our next portion of the exam, whatever that may be."

Unbelievably, Moriah Kirkley added, "The Falcons agree. We've all shared stories about how Ransom and Bowen have showed superior skill."

Elena's face was already beginning to turn red with pride, but then Garrett Vaughn added, "Ransom gave us the opportunity to make the exam a bit easier, but we refused. Bassi, and I have discussed it. We wanted to follow the rules, but sometimes the better choice is not following the directions. We're with her."

Ernest Darnell walked resolutely to stand behind Elena. Slowly but surely, all the members from every Unit walked or hobbled over to also stand behind her. Oscar was left alone.

"What do you say, Hunter?" Declan asked. "Want to help devise a plan to get us all out of here?"

Elena felt like Oscar had absolutely no choice left, unless he decided to be stubborn. She watched him closely. His face was red, either with anger or embarrassment she couldn't guess. He looked around at the rest of the Aves Company standing as a united front. She hoped Oscar would realize that he shouldn't try to contest their unanimous decision. But, as the seconds ticked by in silence, she couldn't help but hold her breath in anticipation.

"If I agree to this, don't think for a second that the Raptors will take blind orders from you, Ransom!" Oscar finally said.

"Of course I don't expect that," Elena replied. "Everyone has a right to their opinion toward our ongoing, everchanging plans."

After that, Elena and Declan talked with Oscar, Stella Grooms from Harrier, and Moriah Kirkley from Falcon about the food and supply distribution from the aerocraft while several others emptied out the fully stocked cargo bay.

One four person tent, four sleeping bags, hunting weapons, medical supplies, enough food for four people to share over the course of one week, and eight canteens of water were sorted and stacked.

"What are we going to do?" Elena asked as they looked over the supplies. "There isn't enough to go around."

After her question, Oscar and Herbie took turns shouting at one another about how best to divide the supplies. Moriah and Ernest inserted their opinions, but they mostly had to speak in raised voices to even be heard over the argument.

Elena watched the entire conversation with mixed feelings of frustration and amusement. She particularly liked that Oscar was red-faced and angry. But, she also felt that the argument was beginning to stretch on too long, and after a few minutes she just wanted them to shut their mouths.

"Can we just give everyone something to carry and figure out how to divide everything up after we find a water source?" Elena asked impatiently.

It seemed that everyone was surprised with Elena's direct, but simple request because no one said anything after that. Several people from each Company simply stepped forward to receive something to carry.

Without the immediate threat of another earthquake, the Aves Company started across the prairie land toward the tree line. When they reached the edge of the forest, they hurried between the trees but soon discovered that it was extremely dense and difficult to navigate.

After an hour of crawling over fallen trees and tangled brush they finally reached a long shoreline of rocks and black dirt. Elena peered off the edge of the island that overlooked the blue sky.

"There's literally no where to go," Elena grumbled.

"But look," Herbie said, pointing across the infinite blue. "That island doesn't seem too far."

Elena followed his line of sight to an object that she presumed was an island, but to her it seemed more like a massive configuration of walls with equal sides. The walls of the structure were shaped into patterns differing in size, and they looked similar to some of the symbols they'd learned in Phonology, as opposed to anything else she's seen in the simulation.

"And it seems a bit lower than us," added Moriah. She looked at Elena and Declan. "Do you think we could use the grappling hooks and zipline our way over?"

"Never gonna happen," Oscar said shortly. "The trajectory on the grappling hooks would never make it that far."

"This does seem like a good place to jump," said Elena slowly. "There's no harm in trying the hooks, right?"

"Maybe we should scout up and down this coastline first to see if there's anything better," Declan suggested.

"Look!" Abria suddenly gasped.

Standing on top of the island near them was an indistinct figure that was waving at them.

"It's Austin!" Elena shrieked.

Austin was trying to shout something to Elena and the others, but she couldn't even begin to guess what it was.

"What's that? What did he say?" Oscar asked Elena.

"I don't know," Elena admitted as she squinted her eyes to try and see him better. "I can barely see him, much less hear him."

As Austin began to make hand gestures and continued to shout at them, all the members of the Aves Company remained as silent as possible.

After several minutes, Oscar and some of the others tried to make guesses about what Austin might be trying to tell them. But, as the noise level grew with the different suggestion, Elena's irritation also grew. She closed her eyes and tried to think.

During their Level 2 training, the Firebirds *walked* through the wall of the simulation to end the exam. This year during Basic, Marshall had the trainees suffer through several weeks of jump training. And now they were on islands had some type of boundaries because Austin couldn't walk to them.

"I think we have to jump," Elena said quietly.

"Interesting theory," Fergie said. "Continue."

"I think we all have to jump together to end the simulation."

Oscar had been talking, but then he seemed to just catch a piece of Elena's suggestion because he turned toward her sharply and scoffed, "Jump? We can't jump that far."

"Not jump to the other island," Elena began. "We need to jump off the island."

Elena heard several people gasp and a buzz of noise as another argument broke out between a few of the leaders, but she didn't bother listening. She looked back to Austin. She could see him waving his arms and acting out his plan. She knew what he was trying to say.

In the blink of an eye, Austin backed away from the edge of the island. Then, he took a running leap off the edge and disappeared into the blue.

Feeling excited, Elena raced forward into the endless sky. She could hear people shouting from behind her, but she never turned back. She didn't even spare a moment to feel fear that there was no ground beneath her.

Then, as she neared the place where Austin had vanished, she suddenly realized that she was falling.

◘ 16 ◘

Harleston Village

Elena felt adrenaline surge through her body. She noticed Austin below her, but it looked as if he were merely resting against a blue sky. The wind pressing her face and ears helped to remind her that she was still falling, but she also experienced the sensation of floating weightlessly. Free falling into nothing but blue seemed to have limitless possibilities. But yet, there was no way for Elena to tell where they were or how far they had to go. The thought of falling and never landing was suddenly terrifying.

Elena wanted to scream for Austin. However, just as she realized that he would never be able to hear her, she felt an intense prickling of electricity. A moment later, she was looking down on the Grimsby campus. She saw the top of Austin's parachute, so she deployed hers as well. Her breath caught in her chest momentarily as the chute caught the wind, tugging her upward. But then she floated easily to the ground, landing in perfect formation.

"That was the weirdest thing ever," she called to Austin who was standing a few feet away.

Then, all around them, the forty-five other members of the Aves Company touched their feet to the ground.

Elena was just about to smile and congratulate Austin on figuring out the riddle of the simulation when she saw three figures marching across the field toward them. Hannibal was out front looking serious and steady with Hopper and Marshall following closely behind him.

"Oh, no!" Pigg groaned suddenly. "Are we in trouble?"

"Aves Company! Stand at attention!" Hannibal called.

As they hurried to form lines, Hannibal stood before them looking displeased. He tugged his perfectly tailored military coat in a downward motion, as if he were trying to straighten it more. He cleared his throat loudly. He surveyed them in silence. Then, surprisingly, he began to applaud.

"Congratulations!" Hannibal praised. "That was truly inspired teamwork."

Elena took a quick second to steal a smile with Austin.

"Yeah, dudes! Neither of the other Companies are even finished yet," Hopper added.

"The Aves Company will go on record for completing this simulation faster than any other Unit in the history of the program," said Hannibal as he smiled genuinely. "The Aves Company has far exceeded Grimsby expectations. You are dismissed for your second quarter break. You have earned it."

At breakfast the next morning, Elena felt tired and thankful that they had a full week break. Declan was busy telling some of the more interesting parts of their exam and was making everyone laugh. But it wasn't until he started doing impressions of Elena cutting Kidd out of the tree that milk actually shot out of Pigg's nose.

When there was finally a lull in the conversation, Austin set his fork down. "So, who wants to go down to the Station to..." he began, but Pigg interrupted him.

"Austin, this past quarter I had to spend more than an acceptable amount of time in harnesses, doing crazy tricks from high in the air; we just got back from an exam during which I was alone with hostile teammates, for several days I might add, and I was forced into several situations that made me so uncomfortable that I've actually begun to have a nervous twitch. See my eye?"

Pigg pointed with his index finger to his left eye, which looked like it was having a spasm. "It's only by some miracle that I'm actually alive today. So, I'm going to Harleston Village to celebrate by stuffing my face until I can't walk. And I'm not going to do anything else."

He looked so serious that Elena couldn't help but snicker. Austin eyed Elena briefly, and then smiled.

"You're absolutely right, Pigg. We deserve a break."

"Really?" Abria squealed. She clapped her hands together quickly and giggled. "Finally, someone is speaking my language."

Elena had never been to Harleston Village, but Abria had been often enough to brag about it so she felt she knew what the city would be like. However, as she stepped off the Grimsby Channel, Elena realized right away that the place was less of a village and more like a city.

Sand colored abodes were ornamented with wooden timbers sticking out of the walls, seemingly there to support the fire-blown, red brick roofs. The streets were lined with red brick and white sand. Flat, stacked-stone lined courtyards and business buildings. She noticed many sparkling pools shaped in elegant designs and fountains of shooting water. The sidewalks were paved with patterned mosaics and whimsically-shaped green bushes.

"Those are called *palm trees*," Abria said as she led them along at top speed. "And those funny little things with the pointy spikes are called *cactus*. Those are just small ones. I'll take you over to Carnival later and show you a forest of cactus that stand thirty feet tall!"

Abria pointed vaguely off in the distance where Elena could see a monumental, multi-tiered staircase that was aligned with flowers, which led down to miles of low land and then strange mountainous rock formations growing out of the ground.

"Oh! And there's my absolute favorite," she pointed in yet another direction. "See those strange, wholly red rocks? Those are called *lava rocks* and the townspeople use them as decoration, the same way that we use flowers and plants in the Galilee Province. I find it so fascinating."

Elena wanted to say that she didn't find rocks fascinating in the slightest, but Abria was already talking about the next thing.

"And OH! Look!" she squealed in Elena's ear. "The jugglers are out today!"

Elena saw a scene that couldn't be described as anything more or less than a festival. Brightly colored flags were strung across streets and between buildings. Jugglers, acrobats, and magicians roamed the streets looking for applause.

Women in brightly colored skirts beckoned people to purchase goods from umbrella topped booths. The air was filled with cumin, coriander, and oregano spices. Red and green chilies were strung on wire, and Optivision signs advertised woven baskets and turquoise jewelry.

Elena could feel people watching her as she moved through the crowd. No doubt her red hair and freckles stood out oddly amongst the black and blonde haired people. She was glad to be with her friends because, similar to school, Abria and Declan seemed to know everyone.

At one cart a woman with humongous topaz earring gave them each a free piece of fried dough with honey drizzled over it. At another cart, Elena dipped a warmed flour tortilla in melted white cheese that burned a spot on the roof of her mouth. And, at yet another wagon, she dunked crunchy, triangular chips into red and green sauces.

"Do you smell that?" Pigg said loudly.

Elena sighed impatiently, "There are a million smells going on here. It's impossible to know what you're..." But before she could finish, Pigg ducked under one of the cart umbrellas that had a sign that read *churro*.

"I know it's good," Abria said. "But we shouldn't fill up on just desserts." She took the rest of the churro out of Pigg's hand just before he took a second bite and handed it to Austin. "There's so much amazing food to taste."

"Abria, let's take them over to that little place with the dancing fountains," Declan suggested. "They have the best food in town."

Trying to keep Pigg from devouring something from each of the food carts they passed was difficult.

But Elena couldn't watch him the entire time because she was in awe over the richness of the blue mosaic tiles that were inlaid into the city walls, the water that spurted out from the street like it was playing a game, the beautifully flamboyant colored clothing that was simple and free flowing, and the loud, unruly collection of voices that rung out through the streets.

Eventually, they came to a cluster of beautifully ornate buildings. Yet another multi-tiered staircase extended between the buildings. These stairs were dotted with people in varying stages of relaxation.

Elena and her friends quickly descended into a courtyard where people were crammed together, sitting around small tables.

"So, they have this amazing thing called mango salsa," Abria began as they squeezed into a table at the far end of the restaurant. "Totally delish! And we can order a bowl of melted cheese and jalapeno, which is a spicy pepper. And whatever you order for lunch, make sure you ask for extra guacamole."

"You just said a bunch of words that I didn't understand," Pigg said. "But I'm willing to try anything you put in front of me."

"Well, I like the green chile cheeseburger with some tamales on the side," said Declan.

"A cheeseburger sounds harmless," said Elena. "But what's a *tamales?*"

"It's meat rolled in cornmeal dough and then wrapped in a, like, corn husk and steamed. So totally yum."

"This place has opened up a whole new world of culinary options to me," Pigg said in awe.

Then, he simply gaped at Abria as she ordered almost everything on the menu. Within minutes, their tiny table was brimming with plates of food. Elena had a hard time making a first selection, but soon enough, her plate was full.

As she bent forward to take a bite of her fried corn tortilla with chicken she had a strange feeling that she was being watched. She looked up quickly. Pamela "Melly" Linus was standing across the room. Her expressive blue eyes were fixed on Elena in a way that made her feel that Melly wanted to hurt her.

Elena almost fell out of her chair, but at that exact moment Pigg let out a loud groan. She looked down to see that he'd spilled the bowl of melted cheese all over the table.

Elena leapt up from the table as Melly turned to leave. She hurried across the restaurant without speaking a word to anyone and into the busy street looking for her former roommate. Elena searched but didn't catch Melly at first sight. She jumped up and down on the balls of her feet, but there were so many people that she couldn't see Melly anywhere.

"What are you doing?" Austin had suddenly arrived at her side.

Elena frowned at him. "I thought I saw Melly."

"Where?" Austin said, searching the streets.

"She was in the restaurant. But, then she just ran off."

Austin eyed Elena seriously. "How could she be here, or anywhere, if she doesn't exist?"

"Maybe she doesn't exist in Crowfield Plantation, but I saw her in the restaurant. I want to know why."

"Well, she's not here now," Austin replied. "Let's get back to the table. We can't do anything unless we see her again anyway."

Reluctantly, Elena followed Austin back to the table to finish their meal, but she was so distracted by seeing Melly that she couldn't eat another bite. She pushed beans around her plate with her fork while her friends discussed shopping and wondered why Austin had been so quick to dismiss the fact that she'd seen Melly.

After a while, Declan slurped his fizzy beverage infusion loudly and said, "So, I've been thinking…"

But before he could continue Abria said, "Uh oh, he has his 'let's get into trouble' voice on."

Elena actually smiled a little and looked at Austin, who smiled back at her. Pigg, however, laughed nervously and stuffed another chip into his mouth.

"Not too much trouble," said Declan. "I've been thinking that we could just go over to Horlbeck Alley to bet on the races."

"What's Horlbeck Alley?" Pigg asked suspiciously.

"It is an arena where patrons go to wager money or property on an event with an uncertain outcome," Fergie said.

"She means it's where all the awesome people go to watch races," Declan said. "I guess *some* people gamble, but we could just watch the competition."

"Students are forbidden to go there," Fergie added.

"True, but no one will find out that we were there if we don't say anything," Declan replied.

"Isn't that where Wheeler got caught flying during our first year of school?" Elena asked, and Declan nodded. "He was almost expelled!"

"We should go," said Austin, pushing back from the table and looking full.

"Austin!" Elena screeched. "I can't believe you're agreeing to this."

"Why? You don't want to go?" he asked.

"Of course I want to go…" Elena said, though secretly she only wanted an excuse to search the city for signs of Melly. "But, we'd have to assume that Pigg won't snitch on us. I doubt that's even possible."

"I won't tell," Pigg whined.

Abria flipped her hair and said, "Oh, like you didn't tell on us in Emerald's class for tasting the flowers from the honeysuckle plant."

"I didn't tell on you," Pigg said defensively. "I was having an allergic reaction to the honeysuckle and had to ask Emerald to see the nurse. I didn't *mean* to tell him that you had tasted it also. And then, once I'd said it, he wouldn't let me leave until…"

"Come on," Declan said, cutting Pigg's story off impatiently. "We're wasting precious time. If we want to go, we've got to get back before the Grimsby Channel leaves."

He began to make his way out of the restaurant and onto the street.

"I don't know, Elena," Pigg said feebly as he grabbed her arm so she couldn't stand from the table. "What if we get in trouble? Or what if we can't get back to the Grimsby Channel on time?"

"You can go back now if you want," said Elena as she followed Declan. Her urge to find Melly was stronger than any argument Pigg could make.

"Well, that leaves me little choice. You know that I'm too afraid to go on the train alone," Pigg said weakly.

As it turned out, Horlbeck Alley looked nothing like what Elena expected. For her, the word "alley" conjured thoughts of small, confined spaces. But this place had three sides of stadium rows to seat people. The fourth side of the arena opened into what appeared to be a desert that stretched into oblivion. The roar of a thousand people speaking filled the air.

"Look, there are the autoflyers!" Declan said excitedly as he pointed down the way toward the beginning of the track.

"What's an autoflyer?" Elena asked, as she took a seat beside him in the stands.

"See those sleek transports?" Declan pointed to a long row of vessels with curved roofs and thin wings jutting out from the side. "The red with silver stripes is a favorite to win at every single race."

Austin pointed suddenly and called, "Isn't that Wheeler?"

Elena turned to the left and, sure enough, Kidd Wheeler was just bending over the hood of one of the autoflyers.

"Yes it is!" Elena said, feeling instantly angry. She marched away from her seat and pushed her way through the crowd of people straight to Kidd. For some unexplainable reason, his presence upset her.

"What are you doing here?" Kidd barked when noticed her approaching.

"I could ask you the same thing, Wheeler!" she spat. "Are you trying to get yourself in trouble again?"

"What's it to you if I am?"

"I could care less if you got kicked out of school," Elena said brusquely. "But the Firebirds have already lost Melly. We can't afford to lose another member. You'll ruin our chances of getting a good spot in Special Ops. And if you think that I want to be taking orders from someone like Hun..."

Kidd didn't give Elena a chance to finish her sentence before he turned and stomped off.

As he walked away, Elena finally realized why it bothered her so much that Kidd was there.

"You ran off again," Austin said, coming up behind her.

"Do you think it's strange that I saw Melly today for the first time in months and Wheeler is also here?"

"Why would it be weird?"

"Listen, we went after the Tablets of Destiny because of the photograph in Melly's closet. Then, Wheeler tells us that he knows that the Tablets are on Tavington's farm, but he won't take us there. It's a little suspicious, right?"

"Are you saying that you think Wheeler and Melly are working together?" Austin asked as he began to direct Elena back to their seats.

"Maybe. Maybe they're even working for Imperator," Elena said, though she was having a hard time thinking about it because of the noise in the arena. "I wish I knew if Melly's parents were in that old photograph of the Renegades. Then, we'd know for sure if they had anything to do with the artifacts."

Moments later, Elena was seated. She felt the arena come alive with the energy of the crowd as the autoflyers took their positions on the starting line. After a flag was dropped, the race began. As the autoflyers took off out of the stadium, massive Optivision screens began to display images from the course and highlights from the various vehicles.

Immediately, it was clear that Kidd was quick witted when it came to flying. He pulled in front immediately. Any time another vehicle got too close he'd purposely turn into them, which caused several collisions. Elena decided quickly that racing was a strange contest along a complicated course of flying through and around obstacles.

"Would you like a chocolate dipped cricket?" said Pigg, leaning toward Elena. He had chocolate smeared all over his face. "They actually *dipped* crickets in chocolate. It sounded so disgusting that I had to try it. Such an interesting flavor..."

"Ew...no!" Elena pushed his hand away.

He shrugged and popped the insect into his mouth just as a wave of noise rose up through the crowd. The clapping of hands and stomping of feet was so intense that Elena covered her ears.

"What happened?" Elena screamed to Declan.

He dropped his mouth to her ear and hollered, "The race is over. And Wheeler actually won!"

Elena watched all the autoflyers stop in a row. Then, the drivers from each vehicle stepped out and dispersed into a dozen different directions. But Kidd strutted toward a small booth and stuck his Trademark arm through a window. Some men grouped around him, looking surly. From her seat, Elena could tell that an argument was occurring.

"What's Wheeler doing?" Elena asked Declan.

"Getting paid," Declan said. "The drivers trade for vehicles and parts and stuff like that. But I don't know who those men are. Looks like they're fighting, doesn't it?"

"I'm not surprised," Elena said.

"We should get back soon," Fergie called out. "The train leaves the station in forty-seven minutes, twenty-one seconds."

However, just as Elena turned to follow Fergie, Austin cried out, "Those guys just grabbed Wheeler!"

▢ 17 ▢

The Tablets of Destiny

Elena noticed that Kidd appeared to struggle against the men that had grabbed him by the arms. A moment later, they all disappeared down a side alley, completely out of sight.

"Should we follow them?" Declan asked Austin.

"What? Why?" Elena said moodily.

"To see if Wheeler is okay, of course," Declan replied.

"We can't go after him," Elena said. "We're not even supposed to be here in the first place. And he certainly isn't supposed to be flying. If we go after him someone might see us, and then we'll get in trouble. Let's just go back to school."

"That's a good idea," Pigg agreed.

"We can't just leave him with those, like, people," said Abria.

"Speak for yourself," Elena grumbled.

"But they could really hurt him," Abria said. "I saw, like, five guys or something."

"In fact, there were seven of them," Fergie said in a formal tone. "I believe we could take a calculated risk to free him from his captors."

"I'm not willing to risk any one of us for him," said Elena stubbornly.

"He's in trouble, Lena," Austin said, looking her in the eyes. "And he's one of us. What would you want us to do if you were in there?"

"Oh, alright!" Elena half screamed. She sighed heavily and added, "I guess we have to get him."

Austin and Declan took the lead across the sidewalks outside the stadium. Elena followed behind them closely through a forest of umbrella-topped marketplace booths. The Firebirds slinked along a side alley in the military style formation that they'd been taught at school, looking and listening hard until they finally heard several raised voices coming from a sandstone colored building with warehouse style windows.

Elena eased down the side of the building, behind Austin and Declan, where they stopped at a low window. She peered through a partially covered pane and saw instantly that Kidd was tied to a chair. A skinny man was yelling at Kidd. Then, the guy raised a fist and punched Kidd in the face.

"I count seven, just like Fergie said," Austin said.

"What are we going to, like, do?" Abria whispered.

"I think we should go back to school," Pigg said nervously.

"No, I mean, how are we going to get him outta there?" Abria said impatiently.

"Wheeler looks like he has everything under control," Pigg said.

"He's *tied* to a *chair!*" Declan said. "And he's bleeding. And he looks half unconscious."

"I don't see your point," Pigg replied.

Austin, who had been assessing the alleyway in complete silence, suddenly said, "I have an idea. Abria and Elena, here's what I want you to do."

Thirty seconds later, Abria pressed some gloss on her lips, fluffed her hair, and then pushed through the door to the room where Kidd was being held. She stumbled over the threshold and laughed loudly like a fool.

"Jane, it's just through, like, here!" Abria shrieked in a girlish voice.

Elena followed Abria inside the room. The situation was grim; Kidd's face was a mess of blood, and his right eye was swollen shut. He was slumped sideways in the chair so it was hard for Elena to tell if he'd even seen that they'd entered the room. The men appeared to be so shocked by the sudden interruption that they hadn't reacted to Abria's presence at all.

"Susan, I think we took a wrong turn," said Elena, putting on her best imitation of Abria's girly voice. She made eye contact with one of the men in the room and forced her voice to remain calm as she said innocently, "This doesn't look like the chocolate shop."

"Excuse us, boys," Abria said sweetly, giving a subtle flip of her hair. "Could one of you give us directions? We're totally, like, lost."

She moved around the men easily. Elena admired her confidence. Then, she stopped at one of the younger men and put her hand on his arm.

"You look helpful."

He smiled at her sheepishly, and that's when the ambush began. Before Elena could react, Abria popped the guy in the face and slammed him to the floor, and then moved on to the man standing beside him. As Elena sideswiped the feet out from under the man beside her, Austin and Declan rushed the room and joined in the fighting. Moments later, the seven men were all on the floor, completely unconscious.

Austin hurried over to Kidd. He pushed one of Kidd's eyelids up to check his pupils. "He's not responsive, but at least he's breathing. Bowen, help me get him to the floor."

Declan immediately began to untie Kidd.

"This is the best place to fix him. If we take him out on the street looking like this we'll draw too much attention." Austin stripped off his armor wear shirt, revealing several zipper pockets that were sewn into the fabric of his undershirt.

"You're wearing a body bubble?" Elena asked, stepping closer to see if she could help.

Kidd had an angry bruise coming in under one eye and a deep gash in his forehead and upper lip.

"After what happened in Turkey with the cave in I started wearing it all the time," said Austin. "Bowen and Pigg, would you watch the door to make sure we're not interrupted?" He pulled some gauze from one of his pockets. "Lena, use this to apply pressure to his forehead while I fix his lip."

Elena watched Austin wipe the blood from Kidd's mouth. Then, he moved the Suturand over Kidd's lip, slowly stitching his cuts. Then, he dabbed some ointment under Kidd's eye and the swelling began to diminish.

"Why would they beat him so, like, badly?" Abria asked.

"I guess those guys didn't like to lose to a *kid*," said Declan.

"We can also assume that Wheeler has won frequently," Fergie said. "Perhaps they grew unhappy having to pay him."

"You mean they were jealous?" Elena asked. "Jealousy sounds like a girl's game."

"Trust me, guys can be jealous," Declan said. "We just handle it with fists instead of gossip."

"Whatever the reason," said Austin, as he began to stitch Kidd's forehead. "At least he's not hurt badly. Because that would be hard to explain to Hannibal or Headmaster Bentley."

When Austin was finally finished, Kidd still had a bruise under his eye, but the laceration on his head and lip were completely gone. He moved the Suturand over Kidd's head. Then, he pushed back the lid on Kidd's unhurt eye.

"He has a minor concussion, but I can't do anything about that here."

"Is he safe to move?" Pigg asked. "Because we might miss the last train back."

"He'll be fine," Austin said. "Bowen, help me get him up."

Soon, Elena and her friends were back on the street headed back toward the Grimsby Channel. Austin was lodged under one of Kidd's shoulders and Declan under the other. They received some curious looks as they walked back through town with an unconscious boy, but no one stopped them. Once they were safely on the train, Austin and Declan sat Kidd upright in one of the chairs and let his head slump over toward the window.

When the Grimsby Channel finally pulled into the campus station, Elena noticed that Hopper seemed to be waiting for something on the platform. When she stepped off the train, Elena realized that he was, in fact, waiting for them because he rushed toward them.

"What happened to Wheeler?"

"He slipped and fell down the stairs at Harleston Village," Elena invented before anyone else could speak. "You know the stone ones with all the flowers?"

"There are one hundred and thirty-five stairs," Fergie added formally. "And I believe that he tripped at step forty-seven. It was not a graceful descent."

"He has a minor concussion," Austin said.

Hopper shook his head and rolled his eyes. "You rugrats are always getting in trouble. Come on, let's get him up to Medical."

As Austin and Declan followed Hopper toward their resident tower, Elena let out a sigh of relief.

"He's right, you know," said Pigg. "We do seem to always be in trouble."

"Maybe Wheeler will be, like, nicer to us now," Abria said brightly.

But, the next morning at breakfast, it was clear that Kidd was still determined not to be friendly. His eye only had a hint of a bruise and he seemed to be in good health, but he wouldn't even acknowledge Elena or her friends. Not even to say thank you.

"Did he make it back to the room last night for bed?" Elena asked.

"Yep," Declan said shortly.

"Annndddd…" Elena said leadingly. "Did he say *thank you*, or anything?"

"Not a word," Austin said.

Elena's attitude toward Kidd continued to get worse as the Firebirds began their third quarter on the first day of the second week of the seventh month.

As she arrived in Booker's classroom, it was clear that Kidd was still planning to ignore them because he was sitting alone in the far corner of the room with his face down.

However, she wasn't able to fixate on him long because her pupil station screens began to come alive as the Instructor presented the class with the longest assignment that she'd ever seen.

"From now until the end of your Level 3 studies you will work on your most intensive project to date," said Booker. "Similar to your Level 2 studies, you will design a simulation that the entire class will experience. Your simulation will be based on a particular event or civilization in history."

Elena's Optivision screen morphed into an image of a round flat object that was the size of the coins they'd studied about in ancient Rome.

"These discs are called *neurolizors*. They are worn on the back of the neck like so." Booker placed the device just below his skull. "When you enter the simulation wearing the neurolizor, the lesson will come alive in a new way to you.

"In addition to the simulation, you will also program a neurolizor for each member of the Aves Company so that they may participate in your simulation."

Elena stared at the little, round neurolizor and began to chew her nails. She felt her confidence plummet. If this project was so complicated that it took two quarters to design, she was sure that she was doomed to failure.

"If you build the character layers correctly, the neurolizor will allow each student to act out the time period of your simulation. Each character must participate in dialogue and a historical activity such as preparing food, crafting weapons, caring for livestock, fighting in war, and the like.

"We will cover the following topics: Imperial Japan, the Mongol Empire, the emerging temple kingdoms in India, the Ottoman Empire..."

For Elena, Booker's voice faded away as she realized that she could get Pigg to help her with the program writing, especially now that Melly was no longer there. She was feeling slightly more cheerful until she realized that Booker was beginning to talk about group work.

"You will be divided into groups of four. Your groups and assignments will be chosen at random. After they appear on your Optivision screen, move around the room and find your group. Then, you may get started on the project as soon as you wish. Best of luck to you all."

Elena's Optivision screen morphed and she saw her face along with Stacia Bassi from Harrier, Garrett Vaughn from Falcon, and Oscar Hunter from Raptor.

Her body convulsed into a full body pout. She absolutely did not want to work with Oscar! And after Stacia and Garrett jumped from the aerocraft during their second quarter exam she wasn't really thrilled about working with them either.

"This is the worst group selection ever," Oscar Hunter said from behind Elena.

"Tell me how you really feel about it," Elena said sarcastically as she turned to face him.

Stacia and Garrett were standing on either side of Oscar looking unhappy as well.

"I really don't see what any of you will contribute to this project," Oscar said rudely. "The simulation I did last year was the best out of the Aves Company. *That* was truly gifted teamwork. So, why don't we make a deal that you three let me handle all the major program writing?"

Stacia and Garrett looked just as offended as Elena felt as they watched Oscar turn and walk away from them.

"Does that mean the meeting is adjourned?" Stacia said.

"No!" Elena replied. "We're responsible for this project just as much as him. And since I don't agree that his simulation was the best last year, I'll be writing at least some of this program."

"Me, too," Garrett said forcefully. "My group had a great simulation last time around. I'm not letting Hunter do it all his own way." Then, he looked at Elena very seriously. "Look, I made a mistake by jumping outta the aerocraft on our last exam. I'm not saying I fully trust your decision-making abilities, but I trust you more than Hunter. So, if you're willing to work together fairly then I'm willing to work with you."

Elena nodded and, to her surprise, Stacia did as well.

"Okay, we have to learn everything we can about the Chinese civilization from between 1300 and 1500 A.D.," said Garrett. "So, we'll work on it during class with Hunter and maybe meet just the three of us in the Media Lab after classes as much as we need to so our project is perfect."

"Sounds like a good idea to me," Elena said.

Elena really wanted to go punch Oscar in the face for being so awful, but instead she asked her friends to meet her at the Firebird Station so that she could gripe about how awful this third quarter of school was sure to turn out.

"I can't believe I have to work with Hunter!" Elena threw herself back into one of the chairs in the main living area. "It's like Hannibal is trying to punish me or something."

"They said the selection was, like, random," Abria said, sitting in a chair across from her.

"Yeah, right." Elena grumbled.

"All the kids in my group scare me," said Pigg from the Station kitchen as he began to make a snack.

"I got that girl from Harrier who has a crush on me. She's always grabbing my arm while I'm trying to use the Optivision screen," Declan said moodily.

"The whole project seems really complex," said Austin. He looked at Fergie and Pigg. "I'm assuming you both understand how the basic components go together to write the simulation and program the neurolizors?"

"Yes," Pigg and Fergie said together.

"Alright. Well, we can just tutor with Pigg and Fergie to get the mechanics down before and after class," suggested Austin. "That way we can all help each other out."

There was a general murmur of agreement.

"Now that that's settled, can we talk about what we're going to do about Wheeler?" Austin said.

"What's to talk about?" Elena said moodily. "We saved him but he's still awful to us. There's nothing we can do about that."

"Some people have a hard time accepting help," Austin said imploringly. "You can understand that, right Lena?"

"I'll never understand him," Elena replied stubbornly.

"Maybe we could bribe Wheeler to take us to Tavington's farm now that we've saved his life," Declan suggested.

"Oh, I love a good bribe and all the, like, scandal that goes with it," said Abria.

"Technically, an offer to Wheeler would not be considered a bribe," Fergie pointed out. "It would be considered *blackmail* because we would threaten to tell Hannibal about his participation in the races in Horlbeck Alley unless he meets our demand of going to Tavington's farm."

"We're not going to bribe him or blackmail him or threaten him in any way," Austin laughed. "We didn't save him because we need something. We saved him because he's our friend, even if he doesn't know it yet."

"I'm glad to hear you say that."

Elena turned sharply and saw Kidd standing in the entrance hallway of the Firebird Station.

"What are you doing here?" Elena asked gruffly.

"Look, you could have left me in Horlbeck Alley with the gamblers, but you fixed me up and brought me back. I owe you a debt and since we already know the price, I figured it would be better to get it over with now."

"Are you saying what I, like, think you're saying?" Abria asked.

Kidd rolled his eyes. "Yes, for those of us that are blonde, I'm saying that I'll help you get to Tavington's farm to find the Tablets, or whatever." He looked pointedly at Austin. "But that's it! Then, we're even."

Austin rose from his chair and crossed the room where he held out his hand so that Kidd could shake it.

"We can't go there without a military style game plan," Kidd warned. "Tavington won't let his artifacts go, and if he finds out we took something he'll hunt us down to kill us."

Pigg let out a gasp. "Seriously?"

"Yes, I'm being very serious. He's a wicked, ruthless person," Kidd moved around the room. "Let's put it this way, Tavington makes Major Marshall look like the pink glitter that Abria puts on her nails."

"So, break it down for us," Austin said.

"First, it would be best if we can make a replica of the Tablets of Destiny so we can replace the real one with a fake one."

"That is achievable," Fergie said.

"Second, we have an issue of getting in and out of his Vault undetected. I haven't been inside since I was young, but I'm sure that it's wired with sirens. Plus, I don't exactly know where the entrance to the Vault is located or how to get inside."

"So, we need a schematic of Tavington's house," Austin said. "Any ideas on how we can get that?"

Kidd shook his head. "I'm not good with all that technical stuff. But I know two people that are." He looked at Pigg and Fergie. "If you could figure out a way for us to watch Tavington for a while, kind of like surveillance, then we'd be able to find out where the Vault is and how he gets inside."

"We will require some time to think about how best to accomplish that request," Fergie said.

"Okay, so even if we can make a fake artifact and we can figure out how to get inside his Vault, we still need a reason to go there in the first place," Kidd said.

"Can't you just say you're home for a visit?" Elena asked.

"No, he knows I hate it there," Kidd said. "I only go back when I have to."

"So, what excuse should we give?" Austin said.

"I've thought about it a bit," said Kidd. "Look, you already have the Amulet, right? But Tavington doesn't know that. So, we say we came to ask him if he knows where the Amulet is located. He's a collector, so the artifact will pique his interest."

"When you say 'we' would tell Tavington, do you mean that all of us would go?" Austin asked.

"No, just me," Kidd said, and then looking steadily at Elena, added, "And Freckles."

Stunned silence settled over the room, until she finally said, "Me? You want me to go with you? Why?"

"Because, you've been there before," Kidd said. "And because Truman Ransom came to Tavington's farm almost every day while he was alive."

⌒ 18 ⌒

Androids

On the sixth day of the first week of the eighth month, Elena gathered with her friends in the Firebird Station.

Over a week had passed since Kidd told them that Elena's dad had been some kind of colleague or accomplice of Tavington's, but he hadn't known much about their business dealings. In addition, he'd seemed reluctant to tell Elena and her friends more about Tavington until they'd formulated some kind of plan for getting onto his farm.

"Pigg and I have spent a fair bit of time deciding how best to perform surveillance on Tavington's farm," Fergie started in a formal tone. "And we have decided on an *android*."

In one hand, Fergie held up a tiny ball that wasn't any larger than a Touchdot, and Pigg stood beside her with a laser pointer. From between Fergie's fingers, little legs sprang forth like an eight-legged insect.

"Fergie and I put a masquerade on each of these little beauties so they will blend into the environment and, oh look at that." Pigg touched the screen on his Touchdot and Elena could no longer see the little dot between Fergie's fingers. "Now it's invisible."

"How did you get this together so fast?" Abria asked.

"Oh, they were already in the Research & Development room," Pigg said offhandedly. "We just made some slight modifications."

"So, Tavington won't be able to see them, but can he detect them in other ways?" Austin asked.

"No, the androids receive a signal from our private Orbitor so Tavington won't be able to detect them," Fergie supplied.

"The androids will attach to your shoes," said Pigg. "As soon as you pass through the door they'll detach and get to work."

"Truly amazing!" Austin praised Pigg and Fergie. "Okay, Wheeler, you're next."

Kidd pulled up an Optivision and a map of the underground of Atlanson appeared.

"Freckles and I will leave from Sector 7 and make our way to Sector 12," Kidd began.

"Huh?" Elena blurted. "Where exactly are we going?"

"This is the way to get to Tavington's farm," Kidd said. "He's not expecting us, but he'll know we're coming once we've entered his fragment..."

"Slow down," Elena interrupted. "Are we talking about the same farm that my dad took me to? The one in the woods?"

"Yes," Kidd replied.

"So, you expect me to believe that there's some kinda forest growing in Atlanson's underground?"

"Yes, it's sorta like that," Kidd said. "But because the farm is inside the fragment it can really be anything that..."

"Wait...wait..." Elena held her hand up. "What's a *fragment*, exactly?"

"I don't know what it is," Kidd admitted. "I only know what I overhear from Tavington and what I've seen with my eyes."

Elena was surprised when no one, including Austin, questioned Kidd about this, but she decided not to press the topic. The whole trip in general made her nervous. Being alone with Kidd on a farm in the middle of nowhere seemed life threatening.

But honestly, Elena barely had time to worry about the trip because her classwork was increasing and the code she was creating for the neurolizors was getting categorically complicated.

Pigg had been a huge help explaining how the code needed to be written to make the simulation and neurolizors synchronize together, but the intricate details of each line of code was almost too much for Elena's brain to handle. She tried as hard as she could to focus during his tutoring, but the whole concept of fitting an entire role-play simulation onto a disk the size of a coin seemed impossible.

Fortunately, Pigg had taught Elena some programming shortcuts so creating the scenery and costuming was a little easier to manage. Still, thinking up activities and dialogue for the forty-six other students in the Aves Company was a challenge. For instance, Pigg would never be good in battle, and she doubted that Abria would ever be accomplished at being a laundry woman. She didn't feel that she had enough creative ability to write enough. The words just wouldn't come.

"I am NOT looking forward to our neurolizor simulation in class tomorrow," Elena grumbled as she closed out the code work on her Optivision screen. She and her friends had been crowded around one table in the Media Lab for over three hours working on their simulations. "Hunter thinks he knows what he's doing, but I've seen the basic code he's written so far, and it looks wrong."

"All the others in my group still scare me," Pigg mumbled.

"Maybe you could take Hunter aside and show him your coding to see if he can tell the difference," Austin suggested.

"Oh, that would be a really pleasant conversation," Elena said sarcastically. "'Hey Hunter, want to come look at what I'm doing so that you can see what a big dimwit you are.' Somehow, I don't think he'd be receptive to my constructive criticism."

"You know, just when I'd finally worked up the courage to ask Frankie Smiley to go to Harleston Village with me on our next break, I completely changed my mind," Abria said absentmindedly. "We've been talking and laughing together a lot lately. In fact, he told this one joke the other day, and I laughed so hard I think I pulled a muscle in my, like, stomach." She giggled loudly, causing some angry glances from students at other tables to come their way. "So, I was beginning to feel like I was 'in like' with him and not just 'infatuated,' but today he told me that he only showers every other day, and I'm wondering if I could really like someone with questionable hygiene habits."

"When is this nauseating story going to end?" Elena said. "Some people at this table have *actual* problems."

"Elena, just tell Hunter that he's a dimwit," Abria said, almost impatiently. "It's not like you have a problem hurting people's feelings." She closed out her session and hopped up from her chair, leaving their table without another word.

"She's right, you know," Elena said thoughtfully. "I don't care about hurting feelings."

"And apparently you are, in addition, oblivious when you cause pain to your own friends," Fergie said.

"Nah, I understood her subtle message," Elena remarked. "But she just got up and ran off so quickly. I don't have the energy to catch her. I'll apologize later for not giving my fullest attention to her riveting story about the ongoing, confused feelings she has about our very own Frankie Smiley."

The others laughed and shook their heads at her.

"Maybe I'll get lucky when everyone in my group sees my simulation and Hunter will be able to magically see the difference for himself."

However, by the following week, Elena's group had been reduced to squabbling over the details of code writing to the point where she decided to give up talking to them about it.

Her simulation program didn't seem to be any closer to getting finished. She secretly wished that she could spend all day writing the code, but her Instructors never relented in the amount of information that they overloaded each day. They had, in fact, even introduced a new style of learning that Elena found absurd.

"The name of the game is *Pandemonium*," Instructor Booker said one day. "I will access the question, which will also then appear on your screen. You will each answer it out loud and as quickly as you can in the language that also appears on your screen. The first person to get the correct answer wins. The points will be tallied as we go along, and we'll determine the winner when we've finished. Everybody ready?"

But, Elena was not ready. She'd barely understood the directions.

Still, that didn't stop Booker from saying, "Compare and contrast the militaristic techniques during the War of the Roses."

Elena's screen filled with the question plus the direction to speak her answer in French.

Suddenly, the entire room filled with student voices answering the same question in completely different languages. Elena tried to pull her thoughts together because she knew she was being graded, but she was finding it so hard to focus with all the noise in the room that was now growing to a roar.

This strange practice went on for weeks and weeks until finally, on the first day of the second week of the ninth month, Instructor Booker started a lengthy lecture about how Henry VII founded the Tudor Dynasty in England after the War of the Roses.

As the Instructor spoke, Elena was far away in her dad's library. Truman Ransom was an ardent student of history. Many times, he'd drawn an intricate timeline of the finer points of European history that forged the way for the Age of Exploration, which in turn led to the largest shift in culture and technology the world had ever seen.

Elena began to smile as she heard his voice in her head.

"Our time on earth is important, but we must always remember the first cultures and civilizations that existed. The first rulers, the first scandals, and the first laws that were broken because all those firsts created something new for everyone. Knowing the beginning will help you appreciate all that was done for people to have a sense of freedom."

Then, with an intense pang in her chest she realized that this week marked the second year anniversary of her parents' death. She felt the room spin slightly and wanted to sit down, but there was nothing to sit on except the floor.

"Instructor Booker," Elena called out, raising her hand sharply. "May I please go and see the nurse?"

Without even looking at Austin, she hurried from the classroom. She walked the halls aimlessly for a while with no intention of actually going to the Medical Station. Finally, she realized there were only two people on earth that she wanted to speak with.

Elena climbed into the nearest Grimvator and selected the "Catacombs" button from the Optivision screen. The elevator slanted upwards, then to the side, and eventually it began to descend toward the Telepost office. Grandpa and Grandma Haddock would understand her need to cut class and call them to talk about her parents, but she didn't even know if they'd be home at this time in the morning. Still, she had to try.

When the doors finally opened, she stepped out onto an eerily vacant hallway. She began to hike toward the backside of the building while absentmindedly thinking about her parents.

At length, Elena came to a hallway lined with doors, each with a light indicator above the frame. If the light was red, that meant the room was occupied, but if the light was green, that meant the room was available for holographic contact.

The entire Telepost office was lit to green, except the farthest door at the end of the hall, which she knew was always lit to red because behind the door was a secret Vault. Just as she began to remember the time when she and Austin had broken into the Vault, the door to that Telepost room began to open.

Feeling panicked, Elena raced off the hallway and flattened herself into a corner of the next room, hoping that whoever passed through the doorway wouldn't turn around and see her. Then, she heard Headmaster Bentley speak clearly, as if he were standing right beside her.

"You're certain that the Feather of Truth is in Egypt?"

"Almost positive," Hopper replied.

"And the Firebird Disc is in China?" the Headmaster questioned.

"Again, almost positive," said Hopper. "Two large continents to search. But we're also hearing reports that the Echelon is somewhere in Italy."

"The Renegades would have strategically placed each artifact..."

Elena crept along the hall behind them as their conversation began to move away from her. She didn't want to get too close, so it was impossible to hear the rest of what was shared between them.

Frantically, she took off down the hall and climbed onto an empty Grimvator. She barely remembered finding everyone, but soon she'd gathered together Austin and Pigg, and had sent a message along with Fergie for Declan and Abria to meet at the Firebird Station.

Once everyone had finally gathered in the Station sitting area, Elena recounted every word she'd overheard the Headmaster and Hopper say in the Telepost hallway

"I'm mean, obviously the Headmaster has been looking for the artifacts this whole time," Elena said in conclusion. "We know he had the Alpha Manuscript in his own Vault. And plus he was looking for the Firebird Disc years ago. Do you think he's working for Imperator?"

"Well, technically we're all working for Imperator," Austin said. "We live in his bubble, remember?"

"You don't really think that, do you? I mean, we know our parents were fighting against him. So, Imperator can't be in charge of *everything*, right?" asked Declan.

"That doesn't matter," Elena said. "Imperator is in control of enough. But it worries me that all of our parents are either dead or incapacitated. Except for Pigg's parents." She looked at Pigg. He had a strange expression of understanding that she'd never seen before. "Your parents are in that picture of all the Renegades, which means that they're in danger. It's possible that Imperator already knows where they are."

Pigg let out a whimper.

"But it also means that they could help us," Austin said optimistically.

"I don't know," Pigg said, sounding uncertain. "It's not like I can go talk to my mom about it. And my dad barely says two words to me when I'm home."

"Maybe we could get Hopper, like, involved," Abria suggested. "He's done so much for us already. Maybe he could help us talk to Pigg's parents."

"I like Hopper, but he and the Headmaster are clearly working on something together. What if he told Bentley what we're doing?"

"Yeah, he may not be the best person to ask to keep our secrets," said Austin. "We're just going to havta go to Atlanson and tell Norman and Emelie what we think. See what they know."

"But, if Mr. and Mrs. Pigg really need protection, where could they even go?" Declan asked.

"We could send them to Fallon in New York City if it is required," Fergie suggested. "Fallon worked with Elena's parents. I am certain he would take them as refugees."

"Okay, it's settled then," said Austin. "During third quarter break, before Elena and Wheeler take the androids to Tavington's farm, we'll talk with Norman and Emelie about the Renegades. We'll ask if they can help us."

"Or if we can help them," Pigg added.

◻ 19 ◻

Mr. & Mrs. Pigg

"I'm so totally excited that I feel my heart is going to burst outta my, like, chest!" Abria said ecstatically as the Grimsby Channel pulled into Atlanson the day after their third quarter exams ended. "I don't know why my parents never brought us to visit Atlanson, but I've always wanted to come here!"

"Yep, you've said that about forty-seven times since we got up this morning," Elena said dryly.

"Okay, okay..." Abria said dismissively. "I know we're here in an official capacity, but I hope that doesn't mean you won't show us around town. I'm dying to get my hands on some of those high collared tunics because I think it would totally compliment my cheekbones. Plus, as you already know, I have quite the palette, so I can't wait to taste absolutely everything."

"Abria, we'll be here for a week," Declan said shortly. "I'm sure you'll have enough time to do everything."

Elena took a sideways glance at Declan. He'd been unusually reserved all morning and was now staring out the window with a frown. Kidd was sitting a couple seats away on the other side of the train also looking resolutely out a different window.

"What's going on with Bowen and Wheeler today?" Elena whispered at Austin as Pigg led the way off the train and toward the platform where they'd pick up their ride to his resident tower. "They both seem so cheerful."

"Oh, Bowen told Wheeler this morning that he'd better watch himself with you while you're at Tavington's farm."

"What? That's weird."

"Bowen said that if he heard that you'd been treated badly that he'd make it difficult on Wheeler when he gets back," Austin said, and then added dismissively, "It was just a stupid guy fight. Nothing to worry about."

Austin pushed forward, grabbing Abria's arm so he could point out some of the finer features of the train station, while Elena was left to wonder just how unpleasant Declan thought the trip to Tavington's farm would be for her.

Before long, Elena and her friends had arrived at Pigg's resident building. She hadn't visited his home in years because she could barely tolerate Emelie Pigg. She was seven years old the last time she'd been inside Pigg's house. On that occasion, she'd accidently knocked over an, apparently, priceless vase. Mrs. Pigg had scolded Elena to tears, and she returned home anxious.

Still, Emelie's frenzied behavior wasn't enough for the Ransom family to stop being friends with Pigg's family. So, they continued to be invited to family gatherings, formal events at the hospital, and government functions.

Elena stepped over the threshold timidly. She detested Emelie's décor. The walls were covered with images of minstrels playing harps, people that were fishing, and others holding exotic birds. Shelves were lined with stone carved busts of men wearing elaborate headdresses or women with high, rounded crowns and strings of jewels around their necks. One display case contained an expensive sarcophagus, which Elena knew contained mummified remains of an ancient pharaoh. It was like the Pigg family lived inside a museum of Egyptian art.

"Gribbin, what are you doing here?"

Elena turned on her heels as Emelie Pigg walked into the living room. Then, she instinctively moved closer to Austin as if she needed protection.

"Good morning, ma'am," Pigg said timidly. "I wanted to introduce you to my friends. You already know Elena and Austin. But these are my other friends Declan and Abria Bowen, Fergie Foreman, and Kidd Wheeler."

Emelie stood, unblinking, with her arms folded over her chest in a disapproving way.

"Pleasure to meet you." She replied so stiffly that Elena was sure it was definitely *not* a pleasure that any of them were in the Pigg home.

"Mrs. Pigg, is your husband here?" Austin asked politely. "We have something we'd like to discuss with you both."

Emelie's eyebrows contracted in a disapproving way. She turned and walked back down the hallway without giving a reply. Austin looked at Pigg expectantly.

"Oh, I'm sure she's gone to get dad," Pigg said quietly. "Let's sit."

Elena looked at the perfectly uniformed sitting area with stiff furniture that looked like it'd never been used and sighed. She waited until everyone else was seated. Then, she stood behind the chair where Austin sat.

Moments later, Emelie returned to the sitting room with Norman following behind her. Elena hadn't seen Pigg's dad very often before. Perhaps it was because Emelie was always so overbearing or maybe it was because Norman was an extremely quiet man.

However, now that Elena and her friends were here to talk about the possibility that their lives were in danger, she couldn't help but stare at him. She noticed right off that Pigg looked exactly like his dad, with ebony black hair, straight white teeth, and even the same nervous look in his brown eyes.

"Mr. and Mrs. Pigg, thank you for meeting with us," Austin started. "We came here to talk with you about an organization you should be familiar with: the Renegades."

Austin held up the photograph they'd taken from the Bowen's apartment in New York City, the one that featured Norman and Emelie Pigg standing beside Elena's parents and the rest of the Renegades.

Norman Pigg's mouth fell open. He crossed the room and reached for the image, gazing at it with a blank expression.

"I found this photograph in my parents' things after they died," Elena lied. "We know that the Renegades were working to remove Imperator from power."

"We're almost certain that Imperator murdered Elena's parents," Austin continued. "Also, last year, Hopper told us that one of our classmates, Kate Bagley, and her parents died. I'm sure you must know by now that Kenneth and Anne Foreman died when the D.E.S. lab burned to the ground.

"But, we also know about another mysterious disappearance of one of our other classmates, Pamela Linus." Austin paused for Pigg's parents to have a reaction to what he'd just told them, but Emelie simply stared, unblinking, and Norman hadn't taken his eyes off the photograph. "We think...well...it's possible that you could both be in danger."

Emelie made a noise of impatience and stated, "Well, this is just the most ridiculous story I've ever heard. Our time in the Renegades, doing the research we did, ended over thirteen years ago."

"Yes, but it's clear that the people who were involved with the Renegades are being systematically removed from society," Austin said steadily. "And we have no idea who will be next."

"Mom, we're just worried about your safety," Pigg said, sounding like a small child.

"Our *safety?*" Emelie replied. "We are perfectly safe, thank you very much. And, might I remind you" — she looked intently at Elena — "That your parents perished in an *accident*. And that the D.E.S. lab burned to the ground because it couldn't withstand the stress after a hovercraft *accidentally* flew into it."

"I know how my parents died," Elena said through gritted teeth. "And I certainly don't need to be reminded by you."

As Emelie cut her eyes at Elena, Austin turned in his chair ever so slightly in Elena's direction. She knew instantly that he wanted her to remain silent.

"We certainly didn't mean to cause any trouble." Austin stood up rigidly. "Thank you for the hospitality, Mrs. Pigg."

Elena was eager to get out of the apartment as soon as possible, so she hurried after Pigg to the front door, but Emelie called out, "Where do you think you're going, Gribbin?"

"With my friends," Pigg replied. "Elena, Austin, and I were going to show the others around town a bit because they've never been here before."

"You're not leaving here with *them*," Emelie said shrilly. "In fact, I would prefer that you don't spend any more time with *these children*...filling your head with all kinds of nonsense when you should be focused on studying and making good grades. I have half a mind to call the Headmaster and request that he move you to another Unit today."

"Mom, please..."

"Gribbin, go to your room," Emelie said firmly.

Out of the corner of her eye, Elena noticed Norman moving across the room. He had a strange look on his face, almost as if he wanted to say something to them. But, when he reached the door, he simply handed the Renegade photograph back to Austin.

"Bye," Pigg said glumly, and then added under his breath, "I'll see you back at school."

Elena and Austin led the others through the city and down Meeting Street. They cut through a back alley between the Rising Loafer Bakery and the Murphy's Paw Kennel to a metal hatch door.

Elena and Austin led their friends through the deep underworld of machinery, electric modems, and power grids to the far corner of Sector Seven where a crude clubhouse stood between stack pipes and silver ducts. She couldn't help but smile when she saw it, the one place in the world where she felt she could be her complete self.

"Okay, now this is awesome!" Declan said.

"What do you mean?" Abria said. "It's totally, like, gross down here."

"Come on, Blondie, you afraid to break a nail after everywhere we've been," Kidd said.

Elena rolled her eyes at Austin as Fergie wasted no time using her Touchdot to set up a pupil station of Optivisions all around the inside of the clubhouse. Then, she opened her tactical pack and began to remove the androids.

"There are fifty androids in all," Fergie explained as she knelt rigidly to the ground and began to place the little devices on Kidd's boots. "As a reminder, once you have stepped over the threshold, the androids will release and move through the house."

"How will they know to do that?" Elena asked.

"I will give them commands from here," Fergie said.

"Fergie has agreed to stay here and work so that Austin can, like, show us around the city," Abria said.

"Not me," Declan said.

"What? You don't want to come exploring?" Abria asked Declan incredulously.

"No, I think I'd feel better watching to make sure that the mission goes as smoothly as possible. We're here the whole week, Abria. There's plenty of time to see things tomorrow."

Abria looked sulky but didn't say another word.

"You should get going if you want to make it back by dinnertime," Austin told Elena and Kidd.

"What are you going to tell Grandpa and Grandma Haddock about where I am?" Elena asked him.

"I did a Telepost with Grandma last week to let her know that we'd be bringing friends with us this time," Austin said. "I told her that we'd explore until dinner. As long as you're back to eat, she won't even know you're gone."

Elena slung her tactical pack on her back as Fergie finished placing the androids on her boots.

"Alright, let's go," Kidd said, heading for the door without even waiting for Elena.

As she started for the door, Declan grabbed Elena's arm to hold her back. "Hey, when you're alone with Wheeler, just don't let him bully you, okay?"

"I never let him bully me," Elena said.

"I know, but you're going to a strange place," Declan continued. "Just be safe, okay."

"I'll do my best to come back in one piece."

Kidd led Elena to the other side of Sector 7, where she assumed they would go on toward Sector 12. Kidd was very quiet as they ducked under pipes and climbed over machines, which suited Elena just fine because normally everything out of his mouth made her crazy with anger.

At long last, Kidd stopped at a door that looked just the same as any of the other metal doors they'd seen along the way.

"Are we taking a break?" Elena asked.

Kidd had a strange look of apprehension and irritation on his face.

"We're going through this door," he said. "Just...be on guard the whole time, okay?"

Elena swallowed hard as Kidd easily opened the door. Then, he allowed her to pass through before him. Her mouth fell open in awe. She was standing in the middle of a field of tall green grass. Above her, the sky was flawlessly blue. In front of her, a small pressed dirt road bent toward distant trees.

Elena turned back around toward Kidd and noticed that he was just closing the door behind them.

"The door is just sitting in the middle of this field?" Elena said slowly.

"Come on," Kidd said as he brushed by her.

He walked surefooted on the road until Elena noticed that the trees were growing closer and closer. Soon enough, the pressed road became a rough dirt path. And finally, dense tree roots and boulders obstructed the path almost entirely.

"It's really creepy back here," Elena said as she crawled over a fallen tree. "Even in the daylight."

"Yeah, imagine growing up here," Kidd replied gruffly.

"I don't even want to think about it." She winced. "I still can't get over the fact that your home is way out here."

"We're not going to my home," he said shortly. "It's just the place I grew up."

Elena closed her mouth, but soon enough, Kidd said, "So, Big Ears has a totally crazy mom, huh?"

Elena bristled immediately. Emelie Pigg was crazy and rude, but Pigg was her friend. The way that Kidd had just spoken about Emelie made her feel as if she needed to defend Pigg in some way.

"I know that Emelie seems strange and difficult," Elena said, trying to remain calm. "But she really loves Pigg and just wants what's best for him. Just like all parents do, you know?" She felt her words start to get all jumbled up on her tongue. "I mean, we can't really judge her if she's just trying to do what she thinks best, right?"

"Oh, okay...whatever," Kidd said shortly.

Elena stopped dead in her tracks and blurted in an aggravated tone, "I thought we were on the same side now. So why are you always so horrible? What could I have possibly done to make you hate me?"

Kidd's typical cocky stature was suddenly overcome with a sag in his shoulders. He sighed deeply and looked away from her.

"I don't *hate* you."

"Excuse me?" Elena said, feeling more confused than ever.

Kidd looked at her in the eyes, and Elena felt for a moment that he could see into her very soul.

"I've liked you ever since I first saw you."

Elena had to think for a moment about when she first laid eyes on Kidd.

"You mean, in the hallway during Level 1 when you called me Freckles for the first time?"

"Not exactly," Kidd admitted, and he actually blushed. "The first time I saw you was that time you came to Tavington's farm. I followed you and your mom around and listened to you talking as you picked berries. You two reminded me so much of my own family. Later, I followed you back to Atlanson and to your resident tower.

"Then, every day after that I walked from Tavington's to Atlanson to see if I could find you again. Finally, the seventh day of the week, I saw you and your parents spread out a picnic in the park. You and your dad were feeding the birds while your mom looked on and laughed.

"Years later I discovered that you, Austin, and Pigg had started building that clubhouse in Sector 7. I would hide down there and watch you. I'd pretend you were my friends."

Elena had never seen anyone look so defeated. She could hardly wrap her mind around everything he'd just said.

"Why didn't you ever talk to us?" Elena asked.

"I wasn't allowed to. After my parents died, I was sent to the farm. Tavington made it clear that I wasn't supposed to have contact with anyone. I had to be homeschooled. I wasn't even supposed to come to Grimsby, but Hannibal insisted."

At this revelation, Elena remembered back to the conversation she'd had with Hopper during her first year at school. Hopper said that the members of the Firebird Unit had been hand selected. Could Hannibal have orchestrated the selection himself?

"Why didn't you just tell me all this when you first came to school?" Elena said.

"It's complicated."

"I think I'm smart enough to understand a complicated situation."

"When I saw you at the farm that first day, I realized that I knew your dad," Kidd swallowed hard, "He saved my life."

Elena realized that confusion must have registered on her face because Kidd continued at once.

"I was born on a plantation where I lived with my parents, two sisters, and brother. My oldest sister was so sweet to me. She was always carrying me around on her hip like I was a doll." He smiled reminiscently. "The first thing I can remember is it snowing outside our house. I'd just turned two. Each night, that winter, I'd snuggle with my family by the fireplace and my dad would read to us.

"In the spring, I played in the corn fields with my brother, and each night we'd sit outside for a picnic dinner. In the summer, my dad took us swimming in the lake each afternoon when the sun was hottest. And then, in the fall, we picked apples from the orchard. My dad was starting to teach me how to fish and trap. My mom carved pumpkins with funny faces and baked pies with my sisters. I was very young, but I remember these things because they are the only happy memories I have."

Elena watched Kidd's face begin to change. His hard frown lines began to transform into grief and despair.

"One afternoon I chased my dog out into the fields, but I got distracted and was gone a long time from home. By the time I got back there was a hovercraft in the yard that I'd never seen before. Droidiers were standing outside the house. I managed to sneak onto the porch. I saw a cloaked figure standing in the living room and my dad was tied to a chair. They were all tied to chairs. Now I know, the person talking to my dad was Imperator."

Elena gasped. She feared what he would say next. She wanted to cover her ears to block out his words, but instead she simply stared in silence.

"Finally, my mom and dad saw me through the window. I could tell that my mom was relieved. And, from the way my dad looked at me, I could tell he wanted me to run. I hid in the fields until I smelled a strange sort of burning.

"When I got back, the house was on fire. I couldn't do anything but listen to my sister screaming my name as the house burned to the ground."

Kidd stopped talking for a long time, and Elena was afraid to breathe out of fear that she'd interrupt his grief.

"After they were gone," Kidd finally said. "I just sat in the barn for hours until finally a man came and took me away to live with Tavington. That man was your dad."

Moments of silence passed. The thought of someone burning alive was inhumane. Elena's heart ached for all the suffering that Kidd had been through. At least when her parents died, she had Austin. But Kidd had been alone and helpless. Elena wiped a tear from her cheek.

Finally, she asked, "What were your parents' names?"

Kidd's face relaxed. "Jonathan and Abigail. And, my name was Joshua. Your dad changed it when he took me."

Elena reached out and grabbed the top of Kidd's hand.

"No, my dad *rescued* you. He gave you a new name so you could live."

"Some life," Kidd said bitterly. "You'd understand better if you had to grow up on the farm alone with Tavington. No friends. No one to talk to. I just learned, ya know, to be isolated."

"Do you think he knows we're here?" Elena asked.

"He's been watching me since we got off the train," Kidd said.

This news made Elena feel very uncomfortable.

"He tracks my Trademark. And he can hack into any of the surveillance in the city. He knows you're with me and hasn't stopped us yet so he must want to meet you."

"If he tracks your Trademark, does that mean he knew that we left the domes?" Elena asked.

"Yes, and he knew where we were, too."

"So, he knows we have the Amulet?" Elena asked, and Kidd nodded. "Why hasn't he turned us into the authorities?"

Kidd smiled bitterly. "He must want something we have."

Elena wasn't sure how to reply so they began to walk again. She thought about how strangely tragic Kidd's childhood must have been. And she was slightly anxious about what to expect next. The barn that she remembered from her childhood was practically falling down with age. She wondered if Kidd had lived in a tent his whole life.

But, as they took a sharp turn through a clump of overgrowth, they came to an overlook, and Elena's breath caught in her chest. A palatial house was set in the valley below them. The place looked like a fortress; it was the grandest residence that she'd ever seen. The grounds were laid with gardens of flowers, mazes of greenery, and dozens of playful fountains.

"You grew up here?" Elena said, the edges of her words full of confusion. "But it's so beautiful, elegant."

"Unlike me who is harsh and slovenly."

"That's not what I meant," Elena said shortly. "I mean, why don't I remember this amazing house?"

"Tavington had it built after your visit."

This information made the hairs on Elena's neck stand up. She wondered again what kind of business Tavington could have had with her dad. And why everything about the artifacts and this farm was so secretive. She remembered back to the one conversation she'd had with Tavington about the Ark that she and her friends had found in the mountains of Turkey. Elena felt sure that he was somehow involved, and she wanted to know everything. But first, they had a job to do.

As soon as Kidd stepped through the front door, Elena saw the androids release from his boots, but he didn't stop walking. She followed closely behind him, marveling at the opulent tapestries, magnificent murals, lavish marble floors lain with luxurious rugs, and extravagant statues and priceless antiques. Elena knew that her mouth was open in wonderment, but she couldn't seem to keep it closed.

After rooms and rooms of grandeur, Kidd finally reached a pair of double doors. He pushed one of them open and stepped aside to let Elena pass through first. She was suddenly reminded of a corner of her dad's library that was rarely ever used; the smell of dust and stale book pages overpowered her senses. The room was lit by a single lamp that was set on a table that was larger than three of the Grimsby Mess Hall tables pushed together.

Under the light was a man who sat in an oddly shaped chair with his back to them. He was hunched over the table in a tense way, as if he were studying, but Elena could not see whatever it was that he was working on. Even though he didn't turn when they'd entered, she could tell that there was something very odd about him.

"That's Tavington," Kidd whispered to her.

"What are you doing here, boy?" Tavington asked in an indifferent tone, without even looking up. When Kidd didn't reply, Tavington said, "I am very busy."

"Doing what?" Elena said impatiently.

Tavington's head rose slowly, though she still couldn't see his face. His chair swiveled around and Elena saw immediately why the man seemed so odd; he was a dwarf. Outside of Fallon's crew that lived in New York City, she'd never seen a dwarf or even knew that they actually existed. This was not the same old man that had talked to her when she'd visited the farm as a little girl.

Besides being a dwarf, this man was young, and his face was hardened with unhappiness.

"Pardon me?" Tavington said, seemingly focused solely on Elena.

"What are you so busy doing that you can't take a few minutes to greet me properly?" Elena said boldly.

Tavington considered her silently for a moment. By the way he looked at her, Elena understood why Kidd seemed so afraid of the man. His small stature seemed unassuming, but the persistence of his piercing eyes was overwhelming. Finally, she had to look away, at which point Tavington looked at Kidd.

"Would you do me the courtesy of telling me why *she* is here, boy?" Tavington said "she" like he knew exactly who Elena was.

Elena looked at Kidd. He seemed reluctant to speak up, almost as if he was terrified in Tavington's presence. She began to hope that the little androids were already in position around the property so they could get out of there.

"We came to ask you for the Amulet," Elena said boldly.

Tavington swiveled back around in his chair and bent over his table once more. "Why do you come asking for that which you already possess? What is your true intention in coming here?"

Elena looked at Kidd for a moment and then said, "We know our parents were part of the Renegades. We're trying to learn more about them, that's all."

"Your parents were murdered. Both your lives were thrown into chaos, yet you still desire to remove Imperator from power." Tavington spoke in tones of polite rudeness. "But look where you are! You are a mouse in a maze. You will never get out. Your parents were foolish in their quest for freedom."

"At least my parents weren't cowards," Elena said angrily. "You sit here in your comfortable cage while there are others out there trying to make a difference."

Tavington turned his chair back toward her. He smirked in a way that churned Elena's stomach.

"You must know a way to get out," Kidd said, suddenly aggressive. "Otherwise, how did you get all those artifacts in your Vault?"

Tavington's face hardened.

"Aw...we have reached the point in time where you disclose your truest intentions. What do you desire?"

"The Tablets of Destiny," said Kidd.

"I do not possess that artifact," Tavington said plainly, and he turned his back on them yet again.

Filled with doubt, Elena took a swift inventory of the room. Besides the books and scrolls that lined the shelving, she could see stacks of wooden crates, rows of strangely carved wooden figurines, a collection of rocks varying in size, and a jeweled case filled with necklaces of different shapes and colors.

Elena's hand closed over the Kairos hanging around her neck, feeling for the first time that perhaps her own necklace came from Tavington's stash.

"What sort of business did you have with my dad?"

"The type of business that does not include the meddling questions from a child," Tavington replied impatiently.

"Ransom has a right to know whatever you and her dad were doing," Kidd said loudly.

"You are a useless, ungrateful boy!" Tavington said sternly and, though the dwarf hadn't bothered to even raise his voice, there was something about the way he spoke that sent a shiver of fear through Elena's whole body.

Kidd suddenly hung his head, like a small child being punished. The scene was more than Elena could handle, especially after everything that Kidd had been through.

"He's not useless!" Elena said angrily. "And if you had any brains you'd know that."

"He has been useless from the day Truman Ransom dropped him on my doorstep," Tavington said steadily. "Imagine for a moment that you are me, a brilliant, historical analyst. Do you believe I wanted to care for a sniveling child, always crying for his family? My time and talents were wasted caring for a boy. Such a disappointing waste."

"But you didn't care for him at all," Elena said indignantly. "You left him to fend for himself."

"This conversation does not interest me any longer," Tavington said tersely. "Boy, take your friend and vacate the property."

Elena looked at Kidd, who seemed so thoroughly defeated. She wanted to yell something to try and get Tavington's attention, but just as she opened her mouth to speak, she felt a hand close on her own. She looked down, feeling stunned to see that Kidd's fingers were wrapped tightly over hers. Without speaking, she followed him out of the room and through the maze of hallways until they were striding through the front door.

"Thanks for, uh, coming with me," Kidd said as they walked back to the edge of the forest and began to hike the trail. "It's hard for me to be around him."

"I can't see why," Elena said sarcastically. She noticed a little smile appear at the corners of Kidd's mouth. "Has that man always looked after you?"

"Yep," Kidd said. "Just me and him."

"It's funny," Elena said. "I thought he'd look different."

"Why?"

"Because, when I was there as a little girl, an old man with a white beard scared me with a story about the Ark," Elena said. "I guess I just assumed that man was Tavington."

Kidd frowned. "I don't know who you're talking about. We never had visitors, except your dad. And no one else lived with us."

"But what about the au' pair you told me about?"

"Oh yeah, but she only lived with us until I was three-ish," Kidd said. "And I'm pretty sure she was just a robot."

They spent the rest of the journey back to Atlanson in silence. Elena's mind was spinning with everything she'd heard and witnessed in the past few hours. She thought about the tragedy of Kidd's childhood, the devastation he must have felt after his family was murdered. She decided not to tell Austin about Kidd's family. She wasn't sure why, but it felt like it might be a violation to share something so personal about Kidd with anyone else.

After that, Elena began to think about the mansion and how it was built after she'd been there with her parents. Only a few years had passed since she'd last been there. How would there have been time to create such a place?

And who would have been enlisted to build such a structure, especially without Imperator knowing about it? She also wondered about the old man that she'd met, the one that told her about the Ark. How did Kidd know nothing about him?

Even though it had been a strange day and her conversation with Tavington had been tense, Elena felt a little more cheerful as she and Kidd walked back to Sector 7. The hostility she'd felt toward Kidd for the past two and a half years seemed to be slipping away.

She'd never taken the time to get to know Kidd before. She'd written him off as a rude boy who didn't deserve her attention. But now, she felt completely different. What would she have been like if her parents had died when she was that young? Or during a time when she didn't have Austin to comfort her? If anything, Kidd's story of losing his family made her feel strangely connected to him.

▭ 20 ▭

Tavington's Farm

In time, Elena and Kidd arrived back in Sector 7 to find that their friends were gathered inside the clubhouse, watching a series of Optivision screens that each displayed a different scene from inside Tavington's house.

"Pigg's still not here?" Elena said after scanning the room. "Emelie must be torturing him."

"How did it go?" Austin asked, sounding eager.

Elena looked at Kidd, but he seemed determined not to make eye contact with her.

"Everything was fine. Tavington was...*charming*." Elena leaned in toward one of the screens and saw that Tavington was still hunched over the desk where they'd left him. "Has anything happened yet?"

"Nah, he's still just sitting at the same table," Declan said, sounding annoyed. He shifted his gaze from Elena to Kidd and back again, and said, "But I'm glad you're back *safe*."

"Can we call it a, like, day?" Abria said, suddenly yawning. "I'm so tired of all this."

"Yep, it's time for dinner anyway," Austin said. "Come on, we'll show you where we're staying tonight. Then, I'm sure Grandma Haddock has all kinds of goodies for us."

Elena and Austin led their friends back through the world of machinery, electric modems, and power grids and onto Meeting Street where a row of Simulab gaming hubs stood together.

Holographic figures patrolled King Street, beckoning people to come inside the stores. The street was lined with ornate marbled columns and mosaic tile floors. The walls flashed three-dimensional advertisements, while Humanoids followed closely to their owners, holding hands with human children.

Abria squealed with delight often, but none more than when they climbed onto the elevator to Elena's resident tower. The thriving metropolis of Atlanson was displayed outside the glass box in all its gleaming glory.

"So, we'll see you in a few minutes," Austin said to Elena after they stepped off the elevator. "Are you sure you don't want to stay with us?"

"No, it'll be more comfortable if we all have rooms," Elena replied as she led Abria and Fergie toward her apartment. "We'll be over in a bit."

Elena scanned her Trademark into the scanner niche, and the door to her apartment slid open silently.

"You know, this is the first time I'll sleep in my room since my parents died," Elena said as they crossed the threshold.

She led her friends straight back to her parents spacious bedroom.

"Are you sure you want us to stay in, like, here?" Abria said as she admired the beauty of the room.

"Of course," Elena said, waving her hand dismissively. "My mom would've wanted someone to enjoy her decorating skills."

"Anne Foreman never really decorated anything," Abria said, running her fingers over the silk comforter that adorned the Ransom master bed. "Your mom had exquisite taste."

"Yeah," Elena said shortly, looking around with a lump growing in her throat. "Wait till you see my dad's office."

Minutes later, the girls arrived at the Haddock's front door. Grandma Haddock enveloped Elena into a generous hug and said, "It's so nice to have you home, Sweetheart."

The rest of the week was filled with Grandma Haddock doting all over them, making tons of food at every meal, and filling their pockets with sweets every time they left the house.

During the day, Austin set up a schedule for monitoring the Optivision screens in Sector 7 so that they wouldn't miss Tavington doing anything, but after a few days it was clear that he never needed to be in the Vault. In fact, he hardly ever got up from his space at the table.

Eventually they gave in to the demands of vacation. Elena and Austin spent most of their time teaching their friends how to skateboard while they waited for Tavington to do something interesting. Or they spent hours exploring the city like tourists. They never saw Pigg, but he'd managed to Telepost them one afternoon to say that he was still alive.

Elena found that she was laughing a lot more than usual. The stale air in Sector 7 coupled with the skateboarding and hours of free time was making her feel more light-hearted than ever. Her friends were talkative and funny, and it was comforting go back to Grandma Haddock's home cooked meals every evening.

After a couple days of non-stop talking, laughing, and silliness, Elena noticed that Kidd acted a lot different from the way he was before. He really seemed to come alive in the Underground as they all rode skateboards and shared stories about school. He talked more than she'd seen him talk in the almost three years that she'd known him.

Plus, Kidd had become so helpful to Grandma Haddock in the kitchen that they started to prepare many dinners together. And, in addition to eating every meal with them, Kidd was now joining Elena, Abria, and the others on shopping trips in town and to Simulabs for gaming.

One night, as the girls were sitting in Truman's library perusing the illegal books, Abria said, "Okay, it's time to spill guts."

"Time to what?" Elena replied, feeling so utterly confused that she looked at Fergie for help.

"It's a, like, expression," Abria said. "It means that you need to tell me everything that is going on in that frizzy red head of yours."

"I'm really not following..." Elena began to shake her head, but Abria interrupted her in an impatient voice.

"I want you to spill guts about what happened with Wheeler at Tavington's farm."

"Nothing happened," Elena lied. She tried to keep from blushing, but could feel her cheeks grow warm. "Why would you even ask?"

"Because, you've been smiling like a fool since you got back. And because he looks a little less, you know...Oh, what's a good word...*grim*, maybe."

"Actually, I think a better word may be *forbidding*," Fergie said in a formal tone. "Or even *foreboding* would work well."

"He looks so different, I might say he almost looks handsome." Abria was grinning from ear to ear.

"Easy there, Blondie," Elena said, using Kidd's nickname for Abria lightly. "Nothing is going on. I just got to know him a little better. Maybe I understand him a little more. It makes one less person on my hate list so naturally I'm a little *less burdened*, but that's it!"

Abria looked at Elena like she didn't believe a word she'd said.

"This is a completely...what's the word..." Elena mocked her. "Oh, maybe, *ridiculous*...yes, this is a *ridiculous* conversation. Wheeler and I practically hate one another."

"That doesn't really matter," Abria said flippantly with a wave of her hand. "I knew this one girl in the Galilee Province...her name was Bethany or something or other..."

"Her name was Kylee," Fergie said matter-of-factly.

"Oh, right. But the point is that she really hated her next-door neighborhood for, like, ever," said Abria, and even flipped her hair once to make an extra point of it. "And then they got stuck on an elevator for three hours and fell in love right then and there. They even got married."

"That's the dumbest story I've ever heard," Elena said flatly. "People don't hate each other and then get married."

"It happens all the time. It could even happen to you," said Abria. "Except...Oh, I really hope it doesn't because...well..."

Elena waited for Abria to say something more, but Abria looked deep in thought.

"Well..." Elena prompted her, but Abria waved her hands dismissively.

"Forget it. Forget it! I shouldn't say anything more." Abria hopped up and dashed out of the room abruptly.

"That was weird, even for Abria," Elena said to Fergie. "What was she talking about?"

"I honestly do not have the slightest idea," Fergie said. "Once in a while, the subtly of Abria's girlish conversation is a mystery to me as well."

Fergie went back to perusing the contents of her book, while Elena found that she couldn't help but stare at her friend. They were sitting in one of Elena's most favorite places in the world, a place that she and her dad shared. Yet, she hadn't really spoken much about her feelings about her parents to anyone since their death. It made her curious about her friend's feelings.

"So, how have you been doing without your parents?" Elena asked.

Fergie looked up from her book, seemingly confused for a moment, but then said, "They were my companions for such a long time. I trusted them for maintenance. They relied on me as their confidant. I must admit that it is peculiar not to have that manner of trust any longer." She surveyed Elena quietly for a moment, and then asked, "How have your emotions fared, this being the second anniversary of your parents' passing?"

"I'm a mess," Elena admitted. "Though you wouldn't be able to guess that based on Abria's portrayal of my happiness." She smiled softly. "It's like I don't want to deal with the pain of losing them so I find things to distract me. Even the one time I was gonna Telepost Grandpa and Grandma Haddock from school because I missed them, I found Headmaster Bentley and Hopper down there talking about artifacts. I could have just let it go, but I got all caught up in trying to solve the mystery."

Fergie considered her for another long moment. "Elena, as much as I am certain it discomforts you to move through the pain, take time to feel the desperation of your loss and grieve their death. Otherwise, you are no different than me. A robot."

Elena felt sad for her friend in that moment. Fergie's condition made it impossible for her to have true human emotion. She only experienced what had been programmed for her. She wondered if it would, in fact, be better not to feel anything. To be a robot. There's was no way she'd ever know for sure, so Elena wrapped her arms around Fergie's neck and uttered the words that she knew were true.

"I'm so glad we're friends!"

■■■

"You're acting ridiculously happy," Declan said the following day as they walked their skateboards out to the track behind the clubhouse. "You're not plotting to have someone killed, are you?"

"I'm not *acting* happy," Elena said impatiently. "Why does everyone keep saying that? I actually feel happy. It's nice to be home for a change. And it's nice to be in Sector 7 all day. You have no idea how long it's been since I felt like myself."

"Okay, okay!" Declan held up his hands in surrender. "I get it. I always feel better when I go home, too. So, do ya want to ride boards, or what?"

"Sure," Elena said, but before she could even drop her skateboard on the ground Kidd came running out to the track.

"Hey! Brainiack thinks she knows where Tavington's Vault is."

Elena gathered with her friends around the dozens of screens that Fergie had open in the clubhouse.

"At long last, I believe that Tavington has finally entered the Vault," she said. "I will need to show you the playback. This surveillance was taken last night while we were sleeping."

Elena watched Tavington leave the table where he'd been working the entire time and walk down a series of passageways. Finally, the dwarf stopped in front of a section of wall that looked exactly like everything else in the hallway. He walked straight into it and disappeared entirely.

"Where'd he go?" Elena said, feeling astonished.

"I believe that he walked through a wall of simulation into his Vault," Fergie said.

"Can the androids follow him into the Vault?" Austin asked.

"We should not take the chance when we do not know what manner of protection he has on the room. If the androids go inside, we might lose all surveillance. However, I believe it could be possible for Wheeler to take his Touchdot into the Vault to scan the space."

"But if we don't have any images of the room, how would he know where to look for the Tablets?" Elena asked.

"I'm pretty sure I remember where they are," Kidd said. "They're easy to get to, as long as he hasn't moved them. Still, it would be good if we could leave something in its place so Tavington doesn't notice that they're missing."

"I have already created a replica set of the Tablets of Destiny," said Fergie.

"You have?" Austin said.

"Yes. After we realized the Tablets were not on the Ark, my parents thought it would be best that we have a second copy, just as they created for the Alpha Manuscript. In fact, their final creation before their death was a replica of the Horn of Gabriel."

Austin beamed at her. "You're really amazing, you know that, right?"

Fergie didn't exactly smile at his compliment, but she did somehow look pleased.

"So, how is Wheeler supposed to get in the Vault while Tavington's in the, like, house?" Abria asked.

"He could wait until the monster is sleeping," Elena suggested.

"First, he hardly ever sleeps. And, when he does, he wakes at the smallest noise," Kidd said. "I once tried to take food from the kitchen in the middle of the night because I was near starving, but he heard and then beat me with a horse whip."

Elena heard Abria gasp loudly. She noticed that everyone was staring at Kidd with their mouths wide open. The thought that a person would beat a child with a whip seemed insane to Elena, and she imagined the others felt the same way.

Kidd seemed to realize that he'd shared too much personal information because his face flushed.

"Wheeler could use that stuff that we used on Melly to put her to sleep," Declan suggested quickly in order to steer the focus away from Kidd. "What was it called?"

"Sleepy Wolf," Elena remembered. "Could you go into his room at night and put the stuff on him while he's already sleeping?"

"That might be worth a try," Kidd said.

"But, we can't really discuss those details until we talk to Pigg about the logistics," Austin added. "Hopefully, his mom hasn't taken him out of school."

Fortunately, Pigg was waiting for them on the Grimsby Channel the day they needed to return to school.

"My mom would *not stop talking* the entire week," Pigg complained as the train hurried toward the school. "She went on and on about what a bad influence you are on me and how you're filling my head with nonsense and all.

"She even called Hannibal, but he refused to move me outta the Firebird Unit. He said we were too close to scoring the third year. Surprisingly, she didn't tell him what we'd told her and my dad about the artifacts or about them possibly being in danger.

"But anyway, that's the last time I'm going home on a school break. I mean, physically going there myself. Obviously, I can just send my Decoy and let the robot deal with her. It'd probably make a better son than I ever could anyway."

On the second day of the second week of the tenth month, the entire Aves Company was seated at pupil stations that simulated a flight environment that included learning to maneuver an aerocraft through oversized rings, around mountains, through caverns, and across oceans. Marshall tried to encourage the students to use more fluidity when making their operating choices, but the more he yelled, the more Pigg's aerocraft jerked around.

"Pigg! Your movements are too robotic," Marshall barked at him often.

Kidd was easily the best operator in the class, while Abria was easily distracted and Declan a little too careless. Fergie's every movement was precise and made with intention, while Austin looked very serious, like he was concentrating too hard.

By the time class was over, Elena felt tired and anxious, but she didn't have any time to rest. She hurried to the Media Lab with her friends to start working on her neurolizor simulation with everyone else.

In the week that followed with what felt like non-stop coding, Elena finally felt that her neurolizor simulation of 15th century China was actually coming together nicely.

The weather systems cipher was working well with the timing of the sunrise and sunset. The buildings were layered with the cityscape in the right amount of detail. The farming and agriculture, trade jobs, and government offices were functioning in a systematically organic fashion.

Still, as she sat with the other members of her group, the back of her brain was jumbled with questions.

"Anybody have any tips about how to give what career to what style of personality?" Stacia Bassi asked suddenly without even looking up from her code. "I mean, how are we supposed to give jobs to the students we barely know?"

At her question, Elena felt instantly relieved that she wasn't the only one that was still struggling.

"Yeah, I'm still having a hard time assigning a storyline and dialogue to the forty-six students in the Aves Company," added Elena. "I mean, I've already decided to make myself the Empress of China, and I created a wardrobe of clothes to make Abria jealous, but trying to delegate tasks to everyone else is challenging."

"I chose randomly," Garrett Vaughn replied. "I put all the names on a list and let the program assign people."

"I did the same thing," Oscar Hunter said off-handedly.

"What? I can't believe you two!" Stacia replied. "I'm trying to match each and every person with what they'd be best at."

"I'm sure most everyone will do one of those two options," Oscar shrugged. "But, honestly, what does it really matter either way?"

Elena cocked her head to the side, feeling stunned. She suddenly realized that the students in her simulation didn't have to be good at one particular job or have to be chosen randomly. She could *make* them excel at anything she wanted. So, while it would have been obvious to put Pigg in a kitchen somewhere, she realized it would be more unique to make him an Admiral.

After she decided this, writing the neurolizor code was a lot easier. Over the next few days, she was able to code faster and write more dialogue than she'd had since the project had been assigned.

This left her feeling more confident about being able to finish the simulation in time for the exam, so she allowed herself to take a little break from coding after one of Marshall's particularly challenging lessons, during which he reduced half the class to tears.

Elena sat in the Firebird Station with her feet up on a table while her friends stood around a series of Optivision screens looking over the plans for Tavington's Vault. Pigg and Fergie had finished writing the program for deciphering the wall of the simulation while Kidd had made some notations about the length of time it would take him to find the Tablets once inside the Vault.

"Do you want to wait until fourth quarter break to go back to the farm?" Austin asked Kidd.

"Actually, I think I should go sometime in the next week or so," Kidd said.

"You said we needed a military style plan to get in and out of there. Are you sure we've had enough time to get ready?" Austin said.

"We should do it now," Kidd insisted. "I'll make up a story about being in trouble or something and just get this over with."

Elena watched Austin for a moment. She could tell that he was wondering why Kidd wanted to go back so soon, and she felt just as curious. He looked at her, and Elena knew that Austin wanted to extend a branch of trust to Kidd in the hopes that he would learn to trust them in return.

Austin nodded confidently. "If you think you can manage it without getting caught then you should try."

"Actually, I don't think I should go alone," Kidd added. "I think Ransom should come with me again."

Kidd looked expectantly at Elena.

"Me? You want me to come *again*? But, Tavington *hates me*!"

"I know," Kidd said, and he was almost smiling. "That's why it's perfect. You'll be a good distraction from what we're actually doing."

A week later, Elena and Kidd left all their friends at Grimsby and took the train back to Atlanson. While Kidd held the door open to the prairie on the edge of the woods, Elena felt the replica Tablets bump against her back as she slung a tactical pack over her shoulder. In next to no time, they'd hiked through the woods and could see Tavingon's mansion.

As they reached the entrance, Elena noticed that the dwarf was standing in the front door in a way that made her feel that he was trying to block them from entering.

"What are you doing back here?" Tavington asked harshly.

"We're in some trouble," Kidd said. "Can we stay the night?"

Tavington waved his hand in a way that Elena didn't understand, but Kidd clearly did because he said, "We'll just be out in the fields hunting then."

Kidd didn't wait for Tavington to reply. He grabbed Elena's hand and led her through the house. They continued down a maze of passages until finally coming to an immense, oaken door. Kidd pushed his way through to a room that was impressively beautiful with an oversized bed, ancient furniture, priceless antiques, life-sized murals, and expensive light fixtures.

"What is this place?" Elena questioned.

"It's my room."

"*This* is your bedroom?" Elena said incredulously. "It's too weird."

"What's weird?" Kidd said, as he began to dig around in a closet that was larger than her bedroom at home.

"Your room is weird. It's so nice and beautiful. I always imagined that you slept with pigs or some pack of wild animals in the woods."

"You've imagined me sleeping?" Kidd questioned. His eyes looked playful and so different from the way he'd ever looked at her before that Elena's face began to flush.

"I didn't mean that I *thought* about you sleeping. I just meant that I wouldn't have guessed that you slept in a bedroom. If I had to guess in the first place, because I woulda guessed that you lived, you know, somewhere that's more..." She stammered, but she couldn't go on because Kidd's smile reached from one ear to his other.

"Relax, Freckles. Let's go hunting, and I'll show you where I really grew up."

Kidd led her down yet another series of hallways to a magnificently stocked kitchen. A greenhouse was stationed just off the kitchen with a garden of herbs, an orchard of lemons, apples, cherries, and pears. This led to a room filled with hunting knives, crossbows, rifles, and fishing equipment.

"We'll hunt rabbit today," Kidd said. "So, choose anything you think you might need."

Elena didn't want to admit that besides the little snares that Kidd had taught her last year during their exam in the wilderness, she'd never actually been hunting. So, she chose an ivory handled hunting knife and some wire for making snares. Then, Kidd led her out the back of the mansion and into the woods behind it.

"How can you tell Tavington that you're in trouble and he doesn't question you?" Elena asked as they climbed through the overgrowth.

"Because he's safe here," Kidd said. "He doesn't bother anyone, and no one bothers him. He doesn't want anyone to interfere with what he does here, so telling anyone that I live here would just bring unwanted attention."

"How does he get water and electricity?"

"He steals it from Atlanson. I don't know exactly how. He's like some freak of nature, magician or something. This whole area, the house and everything around it in a five mile radius, exists inside an undetectable simulation, or so he says anyway," Kidd explained.

"Undetectable simulation?" Elena repeated. "What does that mean?"

"I really don't know or care for that matter," Kidd said. "We basically just ignore one another. And, while we're on the subject, I should go ahead and mention that I'm not allowed in his bedroom. I've never actually even seen the inside of it."

Elena stopped short and said sarcastically, "Oh, great! That should make it much easier."

"It's going to be fine," Kidd breathed. "I mean, it's a bedroom. How complicated could it be? I'm sure there's just a standard bed and dresser and whatever, so we'll just shoot him from as far away as we can. But we'll have to wait a long time. He goes to sleep really late."

"This just gets better and better," Elena replied glumly.

"It'll be fine," Kidd said again. "We'll hunt and gather all day. Then, I'll cook you dinner, and we'll play some Simulabs to waste time."

In the end, Elena actually had a pretty good afternoon with Kidd. They didn't talk about anything personal, but he showed her how to set some delicate snares and situate a trap he'd invented using rope that was camouflaged by fallen leaves.

They also collected berries and mushrooms that Kidd said would taste good in the sauce he was planning to make for the rabbit that had been tangled in one of the traps.

When they returned to the mansion kitchen, Kidd laid the dead rabbit on the counter and picked up the hunting knife. With one swift motion, he sliced the head off the rabbit. Then, he used the pointed edge and began to separate the skin from the carcass.

After washing his hands, he chose a chef knife from a block of wood and sliced the mushrooms they'd picked from the forest and also the carrots and potatoes they'd picked from the greenhouse.

Like an expert, Kidd stirred an assortment of herbs that Elena didn't even recognize into a bowl of white flour. Then, he added the rabbit meat into the mixture. Finally, he carefully dunked the coated pieces of meat into a large skillet of sautéed garlic and onion. The rabbit sizzled.

While the meat cooked, Elena watched him toss a number of other ingredients into another warmed pot that he stirred in rhythmic motions.

"It smells amazing in here. Pigg's gonna be jealous when I tell him what we ate," Elena said. "His mom isn't much of a cook so he taught himself when we were just little kids."

"Big Ears," Kidd started, but then he caught the look on Elena's face and said, "I mean, Pigg is actually something of a prodigy with food. He made that one wild dog dish when we were trapped in Istanbul. I swear I've never tasted anything so delicious."

It was the first time Elena had ever heard Kidd compliment anyone, much less someone like Pigg.

"But don't tell him I said so."

"Why not?" Elena asked. "Why can't you just be nice to him?"

"Being nice is not really my thing." Kidd flipped the rabbit in the pan, which was now beginning to turn golden brown.

"It wasn't really my thing either until I actually started making friends," said Elena, and then she pointed out, "You're being nice to me right now." Kidd only shrugged. "The Firebirds are really good people, I mean, now that Melly's gone and all. You should get to know them better."

When Kidd still didn't reply, she asked, "Do you ever eat with Tavington?"

"Nah, I had to start hunting and gathering for myself when I was really young because he never fed me. Basically, no one cares where I am or what I'm doing."

"I care," said Elena, suddenly wondering why her dad would leave a little boy with such a horrible man.

Kidd let out an awkward, disbelieving laugh.

"I mean it," Elena said. "Austin and the others care, too. You went through the worst thing anybody can go through, and you did it all alone. I understand why it's hard for you to be *normal*, but you have friends if you want them."

"What? You think you're *normal*?" Kidd said skeptically.

Elena smiled. "Definitely not!"

Kidd reached for a ladle. He scooped some of the rabbit and sauce he'd made onto a plate.

He handed it to Elena and said, "Here you are, braised rabbit with mushroom sauce."

After dinner, Kidd took Elena on a walk through the mansion. Each room seemed more impressive than the one before it.

"Is everything in this house ginormous?" Elena asked after they'd just passed through the largest Simulab gaming hub she'd ever seen.

"Everything except Tavington," Kidd said, and Elena couldn't help but laugh and feel lighthearted.

However, her carefree attitude changed slowly to anxiety over the next few hours as she and Kidd waited for the moment that they would attempt to enter Tavington's room.

Kidd had not given her any indication about when that might possibly be, and she didn't dare ask because they were getting along so well.

Finally, at 0200 hours, Kidd said, "Okay, I think it might be okay for us to try his room now."

Elena slung her tactical pack over her shoulders. She felt the weight of the fake Tablets of Destiny against her back and was excited to know that soon they'd be replaced with the real ones.

She followed Kidd down a series of hallways until they reached a pair of sturdy, oaken doors. He stopped for a moment and pulled a long wooden stick out of his jacket pocket.

"What's that thing?" Elena whispered.

"It's a blowpipe," Kidd said simply.

"Okay...I feel really dimwitted that I didn't ask this before, but how exactly are you going to get the Sleepy Wolf on Tavington?"

"I'm going to shoot him. I inserted a tiny dart doused with the serum inside this tube here," Kidd pointed with his finger, "Then I blow on the other end and the dart will shoot out and hit him.

Elena made a face of disbelief.

"Trust me," insisted Kidd. "I've done this plenty of times in the woods with animals."

As Kidd pushed through the bedroom door, Elena had a fleeting thought of Kidd accidentally shooting one of the two of them with the dart instead of Tavington.

"What is that?" Elena gasped as she peered into the dwarf's room.

Tavington's room did not have a bed or a dresser, or anything that a normal room would contain. In fact, it only had one piece of furniture and it looked like a piece of exercise equipment that they'd use during Basic Training. The top of the furnishing was strung with some kind of system of cords that Tavington was secured to by his ankles. He hung completely upside-down and appeared to be sleeping soundly.

"It's like he's a bat or vampire or something," Elena said, sounding horrified.

"What's a vampire?" Kidd whispered.

"It's something I read in a book once...never mind..." Elena mouthed. "Let's just get out of here before he wakes up."

Kidd lifted the blowpipe to his mouth. Elena heard a gust of breath, and waited with baited breath to know if the Sleepy Wolf had actually worked. Several quiet moments passed, and then she distinctly heard the dwarf begin to snore.

Elena and Kidd shared a smile of victory. They eased back out of the room and raced down the halls until they came to the entrance to the Vault. Then, Fergie's voice echoed from the Broadcaster on her wrist.

"Pigg and I have completed the code work that was necessary. You may now walk through the wall."

Elena looked at Kidd actually feeling timid. He grabbed her hand firmly and pulled her through the wall of the simulation. As the room came into focus, Elena saw that it was filled with gold, jewels, priceless artwork, and unusual artifacts.

The Touchdot from her Broadcaster shot out, and she selected the scanning module from the Optivision screen that was now hovering in midair. Without any discussion, Kidd started walking resolutely through the room.

"What is all this stuff?" Elena asked, hurrying after him.

"That pile is gold from the Aztecs; that over there is a pile of diamonds from the Congo; that one is silver from the Lydians, and those differently colored gems are from all over the world, but I can't remember all the places where they come from. Tavington calls it treasure; I call it worthless junk."

Kidd kept on walking hurriedly through the room. Elena had no choice but to follow him.

The next room opened into a grandiose atrium with marbled columns and floors, a reflecting pool, and murals painted from floor to ceiling. Large scale models of the great pyramids in Egypt, the Great Wall located in China, and the coliseum in Rome, Italy, covered the floor in neat rows. But Elena also noticed a depiction of Hagia Sofia in Istanbul, a model of a mountain with a broken ship, and the Empire State Building in New York City.

"Did Tavington build all these models?" Elena asked, feeling amazed at the grand scale of every piece.

"Ha!" Kidd laughed bitterly. "Tavington doesn't have enough skill to whittle a piece of wood. He stole everything in this Vault, from one person or another. He has even killed people to get what he wants, or so he says."

"But, there's something strange about them?" Elena said as she passed a model of the White House in Washington D.C.

"What?" Kidd said, though he sounded completely distracted as he kept walking. He didn't even bother to look back at her.

"Well, we've already been to some of those places," Elena continued. "It's a little weird, right?"

"Huh?" Kidd barely slowed down even though Elena had stopped.

"Why are you walking so fast? Pigg said we'd have all night," Elena called after him.

She started walking again and followed Kidd into yet another set of rooms with treasure.

"Plus, the Touchdot has to get scans of the whole place. We left it way back there because you're going from room to room like your pants are on fire."

"I'm just ready to be done with this," Kidd replied vaguely.

At long last, they reached a far room, much smaller than all the rest with seemingly meaningless objects that were piled unceremoniously on top of each other. Elena saw children's toys, hardcover book bindings, and dusty furniture. Then, for a reason she didn't understand, Kidd began to frantically toss items off the tabletops and shelves.

"What are you doing? Why are you throwing everything around?" Elena asked. "That's just going to make it harder to find the Tablets."

"I'm looking for something," Kidd said absentmindedly.

"Looking for something?" Elena repeated. "Wheeler, where are the Tablets?"

Kidd didn't even look at her as he said, "We didn't come here for the Tablets of Destiny."

ロ 21 ロ

The Trick

Elena's face burned red with confusion. "What do you mean we're not here to get the Tablets?"

"We were never coming for the Tablets," Kidd said, almost impatiently. "I don't know where they are. I just said that to get your help getting into this Vault."

Elena could feel all the lies unraveling in her mind. From the time they were on the Ark in Istanbul, Kidd had known that the Tablets weren't in Tavington's Vault. Then, he'd pretended to be friends with them so they'd help him break into the Vault. He'd even made up the story about his family dying to get on her good side.

Kidd had lied to her. He'd lied to all of them. And, not only had he put them in danger, now they were even farther away from finding the Tablets of Destiny.

"I can't believe you!" Elena exploded as she watched him continue to toss random items around the room.

"But, I just..." Kidd stopped his search abruptly. He took a step toward Elena and said, "I'm looking for something that Tavington stole from me. It belonged to my dad and..."

"I don't want to hear it!" Elena yelled, shoving him hard in the chest. She turned on her heels and stomped away.

"Where are you going?" Kidd called after her.

"I'm not staying here to get in trouble with Tavington for you," Elena said.

She hurried back through all the rooms filled with treasure and out through the wall of the simulation. Elena managed to find her way through the maze of hallways back out through the mansion's front door.

An unusual darkness had fallen over the farm. She grabbed the hololight from her tactical pack and then adjusted it on her back so she could run. She hurried across the yard to the tree line.

When Elena found the door in the center of the prairie, she remembered that Austin and her friends weren't expecting her to get back to Grimsby until the following afternoon. Therefore, she returned home, and collapsed on the floor in her dad's office. She let out a deep sigh, as if she'd been holding her breath for a long while feeling desperately alone.

"I don't care if he ever gets back to school," Elena whispered. "I mean, how could he do that to me? To us? He just lied and I'm supposed to...what? Pity him with his fake little story about his family and how miserable Tavington was to him?"

After a moment of silence, Elena felt a presence in the room. She could only think of one person that would know where she'd be.

"How did you know I was here?"

Austin eased into the room and sat down beside her.

"I left school on the train after you. I've been tracking your Trademark on my Touchdot the whole time. I always worry when you're out with Wheeler."

"With good reason," Elena said. Her eyes filled with tears, but she brushed them away roughly. "He doesn't know where the Tablets of Destiny are. It was all a lie so that we could help him get into that Vault. Tavington had stolen something that belonged to his dad. I'm so mad at myself for believing... whatever...it doesn't matter."

"It does matter," Austin insisted. "Where's Wheeler now?"

Elena closed her eyes. "I have no idea. I left him behind on the farm. I hope Tavington gets a hold of him and locks him in a torture chamber."

They sat in silence for a long time, gazing at the star strewn ceiling.

"How are we going to tell the others?" Elena asked. "We were all so hopeful."

"You'll have to tell them the truth, everything that happened and everything Wheeler said. Fergie will record it for our archives."

When Elena and Austin returned to school, she had a hard time recounting what happened on Tavington's farm to her friends. She'd come to believe in Kidd, to trust him, and having to let that go was difficult. Elena and the others speculated about what it meant that the Tablets weren't in the Vault. She couldn't help but feel completely disappointed.

■ ■ ■

Over the next few weeks, anytime that Kidd tried to talk to her, Elena ignored him. And every time his name was brought up in her presence, she'd leave the room. Her contempt toward Kidd made Basic Training uncomfortable to the point that Elena was almost always on the verge of being in trouble with Marshall.

For instance, during their last jump training class, she'd shoved Kidd away when he got too close to her field of launching. In flight simulations, she purposely tried to make him crash his aerocraft. And during their field training simulation, she'd block his advancement during the rescue mission that the Firebirds had been assigned.

"Ransom! Wheeler is part of your convoy!" Marshall screamed at her more than once. "Stop interfering with his progress."

Each time she caused a disruption, she'd shrug and say that she just couldn't get the hang of the exercise or was having a hard time learning to keep proper control of her aerocraft.

Meanwhile, Elena's constant pursuit of perfection on her neurolizor simulation kept her working late most nights in the Media Lab. Sometimes, Stacia Bassi would join her, and Elena was beginning to realize that she didn't mind Stacia's company.

"You know, I've spent so many hours writing code to describe the Ming Voyages and how admiral ZhengHe had led a series of seven voyages with a fleet of sixty-two large ships and two hundred fifty-five smaller ships that were manned by twenty-seven thousand men that I might just have a touch of sea sickness," Stacia said one evening.

Elena laughed loudly.

"I know. I've been working on the intricate details of the construction of the Great Wall of China and also the construction of the imperial palace in Beijing, which required one million workers and one hundred thousand artisans. I'm starting to feel like someone is standing behind me all the time with a whip so I get my work done."

Stacia put her face done on the pupil station and sighed, "Do you think we'll get done in time?"

"I guess we'll have to at some point or we'll fail the exam," Elena said. "Still, it's not all bad for me. I just got finished yesterday coding the Yongle Canon, which was an enormous encyclopedia with 22,877 volumes and about 370 million words written entirely by hand. That's quite an achievement."

Suddenly, Elena heard light snoring. She looked over and noticed that Stacia had completely fallen asleep. Smiling, she bent back over her coding work.

Elena had been working for over an hour, but she wasn't any closer to getting the dialogue right for the Raptors, which she'd tasked with helping to build the Great Wall of China. And that's why, when Austin suddenly approached her pupil station, she only acknowledged him with a grunt.

"Hey," Austin said as he sat. But then, he was silent for a few moments.

Elena continued on with her work until she couldn't stand him watching her any longer.

"Just spit it out, Austin," Elena said impatiently, looking at him for the first time. "I'm really busy here."

"I have a proposition."

"Does it have anything to do with me finishing this neurolizor so Hunter has to take care of the farm animals? Because I've had a lot of false starts already and I'm starting to get a little crazy. Do you realize how much stuff we're being tested on for fourth quarter exams? It's completely insane!"

"I actually came here to talk to you about Wheeler. He wants to tell us what happened in the Vault after you left." Austin closed his hand over Elena's because she was already standing to leave. "Please hear me out."

"I thought we agreed never to discuss him again," Elena said gruffly. "I don't care what kind of story he told you. I don't want to hear it." She tapped the Optivision screen so hard that Oscar's character did a flip-flop. "Plus, didn't you hear the part about how I'm really busy?"

"How about I help you with this now so we can finish it quickly and then you can come to the Station with me and we can talk to Wheeler."

Elena was already shaking her head. "I don't want to talk to him."

"Lena, just come and at least listen to what he has to say," Austin pleaded.

"No," Elena said flatly. "After what he did, after lying to all of us like that, I just can't try anymore. Can't you just tell me later what he says?"

"I suppose I could," Austin said imploringly. "But that would deprive you of an opportunity to roll your eyes in his face. Please come, for me."

Elena sighed deeply. "Sometimes being friends with you is a bad influence on me."

Minutes later, Elena entered the Firebird Station after Austin and noticed that Kidd was already there. He stood up quickly, looking hopeful.

"Thanks for coming."

"I didn't come for you," Elena said coldly as she walked to the opposite side of the room. She folded her arms over her chest in a protective way and pressed her back up against the wall so she didn't have to look in Kidd's general direction.

In her peripheral vision, she noticed Austin and Kidd share a look. Then, they sat in chairs across from one another. Several tense moments of silence followed, during which Elena considered leaving, but then she heard the Station door open. Her other friends had arrived.

"Is it awkward in here, or is it just me?" Abria asked as she took a seat and eyed Elena suspiciously.

Kidd looked embarrassed but also sincere. "I wanted to apologize for lying and using all of you to get into Tavington's Vault. But, I lied so I could get this."

He held up a round flat object that was the size of a coin.

"This neurolizor belonged to my dad. Tavington stole it from me after I got to his place. I never saw it again."

"Is that what I think it is?" asked Austin.

"Yes, it's my dad's dossier," Kidd said. "My parents were Renegades."

"Why didn't you tell us that before?" Declan asked. "You saw that photograph with all the Renegades. We've had it forever."

"When Freckles first showed us that picture, I didn't want to get involved with whatever you were doing because I'd already lost everything."

"When you say that you 'lost everything' what do you mean?" Austin asked.

"Didn't Freckles tell you?" Kidd's eyebrows raised in curiosity.

"No, I didn't tell them anything!" Elena snapped. She looked at him pointedly and said, "After you betrayed us I figured you made up that whole story about your family just to trick me."

Kidd looked at her sadly for a moment and then said, "When I was two-years-old, Imperator burned my house down with my entire family inside."

Abria gasped and covered her mouth with her hands. Elena's mouth fell open. He had told her the truth.

"That's awful," said Austin sincerely. "Why do you think he wanted them dead?"

"He wanted my dad's artifact. I don't know much about it, just a few details that I've been able to piece together, but someone from the Renegades betrayed my family to Imperator.

"Truman Ransom found me hiding in the barn. He gave me this dossier, and then took me to Tavington's. But the moment Truman was gone the dwarf took the neurolizor from me and put it in his Vault.

"When you told me you were after the Tablets of Destiny, I realized I could sell the idea about getting into the Vault. I knew that Tavington had all that useless junk that he never looked at. So, I made up that story about the Tablets so I could get my dad's dossier back."

"Then, why did you act like you hated us after the whole Istanbul thing?" Elena said, the edges of her words full of irritation. "We could've started working on it right away instead of wasting an entire year."

"I didn't tell you at first because I was doing reconnaissance work. That day you saw me in Harleston Village, I wasn't really there to race," said Kidd. "I was there to talk to an informant about Tavington's farm and why it's unplottable.

"The men that attacked me, they weren't gamblers. They've been following me ever since I started researching Tavington's farm. There's a reason why Pigg and Fergie can't find an electronic signature for it. And I want to know why. Plus, over the years of living there I noticed that very few people are ever able to get onto the farm. I've personally seen Droidiers and Humanoids cross the perimeter and literally disintegrate into nothing."

"So, you're not working with Melly?" Elena asked.

"Melly? What's she got to do with anything?" Kidd asked.

"It's just, I saw her that day at Harleston Village," Elena explained. "I thought that maybe the two of you were working together to try to find the artifacts, or keep us from finding them, or whatever."

Kidd shook his head.

"So, you said that people can't get through the perimeter around the farm," Austin said. "Yet, Elena was able to walk straight on through without any problem."

"Yeah, I still don't really understand that," Kidd admitted.

"Oh, but you were willing to risk my life to find out?" Elena said incredulously.

"No!" Kidd stated. "It's just, I knew you'd been there before, so I just figured that you'd be able to get inside again."

"So, what was your dad's artifact?" Austin asked.

Kidd put the neurolizor on the back of his neck. Then, he opened the Ransom Dossier, the Alpha Manuscript, and an Optivision screen with the images from Truman Ransom's library ceiling. Miraculously, Kidd was able to use his fingers to manipulate the screens and the diaries until an image of a wooden cup appeared. The pedestal and the stem were carved into the shape of a twisted tree trunk. This culminated into a burst of branches and leaves on the well and rim of the cup.

"Imperator was after the Cup of Jamshid."

"He was after a *cup?*" Pigg blurted in disbelief.

"It's believed that the Cup of Jamshid can tell the future," said Kidd. "I think that's why Imperator wanted it."

"Do you honestly expect us to believe that Imperator is looking for a *cup* to tell him the future?" Elena scoffed. "It's just the most ridiculous thing ever."

"I didn't tell you because I expected you to believe me. I told you because I'm going back to my family's plantation to look for the Cup. I was wondering if everyone wanted to come with me."

Elena's eyes narrowed in distrust. Was Kidd actually asking for help? Or was he up to something else?

"My family farm was in the southern part of the United States," Kidd said as he accessed another Optivision. A map of North America appeared followed by a highlighted section in the southern region. "It should take about ten hours to get there. I think the Cup is somewhere on the farm."

"Do you know if there's a Station there?" Austin asked. "That's the most likely place for us to find an artifact."

Kidd shook his head. "The main house was burned to the ground. There's a barn and a fishing depot, but that's it."

"Okay, I'm in," Austin said.

"But, we don't even have a plan," Abria said.

"We don't need a detailed plan this time, Blondie," Kidd said, though he didn't have any unkindness in his voice. "I've already thought it through. I'm just going to fly down there in a day, look around to see if I can find the Cup, and come right back."

Elena looked around at all her friends, wondering if they'd be willing to go.

Kidd must have sensed the hesitation in the room because he said, "Look, I can't get you the Tablets, and I'm real sorry about that, but I can give you this Cup."

"I'll go with you," Austin said.

After Austin agreed to go, Elena knew the others would follow him. But, in the depths of her heart, Elena wondered if Kidd was really telling them the truth.

◻ 22 ◻

Pigg's Not Special

The next morning, Elena dropped her tray of cornbeef and egg hash on the table in the Mess Hall. Feeling tired, she slumped over with an elbow on the table. But then, to her surprise, Kidd sat down beside her.

"Good morning," he said and actually smiled.

Elena looked around for a moment and wondered if she was dreaming, but then Austin and Pigg sat around the table and welcomed Kidd.

Kidd Wheeler had yet another unbelievable transformation over the next few weeks. Similar to the way he'd behaved when they were in Atlanson, before the incident at Tavington's farm, he joined Elena and the others at every meal. Kidd also quit using the nicknames he'd given each of them and called them by their real names instead.

Plus, he walked with Elena and her friends between classes, offering jokes and pleasant conversation. Kidd accepted help from Pigg for his neurolizor simulation when they all gathered in the Media Lab in the evenings. And he made an effort during Basic Training to help any Firebirds that were struggling.

Kidd's sudden presence was so bizarre to Elena that she didn't quite know how to feel about him. However, she did notice something stirring in her heart. A struggle had started between her old feelings of loathing and distrust for Kidd and the new feelings of empathy and hope that somehow he belonged with them.

"Okay, seriously, I don't know what's been going on with Wheeler lately, but it's, like, totally weird," Abria said one evening as she watched Kidd and Pigg studying together across the Media Room.

Elena clicked her tongue impatiently. "He's just trying to be friendly. And, after everything he told us about what Imperator did to his family, we should try to be supportive."

"Look at you being all nice." Abria smiled at her. "Did you hear that he started giving flying lessons to any of the Firebirds that want extra help? And that he actually started tutoring Frankie Smiley on his neurolizor simulation? They aren't even in the same group. Don't you think that's a little much given his surly attitude the past few years?"

"Perhaps Wheeler has ulterior motives," Fergie said formally.

"What's that supposed to mean?" asked Elena.

"Only that, perhaps his change in behavior indicates that he is trying to earn favor for a specific reason."

"Maybe that's true, but can we talk about it later because the guys are coming over...Hey!" Elena turned toward Kidd and Pigg as they arrived at the girls' pupil station.

"Wheeler said he's going to give me flying lessons," Pigg said excitedly.

"Oh, good," Elena smiled. "That will save my back and neck."

Kidd smiled knowingly at her.

"What do you mean?" Pigg asked.

■ ■ ■

The day before the fourth quarter exams began, Elena submitted her neurolizor simulation to Instructor Booker from the Media Lab. She actually felt proud of her work. She'd done a good job and hoped it would be enough to earn her one of the coveted positions in Special Ops.

"Why do we have to turn it in before tomorrow?" Elena asked Fergie as they left the Media Lab.

"A team of assessors will review all forty-seven simulations so that they are able to create a schedule for exam week," said Fergie.

And Elena soon discovered that the schedule was vigorous.

On the first day of the second week of the twelfth month, she was subjected to a wide variety of simulations that were wildly diverse. During one simulation she acted as a farmer in one of the up-and-coming states in Africa during the fourteenth century. In another, she'd been a slave in one of the emerging Temple Kingdoms in India. She'd also been a warrior during the Ottoman Empire.

"I was totally, like, humiliated during that death scene I had to perform during Garrett Vaughn's interpretation of when the Black Death swept through Europe," Abria said after one exam.

"Why?" Elena replied. "Three-fourths of us died during that simulation. You didn't even have to look pitifully sick all by yourself."

"I know, but did you see my hair and the gaunt look on my face? Ick!" Abria replied.

And the week stretched on, leading the Aves Company on a journey through time covering the development of the English language, the historical significance of John Wycliffe translating the Hebrew Bible, the astronomical practices from 12th century Africa, and the state of affairs in the unknown regions of North and South America.

"Each of these simulations take at least an hour," said Austin during one of their breaks."

"I know, right?" Elena grumbled. "This is the most exhausting of all the types of exams we've ever had!"

Despite her misgivings, Oscar's simulation wasn't too bad. He'd chosen the Golden Age of China from 1000-1200 AD and moved the class through the many firsts that this civilization offered the world: the first government to nationally use banknotes, the first permanent standing navy, the first use of gunpowder, and the first discernment of true north with a compass.

Stacia Bassi from Harrier demonstrated massive ship building endeavors, the construction of battle vessels, and nautical engineering, while Garrett Vaughn from Falcon showed the creation of harbors, beacons, and seaport warehouses to support maritime trade.

But none of the three could compare with the richness of Elena's simulation, which was a symphony of colors, light, cuisine, apparel, art, literature, philosophy, and farming. Pigg's tutoring had certainly set her simulation far above those in her group.

She had included beautifully written scenes of society and culture, detailed architecture of the schools and temples for education, and showed how widespread printing helped to circulate Confucian teachings.

She covered welfare programs, women gaining legal rights, the importance of public festivals, the pioneering work in forensic science, the development of mathematics and cartography, and hydraulic engineering.

The dialogue she'd written for her classmates was funny and engaging. Their acting was priceless. Giving students character qualities that they otherwise would never possess was tremendously successful.

Elena was enjoying the entire experience until she noticed something strange as the class entered the scene she'd written about the Imperial City. They were moving through the finer points of the metropolitan construction when she noticed a temple that she hadn't written into the code.

As with all the other buildings, this one had a triangular rooftop with the four corners of the roof edges up-turned, but this temple included a graffiti of an ancient form of Chinese writing on the outer walls. They hadn't studied this style of symbols since their Level 1 studies. To make matters worse, Elena knew that she'd seen this exact same building somewhere else.

Then, as she was beginning to feel uncomfortably confused, the figure of Melly Linus walked out of the building.

"What's she doing there?" Elena thought as her exam voice over continued to describe the simulation to the class.

Elena wanted to chase Melly's image, but her own simulated character wasn't programmed to move anywhere.

As soon as class was over, Elena pulled Austin down a vacant hallway and whispered, "Someone altered my simulation."

"What do you mean?"

"There was a section at the Imperial City, just part of the background scenery really, but there was a temple that I didn't put there."

"Okay..." Austin said slowly.

"The thing is," Elena said in a hushed voice. "I've seen the temple before. There was a model of it in Tavington's Vault. And, Melly was there!"

"Melly was where?"

"She was programmed into my simulation, right in front of that temple."

A look of astonishment lit Austin's face.

"What do you think it means?" Elena asked.

"I don't know," replied Austin. "But we're leaving tonight so maybe Fergie or Pigg could research that while we're on the Independence. If someone did change your simulation they would have opened it using their Trademark. So, maybe we can find out who..."

"I don't really care who did it," Elena interrupted him. "I want to know how they knew what I'd seen in Tavington's vault. And I want to know why they're telling me through the exam. I mean, do you think it could be Melly?"

"Ransom!" Hopper called from down the hallway. "I need to talk to you right now, girl." Then, he noticed Austin and added, "Alone."

Elena's eyebrows creased together in confusion, but she followed Hopper down the hallway and into an empty classroom.

"So, you know how only six from each Unit can graduate to Special Ops?" Hopper asked, and Elena nodded. "We're not supposed to say anything until tonight at the banquet, but you and your friends all made it." Elena smiled, but then frowned as he added, "except Pigg."

"Did you already tell him?" she asked, her heart sinking.

"Hannibal is telling him now."

"I get it," said Elena, laying a hand on his forearm with thankful understanding. "Thanks, Hopper."

Elena got on the first Grimvator she could find and selected the button toward Hannibal's office. She'd been thinking so much about how she wanted to be in Special Ops with Austin that she hadn't considered what would happen if Pigg didn't make it. Technically, it didn't matter to her, but she knew that Pigg was going to have a hard time being left behind either way.

Elena was soon standing outside Hannibal's office. Almost immediately after she arrived, Pigg walked out the door. He locked eyes with Elena and hung his head.

"Oh, hey…" Pigg's face was drawn into a deep frown and his eyes were red with recent tears. "Who told you?"

"Hopper."

Pigg walked past her down the hall. Elena hurried to catch him and tossed an arm around his shoulders. They hopped a Grimvator and rode for a long while until they came to a storage room that Elena had never seen before.

"What's this place?" Elena asked as she watched Pigg walk down a row of stacked crates.

"Oh, it's just a supply room," Pigg said. "I found it during our first year by accident, but Blakely said that it was okay for me to hang out here. It's where I come to get away from everyone else."

Pigg moved through the rows of materials until he finally reached a section of crates that looked as if it'd been arranged for a meeting. He sat heavily.

"I'm a dimwit."

"No, you're not," Elena said earnestly as she sat beside him. "I'm sorry I ever called you that. I'll never call you that again."

Pigg didn't look any happier. In fact, tears began to leak from the sides of his eyes and slip down his nose.

"Look, you're the smartest guy in the school for writing codes and programs," Elena began. "And you can design and create more gizmos than anyone else I've ever seen. You're a whiz at developing all those simulations and your neurolizor exam was perfect."

"I'm just not good enough at survival skills. I'm so clumsy. I'm afraid of heights and water and sloshing through mud. I still can't make sense of which direction to go on a map, and that's with a compass. I don't take any initiative to get myself unlost when we're in the field…"

"Well, that's not totally true," said Elena. "You did fly the aerocraft instead of jumping."

"But I only did that because I was more afraid to jump." Pigg shook his head. "Hannibal is right not to put me in Special Ops."

"It's not a big deal," Elena interrupted him.

"*It is a big deal!*" Pigg said aggressively at first, but then he immediately looked defeated again. "Do you realize that I won't be rooming with the guys anymore. I won't be in any of your same classes, and we'll have different eating times. I'll never see you!"

"So, you'll make some new friends during class, but not too many because I expect you to keep helping me with my homework. Plus, we'll have the weekends to meet in the Firebird Station. I know how much you *love* looking for artifacts." Elena's sarcasm finally made Pigg smile slightly. "You're still a Firebird. That's something to be proud of. You know why?"

"Why?" Pigg asked.

"Because no mistake was made on that. You were *chosen* to be a Firebird. No one can change that."

At that moment, a Telecaster appeared holographically, starling both of them.

"Elena Ransom, Hannibal would like to see you."

Elena looked at Pigg after the Telecaster disappeared and said, "Is it creepy that Hannibal knows exactly where we are?"

"Yeah, it's a little creepy."

"We're supposed to leave at 0600 for Wheeler's farm."

"Then, you'd better go quick," said Pigg.

▢ 23 ▢

The Home of Joshua

"Miss Ransom, come in."

"Hello, Sir," Elena said to Hannibal as she took the seat across from his desk. "So, what did I do wrong this time?"

Hannibal smiled genuinely. "What makes you assume you did something wrong?"

"Because I only come to your office when I'm in trouble," Elena pointed out.

"You didn't do anything wrong. Not yet, at least," Hannibal said. "I called you here because I thought you might like to talk a bit about Gribbin Pigg."

"What about him?"

"About the fact that he didn't make it into Special Ops."

Elena looked at Hannibal steadily. At first, she wasn't sure if she should speak her mind, but then she said, "I think you made a mistake."

"Really? I am quite surprised to hear you say that," Hannibal said. "You always seemed to treat Pigg as if he were in need of your assistance in Basic. Is that not why you almost always partnered with him, to help him get through the Gauntlets?"

That was true. Elena had always helped Pigg because he was clumsy. But hadn't she received equal help from him in tutoring and homework? So, which was the more significant way of giving help?

"You make it sound like physical stamina is all that matters for Special Ops. So, do we leave our brains at the door?"

Hannibal smirked and shook his head. "Pigg is more qualified than anyone to program and run simulations. He is at the top of the Level 3 studies and is more advanced in technological skill than anyone I have seen in all my years at Grimsby, but he lacks the strength to continue in the physical training. You know he does."

Elena looked down at her bitten fingernails. "You knew before we finished our exams which students would move to Special Ops, didn't you?"

Hannibal nodded.

"Then, why put us through the exams in the first place? Why get our hopes up if you already know which ones won't make it?"

"Giving tests is one of the ways we continually assess how students should be ranked," said Hannibal. "Pigg will still receive a certain status, even though he is staying in the same Company."

Elena pursed her lips together.

"I can see that we have reached an impasse," Hannibal said kindly. "So, I will move on to the other reason I wanted to see you. Fourth quarter break begins tomorrow. I was curious about what you are planning to do with your time off?"

Hannibal's casual curiosity felt like a trap. Did he know that they'd left the domes on their last fourth quarter break? Could he know about the trips she and Kidd had taken to Tavington's farm? Or about the discussion they'd had with Norman and Emelie Pigg?

"I'm going home, same as always," Elena lied.

Hannibal surveyed her silently for a moment, but Elena didn't flinch. "You are going to Atlanson?"

"Well...that is my home," Elena replied.

Hannibal paused for another moment. She knew he was waiting for her to break and say something to implicate her in doing something illegal, but she'd once been in a staring contest with Austin for over an hour so she knew how to remain silent and patient when it was absolutely necessary to win.

"I hope you enjoy your time in Atlanson. And that you don't do anything to," He raised his eyebrows ever so slightly, "get injured."

Elena's insides squirmed. What did Hannibal mean? The last time she was seriously injured was the cave-in at the cistern in Istanbul. Could Hannibal know about that? She didn't dare ask.

Hannibal stood and said, "You are dismissed. Have a good holiday."

Elena raced across the campus lawn and into the woods. She was very late getting to the Station now. She wondered if her friends had left without her, until she arrived in the hangar and saw the Independence still sitting there.

"What happened?" Austin asked as she walked into the research lab on the hovercraft. "Pigg said Hannibal wanted to see you."

"Yeah, he wanted to talk about...never mind," she said dismissively. "Why are you still here? Why didn't you leave me?"

"We couldn't leave you behind," Austin said. "But, we should get going. We've got a long trip tonight."

Then, using his Broadcaster, he said, "Wheeler. Elena is here. You can take off now." Turning back to Elena, he added, "Fergie already updated the programming on our Decoys with the pertinent information that we learned this year. She also added some personal anecdotes. The robots have already gone back to the school."

"But, I thought you needed my Trademark to turn the thing on," said Elena.

"One of the new modifications I have created for the Decoys is accepting any Trademark that is entered from my Touchdot," Fergie said in a formal tone. "It is technically more efficient this way."

"So, Pigg and Fergie were just explaining about the program they're writing to decipher the artifact codes," Austin said in a way that sounded like he was trying to catch Elena up quickly.

"We are not quite finished. We fear that we will require all the artifacts to be united before we can complete the program," Fergie said. "However, with the few codes we have, Pigg and I have been able to start the process. Interestingly, the artifact codes are similar to a strand of deoxyribonucleic acid, which means that when they are all combined we will have specific instructions as to their functioning."

"How did you find the time to do so much work on this while we were writing the neurolizor simulations?" Elena asked, feeling impressed.

"I was finished with my simulation the first week after it was assigned. One of the benefits of my *condition* is quick coding work," Fergie said. "We are unable to proceed with the details at this point in time, but we do know there is an artifact out there for us to retrieve, so we will do that and add to the program once we have succeeded."

Shortly after Fergie went to help Kidd navigate the hovercraft, Elena went back to the original cabin that she shared with Austin sometimes. She sat on the edge of the lower bunk, fiddling absentmindedly with the Kairos around her neck.

Elena and her friends were on their way to search for yet another artifact, but there were still more to discover. Headmaster Bentley and Hopper had talked about looking for the Feather of Truth, the Firebird Disc, and something called Echelon. But what those were or where they could be found was completely unknown.

Then, there had been several strange sightings of Melly Linus. Was she part of the mystery somehow? Did she or her parents know something about all the artifacts? Did they have an artifact they were trying to keep hidden? And how was it possible that her image appeared in her exam simulation?

What about Kidd? He'd lied so much but redeemed himself. For inexplicable reasons, she was beginning to feel drawn to him. Losing his family had made him emotionally homeless and possibly incapable of love. Was he damaged forever now? She wondered if that's how she would be if she'd lost her parents when she was that young. Or if she'd be that way right now if it hadn't been for Austin's care after her parents died.

Suddenly, Elena's mind wandered to Pigg again. She wondered if he'd told anyone about how he wouldn't be moving on to Special Ops with the rest of them. She knew that she wouldn't be able to sleep until she spoke with him again, so she got up and found Pigg asleep at the table in the galley with a half eaten fruitcake in his hand.

"Late night snacking again?"

Elena spun around and saw Kidd standing in the doorway.

"Nah, I just wanted to talk to Pigg again," Elena replied. "Make sure that he's still okay about not getting into Special Ops."

As Kidd moved into the kitchen toward the refrigerator, Elena sat at the table beside Pigg. She wasn't sure what she wanted to say to Kidd, but she could feel that they were about to have a conversation.

While she waited for him to speak, she began to relive some of the moments she'd had with Kidd over the past year, like how he built her the pool to help with her recovery when she'd been injured, and hunting at Tavington's farm, and how in their last few Basic Training classes he'd taken the time to work with everyone in the Firebird Unit instead of fighting with them.

"You know," Kidd said, breaking into her thoughts. "I know you thought I lied to you about everything. But I only lied about knowing where the Tablets were." He used a knife to strip skin from an apple and then cut it into bite-sized pieces. "Everything else I said, about knowing your dad and watching your family," he blushed slightly, "and caring about you, that was all true."

"Oh..." was all Elena managed to say as Kidd crossed the room.

He set down the plate of apple slices in front of her. Then, he pulled out a chair and sat across from her. For a long while, they ate in silence.

The following morning at 0500 hours, Elena arrived back in the kitchen feeling exhausted. She'd stayed awake in her bed far too late trying to process the strange new feelings she had for Kidd. She felt a desire to spend more time with him. She wanted to talk to him more. She wanted to know why it seemed that he wanted to help them, but also why he held them at arm's length.

"You look rested," Declan said sarcastically as Elena took a seat at the breakfast table.

Pigg pushed a bowl of warm oatmeal toward her.

"This is always my morning face, no matter how much sleep I get," Elena grumbled. "You should know this by now."

"Actually, right before you wake up you look so peaceful and completely unlike how you normally look. I think I'd call that your *morning face*," said Declan.

"Is this conversation causing anyone else to feel, like, uncomfortable?" Abria asked.

Both Elena and Pigg raised their hands.

"It's almost as bad as last night when Wheeler said he had feelings for you," Pigg said casually, looking at Elena.

A splash of milk shot across the table into Pigg's face. Elena followed the line of spray with her eyes and noticed that Declan was wiping milk from his chin and upper lip.

"Excuse me! He said what?"

"I was asleep at the table, but then I sorta woke up as he was telling Elena that he hadn't lied to her about everything, just about knowing where the Tablets were. And that he cared for her."

Elena's mouth fell open. The entire room went silent so quickly that she could hear her heart pounding.

She dropped her face into the crux of her arm and mumbled, "This is so humiliating."

"I knew it!" Abria squealed. "I knew he liked you. But in all seriousness, Elena, he is too cranky for you."

"Can we *please* stop talking about this," Elena said through gritted teeth.

"Hey!" Austin said, appearing suddenly at the door. "We've stopped. I don't know why."

Elena, Austin, and their friends hurried to the command bridge where Kidd was seated in a captain's chair. He was staring blankly out one of the darkened windows.

"Why've we stopped?" Austin asked Kidd.

Kidd looked decidedly away from the window, but he didn't look at Austin either.

"We're a little earlier than I thought we'd be. What's left of my house is over that way." He pointed out the window without looking. "There's the barn. You're welcome to look around for the Cup, but I've changed my mind. I don't think I can go there."

Elena and Austin eyed one another silently.

"That's fine, Wheeler," Austin said gently. "Thanks for bringing us this far." He turned to the others. "Here, I brought our tactical vests up from the cargo bay last night. I know that it's dark, but our hololights should do alright until the sun rises in about an hour or so."

As soon as Elena and the others were standing outside the Independence, Austin said, "We should spread out, but let's not separate farther than earshot. Call out if you see anything that looks like an artifact or any other relic. Just use your best judgment based on the things we've seen in the dossiers. And don't discount any symbols or special writing that you may see."

Pigg and Fergie nodded and walked off into the dark while Abria said, "I guess Declan and I can start with the barn."

"Of course, I'd love to start inside the smelly barn," Declan said sarcastically.

"It won't be smelly anymore, dimwit," Abria said as they walked away. "There haven't been animals here for, like, years."

Elena and Austin set off together in the direction of where the house had been. Their hololights illuminated an eerie ruin of crumbled timbers. Time had wasted away the area, but they could still see the main foundation.

Elena stepped along carefully through the remaining rumble. A profound silence pressed upon her. Her parents had been burned to ashes in their *accident* so there were no bodies to grieve over at their ceremony in Atlanson. Kidd's parents and siblings had become part of the earth where his house had once stood. No one had been there to mourn them.

"Lena, you okay?" Austin whispered after a long time of silence.

Elena swallowed hard. "It's just that Wheeler told me some specifics about how his family died." She lowered her voice to a barely audible whisper. "I can almost hear his sister screaming for him as she burned."

She covered her hand with her mouth as if she said something vulgar. Austin reached for her and put an arm around one of her shoulders.

"Has your Kairos even moved?"

Elena shook her head, unable to speak because of the lump that consumed the middle of her neck.

"How about you go over there to look around?" Austin suggested, pointing off randomly in the distance. "Just call out if your Kairos moves, okay?"

Elena nodded. She knew that he was trying to be kind by sending her away from the devastation that was once their friend's family. She was grateful for the excuse to get away. As she pursued the darkness, her own grief about her parents' death swam to the forefront of her thoughts. Her eyes began to well with tears.

Elena didn't know where she was going. She was so distracted by her feelings that her hololight hung loosely at her side. She didn't realize the extent of her daze until she was standing in a foot of water. She held up her hololight as high as she could. A shoreline stretched as far as her eyes could see. The clouds broke suddenly, and a bright blue moon shone down. She was mesmerized by it for a few moments until something moved to her left.

Feeling startled, Elena hurried to turn off her hololight. But then, she saw Kidd emerge from the tree line not too far from her. He slung a bag over his shoulder and headed off into the night away from her. She hurried to follow him, until Kidd finally stopped on the edge of the water. He looked out across the lake as if he were waiting for something or someone.

From afar, Elena watched him drop the tactical pack to the ground. He began to pull swim fins and wetsuits out and drop the supplies on the beach. She stepped toward him, holding her hololight high above her head.

"What are you doing out here?" Elena called to him.

He looked up and smiled genuinely.

"I was waiting for you."

▢ 24 ▢

The Smuggler's Station

"Happy Birthday," Kidd said to Elena as he handed her swim fins and a breathing apparatus.

She held them in her hand and said, "We need to work on your gift giving skills. You're a couple days early for my birthday, so we have time to try again."

Kidd smiled.

"You know where the Cup is, don't you?" Elena said.

He nodded. "Are you up for a little swim?"

"In the dark, in a lake I've never been in? Sure, I'm totally excited," Elena said sarcastically as she kicked off her jump boots and pulled on the swim fins.

Elena caught another one of Kidd's smiles in the brightness of his hololight just before he turned and dove into the lake. She gripped the breathing apparatus tightly in her hand and followed him.

The water was cool and crisp and actually refreshing to the soul after the emotional turmoil she'd felt while standing on the ruins of Kidd's old house. All her Level 2 training came back to her instantly as she took full breaststrokes to keep up with Kidd.

At long last, Kidd stopped swimming and turned to Elena.

"Ready to dive? It's a long way, but with the breathing apparatus we should be fine to get there and back."

Elena fitted the device in her mouth and dove under the water after Kidd. As she held a hololight extended in her arm, Elena was astonished to see reefs, rock formations, and strange creatures in the lake. Mud colored fish with striking blue eyes and fanged teeth darted out of their way, while blood red creatures with tentacles and purple eyes seemed to stalk them curiously. Thick-scaled beasts with scary faces sat in the shadows, while a school of smooth, arrowhead shaped fish with eyes on the sides of their heads swam around her.

At first, Elena's brain was working hard to adjust to the feeling of weightlessness. But the deeper they swam, the colder the water became. She started to feel an extraordinary pressure in her chest. Her arms and leg muscles were straining to keep in rhythm with Kidd's every movement.

Suddenly, a series of lights popped in a pattern and a cement structure appeared. Elena couldn't help but gasp, even with the breathing apparatus filling her mouth. She'd seen this building before. She'd dreamed about the building the previous year while she'd been out in the frozen wilderness with Pigg and...KIDD!

In next to no time, Elena followed Kidd under the building. They emerged inside a structured pool. She followed him to a ladder and climbed up onto a cement wharf, which was adorned with wooden slats to help water spill off the runway. The dock was lined with a dozen steel-plated doors. Even though freezing cold water dripped from Elena's clothes, the room was surprisingly warm.

"Your dad called this the Smuggler Station," said Kidd. "I came here with him the day my family was murdered. I thought it was so unique. That is until the first time I stepped foot in the Firebird Station. Then, I realized our dads must have been working together."

Elena looked around in silence. Smuggler Station. A cave of buried secrets. Secrets about how their dads knew each other. Secrets about the work they were doing with the Renegades. Everyone had secrets. As she looked at Kidd, dripping from head to toe, she realized that she had a secret, too.

"I've seen this place before," Elena said. "In my dreams. I guess my dad really wanted me to come here."

Kidd grabbed Elena's hand and led her to one of the ironclad doors. However, when he pulled the handle, nothing happened.

"Locked. It's locked," Kidd said, sounding confused. "I don't know what to do. Your dad just walked right inside."

Kidd pulled his dad's neurolizor out of his pocket and laid it in the palm of his outstretched hand. Elena began to feel the Kairos moving so she striped it from her neck and let it fly out into midair. The sharp angles of the star necklace were moving and sliding automatically.

"Whoa!" said Kidd as the necklace unfolded to reveal a clock-like face.

The hands and symbols on the clock began to spin counterclockwise and clockwise. The dial revolved. The elevated circles rotated around the face while the various symbols lit up at different intervals.

Looking suddenly excited, Kidd placed the neurolizor on the back of his neck.

"I can see it!" He exclaimed. "I can see the way to unlock the door."

As Elena watched him step toward the door she couldn't help but think of the almost supernatural power that Austin had to see hidden simulation walls. She wondered if the neurolizor was showing Kidd what Austin could usually see.

Quite suddenly, the door swung open automatically. Elena eagerly stepped over the threshold, expecting to find the Cup of Jamshid, but instead she saw a room filled with what appeared to be second-hand, unwanted items.

Ugly synthetic sea creatures hung from the ceiling, an elephant sized globe of the earth stood in one corner, and a telescope stood in another. Shelves of vintage bottles, leather-bound novels, old-fashioned clocks, and urns fashioned from different types of materials encircled the entire space. Decaying steamer trunks were placed around the room like furniture but couldn't distract from the umbrellas, head and shoulder sculptures, and captain's ship wheel that were also placed unceremoniously.

"Okay, this is not like anything I was expecting," Elena said. "Is this how you remember it?"

"I've never actually been in here before," Kidd confessed. "Your dad left me in the hovercraft. So, what do you think..." But before he could finish, he gasped.

Elena watched him stagger forward to one of the shelves. She thought he was going to pick up one of the vases, but instead he grabbed an oddly shaped looking instrument that was threaded with strumming strings and was carved with strange symbols. It was a very small object that was threaded like a piece of jewelry.

"What is it?" Elena asked.

"My mom wore this necklace all the time," Kidd whispered. "But how is it here?"

He looked far away for a moment. Then he said, so quietly that Elena could barely hear him, "I remember now. Your dad pulled this from the ashes of my house."

Kidd clutched the necklace to his chest. His eyes filled with tears. "It's like losing them all over again."

Elena felt her heart physically ache. Then, she realized something so important that her breath caught in her chest. Kidd needed a family. And that's what the Firebirds were to her now, a family.

She closed her hand on his forearm. "The necklace is beautiful."

At Elena's touch, Kidd seemed to wake up from reminiscing. He blinked the tears away and rubbed a fist over his cheeks.

"So, where do we start looking for the Cup?"

"The Kairos will show us," Elena said. "At least, it's always shown us before."

She noticed the Kairos off in one corner of the room emitting lights. Miraculously, the necklace Kidd was holding began to transform; the strings of the instrument began to move, and a melodic sound filled the room.

"Homophonic texture," Kidd breathed. "Look, my mom's necklace is an accompaniment to your Kairos."

After he said this, Elena noticed that the Kairos radiated light in specific intervals in concert with the music coming from the instrument necklace.

Suddenly, Kidd walked toward the spinning clock face of the Kairos, as if he were in a trance.

For a moment, Elena thought he was going to grab her necklace. Instead, he reached past it into nothingness. His hand completely disappeared. A moment later, he pulled back and was holding the Cup of Jamshid, complete with its tree trunk pedestal.

Elena looked down suddenly as water came rushing up around her ankles. All around the room water was bubbling up with determined ferocity.

"I guess I should have mentioned that a trap tends to commence after we extract an artifact," Elena told Kidd. "And I really should have remembered because it happens *every single time.*"

Kidd grabbed her hand.

"Come on!" he urged, pulling her through the door and back out onto the dock.

By the time Elena reached her swim fins, they were floating in waist deep water. Elena hurried to push her feet into the fins as Kidd stuffed the Cup of Jamshid in his shirt.

"Ready to dive?" Elena asked, but then she noticed a look of horror flood Kidd's face.

"I dropped my mom's necklace!" Kidd screamed. "I have to get it!"

Before Elena could stop him, Kidd had submerged into the now chest deep water. She followed him with the hololight up so that they could both see the dock. Elena could just make out the shimmer of the necklace lying in between the slats in the floorboard. Kidd's fingers were too big to reach through the slats, so she reached forward to try and help him. However, it was impossible, even for her slender fingers.

Elena's head popped out of the water, but right away she noticed that the room was filled so high with water that she was no longer able to touch the dock. Kidd appeared and gasped for breath.

"The necklace is impossible to reach," Elena said. "This place is about to flood completely. We have to go."

"I can't let it go," Kidd said hysterically. "It's the last thing I have of them. You go back. I'll meet you on shore."

"No!" Elena said firmly. "You can't get it. You must leave it behind."

Without responding, Kidd dove back under the water. She watched him, feeling helpless as he struggled to get the necklace. The water was rushing up to her chin now. Even though she had her breathing apparatus in her pocket, she was beginning to feel suffocated.

Kidd's head emerged after a few seconds. He looked frantic, like he wanted to dive for the necklace again, but Elena screamed, "Joshua!"

At the sound of his name, Kidd's eyes slid into focus, right to Elena's eyes.

"It's not worth your life!"

He looked sadder than Elena had ever seen anyone look before, but he said, "Come on, let's get out of here."

Elena jammed the breathing apparatus in her mouth and submerged again, this time swimming straight for the area where she knew they could exit. Kidd was beside her, holding the hololight in front of him. She worked her arms and fins hard, but there was an intense suction pulling her back toward the Smuggler Station.

Kidd pushed the hololight into her hands. Then, he thrust Elena forward, making his body a barrier between her and the drowning station. She kicked her legs as hard as she could for the surface. Every muscle in her body strained against death.

Suddenly, Elena felt an extraordinary burst of water, as if a bomb had exploded beneath her. The force of the eruption propelled her forward and her head broke the surface of the lake more suddenly than she was expecting.

Then, there was another feeling of suction against her legs, threatening to pull her back down. She kicked hard for where she thought she could see the hololights from the Independence, but still, it was a very long swim to the shoreline.

Elena had to alternate between a backstroke and breaststroke all the way back because she'd exerted so much energy trying to get to the surface. Feeling completely exhausted, she finally felt the ground beneath her feet.

Elena tossed the hololight onto the beach in front of her, and then crawled on her hands and knees until she was able to lie down without her face in the water. She heaved gulps of air, her body screaming in pain.

But then, she realized how quiet it was, even with her loud breaths. Kidd had not crawled out of the water beside her.

She sat up and yelled at the water, "Wheeler, where are you?"

But she didn't hear a sound. Not a trickle of the water. Not the sound of arms and legs swimming through water.

Elena struggled to her feet. Though the sun was beginning to rise, she grabbed the hololight from the beach and held it out over the still darkened water. She screamed again and again for Kidd, but there was never a reply. She was starting to feel desperate, thinking that he must have been pulled down by the suction. She knew the breathing apparatus would work for a while, but would it hold out long enough for her to go back and get him?

"But I can't go back," Elena said aloud. "I don't have enough time on my apparatus for us to both get out of there alive."

Her brain worked in frantic circles until finally she knew what to do. Austin. He would know how to help. He would be able to plan a rescue mission to the boy entombed by water. Just as she turned to run for the Independence, her steps faltered.

"Ransom!"

Kidd's voice rang out. She searched through the dark, but she still couldn't see him.

"Wheeler!"

"Ransom!"

Was his voice coming from the water? Or from somewhere else?

Then, finally she saw a dark figure crossing the beach just south of her. She broke into a run, wanting to jump into his arms, to tell him that she was glad he was alive. He was running for her, too. However, as they got closer he slowed to a stop.

"Are you alright?" Kidd asked.

Elena also slowed to a walk, feeling the moment of terror pass. "Yeah. You?"

Kidd nodded. "I'm sorry. It was really ridiculous to wait that long to try and get the necklace."

"It's okay," Elena replied casually. "I'm familiar with you being ridiculous by now."

Elena and Kidd's eyes locked in the blaze of the hololight. They reached for one another at the same time. Their fingers entwined. Elena felt warmth spread through the tips of her fingers to the souls of her feet. She knew without understanding why that she and Kidd shared a special bond.

"Should we go back?" Kidd asked softly.

Elena looked back toward where she knew the others would be. She could just see the lights from the Independence shining through the darkness.

"Yeah, Austin will worry," Elena said as she gripped his fingers tighter. "But, let's go together."

Elena and Kidd walked hand in hand back toward the hovercraft.

"There you are!" Pigg said, coming through the darkness suddenly. "We've been looking for you. We were really wor..." He stopped short of the sight of them just as Austin, Declan, Fergie, and Abria also appeared. Then, he took a few steps toward Elena and whispered loudly, "Wheeler is holding your hand."

"I know." Elena smiled at his attempt to be covert.

"So, are you two, like, together now?" Abria asked, smiling in a girly way.

Elena looked at Kidd and grinned. "I guess so."

"Why are you soaking wet?" Austin said.

Elena briefly explained about their trip down to the Smuggler Station, but she left out the scary part where they almost drowned. When she was finished, Kidd released his grip on Elena's hand. He pulled the Cup of Jamshid from his shirt and handed it to Austin.

"So, what now?" he asked.

"We find out if this thing can really tell the future," Austin replied. "Though I have no idea how we're going to actually do that."

"Well, that sounds like quite an adventure. But first," Elena said as she locked eyes with Austin, "I'm going home."

Austin threw an arm around Elena's neck, and replied, "Home sounds good."

Elena smiled at her friends, resting in the fact that one day soon they would all be free.

THE ADVENTURE WILL CONTINUE!

What will happen next to Elena, Austin, and their friends?

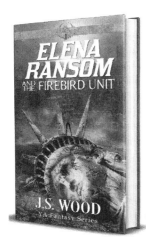  

Follow Elena's story @

www.jswood.me

Made in the USA
Columbia, SC
29 December 2018